THE SECRETS OF CASANOVA

GREG MICHAELS

Booktrope Editions
Seattle WA 2013

Cover Design by Greg Simanson

Edited by Cynthia White

This is a work of fiction. Names, characters, places, brands, media, and incidents are either the product of the author's imagination or are used fictitiously. Any resemblance to similarly named places or to persons living or deceased is unintentional.

PRINT ISBN 978-1-62015-178-5
EPUB ISBN 978-1-62015-274-4

For further information regarding permissions, please contact info@booktrope.com.

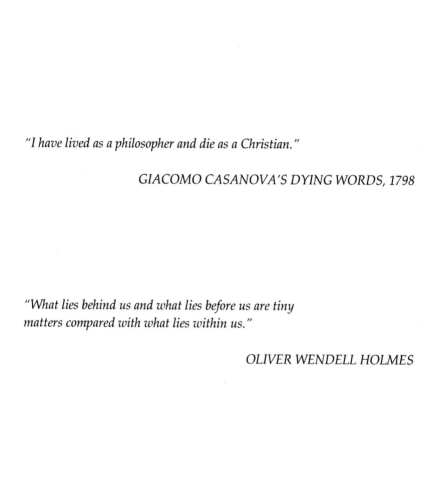

"I have lived as a philosopher and die as a Christian."

GIACOMO CASANOVA'S DYING WORDS, 1798

"What lies behind us and what lies before us are tiny matters compared with what lies within us."

OLIVER WENDELL HOLMES

SPRING – 1755

- 1 -

"I'VE ALWAYS KNOWN THAT VIRTUE'S NOT THE AIM in Paris," Jacques cheered himself. "'Give me too much' is the motto here. And when people live with that philosophy, there's ample opportunity for one such as I am."

Outside the Hôtel du Saint Esprit, Jacques Casanova decided to chance the Rue de la Grenouille. Once before he'd hopped from cobblestone to cobblestone to avoid the mud and the rushing carriages, and although the foul wastewater streams assaulted his nose again tonight, he knew he must brave the streets—for what he utterly craved was food in his belly and a woman in his bed. He tugged at his wig and set off.

Reaching a crowded thoroughfare, Jacques ordered a sedan chair and directed the footmen to a *caffè della Nobiltà*, a "coffeehouse for nobles," where he hoped to sup. He'd had high times here before, but who knew what had changed in five years?

A short while later, he tipped the footmen from the trifling pocket money he still possessed. The café, redolent of garlic, beckoned. The tangy aroma made Jacques think of home; he smiled at the thought while he strode imperiously toward the coffeehouse, where he was met by the chuffy proprietor and a young serving girl, both of whom had black hair in coiled ringlets.

The grisette stepped forward. Jacques assessed her. Light eyes, rawboned features, including a nose quite sizeable for her face. But her cheeks dimpled when she smiled. And she did smile—at him, bidding him to follow.

Passing waves of tables, he was pleased by the social prospects. A blonde aristocrat leered at him, but he found her too abundantly larded. Or perhaps—not.

At his table, the attractive grisette finally faced him.

"How do you do, sir?"

"Surpassingly well," Jacques lied. "I see you serve more than coffee."

The girl leaned forward to light the table's candle, dipping her chin seductively.

"May I have a carafe of the house wine?"

"Will that be one glass or two, monsieur?"

"Let me begin with one glass." Jacques held the girl's gaze until he noticed that the proprietor at the entrance did not appear pleased. "Are you, by chance, married to the gallant near the front door, mademoiselle?"

"When it is convenient, monsieur," she said. "One glass, for now."

Jacques felt a crackle of pleasure in his veins while he again surveyed the crowd. Silk and finery at every turn. Conversations in a half-dozen languages. People drinking and eating with might and main.

As nearby customers puffed on their pipes, clumps of sultry smoke seemed to gobble up the remaining air—just as it had two nights ago at the faro tables of the Palais-Royal. An evening's entertainment for Jacques, a turn of cards, his magnificent wager— *sept et la va*—seven times his original bet. Then, full defeat. Throbbing financial loss. Ruination. And as further insult, his dalliance with the disgusting and toothless Marquise D'Ampie. *Do I sleep these days with anything that snores?*

A carafe clinked on the table. Next, a single glass. Jacques followed the grisette's rough hand to her face.

She smiled. "You know, you're not the prettiest man I've ever seen, but you caught my eye—and held it." She finished pouring the wine, then asked with a grin, "Will that be all?"

Jacques smiled back. He enjoyed the hunt almost as much as the sweet rustle of underclothes. A fleeting memory entertained him when he remembered the singular sweetness of—what were their names? It was so long ago that those two sisters, although pretending to sleep, had allowed his advances. Was a boy's loss of innocence ever so agreeable? Jacques' smile grew wider.

The grisette peeked slyly over her shoulder and whirled away—waving her derrière fearlessly, but Jacques' enchantment was cut short by a croaking male voice.

"And so I tell you—dancers, actresses? Sluts. One and the same."

Jacques had heard that kind of talk many times—his mother was an actress—so it shouldn't have pained him. He turned to see two drunken men at the next table. Neither, it seemed, knew how to stop a belch, but their noble status was confirmed by the jewel-encrusted pommels of their swords and their red-heeled shoes.

One of the garrulous bravos, whose face was severely spoiled from a bout with the pox, felt Jacques' glance. "You, fellow, what say you about dancers and actresses?"

"The company of women is to be enjoyed," Jacques said curtly.

"Flat on their back," the noble laughed.

"Yes, I prize them in bed. But some men prefer to triumph rather than to enjoy."

The pair squirmed in confusion, apparently unable to decide if Jacques had slighted their honor.

The scarred bravo grunted. "Was that an accent I heard?"

His friend, who had bulging eyes, pounded the table with his fist. "You're so stupid," he said. "This man has a Venetian accent."

"You're Italian?" the scarred man asked.

"*Not* Italian," Jacques insisted. "Venice is quite separate—and superior—to those Italian territorial disasters, I assure you."

"Venetian, eh?" Bulging Eyes said. "Venice is clearly under our good King Louis' protection."

"Venice is not—nor ever has been—under France's protection," countered Jacques. "Venice has been a republic for nearly eleven centuries. Eleven. Centuries. A republic."

"Oh, toad," the scarred bravo intoned, "I know something of the world. Your Venice is controlled by a handful of grasping aristocrats who—"

"Every major European state *except* Venice is a monarchy." Jacques' voice began to quiver. "What this means to most human beings who live in these nations is that they're treated like herds of swine by a hereditary king."

"Do I seem a penned pig?" cried the bravo.

Other patrons, sensing the argument, craned their necks.

Jacques felt his gorge rise. "Venice, in contrast, is a republic, and consequently, its people are—"

"—full of pus," slurred Bulging Eyes. His friend howled and slapped the table again and again. The surrounding patrons convulsed in laughter. Raucous, demeaning laughter.

Hot anger seared Jacques' belly. Reaching past the carafe, he grabbed the candleholder and, in one swift move, forced the flame into the eye of the jeering man.

"*Morbleu!*" yelled the scarred bravo.

Jacques flipped the candleholder in his hand and lurched toward the other—who fumbled to unsheathe his sword—striking him with the butt end directly across the temple. Bulging Eyes sank to the floorboards while customers emptied the near vicinity, screaming. The odor of burned flesh filled the café.

Jacques' hand shook violently as it reached his dagger.

At the same time, a well-dressed older gentleman stepped across the incapacitated man on the floor and forced a handkerchief into the hand of the cursing bravo collapsed in his chair. The gentleman cautiously handed Jacques his calling card.

"These two may demand satisfaction from you—although from where I sat and from what I heard, you are to be commended. They should've shown respect for you. And for Venice.

"Undoubtedly."

"Men of their stamp, well, it's perfectly simple. They want for nothing. They believe in nothing. Nevertheless, *sieur*, you are fortunate you did not kill them."

"*They* are fortunate I did not kill them, *sieur*." Jacques slammed his poniard back into its sheath. "I have no need to further defend the honor of Venice, but if these two so desire, they may find me at the Saint Esprit. Tell them I have a dangerous sword, so perhaps instead of choosing to die, they will view this tête-à-tête as a classroom for learning."

"I shall do so. As their uncle, I've had many opportunities to witness their follies." The gentleman glanced at the bravo whose eye socket was now black with charred flesh—and thumbed his chin.

"These two have caused my complete loss of appetite," Jacques grumbled.

"I understand, certainly. By the bye, I overheard, of course, your intense devotion to Venice. May I ask why you don't live there?" Before Jacques could muster a reply, the gentleman's eyes grew wide. "No need to look, but over your shoulder I see a goodly number of men gathering with the owner. It would appear you are to be expelled. Or worse. May I suggest a departure by the back door?" He pointed discreetly, then plopped a coin on Jacques' table. "I'm good for your wine."

"Should I be grateful?" Jacques frowned. He squeezed his dagger, then glanced back over his shoulder toward the mob of patrons and the light-eyed grisette. *Another time.*

The bravo on the floor, lying on his back in a puddle of blood, cursed, "Blackguard! *Jean-foutre!*"

Jacques straddled the man. "I enlighten you, fellow, one last time. Venice is an empire, a republic. Its people are daring, joyful, and above all, free."

These soothing words encouraged Jacques to quickly address the old gentleman. "On my life, it's my most ardent wish to breathe that city's sweet air, where I first smiled at the splendor of the dazzling stars, where my mother cradled me in her young arms. Someday soon I'll return to where I belong."

Jacques hurried from the café.

On the long trudge to his lodgings he regained his appetite. In exchange for reciting a cheerless, extemporaneous verse to a street vendor, he was offered a shank of mutton. "Whether vice or virtue leads me onward, I do not know," Jacques improvised, "yet onward, forward I go." Jacques bolted down the mutton.

His stomach was full. But with little money—and worse credit— he would be thrown in the street tomorrow. And tonight, unhappily, he would spend all alone. But for as long as Jacques cared to remember, he had lived by his wits. Something in that thought buoyed his step.

- 2 -

THE SILK BEDSPREAD FELT COOL and comforting to Jacques' face. Uncurling his body, he reluctantly rose from the bed, coughing an exhale. From the sun filtering into the room, he guessed it was far past noon. He eyed his exquisitely appointed quarters and knew he would be forced to leave.

Over his waistcoat, he strapped on the poniard he always wore; the dagger afforded stealth and quickness.

He picked a simple cravat and took his time selecting a coat from his trunk. The spangles in the embroidery, he knew, would ensure a brilliance of effect during the remaining daylight and a delicate richness by the night's candlelight. Slipping on the jacket, he checked its pocket for his book of quotations by Horace, a poet with whom he often found agreement. The book was there. A good omen. By nightfall, Jacques hoped to have a woman on his arm.

After brushing his hair and setting his wig, several dull thuds in the hallway compelled him to open the door of his room—and to watch his manservant, Petrine, shuffle directly into the wall.

Jacques sighed. "Your condition, Spaniard, is appalling."

"Master, master," slurred Petrine, falling to one knee. "Last night I met—"

"Before I go out, I have a chore to give you."

"Yes, mast—" The manservant dropped his empty wine bottle, pressing the floor with his knuckles to steady himself. His swarthy face brightened considerably as he spoke. "But last night I met a queen. A goddess."

"You confuse me. Is she a queen? Or is she a goddess?"

Petrine heeled over, sobbing. "No one wants me. A lowly mule carries fewer burdens. My life! My life began at the bitter end."

"So you've told me several times." Jacques patted Petrine's shoulder, then stepped around his valet into the hall. "Let me once more remind you that you embarked on the high road two long years ago—the instant you took employment with me. Now, rouse your wits and listen well."

Petrine lifted up his face. Tears channeled his cheeks. He wiped them away.

Jacques made known his desire: to move to a less conspicuous lodging. His only stipulation was that the room have a bed.

Drunk as he was, Petrine knew what changing residences meant: his master's purse had shrunk. Or was empty. He wasn't pleased; he'd felt enough hardship in his life. But for now, he told himself, he was still in work.

The rest of the afternoon passed quickly. Like a hound with a nose for the scent, Petrine found a decrepit inn located in a questionable part of the city and, after transferring Jacques' effects, met up with his master and led him to a new lodging.

Shielding his eyes from the setting sun, Jacques instructed his manservant to visit the Saint Esprit once more to retrieve handkerchiefs that were missing; Jacques then vanished up the narrow Parisian street with "I'll be back."

For the time being, Petrine felt free to follow his fancy, which included ministering to his throbbing headache.

That night, the door of Jacques' room eased open. Petrine leaned into the darkness. A soft whimper marked time with the rhythmic squeak of the bed.

"Sir, it's me," the valet whispered. "A short while ago I ran your errand to the Hôtel du Saint Esprit. I've frightful news."

The squeaking stopped. "If you can see the nightstand, find the candle."

Petrine picked his way across the floor and lit a match, flushing light into the small room.

Jacques shifted upright, huddling under the thin blanket, his long hair hanging loose. Next to him, a curly mound of brown hair mushroomed just above the coverlet.

Petrine stared at his master. "May I speak freely, sir?"

"Of course you may. This is the girl I will most certainly marry."

"Certainly, sir."

"What news?" Jacques barked.

"As it happened, the proprietor of the Saint Esprit didn't see me as I walked in, but it was plain, sir, three men were there to arrest you."

Jacques nodded.

"Your financial obligations, bills of exchange, they said. From your night of gambling at the Palais-Royal? The three men mentioned For-L'Éveque several times."

"For-L'Éveque. What's that?"

"The prison for debtors, sir. On Tuesday, Desgaliers died there."

"Desgaliers? Dead? In prison?" Jacques' voice grew shrill and fretful. "I'll die before I go to prison once more. I'll never again lose my freedom." His face grew stony. "Did the owner inform these men where we now stay?"

"He doesn't know, master—nor, I'm certain, will these men find out."

"Nothing is certain."

While the slight figure under the bedcovers drew her legs into a ball, Petrine searched his master's widening eyes. "Sir, is there good reason for these men to be hunting you? Are your debts so huge this time?"

Jacques' expression told the valet everything he needed to know.

"Shall I pack immediately?" he asked.

"Yes, be prepared to move my belongings at a moment's notice."

"We may be obliged to leave behind your personal pleasures," the valet said gently.

"Such as?"

Petrine gestured to the orange pomatum, lavender water, essence of bergamot, the oil of jasmine, and eau de cologne on the nearest of the three trunks. "We might need to part with your less necessary goods."

"No, none."

"Perhaps that heavy old manuscript?"

"That sacred old manuscript may be the most valuable thing I own. I managed to lug the precious thing all the way from Constantinople—we'll take it wherever we go."

Petrine wrinkled his lips, sighing. "I shall be prepared to move everything, then, including everything old and sacred." He reached for the candle. "It does concern me, sir, that these men knew we'd stayed at the Saint Esprit."

Jacques faltered, confusion wringing his face. "It wouldn't be wise to stay here," he said. "But should we return to my brother's? No, I'll not—I suppose so. Yes. Francesco's. Gather everything and meet me there. I'll see Louisa home."

"Yes, sir." Petrine nudged a short step closer. "Master, I've had little to eat or drink. Might I have a bit of my wage?"

Jacques' shoulders tensed. Petrine retreated. "My stomach can wait, sir. I'll proceed posthaste."

Petrine picked up the candle, then stepped back. The willowy naked girl slithered from the bed and, too quickly, covered herself. Petrine scratched his brow. She might have given him the pleasure of watching her dress.

"One final detail, valet," said Jacques. "After you've taken my belongings to Francesco's, revisit the Saint Esprit. While you're there, summon your acting gifts and make a show of the fact that you and I depart at noon, bound for Pas-de-Calais—no, Venetzia. Venetzia. You understand?"

"Venice, yes sir. A show."

"A show. For an audience smaller than you're accustomed to, but a show nevertheless." Jacques stood. "No gown for me, I'll dress myself."

Petrine grew restless while the lovers stole a last affection.

"Follow me, Louisa, if you please," Jacques said. He opened the door and led her down the hallway.

Petrine quickly decided that congratulations were in order: the girl his master would most certainly marry—looked all of thirteen.

* * *

Petrine stood outside Francesco Casanova's apartment, squinting at the first light of dawn. Before he could knock, the door opened.

"I'm sorry, Petrine, I didn't mean to startle you so," Dominique said. "But I saw you walk into the courtyard from my upstairs window. Did you come to stay with us again?"

"Being frightened out of my wits is a grand way to start the morning," Petrine quipped. "Fear is my friend."

Dominique offered a slight smile. "What brings you back to us, and so early? Where's Monsieur Casanova?"

Dominique's eyes lit upon the trunk he had in tow. She continued, "After you and your master left, I felt I wouldn't see him again."

"As it happens, madame—"

"I changed my dithering mind," came a distinct voice from the courtyard. Jacques emerged from a pack of water carriers ambling down the street. "I concluded I *must* go with Francesco to the Vicomte's this very morning. But first, good day, Dominique," Jacques said, taking off his tricorne and bowing. He stepped in front of Petrine, took Dominique's hand, and kissed it lightly. "My brother has made a fine choice of a wife, don't you agree, Petrine?"

"I do agree, sir. And I'm far more difficult to please than you."

"Not to be the messenger of disappointing news," Dominique said, "but I'm the only one here at the moment. Francesco—"

"Francesco has already left? I'd hoped—on this beautiful spring day—to finally accompany him," Jacques said a bit too earnestly.

"Perhaps tomorrow morning you can join him, master?"

"We'll see, valet. Tomorrow or the next day. Assuredly," Jacques muttered, massaging his chin and gazing at his sister-in-law.

Petrine had seen his master captivate women many times but never had he seen him quite so attentive to one.

"Are you staying with us again?" Dominique asked, indicating the trunk.

"Well," Jacques said, "I felt as if Francesco and I hadn't the opportunity to truly—"

"Just for the night, you told me, sir," Petrine interjected. "Didn't you, sir?"

"For tonight," Dominique said, "or for as long as you'd like, you're welcome. We haven't acquired any children or pets since you left us two weeks ago," she laughed giddily, "so we still have room. I'm sure Francesco will be pleased."

"Good, then," Jacques said. He turned to his valet. "I remind you, Petrine, of your promise to return to the Saint Esprit on the errand we agreed upon," he said. "With Madame's permission, you may take my trunk inside. Then go."

"Yes, sir." Petrine grasped the leather strap of the large trunk.

Jacques took Dominique's arm and guided her inside.

"Might I spend this bright day in your company?" he said. "I have nothing but time."

Jacques spoke the grim truth.

- 3 -

"CLIMB IN, GENTLEMEN," said the coachman.

The brothers took their seats in the fiacre before hearing the crack of the whip and the familiar command to the horses to "walk on."

Just past sunup, the sweet call of meadow thrushes summoned the coach and team of four as it rumbled over ancient ruts. Francesco's apartment was six leagues from the Vicomte de Fragonard's home near the confluence of the Seine and the Marne, through the Vincennes woods. A swift fiacre might leave the apartment in the Carré de la Porte Saint-Denis and arrive at the Vicomte's in little more than an hour.

"I wager there have been no decent roads in this region since the Romans." Jacques folded his roquelaure and laid it on the seat next to him. "No doubt it's good King Louis' pleasure whether or not a road is maintained, but judging from this one, Louis has not taken to heart the superlative secret of Paris: Let nothing be done without elegance."

Francesco, sitting opposite Jacques, offered no response.

Jacques marveled that Francesco still held a grudge—years later—for the boyhood pranks Jacques had played on him. *He baits me with his insolence. But today is the day I'll make peace with Francesco. Once and for all.*

"Why should the Vicomte de Fragonard have an interest in you?" Francesco suddenly blurted.

"Pardon?"

Francesco repeated his question accusingly.

Miffed as he was, Jacques smiled. His brother was envious.

Francesco barked. "I'd scarcely said two words when the Vicomte asked me to bring you."

Jacques sat forward. "*He* asked you to bring me? Are you keeping secrets? Why didn't you tell me?" *Who am I to the Vicomte that he proffers an invitation to his château? Why would he curry favor?* Jacques calmed himself before taking on a comforting tone. "Because you asked me, Brother, I came to see the erotic miniatures. And to glimpse your landscape canvases. Passionate curiosity—the mainspring of my life—spurred this outing."

"Are you telling the truth?"

"I always tell the truth. Except when I lie."

Anger reddened Francesco's face.

The team of bays loped onward while Jacques tried to distract his brother: "This breed from LeBoulonnais are disagreeable to look at," he said, "but they can run for hours and be as fresh at the end as at the start. I admire perseverance."

Francesco exhaled loudly, inspected his large hands, but said nothing.

"You're entirely perfect for executing the Vicomte's landscape commission," Jacques volunteered.

Finally the painter spoke. "The Vicomte, I found out, had been inspired by my copies of Simonini's battle paintings. He eagerly sought to hire me. For my part, I'd hoped to meet influential people through Vicomte de Fragonard, but the more I learn, the more it seems his friends are as old and as strange as he."

"Neither eccentricity nor age should prevent one from cultivating a good patron. If opportunity knocks," Jacques shrugged, "open the door." He peered out the window at a flock of bellicose crows.

"Are you staying with us again tonight?" Francesco asked, rubbing his stubbled chin.

"No, suitable manners deem the Hôtel du Saint Esprit to be my next stop," Jacques lied. "Or I may stay a short while with my acquaintance, the Bishop de Bernis. Five years ago—the first time I met the bishop—he explained the vicious catfight then dividing the royal court. The weighty issue at stake was the superiority of French opera over Italian opera. 'War of the Buffoons,' he called it." Jacques directed his eyes at his brother. "His point, I suppose, was that frivolous issues can sometimes divide even the best of us. That fat old cleric told me tales for hours. He claimed my friendship the very day I made my first foray into Paris proper."

Francesco sneered. "And this time you've been in Paris barely two weeks and you itch to return to the high life with the bishop?"

"Simply-speaking, I appreciate your generosity, Brother, so I respectfully restore privacy to you and your wife."

As Jacques rocked back and forth in his seat, the verdant rolling hills seemed artfully framed through the coach window. During the ride, he'd seen squirrels, larks, hares, flocks of black turkeys, and several stags dotting the countryside. An isolated Latin cross, erected decades before by some unknown cleric, glistened against the sky. Nonetheless, Jacques found himself yearning for the shimmering waterways of home, his beloved Venice. He missed the customary sounds of lapping water that had always seemed to gentle his concerns, dissolve his cares. Somehow the water's magical movement, its regularity, had made him feel still, at peace.

A handful of thatched roofs came into view, turning gold as the sun niggled past a lone cloud. Francesco lowered his window and leaned outside the cab. With his neck arched upward, his long brown hair blew stiff and straight.

"It's the far house of the pair," he roared at the driver, pointing ahead.

"Watering the horses?" asked Jacques when Francesco again sat down.

"That also. But more importantly, buying bread. Dominique somehow found that this particular fellow makes better bread than anyone in Paris. I satisfy my wife's whims when I'm able."

"Fulfilling women's whims. In this, at least, we may agree," Jacques said.

The fiacre rolled to an awkward stop. While Francesco went inside on his errand, Jacques waited in the grassy yard. Nearby two gentlemen in embroidered silk waistcoats—and in animated conversation—escorted a lady arm in arm toward a meadow.

No spirit in her step. Insipid, thought Jacques.

"*Je nie Dieu,*" railed one of the men. "I reject the existence of God, I say. Can you prove to me there is a god or a son of god?" He shook his fist.

"Proof of God? One cannot see the wind, yet everywhere there is proof of it."

These kinds of conversations had become a daily occurrence in France as the *philosophes*, led by Reason in the guise of Monsieur de Voltaire, attacked the official French religion, Catholicism. Indeed, the entire concept of a deity was under fire—as was, equally inconceivably, the institution of monarchy. The times were rife with debate concerning the spiritual and political enlightenment of humankind.

Jacques wondered if he should inform the gentlemen of a proof he was taught at seminary, although he recalled that even as a student, he felt the proof for God's existence to be flawed.

A loud bawling erupted. Jacques trotted to the rear of the house where a man in tattered clothes sat on the ground, his back against a pile of refuse. Just beyond him, a screaming child, covered in filth, appealed to the man with outstretched arms. The man took no notice while he sniffed a pale, dead fish. He split the fish's belly, slung the guts into the mud, and devoured the putrid thing.

Before the pleading child could reach the fish entrails, Jacques snatched her tiny hand, pulled her from the mud, and led her toward the house.

Inside he joined Francesco, explained the situation, and with a loan from his brother, bought two loaves of bread. Satisfied, he returned to the rear of the house, placed one loaf in the little girl's hands and one in the grip of the desperate man. The girl nibbled a few bites from her gift, but the starving man stretched his arm high and pointed at Jacques, shrieking, "You! You! Find it in yourself."

"Sick devil's completely out of his head," Francesco said, now standing behind Jacques. The brothers turned, walking toward their fiacre.

Once the coach began moving, Francesco broke one of the rye loaves, releasing its sharp aroma. Although the brothers had shared eggs and chocolate in Paris, Jacques was famished. Catching his brother's brooding eyes, he extended his hand and was granted a chunk of bread.

The brothers ate, admired the fineries of nature from their coach, and once—watching a reckless bee buzz round and round and out the window—laughed together. When the coach neared the Vicomte's chateau, Jacques took a last bite of bread and wiped his mouth. "In France, nine-tenths of the people die of starvation, one-tenth of indigestion."

- 4 -

"THE VICOMTE EXPECTS ME to be at my work every morning,"
Francesco said. "If a servant is not around, I'm encouraged to enter
the house, then go to the cellar." He opened the front door of the
chateau, and the brothers stepped inside.

The anteroom was finished in a peculiar dark green that was
illuminated by a triangular window above the doorway. The few
articles of furniture were much out of fashion. The vaulted ceiling,
perhaps twice the height of a man, reached its apex at a St. Andrews
cross, its color an oily dark plum.

"I'd call it royal purple—thwarted," said Jacques.

His brother stifled a laugh.

Jacques whispered: "These Frenchmen are imbeciles and madmen,
so light that I wonder they stay on the ground." He fanned his nose
and smiled. "And the bitter odor in this home? Apparently, Vicomte
de Fragonard inherited a perfume business."

A deafening slam startled them. Jacques' hand flew to his
dagger, then eased away when he felt Francesco's reassuring touch.

A raspy voice called out, "Enter the far door, messieurs, and pick
your way down the stairway. I shall join you both below."

Francesco Casanova fetched a key from his pocket, opened the
entry, squeezed past a blazing taper, then teetered down the steep
stairs with Jacques following close behind.

Jacques' foot soon crunched the soil of a cellar floor.

His brother said, "I've found in my previous trips here that this
gloom always brings on my melancholy humor."

Jacques shivered in the chilled air. "Yes, Cloacina, goddess of
sewers, would surely find contentment here."

"Truly."

"Admirable of you to take this on, little Brother. Yet I wonder: Did you bring me to this house to show me the Vicomte's indecent miniatures, as you promised? Or to boost your spirits?"

"We'll find the erotic miniatures," Francesco said. "You weren't brought here for my cheer. You seldom make me laugh."

Jacques' reply was cut short when his face was ensnared in a cobweb as thick as a nightcap. Tearing at it, he felt sickened.

While the two men trod through the duskiness toward a not-too-distant brightness, Jacques shot a glance over his shoulder. No one. He looked ahead. Like a forest of tar-black trees shorn of their branches, support timbers stretched into the dim distance where a speck of light offered relief. Thirty paces farther, a score of lanterns at last erased the darkness. Jacques shaded his eyes against the light and saw easels, canvases, a number of brushes, and an overstuffed armchair.

"Here is my life, six hours a day." Francesco stepped toward an easel. "My commission. I duplicate these two canvases—a dozen copies in oil of this nautilus creature and another dozen of that landscape.

Jacques plucked a handkerchief from his pocket to mask his nose.

"A musty smell, indeed—here," he mumbled while leaning toward the paintings to inspect the precise brush strokes. "The Vicomte must pay you well, little Brother, to paint in these curious conditions."

Francesco shrugged. "Vicomte de Fragonard insists I be tediously faithful to these originals. You know a great deal about art. What do you think?"

Does he counterfeit?

"Highly unusual," Jacques chirped as gaily as possible. "Yet the extraordinary is so much the fashion of the times." He smiled. "To follow the Vicomte's instructions unquestioningly, to copy these marvels of nature will certainly enhance your artistic skills."

Francesco scowled. "Not long ago I was an up-and-coming artist with no need to enhance," he grumbled while setting up his paints.

Jacques moved to the armchair, running his fingers across the oaken chair back.

"Quite the piece," he said, stuffing his handkerchief into his sleeve.

A wraithlike cat materialized from under the chair, drew back her head, and hissed. Jacques stooped and coaxed the animal until she threaded herself about his leg, mewing.

"You are an admirer of beauty of all kinds, even Graymalkin the cat," croaked a disembodied voice.

Jacques strained his eyes to peer into the darkness. "Your Lordship?"

"I don't believe in the formalities of titles and the like. Although some may refer to me as Vicomte, in my heart all men are created equal."

A radical.

The Vicomte de Fragonard limped into the illuminated area of the cellar, his eyes glued on the nautilus painting. He moved slowly but determinedly, relying on a shillelagh. He was hunched but not unduly so for a man who Francesco had called ancient. He wore rouge on his blemished cheeks, carmine on his lips. Carbuncles blighted his nose. He blackened his eyebrows but not his gray and short-cropped beard nor the insubstantial hair on his head.

Jacques blanched. *Will I look like this man one day?* He raked his fingers across the pockmarks on his own cheeks. Old scars from smallpox: a reminder of his first infatuation—and his first rejection.

Francesco acknowledged the Vicomte with a nod. "Vicomte, may I introduce my brother Jacques?"

Jacques bowed. "A pleasure, sir."

"I'd hoped to meet you, Jacques Casanova. I've perused your published account. It's all over Europe."

Jacques' face beamed with pride.

"Can you still find room in your heart for Venice after suffering at its hands?" Fragonard continued. "The solitude of prison can be a great leveler. We come face-to-face with who we are. Or who we might become. But your escape from that Venetian pit, the Leads, must provide you with continual satisfaction."

"Not entirely," Jacques said. "The three members of the *Inquisitori de Stato* who were responsible for my imprisonment—Grimani, Dal Zaffo, and—"

"I am acquainted with the name of Signor Michele Grimani of Venice," the Vicomte interrupted. "Do we speak of the same?"

Jacques nodded.

"Ambitious—Signor Grimani. He seems to want the whole world— that which is not already his." The old man took several steps toward Jacques. "And so, after your imprisonment your travels have brought you here to Paris. In Paris? Well, as you may know, the law of this country has its cruder points. If a man is convicted of a capital crime, his entire family is disennobled and must be deprived of all public employment."

I was not convicted—or even accused—of a crime, capital or otherwise, when I was carted off to the Leads. Didn't I write that in the account? Perhaps Jacques would enlighten the Vicomte—and someday soon, the *Inquisitori.*

"You've earned high regard with your intelligence and your talents," Fragonard said. "Your escape from prison was extraordinarily imaginative."

"My escape has a serious consequence: I may not return to Venice."

Grimacing in pain, the old man leaned heavily on his shillelagh, then turned toward Francesco. "Gentlemen, for the present, I must take my leave. Forgive me, please, as the catarrh continues to plague me."

"Perhaps the root of *Pilule cynoglossus* would help your ailment, sir," Jacques replied. Catching Francesco's frown, his shoulders tightened. *As usual my brother thinks that when I exhibit my acumen, I play the toady.* "I'm speaking of hound's-tongue, sir," he clarified for the Vicomte. "I'll be glad to send some with my brother on his next trip here."

Francesco shot a concealed glare at his brother before he bent toward the canvas before him.

The old man's lips drifted into a smile. "I will consider your cure, Jacques Casanova, though its utility I doubt, as I frequently work with a number of chemicals. Those chemicals—and time, of course—are my adversaries." He raised his shillelagh, tapped the oak fauteuil, and turned toward the canvases. "Please commence painting, Francesco. Call out to my majordomo if you have further requirements. As for you, come here, sir."

Jacques stepped toward the man, stopping at a respectful distance.

"Closer, *s'il vous plaît.*"

Jacques complied until he was an arm's length away from the Vicomte.

"Should you be wondering, Monsieur Casanova, I permit you in this workplace solely because of your abilities. And your needs." The old gentleman leaned in close. "And you're someone who may be suited for a need of *mine,* far greater than a simple medicament. I've a startling opportunity for the right man." Fragonard eyed Jacques intensely before whispering, "I am the depository of a vital secret of which I am not free to dispose. As yet."

"Opportunity, sir?" asked Jacques respectfully. *What opportunity could this odd man provide?*

Fragonard straightened up, his whole body puffed by some new feeling, a new confidence. He placed a finger across his lips, turned, and walked gracefully back into the darkness, calling back to the brothers.

"I'll not attend the main meal with you but will return late this afternoon to see you both," he said. "You may bring the hound's-tongue, Monsieur Jacques Casanova, on your next visit."

"Yes sir," Jacques called out. *If ever I come again. Why would the Vicomte's needs interest me?* Jacques knew what his own necessities were, and nobody could judge them better than he.

Francesco mixed paints onto his palette and slipped into his painter's pose of absolute concentration. Jacques sat in the armchair and looked at the canvases to be duplicated. The nautilus cross section, although one of nature's strange wonders, seemed a peculiar subject to copy. As for the landscape painting, it was craggy, distinctive, but of scant aesthetic interest. What artist of worth—which Francesco was—would paint *any* landscape? And why have Francesco paint them in a *cellar?*

Before long, the majordomo summoned the Casanova brothers upstairs and outside, where a magnificent sycamore provided shade for the main meal of the day. The brothers shared several glasses of Chianti, some mutton, cheese, figs, and apples.

"Now that our bellies are full," Francesco confided, "it's time to locate the indecent miniatures."

"As you promised."

"Several weeks ago while I strolled the house looking for a servant, I accidentally came upon the room containing the miniatures. I want to see the room again alone—or with you, but I'm not asking anyone's permission. I'm not sure the Vicomte would want me there at all." He whispered, "Common sense says I'm risking my painting commission, and maybe more.

Jacques patted Francesco's shoulder. "Daring guides us, Brother."

Francesco began mumbling reasonable defenses, should he and Jacques be detected wandering the interior of the house.

"Remember this," Jacques smiled, "the primary pleasure of life is to do what's forbidden."

He handed the bottle to Francesco, who gulped down the remainder of the Chianti while they stalked to the house.

Exploring the old chateau was not a simple task. Either from the Vicomte's frugality or from the servants' idleness, few of the halls were lit. Outsized furniture scattered haphazardly created formidable obstacles. Hulking armoires appeared to prop up canted walls. Buffets jutted at odd angles, presenting unusual impediments. As the brothers picked their way to the upper floor. the stairs creaked woefully. In one moment of crisis, the two were able to throw themselves behind a massive armoire when a manservant unexpectedly crossed the room ahead.

The wine contributed to the elation of their venture. What occupied only a matter of minutes took on the timelessness of a dream where each moment elongates itself.

"I, for one, feel boyish again," whispered Francesco. "When we sneak about, I'm a warrior."

"The Chianti goes to your head," Jacques whispered back, smiling. "But cover my sins with darkness and my cunning with a cloud."

Nervousness soon replaced excitement as Francesco found that, although he'd partaken in mischief during his youth, his skills had dulled with lack of practice. The longer the brothers explored without reaching their goal, the more the aged house seemed an unending maze of redoubtable staircases, groaning floors, and unlit hallways.

Although Jacques' nose was beginning to revolt from a harsh odor in one hall, he relished the game. Watching his brother stop at the end of the long hallway, he tiptoed to Francesco and saw a door some distance away with a brilliantly polished lock fastened to a gleaming hasp. Easing toward the door, Jacques pinched his nostrils. "Now I know from where the bitter smell of castoreum issues."

"Jesus-Mary, it's pungent," said Francesco, aping his brother's nose pinching.

"No, this isn't the room that holds the miniatures," he said in a hushed tone. "There was only a very faint smell when—"

"Then why is it fortified with such a lock?"

"It's not the room, I tell you. But even if it were, we can't get past that lock."

"Nor would I want to, with that odor."

"We've failed. We'll see no miniatures."

"We hail from Venice," Jacques replied. "Failed? Why, as Venetians, we don't know the meaning of the word. Did not our forefathers, in fleeing Attila the Hun, hide themselves in the godforsaken swamps and lagoons? And by using their daring and resourcefulness, did they not only survive but grow into the prosperous republic of Venice? Aren't we, as sons of this remarkable city-empire, as ingenious as our ancestors? Failed?" laughed Jacques as he rapped Francesco gently on the head. "There is *always* the main chance, Brother. And we have all the time in the world."

"But *not* today," Francesco frowned. "We must get back so we won't be missed."

Reluctantly, Jacques agreed. "Not today." Again he eyed the door. His curiosity burned. *But what might that stinking room hold?*

- 5 -

JACQUES AND FRANCESCO MADE THEIR WAY back to the sycamore tree where, in due course, they were summoned by the majordomo. Before the brothers began their walk toward the chateau, a cat mewed. Jacques mewed back.

When his shoe reached the hard ground of the cellar and the door behind him shut, a momentary shiver came over Jacques. *In the solitude of prison, I withered like this.*

The brothers trudged through the darkness to Francesco's workstation. Startled by a clomping noise, Jacques turned to see Vicomte de Fragonard hobble into view, pushing hard on his shillelagh.

"Good afternoon, young gentlemen."

Without turning, Francesco defiantly thrust a fistful of brushes into the air over his head.

Embarrassed by his brother's gesture, Jacques took several steps toward the Vicomte and offered a short bow and a "Good afternoon, sir."

"I felt it urgent that I be here," the Vicomte said, limping toward the armchair.

Jacques noted the almost-threadbare waistcoat and pants worn by Fragonard. The man's faded velvet jacket was long ago out of fashion.

The Vicomte caught Jacques' gaze. "Is it my garments you disdain? I tell you, sir, there are matters far more considerable than a man's raiment."

Jacques lowered his eyes and bobbed his head politely. In the musty air, he felt a bead of anxious sweat moisten his temple. He twisted toward his brother, who had obviously seen the exchange, but Francesco coolly returned to his work.

Vicomte de Fragonard soon initiated a conversation as if nothing inharmonious had occurred: "Have you perchance seen the Château Vaux-le-Vicomte on your travel here?"

"No, I haven't."

"I should have my coachman take you on that route. Magnificent château, built over a century ago by Nicolas Fouquet, Louis XIV's finance minister. Do you know Fouquet's story?"

"No, sir. I know much of your French king, but I know nothing of Fouquet."

"When the eighteen thousand workmen finally completed their labors on the château, Fouquet invited the young king to a resplendent celebration. King Louis seemed well pleased, yet a short time later Louis had the man arrested. Although the official charge was embezzlement, the real reason for Fouquet's arrest was that he refused to divulge a secret to the king, a secret of spellbinding significance. Louis ordered Nicolas Fouquet's head bound in a mask of iron, and he was locked away for the remainder of his life. King Louis, it is certain, never obtained the secret."

Jacques' gut wrenched at the thought of an iron mask on a human head. But then his mind began to race. *Is the old man about to reveal his vital secret?*

"You will visit Fouquet's wondrous château, Monsieur Jacques Casanova?"

"Certainly, Vicomte."

Fragonard, momentarily transfixed by a flitting moth, extended his index finger before him, where the moth alighted before fluttering away toward the row of lanterns. "Your brother, sir, has told me you are unmarried."

"Unmarried, yes. Willfully so."

"I also was heedless in my bachelor days. We roués, a dozen of us, squandered small fortunes in venery. We furnished our homes with expensive art, sexual stimulants, and extravagances. Can you imagine a twenty-year-old Frenchman requiring cantharides to fornicate? I remember Duclos—he later died a horrible death from the pox—once spent over ten thousand louis on a gilded *siege a deux* so he could, from that golden armchair, seduce a new debauchee every night. What an era of indulgence."

The Vicomte stared at Jacques as a crack of thunder sounded in the distance. Then with a calm matter-of-factness, he asked Jacques, "You are a libertine, are you not?"

"I greatly *enjoy* life," Jacques said with a smile. "If others accuse me of excess, so be it."

"Indeed," Fragonard said. His eyes gleamed brighter in the lantern light as he stared resolutely at the landscape canvas Francesco painted.

"Your gifted brother is executing divine and worthy work, I assure you."

Francesco, hands on hips, eyes on canvas, seemed impervious to the compliment.

Though Jacques put little capital in the Vicomte's stories, could he forestall his now-growing curiosity of the old gentleman's secret? Should he broach the subject in private to the Vicomte and risk Francesco's anger? When, if ever, might the Vicomte reveal his hand? Jacques wondered if he could check his own irritability at being in this dark, dank below with little to do. Patience was not one of his strengths, but he decided he would bide his time, at least until the circumstance might be more suitable.

The Vicomte spoke. "I believe Francesco told me you have other siblings?"

"As well as our Mother, Zanetta—"

"Living somewhere in this world—far away from us," Francesco muttered.

Jacques continued. "Speaking of the world, Vicomte, you seem a man who has seen quite a bit of it. Why—"

"I moved to this mansion with my wife. Consequently, I built my wealth with my wife's fortune. Perfectly shameful."

To Jacques, the old man's guilt was mystifying. Marriage was assuredly intended to further a man's fortune.

"Now I live in this out-of-the-way place," the Vicomte said. He sat down, laid his shillelagh across his lap, and patted his short beard. "This corrupted flesh has led me to places that I, as a young blood, would never have dreamed. I was a perfumer's son who, being crippled, forfeited my right of primogeniture. Shunned by the military as well as by my father, I became a surgeon. I confess there was not much occasion to practice my profession here in this remoteness, except to bleed, to cup, and to advise bed rest and medicaments. How was I to know that I would be led in midlife to embalming? And to serve mankind?"

Jacques and Francesco glanced at each other, surprise on their faces.

"But long ago, after my wife died and after a certain extraordinary and crucial experience, I decided to remain in this place, this distant place. As I participated less and less in the world, I became, finally, a philosopher—a pursuit that aids the spirit and men's hearts." The Vicomte cleared his throat. "So this day you have heard a large piece of my story."

"Intriguing, sir."

"Significant is a better word."

Jacques blinked at the peculiar statement. *Leading an embalmer's life, what could be significant?* The old gentleman made everything sound substantial, when all Jacques wanted to know was his secret and what opportunity might be in store.

He peeked at his brother, then drew a breath to speak, but the Vicomte spoke first.

"I am to understand that you are a man of mathematics, Jacques Casanova. And every man who has an exacting mind must bow to the idea of 'first cause'—God."

"I don't agree," Jacques said loudly. "Even if a mind could admit to the notion—the concept of deity—the reality does not necessarily exist."

"I honor your sincerity. However, I prefer not to debate. We risk becoming entrenched in our positions without opening the question for authentic exchange." Then in a whisper: "But mark my words, sir. I have met God. Here, on earth. And one day perhaps you, too, shall meet Him."

The thin peal of a bell sounded from the darkness. A moment later, the majordomo appeared bearing the instrument and rang it softly again before helping the Vicomte to his feet.

Leaning on his manservant, the old man limped away.

- 6 -

THE BROTHERS WERE FORTUNATE while they explored. A summer rainstorm muffled the telltale creaks of the house, white flashes of lightning firing wild shadows across the windows. The search drew the brothers farther into the home until, on the third floor, they were near losing hope.

"Over there," whispered Francesco, indicating a polished door in the far corner of the long hallway.

"Ah," said Jacques. His heart raced with exhilaration.

They scurried to the door. Placing their ears to the cool wood, they heard nothing. They tried the knob. When it turned, they took two candles from their pockets, lit them, and entered. A garret-sized room met their eyes, its space brimming with erotic paintings, salacious statuary, and art pieces, all neatly displayed on two huge tables.

In moments, the brothers were pawing the private collection of miniatures belonging to the Vicomte Honoré de Fragonard.

Though in the last hundred years or so art had become accessible to the masses, the vast majority of good art was still housed in private collections. There was no collection, however, that Jacques had viewed—and there had been several—as extensive as this.

"Fragonard says this room holds artifacts from his former life," Francesco said flatly.

"Oh, my delicious gods," squealed Jacques, peeping over his brother's shoulder at the dusty ivory tablet he held. The pale oval, no larger than a man's palm, displayed a nude woman on her back, being ravished by a satyr. About to crown the lovemakers with an olive wreath was another naked girl, her voluptuous breasts peeking through her long hair. The satyr squeezed the budding nipples of the supine woman while sharing a tongue kiss.

"Stimulating," Jacques bubbled.

"I hope so."

The brothers were immovable for some time until Jacques gorged on a different miniature, a vibrant statue of a woman astride her partner, both lost in the uttermost moment. The artist had done his job skillfully, and although the swirling bed stuffs well hid some of the couple's anatomical delights, there was no disguising their rapturous glory.

"Have you created pieces such as these?" Jacques whispered.

His brother shook his head, apparently despondent. "Battle scenes are what I paint."

"Admittedly," Jacques went on, "erotic work such as this requires money for models but—"

"I had expected these to … but they're no help." Francesco's voice had a strange yearning.

"Oh," Jacques said, looking up. "You sound as if the miniatures are life and death to you."

"They may be."

Jacques wanted to ask what Francesco meant. Instead, he shot a quizzical look at his brother, then unveiled a draped easel. "Ah, the creamy-fleshed, rosy-cheeked nymphs Monsieur Boucher paints," he said. "And all have the unmistakable baby face of Madame Boucher."

Francesco gave a halfhearted smile before staring at the table full of erotic work. He selected a miniature and held it in his hand.

"I know I'm capable of this." A clap of thunder startled him, and he returned the piece to the table before looking to his brother.

Jacques smiled, pointing to his swelling crotch. "Psst," he whispered.

"Is that humor?" Francesco growled. Instantly, he wheeled about and tramped toward the door.

* * *

The quietude of the cellar, combined with the surrounding darkness, captivated Jacques. The lanterns created a glittering effect so that the pale russet chambers of the nautilus seemed to expand and contract, shifting into extraordinarily vivid colors. The canvas itself at times seemed to undulate. Francesco's intense concentration—the fluid motion of his painting arm, the confidence of his brushstrokes—all added to the spell.

Soon the old Vicomte entered, thwacking the thick support timbers with his shillelagh. He put on a proud air and took a seat in the chair Jacques had vacated. All but swallowed by the cavernous armchair, he said nothing. Occasionally he leaned forward or waved his finger as if it were a baton, tapping it rhythmically on the fauteuil's arm, while his eyes searched every inch of each canvas as if it held some long-lost secret.

The two brothers shared a glance before Francesco mumbled something and refocused on his canvas.

At last the Vicomte spoke. "I sought fame—or infamy, some might say. I wanted my song to be heard, perhaps above others." His voice held much sadness. He thrust his shillelagh towards Jacques. "I recognize that very characteristic in you, my son. Vanity drives you to indulgence. Your compulsion to have your song heard is your cross, a burden you will not or cannot lay down. I was of that nature. But you shall perhaps discover it's not a true path." He leaned back. "For me, in one astonishing experience, only in an instant, I was able to recognize much of my authentic nature, and I was transformed. Profoundly, believe me. And Jesus of ... well, I had much to learn."

Jacques pulled out his snuffbox, offering its ingredients to his brother and the Vicomte. Both declined.

"I am decided," Fragonard said to Jacques. "I am decided."

He pointed his shillelagh at Francesco. "Because I am paying wages to this talented artist to paint and not to prod in other business, and as you," he pointed his stick at Jacques, "are the one whose character I feel free to dissect, you are chosen to accompany me. I invite you alone."

Jacques, wondering how soon he would be visiting the erotic miniatures, reminded himself to be surprised when the old owl showed them. He bowed.

"I gratefully accept, Vicomte de Fragonard, and look forward to your company."

Fragonard lifted himself from the chair and retrieved his shillelagh.

"No doubt that much of what I have said seems to have little importance from your vantage point, Signor Casanova. But grant credit to a man with many years and some wisdom. Truly, I confide I've had an experience that most men may only imagine."

"My inquisitive nature, sir, near overwhelms me."

The Vicomte beckoned the younger man with an outstretched finger.

*   *   *

Once into the upper house, the Vicomte and Jacques made their way with only a single candle between them and an occasional wall sconce for illumination. Jacques' nose was beginning to react to a familiar odor.

"I rely on your reputation as an understanding man and a citizen of the world," the Vicomte said as he stepped into the dark void of a hallway, a rash of thunder echoing from the storm outside.

Jacques was anxious; he didn't recognize where he was. Certainly it wasn't the corridor that led to the miniatures, but while he and the Vicomte lumbered down the hallway, he stayed abreast.

The unmistakable smell of castoreum engulfed Jacques. In moments, the sight of a gleaming lock told him he was standing at the door that had first attracted his attention that day. He heard a creaking sound and lifted the candle to see the Vicomte replace a key into his vest pocket. What lay behind the door?

"Remove the lock from the hasp, if you please," said the Vicomte, "then stand aside."

After Jacques complied, Fragonard spoke. "I invite you to view my cabinet of curiosities, Signor Casanova. Few others have seen this work of mine. But you are a freethinker. What I have gleaned of your character interests me—and more importantly, what I intuit to be true of you confirms your usefulness." The Vicomte de Fragonard edged toward the younger man. "Earlier I readied the cabinet. Now I ask your opinion of my creations."

The Vicomte pushed hard, and the door swung wide. A jewel box of iridescence blinded Jacques, and in the moment he tried to regain sight, the sickly sweet smell nearly overpowered him.

The Vicomte ushered him into the chamber while Jacques shaded his eyes against what seemed a ceiling full of candles. When he stepped forward, his slowly returning vision was drawn to the far end of the room where, high at the ceiling, a black scrim draped downward, partitioning a portion of the large space.

He followed the scrim to the floor. His chief view was the dark outline of a stationary horse, a rider seated upright, arms flexed as if to grasp reins. Moving slowly into the room, he saw the horse had no skin. Every cord of its musculature was visible.

Jacques' throat dried. He was sickened but couldn't keep from looking. Neither man nor horse was a skeleton or a corpse but an amalgamation of red veins, brown ligaments, and yellowish tendons— all power and rawness, frozen in grotesquerie. The rider's teeth were gritted, his nostrils flared, eyeballs expressionless. A nightmare of fiendish vulgarity.

"What is the purpose of ..." Jacques stammered, nearly voiceless.

The Vicomte said, "I, naturally, cannot disclose my recipe, though I have, by determined experiment, improved upon a Templars' formula, which was revealed to me many, many years ago. My écorchés are preserved, I may reveal, by soaking the cadaver in eau-de-vie, mixed with aloe, myrrh, and pepper, among other substances."

"What I meant was—"

The Vicomte broke in. "After draining blood and removing the vital organs, I employ my prescription, then inject the arteries, veins, and bronchial tubes with tallow mixed with turpentine. Sometimes arsenical salts. I then—" The Vicomte stopped, frowning. "No, I forbid myself to give away the embalming process. That is my private domain. I will say my method is far, far superior to, say, that of Czar Peter, who knew how to decapitate his unfaithful lover but knew only to put her head in spirit of alcohol. Spirit of alcohol. Primitive, do you agree?"

"So the castoreum I smell—?"

"Covers the occasionally distressing odors from my work. Sometimes I use ambergris or styrax for a sweeter fragrance." While the Vicomte ambled forward, he spoke. "You realize, of course, that in France we anatomists receive convicted assassins for dissection. That is the law of the land. *Fiat experimintum in corpore vili.* 'Let experiment be made on a worthless body.' The gentleman you see here was in several pieces when the authorities turned him over to me. It seemed he had become an acolyte of the diocese, but the Sacred Orders refused to accept him in the priesthood. The distraught fellow attempted to murder the bishop outside his episcopal quarters. The attempt failed, and in due course, he was sentenced. His fist was broken on the stake. His arms, legs, thighs, and loins were broken on special scaffolding. And his body, which was to be reduced by fire to cinders and scattered to the wind, was instead given to me. How one may suffer from the boot heel of the Church. But as you see from this bust, I was able to retrieve some of the ..." The Vicomte threw his arm wide. "These are my écorchés."

Staring at the stark remains, Jacques felt his face grow blisteringly hot. *Is man no more than this?*

"As to the purpose about which you asked? There is a far greater intention to my work than one would suppose," the Vicomte admonished.

Beside him, a menacing figure, possibly once human, was posed midstride, brandishing a large mandible. The pit of Jacques' stomach grew cold and hard. Yet almost against his will, he found himself following the Vicomte into the larger chamber beyond.

In its corner, beyond more than two dozen gnarled demi-beasts of exposed viscera and swollen veins, hung the dark scrim. Approaching, he recognized the sweet smell of ambergris before stepping around the curtain.

A figure with skeletal hands, palms pressed together, reclined in a bath of fluid. The being, slumbering on his back, had not been managed or mangled like the rest. Jacques stepped toward the figure. *This once lived as a man; amid all the hellish figures, this one alone is transformed.* The face had an enigmatic, almost serene expression.

Jacques turned upon hearing Fragonard clubbing across the parquet floor.

"All the other écorchés you have seen are my earliest experiments," the Vicomte said, "rudimentary labors in progress, really. This is the zenith toward which I have worked. He was created from a devout inspiration of the spirit, born from an experience that changed me once and forever."

"I find myself oddly touched by him," Jacques admitted.

"That is vastly pleasing." The Vicomte's face softened. He made one final review of the chamber, punching his shillelagh in staccato thrusts at airy nothings, then strode toward the door.

Jacques followed.

- 7 -

DOMINIQUE CASANOVA WAS FASCINATED. She didn't wish to be. But her kind and inquisitive nature found her houseguest fascinating. Jacques' stories of faraway places, of charlatans he'd met, of bluebloods he'd known, as well as his variety of occupations— adventurer, gambler, secretary, soldier, preacher, musician, writer— all excited her.

He talked. And he also listened, though she knew the dullness of her daily routine provided slim fodder for interest. Their conversation and his attentiveness were all too stimulating.

This morning while he and Dominique shared Francesco's two-day old bread, Jacques discussed the brothers' recent trip to Vicomte de Fragonard's; without mentioning the indecent miniatures, he accentuated his generous gift to the child, the "rewarding time with his brother," and the Vicomte's eccentric manner.

For Dominique, these stories pointed up her separateness, her loneliness.

Too, she was disturbed by her interest in —her attraction to—her husband's brother. So that she might not grow further distraught, she determined that her best course was to rediscover Francesco's charm. And after seven years with a man who seemed more married to his art than to her, she knew she must, without delay, have an answer for her deepest desire of all.

After Jacques left for the afternoon, Dominique knelt beside her window, anxious to speak with her god. Fingering the ivory cross hanging from her neck, she attempted to hold back her tears.

"My master, Jesus, I come in humility to ask ... not been to confession, and ... feel weak. Show me the path ... goodness ... sweet Jesus, You keep us pure, create us anew. Encompass my heart in ... grant an answer for my confusion. In my master's name, Jesus the Christ. Amen." In the fading rays of daylight Dominique genuflected, kissed the crucifix, tucked it back into her dress, and wiped her eyes.

She knew what she must do: ask Jacques to find another lodging, to leave.

But it was Francesco who arrived home first.

"You're back from the Vicomte de Fragonard's early?" Dominique called from the door of her room. "I'd hoped you would be."

"Tonight I paint at home, not in a cellar," Francesco grumbled, coming up the stairs.

"And we'll have privacy. Jacques and Petrine may not return until late so—"

"For once."

"But I enjoy their company." Guilt colored her voice. She stumbled on her next words. "May I join you, husband—to see your progress?"

Francesco said nothing while continuing up the stairs.

Dominique soon entered the loft, where spiraling shadows—spawned by crude chandeliers—revealed a myriad of creatures on canvas. The walls of the loft seemed a gargantuan speckled honeycomb of sketches, half-finished colorings, blank canvases, and paintings.

With help from the substantial slice of moon streaming through the overhead window, Dominique crossed the long room, pondering the various portraits, animal depictions, and scenes of war that her husband had painted over the years. She sucked in a breath of air tinged with turpentine and dared a look at several paintings Francesco had slashed; although she found his actions disconcerting, what upset her further was his insistence that his defaced works remain on the loft walls. To Dominique, it was a reminder of his sullen frustration.

She set her tray of bread, cheese, and wine on a small table, then took a seat on her favorite stool while her husband finished lighting the chandeliers.

When Francesco walked by, Dominique tugged playfully at his finger, but he drew back his hand. He climbed the ladder that was set against his large canvas, closed one eye, and began to paint, adding silver highlights to the sabers of a troop of soldiers attacked on all fronts by a fierce enemy.

Several minutes passed while he worked.

"I should take a saber to that brother of mine," Francesco grumbled, eyeing Dominique. "Am I unwise to say so, my wife?

"Such an imposing canvas," was all that Dominique said.

Francesco stubbed the palette with his brush, shook his head, then descended the ladder.

"My brother is a singular character whose extravagances make many steadfast allies—like his bishop friend—and many avenging enemies."

Dominique supposed her husband was correct about Jacques. He had many enemies—and no one to protect him.

Francesco gobbled a hunk of cheese, then lumbered back to his work. He crouched by the corner of the large canvas, running a finger across a tree he'd sketched months ago, before climbing the ladder.

"Did I tell you when my brother was twenty, he was so enamored of a girl that he decided to bake locks of her hair in a sweet confection— a not uncommon practice where we grew up—and present it to her?" Francesco rattled on, now splotching vermilion on his field of battle. "The whole love affair foundered, died. By sheer chance, our mother was in town, and she comforted him in his utter misery— while during those few days, a different calamity had befallen me that put me in worse agony than he. But Zanetta ignored me. As always."

Dominique caught her husband's dismay. "I don't ignore you, Francesco. I want us—"

"Don't," he barked. He speared his paint palette with his brush as if he were impaling a bug.

Dominique stiffened and remained silent for several moments before speaking. "What do you want from *me*? I don't understand."

She clamped herself to her stool, a sharp agitation within her driving her to leave the room. This agitation stemmed a secret, a truth that she knew dwelled in her, but one she couldn't seem to dredge from her depths. Although long ago Dominique had decided she'd not confide each and every one of her confidences to Francesco, she'd always felt an unspoken permission to do so, if and when she cared to shed another layer of guard. She knew Francesco, in his bearish manner, accepted her even if her secrets were her own.

But this unidentified unease she felt seemed more a secret from herself than from Francesco. *Free this secret. Pry it loose. Open it, Jesus, to my heart.*

She pinched at her crucifix while Francesco, balancing on his ladder at chandelier height, smeared a dark indigo on his canvas. No emotion was perceptible now on his face, nothing that might betray what he was thinking or feeling. He was finished talking. Dominique had learned this. She'd become skilled at reading his minute gestures, in gauging his utterances and moods. She sometimes understood his eyes, but not when they were in the throes of despair.

Francesco stared at his canvas, rubbing his forehead as if he wanted to erase his flesh. He climbed down the ladder.

Dominique knew. *He grows dispirited. His black humor encases him.*

She weighed whether to address him.

Francesco set aside his palette and stood alone, brown hair shrouding his brow.

Our strength is friendship, Dominique soothed herself. But a strange instability disturbed her with this thought.

"Friendship, our strength," she said aloud, as if an invocation. The inflexible wooden stool pressing against her gave her pause.

"Friendship," she reiterated, now beginning to question her statement.

Suddenly new words, as if furnished by another voice, arrived on Dominique's lips, and although she wanted to deny them, subdue them, reject them, they pushed coldly and quietly out through her mouth.

"Friendship's our deadly weakness. It cannot be the only way I love you. No longer is ... meager friendship ... enough. I resent that I don't have a husband." Instantly, she knew this was the plain, earnest truth whose declaration she'd hidden for such a long, long time. And she knew the truth was hurtful.

Stunned, Dominique stared at Francesco before continuing. "I need my husband. And I want children."

His dark, unwelcoming eyes confirmed his understanding of what Dominique had just said. Slowly, his lips crooked into a glum, impassable grimace.

Grasping her crucifix, Dominique shoved aside her stool and moved closer to Francesco. She touched his hand. The pain in his eyes was crushing. Nothing would comfort him.

She turned and walked away.

* * *

It was just before midnight when Jacques barged into the loft, shouting gaily. "Petrine and I scoured the downstairs. And here you are, Francesco. Let's have a fight. It's been—I don't know how many years." Jacques crossed the wide loft, followed by Petrine, clutching a mahogany case and small cloth bag.

Francesco leaned on his haunches, back against the wall, hands on cheeks, gazing at his canvas. The ladder lay next to him.

Stopping several paces from his brother, Jacques glanced up at a battle painting. "Of all the splendid art in this huge room, I like this one best. And I see you're almost finished."

"I'm just in the humor to duel," said Francesco.

Jacques spoke to Petrine. "My brother has the bold countenance of an eagle, don't you think?"

"While you, Brother, are a fine line away from ugliness," Francesco replied.

"Perhaps so," Jacques said sincerely. "Yet it seems my bright eyes persuade women that I'm handsome. Shall we fight?"

Francesco smiled wryly, stood suddenly, and stripped off his shirt. Jacques did likewise.

"Perform your duties, valet."

Sweeping his hair from his eyes, Petrine bowed to his master and presented the long rectangular case cradled in his arms.

Francesco clapped Jacques' bare shoulder and pointed to the numbers carved on the mahogany lid.

"Seventeen forty. Mother gave us these swords fifteen years ago."

"On *my* fifteenth birthday," Jacques said. "They're *mine*."

"When I plant this sword in your chest, you'll have my weapon *and* yours—full custody of *both*."

Jacques wagged his head.

"What a gift these were. Born common, and yet to possess our own swords! Do you remember how excited we became? We knew it cost Zanetta dearly, and we kissed her hands for hours."

Petrine stood midway between the two shirtless men while he unfastened the latches on the mahogany case and opened it.

"Your choice, sir?"

Francesco studied the two weapons, walking his fingers across both hilts before selecting one.

"This lancet suits me well," he said as he withdrew the elegant sword.

The valet submitted the case to Jacques, who removed the remaining weapon.

The smallsword was wicked perfection: its triangular shape gave the sword lightness and durability; its edges tapered to a deadly, needle-like point.

It was said triangular blades produced wounds that were particularly difficult to stitch back together. Most smallswords were not made to have a cutting edge. These two were.

Petrine laid the case on the table next to him, then after digging in his bag, offered leather gloves to each brother.

"No blood, please," the valet smirked. "After our long day in Paris, I'm in no condition for more work."

Jacques glared. In the splaying light and shadows, he examined his "sharp," pinched a bit of crab's-eye tobacco and snuffed it, then slid his right hand into a thick leather glove. He and Francesco took a dozen steps and stood opposite one another, both standing just outside the range of each other's deadly steel.

"When we were boys," Jacques said, "well, I recall that we fought less and less after you began to dabble with paint and palette and I began to dabble with maids and maidenheads."

Francesco's sword blade hissed through the damp air.

Jacques rolled his eyes.

"Testing my arm."

"As I was saying," Jacques continued, "my passions are different from yours, but you mustn't think I'm a slave to them. *Animum rege, qui, nisi paret, imperat*, says Horace. 'Unless the heart obeys, it commands.'"

I never let my passions command. I keep my defenses strong at all times. I allow passion its place, of course, but I remain composed. And that's how I shall best you." Jacques pointed his weapon at Francesco as an affront.

Francesco, squaring his body with Jacques, leveled an intimidating stare. "Tonight I will merely wound you."

The two men remained rock still. From the high walls, wild eyes of painted horses glared at them, dazed and dying soldiers wailed silently, and from his canvas domicile, the stern visage of some long-forgotten saint appeared to comment on the follies of men and swordplay.

The brothers raised their swords and executed an elaborate salute. Both took a *tierce en garde*, then began circling and countercircling, each attempting to maneuver within striking range.

"O elder one," Francesco declared, "I would paint your limpid eyes—"

"What did you say?"

"I said I would paint your liquid eyes …"

A flash of anger crossed Jacques' face. "Beat, attack," he shouted as he swept aside Francesco's steel with his blade and made a thrusting assault to the shoulder.

"Parry, riposte." Francesco blocked the attack, then thrust at Jacques, who narrowly evaded the point.

Petrine slid tighter against the wall where he'd placed the sword case.

"It's not the sight of blood; it's just so impossible to scrub it off a floor," he yelled at the adversaries. He then spoke to himself. "If my master is killed, I'll be forced to seek another paycheck."

Francesco, caught off guard, executed a counterparry and dodged another harrowing flurry of steel before regaining his fencing stance. He advanced, thrusting at Jacques' torso. Jacques gave ground.

For an instant, both stood stock-still, swords apart. Sweat clouded their eyes. Each duelist wiped his brow before edging forward and back in a deft dance. Francesco initiated a number of spirals— *doublés*—with his blade, forcing Jacques to do likewise.

"Like all men before me, someday I'll die," Jacques said. "But before that, I'll damned well live. What I've learned from life is that the only significant difference between an animal and me is that I know more personal pleasures."

Francesco scowled. "Have you never once searched your heart for—"

"I say that a man who asks himself too many questions is an unhappy man." Jacques smiled and resumed his *en garde*. "I live to satisfy my senses. Why should I deny myself pleasures?"

A female voice rang through the large room. "You'd better be playing, you two," said Dominique, walking through the far door and stopping at a safe distance.

Without replying, the brothers renewed their feverish thrusts.

"*Et la*," shouted Francesco. "And there."

Jacques' body braced. He stopped and looked down to watch the sword's point pull away. He barely heard the gasps from Dominique and Petrine while he surveyed his chest. When a languorous course of warm blood seeped from his pectoral, he sank to his knees.

"To possess our own swords," he muttered.

Petrine and Dominique helped Jacques stand while Francesco relieved him of his weapon, setting it next to his brother's feet.

"Are you hurt?"

"I merit I am, ass." Jacques opened his fingers cupped over his heart, and pulpy red blood bloomed from his chest.

Dominique swabbed Jacques' wound with a handkerchief. "Monsieur, it looks horrible. Horrible. Make your peace. Now."

"What, what?" Jacques cried with terror.

She turned back to Petrine and Francesco with a grin. "A wound, perhaps. But I would judge it only a prick." She laughed.

Petrine bobbed his head in agreement. "Won't be mopping up much blood from that wound."

Jacques cautiously rechecked his upper body. "Not as wide as a yawning grave, I suppose, but it will do."

Petrine scurried to the far wall and returned with two shirts, the sword case, cloth bag, and snuffbox.

"I might have died," Jacques said in a barely audible voice.

"I only wounded you, libertine. Maybe I should have killed you." As he extended his point, Francesco's eyes glinted.

Jacques' belly tingled with a queer feeling of alarm.

"I once again claim victory," Francesco said. When Jacques huffed, he added, "Must not let the passions command. Is that not your precept?" He took his shirt from Petrine.

Jacques brimmed with humiliation. He seized his sword, but Francesco drew the hilt of his smallsword to his face and, offering a polite salute, ended the combat. Jacques had no choice but to do the same. Good manners demanded it.

The two brothers, following their personal custom, then faced Dominique and saluted with their weapons.

The woman's eyes glittered like translucent gems.

Petrine produced a cloth, accepted Francesco's smallsword, wiped clean the blade, and set it in the case while Francesco headed toward the loft entrance.

"Are you coming to bed soon?" he asked without turning around.

"No," Jacques and Dominique said in unison. Dominique's stately manner disappeared when she laughed.

"No," Jacques repeated. "I'll write late into the night, as is my habit."

"I was speaking to Dominique, elder Brother. Good night, then. See you on the morrow. I'll keep the candle lit, wife." He left.

Jacques examined his naked chest with intense consternation, paying little heed to Dominique. Petrine, who stood in a patch of moonlight shining through the overhead window, cleared his throat.

Jacques glanced at his valet. "Hang my shirt on that painting. Take my blade. Then place the sword case and gold snuffbox in my room. Wait there."

Petrine nodded while Jacques' attention returned to his wound.

"I think you've thoroughly mended," teased Dominique. While Jacques stroked beneath his pectoral with a fingertip of saliva, she continued, "Your stamina is astonishing. You say you write tonight?" A brief smile played upon her lips. "What else do you accomplish late in the night?"

There was no response.

She shrugged her shoulders. "If you write late into the night, it would appear you possess a vigorous intellect," she tried again.

"I continue working, madame, on the squaring of the cube. Many philosophers, as well as Messieurs Descartes and Newton, have labored ineffectually on this extraordinarily vexing problem, but I intend to find the mathematical solution."

"You will, without a doubt, be successful with this extraordinarily vexing problem," Dominique replied with a smile. "You say you live to satisfy your senses, yet your intellectual curiosity seems paramount. Beyond your intellectual endeavors, have you other pursuits?"

Jacques looked up, then stepped close. "None as important as the one who stands before me."

Dominique drew a sudden breath.

"You may have to teach me," he said.

Spellbound, Dominique whispered, "Teach you?"

"Yes, teach me." His words lingered while he brushed away a lock of hair on Dominique's cheek and leaned forward.

She blushed deeply.

Jacques smiled at his thoughts; unhurriedly, he withdrew from her. "Yes, you may have to teach me the lunge, the fencing move which gave your husband victory."

A gush of silver moonlight overwhelmed the loft for several moments, enough time for Jacques to catch Dominique's emerald eyes swell large and bright.

"Besides the squaring of the cube," he said, turning away, "I'm also expanding my old doctoral thesis: 'Any being which can be conceived only abstractly can exist only abstractly.' For devout religionists, it's a dizzying concern."

"Your sarcasm puzzles me," Dominique replied. "You puzzle me. Shall I take it that you are a good member of the Church?"

Jacques picked up his linen shirt and slung it over his shoulder. He began to leave but abruptly spun back.

"Madame, I was not born to be redeemed."

Then and there, Dominique decided she'd much to teach this man.

- 8 -

WITHIN A DAY, DOMINIQUE FOUND herself sitting on a grassy knoll face-to-face with her houseguest, listening to a tale that some in Europe already knew: Jacques' escape from I Piombi.

Jacques tented his fingers around his knee and leaned back, resting against a tree. Shining just over his shoulder, the sun was preparing its departure.

"I don't know why I'm telling this," he said.

"Because," she smiled, "I asked you. I'm interested."

Jacques laughed. "I should've been interested in the warning my patron, Senator Bragadin, gave when he advised me to leave Venice." He looked into the distance. "Three years before that, you see, I'd saved the senator's life, and I soon convinced him that I possessed profound occult powers. Now, know this: Senator Bragadin is no fool. On the other hand, there isn't a man in Europe, including me, whose mind is entirely free from some superstition.

"Most men carry many such mindless notions: belief in gnomes, undines, and sylphs of the mystical cabala; a yearning for the philosopher's stone to cure all disease or to transmute base metal into gold; the conviction that some astrologer can make known a man's destiny; a faith in magic elixirs, in alchemy, in … the list goes on.

"Like all men, Senator Bragadin wanted to believe in something. This I knew. So my knowledge of the occult helped me cement the role of—more or less—adopted son. It was a position that placed me in the upper chamber of Venetian society with gentlemen's clothes of silk and sufficient funds for endless gambling and the procurement of the most delicate treasures. Signor Bragadin was generous and tolerant, even while insisting that someday I would pay the price for my perilous behaviors.

"You can understand why it was wholly inconceivable when this evenhanded man came to my room to explain the Inquisitori's methods and to feverishly pronounce the warning to me: Leave Venice this minute.

"I chose not to listen. The very next morning, my lodgings were invaded by three dozen Venetian policemen. Looking back, I suppose it pleased my pride—that the Secretary of the Three deemed me dangerous. Or so I thought."

In the telling, Jacques' voice was soft and simple. He thought he saw in Dominique's eyes a question: *Do you seek to lead me astray?* He laughed at his notion and let the spring air warm his lungs.

Dominique bade him continue his story.

"On the first day of my sentence, I remained in good spirits while entering the Doge's palace and the prison within it: I Piombi, the Leads. Spirited was I—even while I passed the garroting machine, the torture instruments used for tearing out teeth and tongues, and the tool for skull crushing.

"But …," he paused. "I hadn't been informed of charges nor been told the length of my sentence. I crouched in that cell—lower than my full height—feeling utter confusion." Jacques bent his head forward. "All was dark except for one corner of the room that had an undersized window that offered some dingy light. Rotting in a cell, you don't tire of living, you tire of slowly dying. Deeply frightening, I assure you. It speaks to my fear that I didn't have a bowel movement for half a month.

"'Why am I in prison?' I asked myself again and again. 'I'm blameless. Guiltless.' Soon I did not so much wonder *why* I was there but *how* I would escape the place." His eyes glistened.

"How … how *did* you escape?" Dominique's lips were parted in astonishment, her eyes unblinking.

WHOMP! Jacques' hands clapped shut.

Dominique immediately took up a defensive posture, her expression vulnerable but not helpless.

"The slamming of that cell door scared me as badly as I scared you!" exclaimed Jacques.

The pair exchanged a silly laugh.

"Here—in brief—is my escape story: I donned a hat and walked out the front door of the Leads."

Dominique showed a glimmer of glee that ended with a smile. "Tell me all, or you'll get no dinner tonight."

"For your pleasure, madame," he said, straightening out his legs. "In the beginning, I was put in solitary confinement. Little did I know I would stay there ninety-seven days. In unremitting hell. Keeping company only with what thoughts I had. I, who thrive on the pleasures of social discourse, on the sweet joys of food and drink, on the ... reduced to a dark, dank cell with rats as big as rabbits.

"By late autumn, I was given cellmates from time to time. The head jailer, Lorenzo, began to feed me decently and soon granted me an armchair. For reading material, I was given *The Mystical City of God*." Jacques' face screwed up into a graceless expression. "Interminably long and catastrophically boring."

Dominique laughed.

"I knew these privileges of mine were granted only because of the entreaties of my benefactor, Senator Bragadin." Jacques frowned. "But most everything, it seemed, added to my severe melancholia. Fortunately, better things were to come: eventually I was granted walks—for exercise—in the prison attic. It was there I discovered a piece of polished black marble and an iron spike the length of my forearm. Although at the time I'd no idea what good this might do, I secreted the spike and marble in my armchair. Then one dream-filled night, a plan came to me.

"Quite soon, I began to complain of chest pains and bronchia to Lorenzo. I persuaded the prison doctor that my cell must not be cleaned because the dust might kill me. I kept this up for some time, during which my difficult work started: In those periods when I was absent cellmates, I'd sharpen my iron spike by honing it on the marble, using spit for lubrication. Stiff arms, a huge blister, and a month's work—that's what the pointed spike cost. Convincing myself that my jail cell was above the chamber where the Inquistori held court—and my best bet for escape—I began to bore through the cell floor.

"Ever so slowly and painfully, I worked through the wood, the marble terrazzo—using vinegar from my salads to soften the terrazzo—then more wood."

"They didn't discover the hole you were making?" asked Dominique.

Jacques offered a sly smile. "My cell was not entered once, not cleaned a single time—for as you know, the dust would most certainly harm their prisoner."

Dominique glanced away, rolling her eyes.

"It was the height of summer, blazing hot. A sweatbox. I worked naked, sweat pouring from me. One night, the bolt on the outer door squeaked. I hurled my spike in the hole, brushed the wood splinters in, all before pulling my bed over the hole and covering myself.

"A man entered. A new cellmate."

Dominique gasped.

"Luckily, he stayed for only a week. After he was gone, I continued my work. At last I punched through the floor. But ...," Jacques' tone lowered. "But my secret breach was too close to a stout ceiling beam. The hole could not be enlarged any further for my body to slip through.

"Miserable, I nevertheless resigned myself to drill again, farther over, making sure that none of my scraps would fall into the Inquisitori's chamber below and that my lantern's light would not be seen at night by a watchman. I planned to break out during a Venetian festival in August, when no one would occupy the room below.

"By the twenty-fifth, my new escape hole was almost finished. It was then, three days before my planned exodus, that Senator Bragadin thought to make my incarceration easier; with his influence, I was to be moved. To a better cell. One with *two* windows, more light, a view.

"Nearly fainting, I told Lorenzo, the jailer, that I couldn't budge, that fresh air was bad for a man with bronchia, that the feral rats had become my friends. I pleaded to stay in my cell. Lorenzo thought me mad."

"What happened?" asked Dominique, touching his hand. She was enthralled with his story, sympathizing with him for the trials he'd undergone and perhaps exulting in his tiny victories.

Jacques continued. "Into the new cell, the armchair was moved—iron spike well hidden in it. In the chair I sat, a wretched lump, until, as I feared, a raging Lorenzo arrived—he'd discovered my escape hole—and now threatened torture and death if I wouldn't divulge the whereabouts of my tools.

"I'll never quite understand how in my bewilderment I was able to respond, but because I knew jailers were easily corrupted, I simply replied, 'You, Lorenzo, provided the tools the moment I offered a bribe, and when I'm forced to confess this, the Secretary of the Three will not be pleased.'

"Lorenzo shut his mouth. Because no one else knew of my attempt, well, he must've figured he yet had the upper hand—he still held me prisoner in his jail."

The sun seemed poised on Jacques' shoulder and appeared magically to remain there.

With bitterness ringing in his voice, he explained to Dominique that he was soon given another cellmate, certainly a spy sent by the Three, who by this time must have been alerted to his escape attempt. "Although I still had possession of the spike, I was now under constant watch. I felt defeated.

"Nevertheless, I decided to risk another escape, figuring to employ Father Balbi, a renegade priest in the adjacent cell, as my accomplice. To advance this fresh plan, the jailer was ultimately persuaded to exchange reading books between Father Balbi and me; the jailer was hoodwinked when he unknowingly transferred my spike to the priest by way of a heaping plate of pasta he balanced precariously on a large folio Bible.

"As for the spy in my cell, I played on the man's superstitions and terrorized him into silence while Balbi, over a period of time, bored a hole with the spike in the ceiling of his own cell, climbed across, and in due course produced a similar hole in my ceiling.

"The night of the escape came. Based on observations of the jailers' schedules as well as the Inquisitori's chamber sessions, Jacques knew he and Balbi had nineteen hours to complete their flight. The pair lifted themselves up through Jacques' ceiling, knowing that should the spy cry out, there would be no one in the Leads—at this handpicked hour—to hear.

"Prying up the wood and the lead plates of the palace attic," continued Jacques, "I discovered a thick fog shrouding the sloping roof and much too long a drop to the canal. Balbi and I returned to my cell and spent hours cutting up sheets, coverlets, and bedding that would act as rope.

"Returning to the roof, we were immediately struck by a brilliant crescent moon, so bright that our shadows might reveal us to anyone on the Piazza San Marco. For safety's sake, we waited another three hours until the moon disappeared.

"After we struggled back onto the roof, I exhausted precious time in exploration but found no way down. As a last resort, we decided that we must slip back inside the palace where it was not a prison, then complete our escape when the building opened in the morning.

"Fanatically determined, I pried open the grate over a dormer window, broke the glass, then with the aid of a repair ladder I'd found on the roof, made preparations to descend into the room below. Before I could do this, I lost my footing on the slick lead sheathing and slipped to the edge of the parapet as far as my chest. The nearly fatal mistake required great courage to correct, but awhile later Balbi, and I lowered ourselves to the floor of the chamber below.

"I slept for three hours until the blathering Balbi awakened me. Overcoming additional hardships, he and I broke a small lock on an exit door, passed through the empty palace, and in a hastily improvised disguise, blustered past a guard and out a door at six that morning. We made our escape by gondola.

"Free at last, I admit I broke down, sobs racking my worn-out body.

"I'd suffered fifteen months in Piombi prison—and was now essentially exiled from Venice."

"And you said," Dominique cooed with tenderness, "for your escape you just donned a hat and walked out the front door. Nothing to it."

- 9 -

TWO DAYS PASSED. On the third morning, a strand of sunlight, diaphanous and delicate, pushed through the open window; soon the room shimmered with dawn's glow. On the window's ledge perched a pair of wind swifts, chirping mischievously, tallying perhaps the lovers' sighs that issued from within.

Dominique's feelings swirled like parti-colored ribbons round a maypole. Her flesh felt scorched by Jacques' naked body atop hers. Their lips touched, kissed, and for a great while held them fast.

Soon Jacques' soft mouth began to glide across her cheek, warming her face wherever it settled. Slowly, he brushed her ear, and she succumbed to the delight that flooded her. He proceeded silently, placing kiss after kiss on her neck; she tingled with need.

He asked her to cover her breast with her hand, then coaxed his tongue between each finger. She gasped at the unexpected pleasure and moaned into the pillow beside her while he continued his exquisite teasing. Shifting Dominique's hand, Jacques sucked at her nipple, sending a rush of chills throughout her body.

Dominique raised her head. Her eyes held his. She felt frozen, suspended, as though one further touch might bring unbearable ecstasy.

Jacques stopped and let go her body. He rested himself on her shoulder, sniffing her sweet skin.

Her senses reeled. She tugged his hair with both hands, but he did not rouse. She pulled at his ears, lifting his mouth to hers for one searing kiss before she pressed him downward.

He offered little resistance as he slid his face between her thighs. Her moans, in turn, fostered even stronger action from him.

Rocking, pushing, aching, she continued her quest, her body racing toward the summit at the urging of his pliant tongue.

Oh, now! Now! Her body heaved. Storms of release rolled from deep within. Flash of color. Divine light, oh, precious light. Lust, love, domination, surrender—all mingled together now. She was beyond herself—beyond it.

She fell back on the pillow, closed her eyes, and sighed. Countless waves of pleasure played within her. There was a measure to the world again. All seemed robust, yet also whole and serene. She drifted in tranquility.

When she opened her eyes, she found him gazing at her.

"I lie here," he said, "to admire the fullness of your lips, your high and even cheeks, the blonde hair that sweeps your neck. The hue of your eyes, it seems, might put an emerald to shame."

With her long, supple fingers, she stroked Jacques' face and hugged him close.

"And here, this first time—so gratifying that your body fits perfectly with mine," he added in a whisper. Then, showing a grin, he spoke louder. "Of course, I need to remind myself that my brother is married to a strong, sturdy dancer, and that it might be wise to protect myself from her vigor."

"A *former* dancer, Monsieur Casanova." Dominique shoved Jacques to his pillow and returned his wide grin. "And to think that just weeks ago you were lodging at an inn! What kind of hostess does that make me?"

"Well, you've been quite courteous this morning."

The lovers chuckled.

Dominique sat up and leaned back against the headboard.

"I'll be forthright," she said. Shifting slightly, she pulled Jacques' hand to her stomach and held it. "I realize that in no way have I the right to inquire—"

"But you have rights," Jacques interrupted, "the same as I. The rights that polite society grants to all its members. So speak to me. But I caution you. Should this be a finely tuned inquiry, I may choose to conceal certain sentiments."

He stole a quick kiss. Dominique's stomach eased under his touch.

"I want to know. How is it women grant you their favors? Do you have methods to—" She covered her mouth. "What are your means to their charms?"

"Means? A subtle question, indeed, Madame Tigress," he laughed.

Dominique pulled the bed sheet tight to her shoulders. The morning sun's rays glistened through the half-empty wine bottle on the table next to the bed. She smiled when Jacques gently laid his head on her leg, and a slightly questioning expression crossed his face.

"If you're wondering, Francesco had a taste for his models," she said. "But after all, he's an artist, we live in Paris, and he may take a lover. And so may I." Rearranging the sheet so that the breeze from the open window would not chill Jacque's naked body, she stroked his thick hair from his forehead to the nape of his neck. "Now, *mon ami*, are you willing to answer my question?"

"Yes," Jacques replied, but then proceeded to lie in silence.

"By century's end?"

Both laughed.

"All right, all right. What is my method? How is it I ..."

He picked up the empty glass standing on the floor next to the bed and passed it to Dominique, who filled and returned it. Reclining, he steadied the drink on his chest.

"I once seduced a wonderful girl by playing my violin."

She slid under the sheet beside him. "Tell me more."

"Well, I discovered as a young man that I had not beauty but something far more valuable, though I can't define it. Perhaps an unbridled confidence. Certainly a clip of courage. And always the benefit of good fortune. Even while recognizing that love is a grand game, I took seriously those attributes which nature bestowed upon me." He ran his hand down Dominique's silky arm. "I've always believed that seduction is one of the higher arts, but higher still, in fact, is the art of making others laugh—not by coarse or vulgar means but with wit and artfulness, from a joyful observation of humankind."

Dominique poured herself another glass and clinked the bottle against his.

Jacques continued. "In seduction, I'd like to believe I've never been calculated; I feel that would imply a cold detachment. I have been meticulous on occasion. Sometimes that's required, and it's certainly in my nature. Improvisational, too. One must be able to improvise." He put his glass to mouth but took it away before drinking. "It goes without saying, a successful seduction must end with physical proof. Consummation."

Dominique's face flushed.

"So," Jacques added, "when first meeting a woman I wish to have, I allow her physical and emotional impression to work upon me. I want her magic to inspire me. I guess her dreams and desires and attempt to achieve my aim through the direct attentions I pay her. Not words. Words alone are a fool's game. When I haven't the leisure to pay her my attention, I present an appropriate gift, maybe a chemise, some lace, cambric for handkerchiefs, dimity for petticoats, sometimes something golden. Gold, you see, is a powerful god who can often perform miracles. What I'm saying is that a well-conceived gift is visible evidence I've meditated on her person. I've listened to her, then revived her in my thoughts in order to select the perfect bauble. A woman's nature dictates she be foremost in a man's thoughts and heart."

Jacques drank the remainder of his wine. "When all is said and done, time is truly the most valuable commodity we share with another human on this earth. This is the significance of the gift—which lends itself to, but does not guarantee, a seduction."

"But, monsieur," she pouted, "just this morning you seduced me without a single gift. What does that say?"

"I seduced you, madame? I believe you seduced me."

"Rascal. Why on earth would I seduce you?"

"*Nitimur in vetitum semper cupimusque negata.* 'We ever strive for what is forbidden and desire what we are denied.' Ovid."

Dominique blew a tress of hair from her face. "If it's true I lured you, why would I do so?"

"Reputation, of course—my reputation."

"As a libertine?"

"Yes."

"In the beginning, Francesco called you 'the chaste.' I actually took him seriously then."

Jacques lips curled upward.

"Francesco, of course, is not easy to read. When I confessed that I'd misunderstood his irony, he confirmed in great detail your dissolute manner. I began to form an image of you in my mind's eye. My imagination fired my desire. I'd never known a man who was a lover, a lover of many. A man ..." Her voice began to falter. She spoke low. "A man who—"

Jacques lifted Dominique's arm and gently flapped the bed sheet so it billowed between the bedposts.

"Reputation, reputation, reputation," he repeated as the cool sheet molded over their forms and faces. Jacques spoke softly beneath the sheet. "Before I ever arrived here, I knew Francesco would tell you of my past, glorious and galling as it may be. Your husband is, after all, a younger brother who looks for my lead, who admires my exploits— although he'll most likely never admit to it, even to himself. I felt then you might be tempted to discover—or rather uncover—my nature for yourself. Is that true?"

"You and Francesco are indeed fruits of different vines." Dominique's laughter carried through the sunlit room. "It appears that when I have the purple grape, I prefer the green grape; when I possess the green grape, I want purple."

"Fickleness," Jacques hooted. "Grapes! Madame Tigress is not to be contented then?"

"Contented? Contented, Monsieur Jacques Casanova? Let me put a stop to this bloated conversation in a language you will clearly understand. *Il cazzo non vuole pensieri*. 'The prick does not want to think,' is that not so? But for my delight in the days ahead," she added, "I'll be pleased to hear of more seductions from you." With that, Dominique whipped the sheet high, ballooning the canopy of coverlet above her and Jacques.

Jacques' face was altogether mock astonishment as he leered at Dominique's nude body. "Ah," he gasped. "Is *that* all for *me*?"

- 10 -

THE BED GROANED AS JACQUES SAT UPRIGHT and lowered his feet to the floor. He yawned, stretched, and slipped off his nightcap just as the golden belly of the sun made its appearance in the eastern sky, which meant that, rising earlier than usual, Jacques might find time to answer the stack of letters on the secretary. Wherever he lived—which had been many places—correspondence arrived by post nearly every morning, and he felt a desire to exchange ideas and fond feelings with his friends, as well as the latest gossip of the day.

He'd adventured throughout the thousand duchies, fiefdoms, and bishoprics of the Holy Roman Empire, the kingdoms of France, England and Italy, throughout Bohemia, Poland, and Switzerland. He'd had extended stays in Spain, Holland, and even Russia.

Letters he received from royalty, from poets, from philosophers and mountebanks, from ecclesiastics, light women, and chancers were proof of these journeys. He prided himself on his ability to make a legion of acquaintances from many and sundry walks of life.

Three years was a long time to be on the move, but it seemed clear to Jacques that Paris would once again elevate his fortunes.

He shook loose his mane of hair, glanced into the sizeable hand mirror he always carried, and sat next to his bed stand, where he saw his previous evening's study, his doctoral thesis. Hunting beneath it, he found his treatise on the squaring of the cube. He paraded bedside, flipping page after page while morning sunrays snuck into the room, reminding him that his brother was seeing the sunrise from the inside of Fragonard's coach.

"Owww." Jacques dropped his papers, grabbed his foot, and plopped back down on the bed, a splinter from the floor fixed in his toe. He tugged his foot toward his body and removed the annoyance. In that instant, dread returned.

"The écorchés," Jacques shuddered, recalling the dream from his far-too-short sleep. He'd danced away the night with a dozen demi-beasts! Each jabbering creature hobbled toward him, slithered its hand into his, and began a chaotic whirl. The nightmare had ended when he'd gazed into the face of the reclining écorchés. *He, the serene one, dispelled the phantoms, eased their ghastly rants.*

"Sir," called a voice from the other side of the door.

"A moment, Petrine. I'm awake far too early." Jacques pinched a drip of blood from his toe.

"I've brought your coffee, sir. Are you ready for your toilet?"

"Yes." Jacques retrieved his papers from the floor and, after replacing them on the bed stand, rubbed his toe a final time as Petrine entered. "Ah, the obedient valet," huffed Jacques.

The Spaniard had a pleasant look on his face, a quality his master appreciated in early morning. Petrine rarely spoke at this hour unless his opinion was requested; for this, Jacques felt absolutely blessed. He had acquired other servants in the past who chattered incessantly and on matters without a grain of substance. Jacques didn't value idle talk from valets. At least not at sunrise.

"I will wear the embroidered garters with the gold clasps on my stockings today, Petrine. Also, you may remove those shoe buckles from that case," he pointed. "I'll have those." Jacques stole a look at the jewel box on his toilet table and decided to wear only the sapphire ring. "No periwig today, but powder my hair, if you please."

An hour later, Petrine had dressed his master's hair, shaved him, brought eggs and more coffee, and polished the ever-dirty shoes.

"It was genius of me to hire a valet who once upon a time was a hairdresser," Jacques said while admiring himself in his mirror.

"Let us not forget, sir, I was also an actor of some renown."

"Of *some* renown."

Jacques caught Petrine's reflection in the mirror—screwing his mouth into some overworked expression.

"What's your favor today, sir?"

"Until the main meal, I'll answer these letters here. Please find me more paper and sharpen the quill." Jacques laid his mirror on the bed and fiddled through his personal items on the secretary. "I've enough ink and—let me see, yes—enough sand for blotting to last the morning. This looks to be a fine summer day, although I'm not in a particularly fine mood." Jacques scratched his head. "Is the mistress of the apartment awake?"

"Not to my knowledge. But, if it's your wish, I'll make it my business to spy on her," grinned Petrine.

"I'll make it my business to have you whipped, rascal." Jacques took a step toward the valet, which was enough to hurry Petrine toward the door, laughing. Before reaching the knob, he swiveled on his heels, facing Jacques.

"There are no signs of the men from the debtors' prison, sir. But," he continued, knitting his brow and shaking his head, "as you yourself said, nothing is certain."

Jacques sucked in a hard breath.

Tiptoeing toward his master, Petrine persisted. "Sir, while we're talking—if I, sir, may wonder aloud—"

"Speak plainly, Petrine."

"Well, yes, master. Yesterday's conversation—you mentioned that the old Vicomte offered you an opportunity. You implied it was balm for our—for your—financial problem. Can that be true? I mean, is it even likely that the Vicomte—"

"There is a rumor of immense wealth surrounding the Vicomte, I have it in confidence."

"In confidence? From whom?"

Jacques crossed his arms. "What concern is it of yours?"

"None, master," Petrine said, and bent over awkwardly to scrape mud from the top of his boot. "But since you have often scolded me that I look out for *myself* foremost …"

Jacques thumped his fingers against his arm as if to a fast fandango. "Complete your theme."

"Well, sir, if Vicomte de Fragonard is, as you say, balm for your problems, I can assist you in your friendship with him."

"Why would I need—or want—your assistance?" Jacques barked. "Oh, I see now. If there's no bounty forthcoming from the Vicomte—

and the authorities clap me in irons—*you've* no employer and will be out of ready money. Perpetually concerned with your own skin!"

Petrine meekly jerked at his sleeve and nodded.

"No more talk this morning." Jacques snapped his hand hard against his leg, then busied himself with his manuscript. A moment later, he glanced at Petrine, who stood close by, eyes downcast.

"Forgive me, Master Casanova. I desire only what's best for you."

Jacques glared.

"And *me*," Petrine admitted coyly. He threw back a shock of black hair that covered his eye. "I'm here to sustain you, sir."

*   *   *

The morning hours passed quickly as Jacques wrote one letter after another. Many of the letters he composed were to women who had shared their favors with him and who were now married and in far-flung places, though, as he knew, they would again share themselves when he arrived in their town. Other letters relayed recent tales of Jacques' life of adventuring to old friends, companions, and even rivals.

One never knows when a rival might become a confederate, Jacques thought as he signed his name with a flourish to the page before him. He was leaning forward in the secretary chair when a knock on the door stopped him; he looked up, wondering what time it was.

"Are you in?"

"Yes, Dominique."

"May I interrupt you?"

"Only for wickedness."

Dominique entered the room, uttered a terse "Morning," and quickly shut the door. It seemed to require some effort on her part to muster a brief smile. Nevertheless, the woman looked especially appealing, her abundant blonde hair banded and pulled toward the back of her head.

Jacques sat relaxed in his chair. "How do you do this beautiful morning, *Fragoletta*, my little strawberry?"

"Well enough," answered Dominique, tousling her sack dress. She stood still and fairly glowered. "I've been preparing a list for the market, which I added to yours and gave to Petrine. And that's why I'm here; because Petrine and I managed to quarrel over market money, I learned some very irregular things. Of course, I, for one, never take a servant's word when I can find out the truth from the master." She strode to the bed, plumped the coverlet and sat down on the corner. "So I now ask you: Is it true that when you returned to Paris, you called on your brother only as a courtesy, then left us for the highlife, gambling away everything you owned in this world? Next you came back to us, lying about why you returned. Lying? To us?"

Jacques sat in silence, squeezing his chin with his fingers, trying to manufacture an answer. Perhaps he'd whip his valet after all. He listened to the uneven tapping of Dominique's foot on the wooden floor.

"Petrine wept," Dominique said. "'God help me. *Valgame Dios*,' he cried. 'I'm too poor and my master is destitute.' Does Petrine speak falsely? You have no money whatsoever?"

Looking into Dominique's green eyes, Jacques pawed his cheeks' scars. *I'd rather be looking down the bore of a loaded musket.*

"What I have—what I still own is my gold snuffbox, a religious manuscript I smuggled out of Constantinople, my pistols, and one-half of a case of smallswords worth fifty louis. The snuffbox and sword were gifts from Mother, and I'll go to the grave with them. But my prized manuscript may bring a price, possibly. At least the paleographer whom I hired long ago—and who authenticated it—thought so. I have sent several pages of the manuscript to Voltaire, who claims he'll purchase it. He is, in equal parts, a flatterer and philosopher, and in his letters for the last two years, he's offered me extravagant praise in an attempt to possess the relic. The French lion is arrogant and vainglorious, but his quest for knowledge is unquenchable."

"What about these?" Dominique stroked the precious stones in the jewel box on the toilet table.

"Those are imitations, all imitations." Jacques glared at the gold clasps on his stockings. "Even these—elaborate fakes." He gouged his finger into his palm as the hot words came pouring out. "Just five years ago, I was my own man. I had friends, a furnished home, a country house, a carriage at my disposal, an excellent cook, three manservants, and a housekeeper. Now I have Petrine. And he stays only for a wage."

Dominique's green eyes flared. "He stays for adventure, he claims."

"The truth is that my personal standing is at stake. And my freedom. Two bills of exchange are due from my gambling debts. Oh, I have friends, many friends—who are scarce, now that I have a need. This time I'm indeed ruined." Jacques turned away. "This has never before happened. Never."

Glancing up at Dominique sitting on the corner of the bed, Jacques supposed he might propose a joke, but he could not marshal one. "I came to your household to ask Francesco for a loan. My little brother—his manners not polished for good society—said nothing to me when I made my request. His manner—"

"Francesco is polished enough."

Jacques swallowed hard and forbade himself to tell Dominique that once, some years back, when he had stood security for Francesco, he had been forced to sell his horses, carriages, and all his furniture so that Francesco might repay his debt to a landlord.

"Perhaps Francesco didn't answer you," Dominique chided, "because he didn't want to refuse you. Finances are difficult, even for a capable artist like Francesco. We've little money but many creditors whom we barely keep satisfied. To let these three rooms and Francesco's painting loft is not cheap. His dream to go to Dresden as an artist is fading. He paints at Vicomte de Fragonard's for a pittance, and he despises the work besides. And, yes, you might have noticed he's been riding rather high since you arrived, had you cared to look. But I fear—I fear the terrible lows, the blackness he more often knows."

"He *is* painting. He's an artist. What more could—"

"He's painting?" cried Dominique. "Copying. Mundane mountain landscapes. Do you think that suits an artist of his temperament? You think that with his talent and experience it's his artistic ambition to scratch out sea urchins over and over?"

"Now, I know my brother—"

"You know Francesco. Phht! I hardly know Francesco," she said, her mouth creasing spitefully. "Do you recognize his artistic dreams?" The woman's face hardened.

"If it were me—"

"You, you, you," shouted Dominique, rising from the bed. "Pardon me, Jacques, but you're selfish. Self-serving. You act like a child, not a middle-aged man. France is choking with men like you. Self-serving, deceitful." Her eyes reddening, she turned away. "God help you. God help France."

A housefly buzzed around her; she swung twice, catching the insect midflight before hurling it to the floor.

Jacques balled his hands into white-fingered fists. He rose from the chair, walked slowly around Dominique, and stared out the window. He recalled when money was no object, when he'd been the toast of Paris, an advisor to the government, the man who had succeeded in raising millions for King Louis by instigating the Parisian lottery.

"Five years ago, I turned the king's debts into gold. I succeeded in transforming—"

"So you're an alchemist."

Jacques faced Dominique. "As you see," he pointed behind him to the secretary, "I've been writing my patrons and my supporters. I've certain plans: I have vast knowledge of mining and geology, a feel for the silk industry. More. I would need capital, naturally, to begin these keen business ventures. I would need ..."

He stopped talking when he found Dominique's eyes riveted to the bed between them. Neither said anything for a great while.

"This debt business could cost you your very life."

"It could." Jacques' voice lightened. "It's said that he who is without money, means, and contentment is without three good friends."

Dominique offered no reply.

"What are we to do then? We have no money to speak of." Jacques stressed the "we," careful not to use "I."

"Sit down on the bed."

Jacques did so.

Dominique stood next to the chair, her fingers strumming its spindles.

"I grew up poor," she said. "I've felt the constraints of penury most of my life. For that reason I've put aside small sums of money from time to time. This savings we'll use for food for this evening. As we're at the end of the week, Francesco will be paid. We'll solve our problems one at a time. And," she added, "I appreciate your small generosities. Although I wonder how you manage to provide them."

When Dominique slid into the chair opposite Jacques, his eyes softened.

"I, naturally, am prepared to pawn all the rest of my fineries," he lied. "That will aid us."

For a time, they talked. He spoke of when he had been young, of his roguish life in Venice, of his brother and family. "As for freedom," he said, "I have prized it above everything else. And freedom, in some ways, has forced me to this woeful financial precipice."

Dominique nodded.

"I've considered selling the manuscript to Monsieur de Voltaire. I've considered selling even my gold snuffbox and my smallsword and pistols. But I can't bring myself to part with them. I may become a fatality to my sentimentality."

Dominique laughed at his inelegance.

Jacques felt ridiculous, but he found his lips curling upward into a grin.

He was pleased when Dominique spoke—not so much of her past—but of her learning. "I was inspired by my father, who labored continually, a cobbler by day and at nightfall—not so much a scholar but a man of intelligence, intent on satisfying his questions about the world. He borrowed books, he solved riddles, he conversed with learned clients—anything to challenge his mind and soul. That he barely scratched out a living never seemed to matter. He always spoke of his 'authority of inward assurance,' which is a phrase, although I may be mistaken, from John Locke, the English philosopher. My father, it seems, had that assurance. I perhaps inherited it from him and Mr. Locke."

The noonday sun had by now passed the window. Francesco would not be home from Fragonard's before dark.

The conversation, more relaxed, seemed to be winding down. Dominique again bathed her hands in the strongbox full of imitation stones. There were red ruby rings, yellow chrysolite, sapphires, diamonds, oriental topaz, and at least two women's brooches with inlaid lapis lazuli.

"How does one know if a jewel is genuine?" she asked.

"Well, with a diamond, for example, I would lick it. Stones are cold to the tongue. Composition is not. The lapis you hold, of course, is genuine."

Dominique's green eyes flashed slyly as she placed the stone back in the pile. "You've not brought me a pretty bauble, monsieur."

It took a moment for Jacques to comprehend her meaning. "On the contrary. All the baubles now at your fingertips are yours, if you desire. And further, for you—the seasoned maiden who stands before me—I'll impart yet another seduction, as you requested at our first amorous meeting."

"Yes, that's my wish." Dominique stood up, and wandered toward the window of the small room, interlacing her fingers behind her.

Jacques lay back on the bed, propping himself on an elbow. "I've used this course of action more than once, although there's no guarantee that consummation will necessarily come from it."

Dominique smiled again. "Certainly. No guarantees. And, please, no more of your law school language."

"Fair enough," he nodded. "I begin my intrigue with a shy waifish girl, she of the ripening figure whose expressive brown eyes show kindness and trust. One late afternoon, I slowly and earnestly convince her that it is her duty as chambermaid to scrub not only the floors but also her lodger. In this case, me. It took some chat on my part, and a small gift of a ducat in her palm helped my cause.

This is all for cleanliness' sake, I say, and she agrees. Gabriella, let us call the waif, draws the hot water I require. I stand and casually peruse the gazette, at all times maintaining the appearance of propriety. Finally when the bath is ready, I ask her to turn her back while I go behind the screen, remove my clothes, reappear in a towel, and at last, dip my nude body into the warm water. I make sure that my masculinity is covered by soap bubbles or a cloth so as not to cause undue consternation on Gabriella's part. It's true I wanted love's reward from her, but more importantly, I wanted her love. Without love, this seduction business is a vile thing."

Jacques watched the sunlight, gauzed by the window curtains, dance across Dominique's face. *How fetching this woman is,* he thought.

"Reminding myself that the chase is more than enough adventure, that the crowning moments may never occur—or only in due course—I request she wash my neck with the sponge. I relax, even with her tentative gestures. From time to time, I let out an earnest sigh, always encouraging any true pleasure she may innocently bring by washing my hair, my neck, my arms and back. It's at this point, I recall, that I ask her to sponge my chest. She's reluctant. I speak of her efficacious manner. I talk of her professional diligence. I quote Ariosto. My waif gives over to the moment.

"At the first touch of my nipples, she says nothing, but I myself cannot contain a delicate moan.

"It's plain to us both that by now I'm the schoolgirl, you see. Gabriella, the waif, realizes she dominates the state of affairs, and that nothing may get out of hand without her consent. This chambermaid feels supremacy, maybe for one of the few times in her life.

"I make one last request: that she bathe each of my legs. I help the process by extending my legs from the bath while continually making sure that the wet cloth covers my love prick. I am discretion itself.

"Finally, I ask her to again turn her back. I take the towel, dry myself, and lo and behold, realize that liberality must carry the day; I tell her I feel compelled to return the favor. To bathe her. She, of course, is hesitant. But she wavers when I subtly convince her that she's in no danger—is, in fact, in complete command of her faculties and of the situation—and is bound, moreover, by courtesy to receive a pleasure in return.

"Still I remind myself that the final outcome of the rendezvous is not forecast."

Dominique started. Holding her breath, she withdrew herself from the window and trained her eyes at the courtyard below.

Jacques' heart chilled. But his ears told him the clatter below didn't belong to Francesco's coach.

Moments later, she relaxed her fists, allowed herself a gentle exhale, then lay on the bed next to Jacques while he casually resumed his story.

"Dressing hurriedly—and only in my breeches—I make as if to button up but, in fact, expose a bit of my masculinity to her. I pretend not to notice that Gabriella has perked up, and I quickly begin my work: first of all, to talk her out of her clothes. I persuade her, turning my back, and my waif slips hurriedly into the bath.

"I pour ever more warm water from the ewer and continue the game, not by delighting her senses but by delighting her soul. Small compliments are coupled with soft touches. While talking, I lightly dote on her, nosing her hair, her neck.

"In truth," Jacques said, "it's the scent of a woman that entices me to heaven." He glanced at Dominique. "I face her, then begin the washing of her hair in tantalizing fashion, careful not to allow my building passions to overstep my artfully-laid boundaries. After a time, however, I make no pretense; I observe her body in the bath. She feels my admiration, and her excitement grows. As does mine, although I am determined to mask my ardor.

"Therefore, I bar myself from washing her breasts but instead move to the front of the tub, taking each extremity and bathing first the foot, then the calf, then the thigh. I surmise Gabriella is tingling in the special spot, but I do not give in to lust; I continue a quiet conversation, allowing myself to gaze into her eyes while they're open and when it seems appropriate.

"Once her eyes shut, I know she's enthralled. She enjoys this understated game of domination and no longer has a care as to who is now to be victor. I feel she may join me in the blossomed world where we shall both welcome triumph—bodies blending, senses blinded."

Jacques saw in Dominique's expression that, although her delicate curiosity might now be satisfied, her desire had mounted.

Their eyes locked. Slowly, Dominique pulled the bed coverlet over Jacques' face and began to kiss the sheet where she guessed his mouth to be. Moments later, she pulled his shirt above his breeches and stretched her hand toward his warmth.

"To feel your hardness. How it thrills me."

Jacques was aflame with passion. He threw off the coverlet and, lifting up Dominique's simple dress, found the sumptuous favors she was eager to bestow.

"Dominique, Dominique," came the call.

She madly leapt to the doorway.

Jacques wrested himself on his back, fastened his breeches, stuffed in his shirttail, and straightening the coverlet, flipped to a sitting position on the bed.

"I'm in the hall," she sputtered, "talking to your brother." She stood primly in the doorway, trying to keep her watering eyes from giving her away.

"Then, of course," Jacques began, "I commanded two hundred francs, twelve thousand scudi in jewels and precious stones, and nearly forty thousand florins. This was the result of several good business opportunities in Amsterdam when I was hired by the French." He fluttered his hand briefly to reassure Dominique.

A heavy clomp of boots.

Arriving at the door Francesco looked queerly about.

"My husband." Dominique gave Francesco a slight hug. "You're home early today."

"I am," snarled the hulking man, "because I've been puking."

"You're sweating badly, too," said Dominique, pressing her hand to his forehead.

Jacques, spying the wet sheet where Dominique had kissed him, slowly shifted his hand to cover the spot. His face grew suddenly hot. "Good time for a brotherly duel?" he quipped, scratching his chin. From the way Francesco scowled, Jacques couldn't be sure if the man was going to retch or if he'd found them out.

"You're burning up, Francesco," Dominique scolded. "We must cool you down. Into a bath you'll go."

Jacques barely squelched his laugh, wondering if Dominique's bath comment was intentional or not.

Francesco wheeled back toward the hall, arm slung over Dominique. The pair trod down the hallway till there was not a sound to be heard.

"Does he know?" Jacques asked himself.

SUMMER – 1755

- 11 -

DOMINIQUE OPENED HER EYES, smelled the sweet night air, and felt the pillow warming her cheek. She was excited. In little more than a day's time her prayers had been answered.

But who could she tell? Jacques was out, she remembered, and she was loathe to divulge her new idea to Francesco. Yet to succeed, her plan would have to be told to both brothers.

She climbed from the bed and paced back and forth across the room.

There was a rustling of bedcovers in the darkness. Francesco mumbled. "Is that you? Wife, is that you tramping about?"

Dominique stopped still.

"You're not next to me snoring," snapped Francesco, "so I know you're awake. Come lie down." The straw mattress crackled as he rolled to his side. "What hour is it?"

"Not late. Not too late." Dominique opened the curtain that covered the doorframe, lit a candle, and placed it in the hallway sconce so that it shone dimly on Francesco's face.

He strained to see.

Goodness, she thought, *he looks like death with his hair poking every which way.*

Taking a bristle brush from the bedside table, she seated herself on a chair at her husband's back but decided against grooming him. Instead, she brushed her own hair. Each stroke reinforced her courage.

Although for some time Dominique had held vague notions on how to advance her husband's success, she now had the leverage to make her plan work. Leverage—in the form of Jacques' antique manuscript—was the element she'd been missing.

"I've an idea, dear Francesco. A plan that helps you. And that will also help your brother." She took in a heavy breath. "God has answered my prayers."

"Prayers. Claptrap."

Dominique stopped brushing but ignored her feelings and continued. "I have to make certain inquiries beginning tomorrow morning, and all must go according ..."

Francesco rolled over to her, but before he could finish his yawn, she added, "I ask you to listen to me. As you know, I'm not a silly woman who involves herself in folly."

Somewhere in the Parisian street below, a pack of dogs began barking.

"First," she began, "I'll find out the value of a religious manuscript your brother owns and have him alert Monsieur de Voltaire by swiftest post that the manuscript at last can be had. Then using Voltaire as bait, I'll exact a promise from a reliable patron to host a ball at his country chateau.

"Patron? What patron do—

"Please listen, Francesco. At this fête, this ball, you'll exhibit your best paintings, not your copies of other artists. When your originality is admired—and purchased—well, it may—"

Francesco growled, and in his state between sleep and wakefulness, words tumbled heedlessly from his mouth. "You're not frivolous. But you're full of extremes. What! A ball, a fête? You're not royalty. How will you throw a ball?"

Dominique brushed her hair harder, doubt clouding her mind. Why set upon this daunting plan to help the Casanova brothers?

It took time for an answer to come, but at last she knew. She was a woman who had a duty in life, although at the moment she wasn't exactly sure just where her duty began and ended.

"I'm twenty-nine, Francesco, yet even when I was younger, I felt certain obligations. If I can't fulfill these obligations to myself or the ones I love, I can have no self-respect." Dominique set the brush aside and placed her hands on her knees. She arose from her chair, seated herself on the bed, and gently tucked the cover around her husband's shoulder. She briefly caught Francesco's glinting eyes. "I must tell you," she said, "to put on the ball, I'll seek the help of Signor Grimani."

"Grimani? You'll not have anything to do with—"

"I refused him years ago. Unlike the other dancers. You know that. You needn't think otherwise."

Long ago, Michele Grimani had supposed his money might obtain Dominique's favors, a thought that did not upset her. Their slender connection over the years had been one where he politely offered and she resolutely refused. While prone to attacks of grandiose behavior, Signor Grimani had always been a gentleman with her, although she wondered why—when he had not been so with others. She concluded that he admired her strength of character, that deep in his heart he knew a gift of money couldn't weaken her principles.

Francesco filched his shoulder from Dominique's touch, burying his face in the bedding so that she could barely see his profile. *"Quand'ero in parte altr'uom da quel ch'io sono."*

"Kindly tell me what you just said. In French."

"When I was in part a different man from the man I am," spat Francesco. "Ten years ago. I was a *man* ten years ago."

"And I want you to be that man again, Francesco. You and I, we deserve a family—"

"It won't work. I can't …"

"It's not your fault."

Dominique could find no more comforting words on the bitter subject. She sat quietly for a time before speaking.

"It's important for you to know, Francesco, I'm firm in my belief that my idea will succeed. And to achieve this success is to involve Signor Grimani. As well as Voltaire. I will—"

"I *thought* you'd said Voltaire a moment ago," Francesco spouted, turning to face her. "Voltaire? The exalted Voltaire! How would a woman of your station reach such a luminary? Why, the man doesn't even live in Paris. Or France. Are you without wits?"

Dominique felt her choler rise. "Am I—? What of the Casanova brothers? Overgrown children! Who both require help. And I and the good Lord will help them, regardless of their wayward natures."

Dominique stood up, tramped to the hallway, and slung the room curtain closed. She seated herself as best she could in the hall with the lit candle as her only companion. "Gather your notions, Dominique," she said. "The Savior will direct you."

In her mind, she began to compile a list of tasks. Hours passed. When at last she finished, she calmly opened the curtain to the bedroom where the sun was beginning to share its yellow rays. Back into bed she crawled.

- 12 -

PETRINE, TRYING TO KEEP HIS SEAT on the rear of the rumbling coach, hugged a small barrel. Inside the coach sat Jacques and Dominique in morning dress, both sweating profusely from the heat.

Fate demands a sacrifice—my manuscript. That it should come to this!

Dominique ruffled her hair. "And so within one week, Jacques, my prayers are answered," she smiled, "and it's likely the Casanovas' problems can be resolved if you still agree to donate your manuscript to the cause."

"But I'll be paid to do so?" Jacques asked, pursing his lips anxiously.

"Yes, I've requested a sum of gold from our patron for your donation to Voltaire. As I said, your valued manuscript is the lure that attracts the famous philosopher—who attracts, in turn, our wealthy patron—who'll sponsor the ball. At the ball, Francesco can market his paintings, and after your donation of the manuscript, a bag of gold—from the patron—will be your reward." Dominique threw her hands in the air, laughing. "I'm excited."

"I'll admit it would an honor to meet Monsieur de Voltaire face-to-face. To bask in the glow of his genius. But he reads and comprehends the strange tongue of my precious manuscript while I always delayed learning that language. To me, it's disconcerting to give away something whose value I don't even know."

"If you choose to help your brother—and yourself—the only hope we have is your religious manuscript."

Jacques felt a lump in his gut. Should he bank on this plan of Dominique's? It had the possibility of fortune. And some distinction. Whereas to consider Vicomte de Fragonard's proposal ... *The smart move is to keep all avenues open and pursue the plan that promises quicker benefit.* "As I said, I'm *willing* to give up the manuscript."

"Please promise you'll not withdraw your offer, Jacques."

A moment passed before he answered yes. It behooved him to agree for the time being.

Oh yes," added Dominique, "our patron, Signor Grimani, is already acquainted with Monsieur de Voltaire. But let Signor Grimani explain. He's—"

"Grimani, you say? Michele Grimani?" Jacques felt the heat rise in his veins.

The woman nodded.

"Dominique! What have you done?"

Dominique drew a quick breath. "What's the trouble?"

"Cavaliere Michele Grimani?" he asked, his hand wiping sweat from his chin. "Cavaliere?"

"I think. Perhaps."

"*Cavaliere della stola d'oro,*" Jacques muttered, trying to restrain his growing alarm. "The title 'Cavaliere'—plus the 'golden stole'—is only conferred on Venetian bluebloods who have distinguished themselves in public office. His family's been listed in Venice's *Libro d'Oro* of notables for hundreds of years and—"

Dominique hurriedly interrupted. "Signor was fond of my skills when I danced in the *Comedie Italienne* in Paris. From time to time, I've reacquainted myself with him. I'm only using my connection … you and I will do the hard work and borrow his chateau and ballroom. He'll receive the credit but he's—"

"He was one of three members of the Inquisitori de Stato who sentenced me to prison."

Dominique gasped, her eyes glossed with wetness. She placed her hand on Jacques' leg. "I'd no idea this journey would—"

"Yes, Grimani." Jacques glared out the coach window into the distance. "A brilliant politician, an inveterate gambler, a great epicure, and a gentleman highly regarded in the art of fence as well as dance. In short, an aristocrat of vast wealth, immense power, and superb family name." He turned to Dominique, tugging his wrenched brow. "I was carted away to Piombi prison without ever meeting Grimani face-to-face," he said grimly. "And now I'm surprised and stunned once again!"

Dominique was speechless, shocked. A bead of sweat dripped down her nose. "All I could think about was him lending us his country home, his *French* summer home. I've known him so long, it never crossed my mind that … I'm embarrassed. Mortified."

Jacques looked hard into Dominique's pained eyes. "Let us meet our patron Michele Grimani. Until then, I'll withhold my opinions." *I've been duped. I must keep my wits to learn their design.*

Within a short while, the coach moved beneath a dense canopy of towering trees, and when the wheels left the dirt road and clattered across cobblestone, Jacques and Dominique, as if on cue, peered out. On the gently rolling hill in the distance was a structure of nearly cathedral proportions, glistening in the morning sun. The tall, straight lines of the mansion were softened by the sea of artful foliage that surrounded it; the entire home appeared to float atop a multihued cloud of budding flowers. No mere summer home, this mansion appeared a strikingly beautiful shrine to a powerful family.

Almost before the coach rolled to a stop, Petrine came forward to the window, where he held a private conversation with Jacques. After the valet stepped away, Jacques spoke.

"I've found it practical, Dominique, in my various and past travels, to retain a valet who can, not infrequently, act as my security. Petrine is comfortable with his role as eyes and ears for me, and in this unique instance, I most certainly shall ask him to play his part."

A flock of liveried servants appeared as if from nowhere, and in short order, Jacques, Dominique, and Petrine were ushered to a side door of the great home by the maître d'hôtel, a man of impressive bearing who was richly clad and who flashed a ring studded with a variety of gems.

Jacques fretted. *Side door? What practice is this? Will the host clap me in chains and smuggle me back to prison?*

Upon entering Grimani's mansion, Petrine and Dominique were struck by a prominent feature: the archways, enfilade, created an unobstructed view from this part of the house. As each room opened into the next, the three guests marveled at the fine china, linen, and grand furnishings. Affixed to one entire wall was a collection of magnificent basket hilt swords. "Slavic mercenaries hired by the Doge of Venice wielded those," Jacques whispered in Dominique's ear. "Are we to be impressed by Grimani's tie with the high and mighty?"

Her casual reaction told him nothing.

The maître d'hôtel stopped. "The Cavaliere shall attend you here in the library."

While Jacques pretended to look at the handsome lacquered bookcases, behind his back he squeezed his fist until the skin grew taut.

No sooner had the maître d'hôtel escorted a reluctant Petrine to the far corner of the room than in sauntered a gentleman.

The man was not of lordly stature but of genteel comportment, appearing fit and well proportioned in his unadorned coat, embroidered waistcoat, and breeches. Thin lips, aquiline nose, and piercing azure eyes perched on a moonish face. His skin was pale with snatches of gray hair protruding from under his neatly dressed and powdered brown wig.

After the unpretentious man passed his maître d'hôtel, he momentarily fingered a calling card Jacques had presented upon arrival. Pocketing it, he continued his leisurely gait past Petrine.

Watching Dominique rouse her weary body, Jacques wondered what Michele Grimani meant to her.

A short distance in front of Dominique, Grimani stopped and lowered his eyes, his full attention showering her. He bowed vigorously, accepted Dominique's hand, and kissed the air above it. Dominique blushed pink.

Jacques bristled. *Grimani treats her as an equal, though she is not of his class. Exceptionally decorous.*

Dominique smiled, as did her host: "This girl's beauty reduces me to slavery each and every time I see her. And her vivacity enslaves me even more."

In his gut, Jacques felt the insistent tightness of cold jealousy.

"Madame Casanova," said Grimani, "please present your chaperone."

Dominique took in Jacques' blazing eyes and spoke. "*Con grandissimio piacere.*" "With great pleasure." Her voice grew honeyed while she reeled off what little Italian she knew. "*Cavaliere, ti presento il Signor Don Giacomo Casanova veneziano amico mio.*"

"Your friend from Venice? Ahh." Scarcely turning in Jacques' direction, Grimani nodded.

Jacques held his tongue, hoping to see what gesture of war or peace the man might make.

After introductory formalities were completed, Jacques could no longer resist. "It's well we meet, Cavaliere. I knew you by reputation when I was younger and yet able to reside in our homeland." Jacques heard Dominique's sudden inhalation.

Cavaliere Grimani opened his arms wide and laughed. "Is that a refined way of saying that I'm older than you?" He crooked one arm back toward his barrel chest and, with a tap of his finger, summoned his maître d'hôtel to his side. "Send Signor Casanova's valet to the kitchen to have some food. And please show Madame from this gloomy library to our ballroom. Signor Casanova and I shall join her there momentarily."

Cavaliere Grimani once again bowed to Dominique, who, with a baffled expression, was immediately escorted from the room.

Jacques' hackles were up. He threw a quick glance at the departing Petrine.

"Now that we are alone, Signor Casanova, will you join me?" Cavaliere Grimani extended a snuffbox of light-colored tortoiseshell encrusted in gold. Jacques grudgingly accepted, inhaled the tobacco through his nose, and handed back the box.

"Fine Spaniol, is it not?"

Jacques nodded. As he did so, Grimani, swift as a snake, slapped him hard across the face.

Jacques seized his stinging cheek, then reached for his dagger.

Grimani, already two steps away, faced Jacques. "Drawing that poniard would be an egregious error," he hissed in a withering tone. "Do not presume to enter my home and insult me. Insolence." He clapped his hands together as if he were quashing a fly. The man paced angrily and continued his vociferous cry. "You *deserve* exile from Venice. You earned imprisonment."

"I did nothing to—"

"In some circles you are a champion—for your escape—and because of this momentary notoriety, the government shies away from jailing you. But in better circles, people ask the cause for your imprisonment. Always they reach the correct conclusion: you're an affliction who should be gotten rid of."

Even as he snugged his dagger back into its sheath, Jacques felt the harried rush to redraw his steel. "It's only for Dominique that I restrain myself," he barked.

Cavaliere Grimani spread his legs wide and smoothed the peruke on his head. "I know of your career as adventurer, as some call it. Vanity, boy. You possess only, as the French say, *nostalgie de la boue*. 'Homesickness for the gutter.' Your notion is to spit constantly on the world, then expect the world to reward you. As a renegade from the Venetian Republic, you have been a personal embarrassment to me for years. If Venice cannot presently sit atop the world order as it has for past centuries, it's because of presumptuous vulgarians such as you."

Jacques checked his fury. "I'll quit this house—and neither you nor Voltaire will ever possess my manuscript."

"Do as you please. But from the inquiries I've made, you are one short step away from debtors' prison. Your abysmal behaviors poise you for death."

"So you have tentacles everywhere."

Grimani ignored the affront while marching back and forth. "What did you expect from this little plan of Dominique's? Ho! Signor Casanova, the worm, now has the opportunity to become a butterfly! He's been given the main chance to consort with French society as he did some years ago. To be able to visit the consequential salons again where one hears the real news that allows clever speculation on the market, or induces one to take the correct step at the opportune moment. Signor Casanova has need of fresh opportunity. A fresh victim. To latch like a parasite upon some great personage. To suck them dry. As you do to that fool, Fragonard."

Jacques' face burned hot. "Fragonard? How—?"

"Tentacles everywhere!" Grimani grinned icily, then regarded Jacques with renewed ferocity. "To desiccate each and every victim. That's what your adventuring entails, does it not? To flourish, you need Dominique's plan. You therefore need *me* to provide a favorable circumstance. Me!" His voice rose to a terrible crescendo. "Do not pretend otherwise."

"It's true that fate provides the circumstance," Jacques lashed, "but I repeat—I own the unique manuscript on which the whole of the plan relies. Without the enticement of my manuscript, Monsieur de Voltaire won't return to France for the fête, nor will the house of Grimani be honored for his return. And as for adventuring—sharp wits, multiple resources, and adoration from fickle Fortune—these are the ingredients of adventuring, I assure you."

Grimani turned his back and took several steps away. "As you and I well recognize, signor, you need money, you need this fête." He lowered his voice and faced Jacques. "Now ask why I deign to open my villa for Madame Casanova's arrangement? I have one solitary reason: my great regard for Madame. I have always honored her requests, no matter how misguided."

Jacques eyed the man whose gray hair now jutted from under his peruke in ever-larger snatches. "As you say, let us not deceive one another. To be able to coax the great Voltaire back to France after his self-imposed exile is an enormous feather in any man's cap, even in the cap of a Cavaliere della stola d'oro. The king himself shall assuredly attend this celebration to reacquaint himself with the renowned Voltaire."

Michele Grimani lightly applauded. He ran the fingers of both hands down his waistcoat, took several steps toward Jacques, and spoke in a carefully modulated tone. "For now I say let business be business. I shall assist Madame Casanova in her plan, and no one, including her, will be privy to my judgment of you. But make no mistake, Casanova. To me you are neither a fellow Venetian nor a friend. And you shall not consider me either, for I am your enemy."

"You have put me in mind of a further contract I'll need. Before I engage in this business arrangement, I shall want a letter of permission, as it were, from the Inquisitori. From you, Cavaliere Grimani. Permission to return to our homeland, Venice."

"You know that I alone do not possess such authority."

"But you, powerful and prestigious, will smooth the way nevertheless."

Grimani drew in a long breath, but Jacques fixed him with a stare. The man slowly and coldly nodded.

"Perhaps."

"Be advised, Cavaliere"—Jacques snarled the word—"that I cherish La Serenissima—Venice—my home. On my return, 'many there shall be restored that now are fallen, and many shall fall that now are in honor.'"

Grimani shifted his eyes and smiled. "Horace." He turned, obligating Jacques to follow him out of the library.

In the ballroom, they found Dominique standing alone and quiet at its center.

Pacing beside Jacques, Cavaliere Grimani showered sweet words. "And thus we have an opportunity for the coup of the century, Signor Casanova. After his self-imposed exile, Monsieur de Voltaire's return to his native land will be momentous. By the bye, Voltaire's paleographer, after examining the pages of manuscript you submitted to him, has assured us that the date and authenticity of it are what Voltaire hoped it to be. The great man will happily accept your valuable gift, Signor."

All the while Jacques remained still as a tree. He thought Grimani a true politician who did not allow his passions to impede exacting business.

The Cavaliere ushered Jacques to Dominique's side, gazed at her, and cooed. "I find that this lady's only fault is not being rich, but she only feels how great a failing it is when it prevents her from being generous."

I must stave off the stinking odor of this dog. Jacques slipped his handkerchief from his sleeve and stuffed it under his nose. *And I must be on guard with this woman.*

Dominique arched an eyebrow at him while pinching the corners of her dress to perform a curtsy.

"But to the affair at hand, madame," the Cavaliere continued, his strident voice creating an echo in the cavernous ballroom. "Since I'm supplying the money to purchase Signor Casanova's manuscript gift for Voltaire, because I've sway with Monsieur de Voltaire, and as I'm lending my home for the fête, I'll expect the occasion to be flawless perfection. As you may know, madame, I—and my heralded family—are known to succeed brilliantly in all manner of things." The Cavaliere's eyes were now alight. But then, while he whispered almost to himself, his expression greatly altered. "My family, my potent family—well, I do *not* brook failure. Never. None."

"We understand, Cavaliere," Dominique said quietly.

Grimani flicked a finger toward Jacques. "Madame, you and your chaperone will plan and carry out the affair with aplomb. I, of course, shall have the final say on all matters."

Dominique laughed. "Just this moment I've created a name for our fête. L'affaire de Voltaire." Her green eyes gleamed with such joy that both men were obliged to concede a smile.

Jacques gestured grandly toward Dominique, then turned toward Grimani to establish the full measure of his height. "L'affaire de Voltaire. So it shall be."

Shifting a step backwards, Grimani pushed his palms together. "L'affaire de Voltaire," he muttered. "Well, I'm in unqualified agreement."

The Cavaliere congratulated Dominique on her choice plan, then walked his guests to a private study where they seated themselves around a gilded desk. For the remainder of the afternoon, the trio worked on preliminary details. July 21, midnight, was set as the date, a mere three weeks away.

"One item more, Cavaliere," Dominique said. "When we reach the final preparations, may I suggest that you hang my husband's most valued piece in the balcony just above where the musicians are to perform? All eyes will see the painting there. Dramatic. Ideal. N'est-ce pas? "

"Oui," said Grimani.

"Marvelous. And Francesco's work in each and every corner of your ballroom? I know just the paintings he'll choose." Dominique's expression left little doubt she was greatly excited.

"My majordomo will supply the necessary ropes and block and tackle to hang the piece in the balcony."

A short time later, Jacques, walking Dominique toward their waiting coach, expelled a lungful of air as if he were whistling a harsh, silent tune. He watched Petrine climb on the back of the coach before helping Dominique inside and sitting opposite her. The orange rays of a slowly sinking sun seemed to heighten her cheer.

While she peeked out the window, Jacques pressed a hand to his forehead, pushing his hair backward as if he wanted to pry it from his scalp. When she turned, he immediately loosened his fingers, running his palm down the back of his neck.

"I'm so hopeful," she beamed, leaning forward to touch his leg. "And I must tell you, Michele Grimani made us a small monetary gift for immediate needs."

"An unlooked-for addition." Jacques shrugged and managed to shape a smile on his face.

So, Grimani would receive social acclaim for enticing Voltaire back to France. Francesco would exhibit and sell his art. And Jacques, to his benefit, would gain access to the very best of French society, as well as obtain a purseful of gold from Grimani for his manuscript gift to Voltaire. Most importantly, Jacques would also acquire Grimani's letter to ease his entry into Venice.

Dominique, of course, had devised all of this in her lovely head, although she would answer that her god was solely responsible. It seemed she was never happier than when able to give to others. Such was her nature, and such was the course she was on.

A jolt of the coach roused Jacques. *As for Vicomte de Fragonard's opportunity—whatever it is—it must, after all, take a far backseat.*

On the ride home, Dominique engaged Jacques' interest about everything from the invitation list to the floral decoration for L'affaire de Voltaire.

"This ball," said Jacques, "will not take place in Versailles with three or four thousand people. We will make it intimate with three or four hundred."

"Intimate? Four hundred," laughed Dominique. "And all ladies and gentlemen of the highest nobility."

Jacques knew that the fewer invitations he, Grimani, and Dominique doled out, the more prized they'd be—adding to the event's cachet as well as to the reputation of Jacques Girolamo Casanova.

"And why deny the king our presence?" he asked.

Dominique squealed excitedly. When she quieted, Jacques felt her eyes fasten on him.

"I'm imagining," she said, "your sweet mouth on mine."

"Must you have physical proof?"

Dominique at once sat forward and kissed him. The coach bounced, separating them. He watched Dominique playfully wrinkle her nose.

"What?" he asked.

"A kiss like that leads me to consider ..." She did not finish her thought, but the communication was clear.

"In the service of the queen, then?"

"What?"

"Why, this must be our pet name for the sweet delights my mouth and tongue will provide to you. In the service of the queen."

Dominique fairly blushed, glanced hurriedly out both coach windows, then leveled her gaze to Jacques. "Yes, our pet name for my *second* favorite pleasure, yes," she purred. "Please, in the service of the queen."

It was not long before the shameless words "must have you" flowed from Dominique's lips.

Jingling laughter punctuated by sighs of ecstasy spilled into the twilight while the coach bumped onward to Paris.

- 13 -

TWO DAYS BEFORE THE FÊTE, Dominique lay on her bed, speaking more to herself than to Jacques who rested beside her.

"This morning Madame de Gigot told me that she'd given away the costume she'd promised to loan me. Inconceivable that she would do that! Saturday is almost here, and I've no outfit." Dominique sucked in a deep breath and mantled her hands against her stomach. "But it's important to remind myself, I'm privileged to attend this ball; I'm not, after all, nobility. Further, it's not likely I'll ever again attend a magnificent gala, costume or no costume."

"Dear Lord Jesus," smiled Jacques, "please bless this sinner with yet another grand idea."

Dominique did not return the grin.

Jacques sat up. "Let's not forget it was my brother who proposed the fête be a masquerade. For his idea, he should be thanked."

"Yes, very much so. Although you realize he was dryly sarcastic when he made that suggestion?"

"I hadn't." Jacques rose from the bed with a loud yawn, his voice ringing through the room. "I think I hear Francesco's coach, dear Fragoletta. What—"

"Oh," wailed Dominique, "I've just remembered his remaining piece of artwork. He'll fall into his deep, black hole if we don't—"

"I've seen to it," Jacques said calmly. "I sent Petrine to Cavaliere Grimani's earlier this afternoon with it. My brother will only have to suffer the torments of not knowing if the painting's hung precisely as he wants. So be it until Saturday."

Dominique blew a strand of hair from her face. "Yes, Saturday—the ball and—"

"You'll have no costume. I know."

Dominique hissed lightly.

"I relish the thought of you attending the ball—a mere garland as your attire."

"How can you joke?"

"Ah," whispered Jacques "I believe I hear the artist of the castle plodding up his steps. When he arrives, I'll surprise you both."

"Surprise us? How? How?"

Jacques quickly stepped into the hallway, followed instantly by Dominique. "Brother, is that you?"

"The Vicomte de Fragonard sends his warmest wishes," harrumphed Francesco as he cleared the last stair and entered the hall. "Hopes to enjoy your company again soon, he claims."

"Thank you, Brother, for bearing his message. Will you and Dominique both wait here a half moment?"

Jacques entered his room and immediately returned to the hallway, handing a bottle of Cyprus wine and three glasses to Francesco, who made a drama of refusing before Jacque's insistence overcame his objections.

"Please take Francesco to the loft hall, Dominique."

The woman, a quizzical look on her face, complied by scooping up her husband's hand and leading him toward the door.

Jacques shouted. "Drink up, you two. Don't wait for me." The stratagem he'd concocted demanded that the pair soak up some wine.

Not long after, the loft hall echoed with Jacques' footfalls. There was a gentle spring in his step. Dominique, he found, was seated on her favorite stool while Francesco lounged on the floor. A glance at the bottle told Jacques they'd drunk a goodly amount, so without a word, he stepped back outside the door, then reentered, carrying a large trunk. Throwing open the lid, he pulled out men's breeches, waistcoats, shirts, hose, and coats—strewing them across the floor. With a swell of pride, he proclaimed, "These are our costumes."

When Jacques held up a blue velvet coat with white satin lining, Dominique covered her mouth in alarm.

"For Grimani's ball?" Francesco sat up, laughing unkindly.

Dominique's voice grew heavy. "The nobility will all be wearing masquerade costumes, while we'll be wearing *these?*"

"You want my wife dressed as a man? As a royal?" Francesco cried.

"This fine, precious jacket—perhaps—well, since you don't appreciate my idea, Francesco ..." Jacques drew his dagger and angrily jabbed through the pocket.

Dominique's jaw fell open.

Jacques stabbed again at the coat. He inserted his fingers into the holes and tore them wider.

Francesco sat stunned.

Jacques slugged a mouthful of wine. "After the ball, I'll have no need for stylish clothes, because I will be the king's favorite and be permitted to cavort wherever, whenever, and *in whatever* I please."

Francesco whistled wildly. "You're mad."

"Close to it," Jacques said, sheathing his poniard. He took several swigs of wine and passed the bottle to Francesco. "I've a plan, of course," he said, offering a conniving grin. "You now see our *almost finished* costumes. Which promise to be the triumph of L'affaire de Voltaire."

In an instant, Dominique digested Jacques' design. She shouted in glee, infecting her husband with her abandon. Catching her drift, Francesco howled like a savage animal. He jumped up, and with his strong hands, ripped the sulphur-yellow jacket away from his brother, then jerked Jacques' dagger from its sheath and began gashing the short-napped coat. Soon the batiste shirts with their fine lace cuffs, the elegant silk stockings, the breeches, the vests—all the splendid garments had been gashed.

Jacques quickly produced three sets of needles and threads and various colored patches.

"We'll sew these to the garments to give even more humorous appeal. And lastly from my bag, three fine hats and three ceramic caricature masks with exaggerated faces. These masks of desperation, as I call them, and these gay—if ripped—costumes will show the haughty French nobility that we've taken the most sumptuous clothing and despoiled it. They'll believe we've absolutely no regard for expensive finery, and unless I've missed the mark, they'll share our recklessness—and laugh."

"We're insulting the aristos," brayed Francesco. "Good."

Jacques nodded, smiling.

Insulting, indeed! Jacques had thought ahead. He knew that in France, the aristocratic men were slaves to women, and that women were slaves to fashion. By wearing tattered costumes, he slyly winked at the fashion of the hour, and his travesty, he hoped, might have the effect of actually attracting many noble sheep to his fold. However, if the nobility took offense ...

Tittering with joy, Dominique kissed Jacques on the cheek.

"Thank you, madame," he said, carefully checking his brother from the corner of his eye. "But one word of caution. Be certain that the Cavaliere has drunk a surplus of champagne before he spots you in this, his own clothing."

Francesco began a callous laugh and pointed the dagger at the vest he held. "Grimani's clothing? Truly?"

"Yes. Truly. I coaxed these from the Cavaliere's wife when last we visited him."

"Using your charms? Perfect," Francesco cried, slashing the vest.

"One other thing," Jacques said. "I must confess that I persuaded Madame de Gigot to mislead you, Dominique—to say that the costume you were to borrow was given away. However, if you'd really like to wear her—"

Dominique's eyes widened in elation, her mouth opened in laughter, and she ran out the door with a waistcoat, breeches, and jacket draped across her shoulder. "No need! Going to try on my *new* costume," she shouted.

It was only a short while before Francesco put the dagger aside, massaged his scalp, and gawked at his paintings on the loft wall. Jacques watched in vain while his brother tried to recreate his earlier enthusiasm, but the wine had ceased playing its trick. Francesco stared at his canvases and wondered if the paintings—his children— were stillborn.

Finally, he stirred from his reverie. "As usual, you've been extravagant, brother." He pointed at Grimani's vest. "All for a man I neither care for nor trust. For a fête that disgusts me."

Jacques looked at the numerous portraits, still lifes, and battle paintings on the loft wall. "At the fête when your artwork is purchased by the nobles—"

"My artwork? Bloated. Like the bluebloods who'll gape. I abhor it all."

Jacques smiled cunningly. "You revile *everything* then? Even boudin noir—the blood sausage I procured especially for you, to be served at the ball."

Francesco turned away. "Yes, Brother, I revile even your blood. Sausage."

- 14 -

ON JULY 21, A HALF HOUR BEFORE THE BALL was to begin, Dominique, Jacques, and Francesco Casanova arrived in fulsome style at the Grimani summer mansion. Grimani, as pledged, had provided the Casanovas his coach—a conveyance whose cab and horse trappings were decorated with the family coat of arms and—complementing the livery of the coachmen and postilions—embellished in the family colors of argent and crimson.

When the rumble of the coach wheels faded on the smooth stone of Grimani's private road, Jacques adjusted his costume and made a funny face at Dominique and Francesco. Squealing with eagerness, Dominique smiled at the brothers and turned quickly toward the window. Her lips parted in surprise.

In the distance, the grounds of the Grimani mansion blazed with torches that swarmed like fireflies up the rounding hills. Between these fiery flambeaux, giant puffs of flowers bubbled a host of colors while stanchions of fluttering pennants—argent and crimson—teased the eye. Even the dark, low-slung clouds that embraced the mansion's towers seemed complement to a pageant of brilliance.

Once the coach wheeled closer, the night sweetened further with the lively music of strolling musicians, the traffic of liveried servants, and the gay chatter of packs of costumed nobility.

Jacques had hand-chosen many of tonight's guests; five years ago he'd gamboled with *la crème de la crème* of polite society, and he supposed that many of these Parisians still remembered him. But the French were provincial—maybe pragmatic—regarding failure: when Jacques had lost his lottery fortune, he'd lost the interest of the well-heeled.

Tonight he had the opportunity to redeem himself. Feeling a trifle pressured, he buoyed his spirits: *By dawn the name Casanova will be sounded from the lips of all Parisians of prominence.*

The coach came to a rest. The cab door opened.

Dominique, reveling in the warm night breeze that caressed her face, was helped down the coach steps by a servant when, abruptly, her hand was taken up by a person wearing the black-and-white diamond-patterned costume and half mask of Arlecchino. Assisting Dominique to the ground, Arlecchino then retreated several steps before his sword hissed an elaborate salute.

When Dominique rose from her curtsy, the splendor of the mansion grounds animated her once more. She squealed again.

"Madame Casanova is pleased to attend L'affaire de Voltaire?" asked Arlecchino.

"Since I've never before heard my wife screech, I presume she's either delighted or injured," Francesco snapped, exiting the coach ahead of Jacques.

"Delight is the order of the evening," Arlecchino insisted.

"So says our host, Arlecchino, the crafty manservant from Bergamo," Dominique said, and broke into tinkling laughter. "I know your voice, Cavaliere Grimani! I knew it wasn't your maître d'hôtel behind that mask."

"This disguise doesn't serve me?"

"Serves you well," Dominique replied, "but only under these clouds. You'll be easily recognized beneath the ballroom's candlelight."

Jacques' foot met the ground. "The Cavaliere wears many masks. Of that I'm sure."

Grimani smiled strangely. When he began to raise his sword point, Jacques knew he'd exacted flesh from the man. *With this man, I will watch my front and my back.*

Dominique had a ready word. "And what do you think of *our* costumes, Cavaliere?"

Behind his half-mask, Grimani's eyes narrowed—when a female came skipping awkwardly to his side. She seemed all rouge and hair.

"May I introduce my saucy sweetheart, Columbina?" Grimani said.

The costumed female flaunted her multiple rings, curtsied, and in a comic falsetto voice, trilled a high note.

Jacques bowed. "I'd recognize that voice anywhere."

Everyone, except Francesco, laughed.

"Allow me to introduce this worthy woman—my wife, Signora Grimani," said the Cavaliere, sheathing his sword.

Francesco bowed unenthusiastically and turned slightly away while Dominique curtsied to the woman.

At that moment, two youths made their way into the circle of revelers.

"And these gentlemen," Grimani said, "who follow my wife as chicks to the hen, are my two sons. My oldest, Alvise, rides well, plays the flute excellently, and dances and fences in a nimble manner. Antonio is our erudite son who will demand you test him in heraldry, a science so necessary to a nobleman. Both sons, we know, will carry on the supremacy of the Grimani name." The Cavaliere batted his taller son on the shoulder while pleasantries were offered all around.

An enchanting madrigal obliged the group to face the troupe of performing singers. After the song, Jacques stepped under the dancing blaze of a flambeau and opened his arms wide to the glittering summer home and his high-spirited collaborators. "Signora Grimani, you have fashioned a most worthy welcome for the French sage whose reputation shimmers throughout Europe."

"Yes. The wondrous Monsieur de Voltaire."

"And does the king come?" Dominique asked earnestly.

Jacques felt his knees weaken. *Should the king attend, my stock surely soars.*

"Oh, King Louis," Signora Grimani said. "If that boorish man refuses to appear, I'll not be displeased."

"Never you mind what my wife says about the king," the Cavaliere said. "She'll be the first to bend her knee when he arrives."

Signora Grimani waggled her finger in the air. "No, I will not. Neither to him nor to his consort who—even with her gold lice needle— remains unquestionably a commoner."

There was silence among the group.

Francesco's head bent low. His voice shuddered. "Commoner? Then am I not a man? Is *my* blood not prized?"

Cavaliere Grimani placed a firm eye on Francesco. "It need only be said: it is sure that France depends on *everyone's* sedulous actions here tonight." Huffing breathlessly, he tugged a watch from his costume. "Nearly midnight. Time's wasting. Before more guests arrive—late, I suspect, as is the French fashion—I must check the details of the ballroom. Oh, Casanova, if you've brought your valet, post him in the kitchen where he can be out-of-the-way—and fed."

Jacques reluctantly nodded.

The Cavaliere continued his palaver. "The servants must transport the dozen closestools I ordered to wherever necessary. These Frenchmen may defecate in the galleries at Versailles, but not here!"

"What?" Francesco snapped. "Don't tell me these people are vulgar commoners?"

Dominique glared. "Husband, aren't you," she began, her voice growing out of tune, "aren't you privileged—aren't we all privileged"— she gestured frantically to everyone in the circle—"to celebrate this historic occasion when Monsieur de Voltaire returns to France's heart?" She forced a smile. "Let us proceed, Cavaliere Grimani. We're ready. All of us."

Jacques spoke up. "Oh, but we ask one final time, Signor Grimani: what is your opinion of our costumes?"

Dominique moved closer to the torchlight and began a slow pivot, showing off her jacket and breeches, beaver tricorne hat, and ceramic mask.

"Ah, your costumes? Of course." Grimani posed hand on elbow, chin on palm—as a tailor might study attire—and surveyed all three revelers. "Your costumes? Unconventional, certainly." Grimani suddenly recognized his shredded garments and sputtered irritably. "Audacious—"

"Au courant," piped in Signora Grimani, who now identified her husband's clothes.

"Stylish? That's what we felt," said Dominique, laughing gaily.

A cackle broke from Francesco's mouth. Signora Grimani joined in. At once, Jacques felt a satisfaction in his belly: his costume idea had stung the Cavaliere.

"Shall we attend the masquerade?" asked Signora, taking the arm of her glowering husband.

"Francesco and I will join you in a few moments," Jacques said. He pinched Francesco's sleeve and waved off the rest. Together, they watched the revelers float toward the entrance of the mansion.

"A word, please?" Clearing his throat, Jacques gently led his brother beneath a high torch. "You, your wife, and I—all have much to gain tonight." He pitched his eyes toward the diminishing figure of Dominique, looked back to his brother, and hushed his voice. "I recall you telling me of the first time you ever saw her, Francesco. Wasn't she walking a colt through a lush, yellow meadow?"

Arms lank at his sides, Francesco stared eye to eye with Jacques.

"You couldn't see her face, yet her walk captivated you. Isn't that so? You noticed her turned-out feet and knew she must be a dancer. There was something bold and joyful in her step. She possessed a confidence. A lusty confidence, you told me. I plainly say," Jacques said, his voice filled with sincerity, "remember who this woman is. What she's done for you. And how she maintains— well, you and I—because of her, you and I stand to achieve much success by night's—"

"My insolent ways." Francesco's eyes misted momentarily, but he said nothing more.

"What?" Jacques asked. "What? Talk with me, Brother."

A mischievous flame from the flambeau darted toward Francesco. He dodged low, then wheeled back and, coming to his feet, veered away, stalking toward the Grimani residence.

Jacques twisted his fist into his palm and took a step to follow.

"Brothers Casanova? Are you coming?" Dominique wandered in from the dark, stopping at Jacques' side. "Where's my husband?"

"He went to inspect his paintings," Jacques lied. His voice grew reassuring. "He's in good humor. He and I have an understanding."

"I'm anxious for tonight," she said with a slight catch in her voice. "For success."

"As am I," Jacques said. "Shall we start with this view?" With a gentle touch to her elbow, he turned her in the opposite direction.

Scanning the huge courtyard, Dominique was awestruck by the partiers now fanning from the opulent coaches. The costumes were more varied and astonishing than in her imagination. Knights in armor, ballerinas, unicorns, pirates of the Spanish Main. And the omnipresent fragrances of the flowers seemed as if they might transport her to heaven. She turned to Jacques, her voice leavened with pleasure. "To the reception vestibule! I'm excited to watch the nobility announced. We'll join Francesco inside."

"We shall."

Keep on your guard. Jacques tightened his mask and gave Dominique a playful squeeze on the arm. A clap of thunder boomed while they slipped into a throng of drifting partygoers.

Once inside the ballroom Dominique gasped. "A transformation indeed! Just as Signora Grimani boasted."

The walnut ceiling decorated in silver and gold now repeated its pattern on the floor. Pale blue area carpets contrasted with the ormolu scrolling, and all reflected in the finely wrought serpentine mirrors lining the walls. A joyous tune from the balcony orchestra wound its way through the ballroom where in every corner of the huge room hung Francesco's art. High in the balcony, too, was the artist's most colorful canvas.

From the corner of his eye, Jacques noticed a guest slink past, his peculiar gait displaying cunning malice in each step.

Certain that Dominique was tucked safely behind him, Jacques edged alongside the man outfitted as Pierrot: full mask, frilled collaret, loose blouse, pantaloons, and dunce's hat. He leaned close and spoke. "You'll not wreck this ball. You'll behave."

The man turned, his eyes shining through his face mask. "Why, the last time I saw the detestable Casanova, I was—"

"At the point of my dagger, which sits even tonight at my side."

"Particularly humiliating, that dagger experience," growled Pierrot.

Disregarding Dominique, Jacques grasped the man by the arm and shuffled him away from the crowd. "*I* made up the invitation list and *you*, it's certain, weren't included. How did you manage—"

"Please keep your voice down." The man cocked his masked head, jaw jutting upward at Jacques. "And how, friend, is the life of adventuring treating *you*?"

"I might ask you the same, Brose," Jacques barked. "Again, how did you manage to gain entry?"

"Ingenuity." Brose pointed over his shoulder. "And the fact that I diddle the blue-blooded slut lolling against that far painting."

Jacques glanced toward the corner of the ballroom and saw a woman leaning against one of Francesco's large paintings, purple fan limp at her side.

"One of the richest widows in Paris—she was included in the invitations, was she not? Oh, by the bye, how is it that you, one of the rough trade, were allowed to assemble the invitation list?"

Jacques felt Dominique draw next to him. Still staring at Brose, he spoke to her. "I won't introduce you to this pimp, poetaster, and thief, for if you were to examine his physiognomy beneath that oversized mask, you would see he stands for duplicity and cynicism. Above all, Carlo Brose hates life. For that, he can never be forgiven."

"Charmed, madame," intoned Brose, shaking his arm free from Jacques' grip in order to bow. "I see from the identical ceramics you and Signor wear that you're a matched pair." He pointed at Jacques. "This man hasn't the heart to introduce his wife to a well-known rival."

"I'm his *brother's* wife, signor."

"Brother's wife?" Brose repeated slowly. "How practical. So at hand."

Jacques glared. "Watch your tongue, or I'll cut it out and feed it to you."

"You'd do that? Why, if you were to complete even a portion of what you *say* you'll complete, you might claim accomplishment."

Dominique fixed her stare on Brose, then Jacques. "I'll find my husband." She turned on her heel and marched away.

"Calm yourself, Casanova," said Brose. "I've reason to behave tonight. If I suitably dote on the Marquise all night long, she'll marry me tomorrow—and the day following, her pretty fortune will be at my command."

"Phhtt!"

"In your eyes, I see envy."

Jacques took a long moment gritting his teeth before he looked away.

"Then doting I shall go." Carlo Brose waved coyly and loped toward a mass of onlookers.

Jacques' attention was mastered by a new sight: Cavaliere Grimani strutting down the steep balcony stairs to the middle of the resplendent ballroom. When Grimani began his speech, Jacques quickly fell into a lighter mood, amused at the pompous voice stemming from the man in Arlecchino tights.

Jacques now considered: introductions to la crème de la crème, he told himself, would be far more beneficial *after* his manuscript presentation to Voltaire, so the adventurer began to flow casually around the outskirts of the crowd, nibbling the food, listening to conversations, taking in the gentlemen and ladies decorated in gold braid, tassels, frills, ruffles and ribbons, plumes and puffery. The glittering hues of painted faces, masks, and costumes, the redolent perfumes, the rapid movement of a hundred fluttering fans—all seemed to intoxicate Jacques.

Two women dressed as butterflies flitted by, chattering. "Apparently this Monsieur Casanova's so-called religious manuscript may have views capable of upending the Church."

Jacques chortled. He was exceedingly pleased. *Upend the Church? Let these butterflies wing through this party and exaggerate my deeds until all the well heeled know my name.*

The Cavaliere was ending his speech. "I look forward to meeting each and every one of you this evening."

"As do I," Jacques said quietly to himself. He climbed several steps up the balcony stairs for a better view.

Cavaliere Grimani bowed to polite applause while the orchestra filled the room with music, obliging him and Signora Grimani to open the ball with a polonaise, a simple but majestic procession that gave the couples a chance to show themselves. Immediately after, the orchestra struck up a minuet, whose tune was soon augmented by thunderclaps. Jacques would join in good time.

Feeling fully confident, he sipped his champagne while a faster dance—the fandango—began. He savored the fanciful costumes, like spinning fireworks, as they flared across the ballroom mirrors, while beneath the thousand ceiling candles a throng of partygoers pressed in upon a gentleman dressed in a Roman toga.

- 15 -

AS THE RAIN BEGAN TO PELT OUTSIDE, the orchestra picked up the tempo of its fandango. A crush of guests swarmed toward the entrance. From across the room, Jacques easily recognized the man he'd seen in countless engravings: Francois Voltaire. Thin lips, nose, and face, but bright, bright eyes beneath nonexistent eyebrows. And tonight—poking from his toga—arms and legs as thin as capellini.

Voltaire. Brilliant thinker, writer, and prodigy extraordinaire.

During their correspondence, Jacques had envisioned meeting the esteemed philosopher a hundred times, but always his fanciful scenarios were fraught with unease, for it was said that Monsieur de Voltaire on occasion took joy in skewering men with his caustic wit and scalding humiliations.

Jacques tensed while his mind piled high wild thoughts. Examining his warm and clammy palms, he wondered: *how do I expect to earn respect from the most exceptional man in Europe when I've chosen to wear torn and tattered rags?* What if—somehow—the great Voltaire made known that Jacques was the son of Zanetta Farussi, actress? Among this crowd, Jacques' shame would be total.

In due course, he forced himself to move to the edge of the crowd that surrounded Voltaire.

The partiers quieted. Monsieur de Voltaire began to speak. "I'm long, lean, and fleshless," he spouted while tugging at his wig. "Furthermore, I'm without buttocks. I need heat."

The spectators cackled.

"And there is nothing of which abuse has not been made. The kiss, for example, designed by nature for the mouth, has often been prostituted to membranes which do not seem made for this usage." Voltaire lowered his voice to a throaty whisper. "One knows of what the Knights Templar were accused."

Hoots of laughter echoed through the ballroom while Voltaire clucked away. If a stolid, moralistic sage was anticipated, expectations were now shattered.

I can converse with Voltaire on this bawdy level, at least.

A gruff voice in the middle of the throng sounded. "Monsieur de Voltaire, what do you think of the three youths in Lyons who—"

The philosopher raised his hand. "Yes, I know what you ask. The boys who read some of my anti-Church raillery, and then decided to mutilate a cemetery crucifix and smear ordure on another. What is one to say?" he sighed. "The three are now sentenced to torture, to death, and to oblivion. I'm shocked to the core of my being at the community at Lyons who, as Christ's good Catholics, are commanded to turn the other cheek. I agree, yes, some punishment is needed for the boys for destroying property. But torture and death?"

There was not a movement in the crowd as Voltaire's jaw shook uncontrollably.

He wiped his hand across his forehead, then as an afterthought added: "Frederick of Prussia thinks the young men should suffer a fate worse than death—to be condemned to read Thomas Aquinas' entire *Summa Theologica*. An acid smile crossed his face until he raised his hand to cut off the mounting laughter. "Yet I must not jest in the face of such barbarity."

The flutter of a fan caught Jacques' eye at the farthest part of the crowd. A woman wearing a wimple and a face mask flipped her purple fan closed and circled it teasingly in his direction, allowing Jacques to recognize the startling sapphire rings on her lithe fingers. Beneath the brocaded mask were rheumy eyes he knew—those of the Marquise D'Ampie, the woman whose impassioned charms he'd shared two months ago—and with whom he'd scarcely traded a word. The hairs bristled on his arm as he recalled his late-night tryst with the toothless woman. *What was I thinking when I invited her to this select affair? And to boot, this is the harridan whose vast fortune will shortly belong to Carlo Brose.*

Jacques shook his head at the Marquise. He gestured emphatically toward Voltaire, turned away from the woman, and launched his champagne glass to his lips, hoping the drink would soothe his disgust.

"Signor Casanova? Signor Casanova?"

While Jacques guzzled, the voice again rang out.

"You are Signor Casanova, the Venetian, are you not?"

Jacques' ears turned to fire. His pulse battered his brain. Francois Voltaire addressed him from across the room. The crowd parted in halves.

Jacques forced a stiff bow and replied. "I'm he, Monsieur de Voltaire. You do me honor." The guests immediately hushed in apprehension.

"Although you and I, good sir, have exchanged our thoughts by post, we've never had the pleasure of meeting face-to-face."

"You are correct, monsieur," Jacques answered, his voice cracking badly.

"Signor Casanova, I'm reminded of a not-insignificant feat of yours: that some time ago you escaped an inescapable prison, and that this bold action has astounded much of Europe."

"My bold action most certainly astounded the authorities." A round of laughs issued from the crowd.

"And now, Signor Casanova, no one in Europe trusts you. That is, in their prisons."

"No more prisons for me, sir. My present opinion is that studying the world on the run—instead of from a history book—suitably amuses me."

Many faces beamed approval, but Jacques felt his mouth go dry. *These blue bloods nod, encouraging Voltaire and me to continue our sallies, one at the expense of the other.*

"Signor Casanova, since you bring up history, what is your opinion? Is history—the history of mankind—created by God?"

Jacques' eyes raced along the rows of chandeliers that crowded the ballroom ceiling. The last thing he desired was a religious debate with the sage. If Voltaire bested Jacques, Jacques would lose any standing he might have already gained. If Jacques bested Voltaire, he insulted the guest of honor. Jacques felt four hundred heads bend in his direction. *They must not laugh. I cannot stomach their scorn.*

Sweat bubbled across his brow. "I believe that a history—for God—was invented by men. I believe we've imagined Him, created Him, mythologized Him for such a long time that most men dare not live without Him."

"Do you dare live without God, Signor Casanova?"

There was an awful silence in the great room.

"I dare, sir."

Voltaire quieted the growing murmurs. "Say you this to placate the old man who now questions you? Or say you this to spite God?"

Jacques gulped a breath. "For many Frenchmen, Monsieur de Voltaire, you *are* God."

Muttering filled the air. And nervous laughter. Also light clapping.

Monsieur was pleased, no doubt, yet had another ready reply. How long could Jacques continue this game?

But then a tumult arose from the entrance staircase, and before the crowd's attention left Voltaire, Jacques turned to watch a number of tall, stout men—sopping wet—quickly enter the room.

"*Vive le roi.*" someone shouted. "*Vive le roi.*" The crowd picked up the cue, and turning toward the entry doors, gentlemen bowed, ladies curtsied.

Jacques' pulse notched higher. *He's here. The king has come. He and I—we'll soon be reacquainted!* He lowered himself to a bow, his eyes scanning the scene.

Into the middle of the ballroom strutted *Louis Quinze* in golden frippery and exotic feathers, a haughty smile on his face. Accoutred to resemble an unusual bird—perhaps a cockatoo—Louis was, even in this ostentatious costume, truly majestic. Vicomte de Fragonard had claimed that he'd met God. Perhaps it was Louis XV he'd met.

It began with the physical. Louis' head, ravishingly handsome, was set on his neck to perfection and it was often said that women fell in love with him on first sight. In the forty-fifth year of his life and the fortieth year of his reign, King Louis was yet adored by many Frenchman.

The guests lauded their monarch with spontaneous and gentle applause. A tingle raced up Jacques' arms, but at the same time, he couldn't hide a frown when he considered that Louis' inherited position of power gave him dominion over every single creature in France that had a beating heart. A monarchy, certainly. Not a republic.

Jacques' mood elevated when he noted that situated between the king and circling nobility were the stout men of Louis' Swiss Guard, all drenched from the rainstorm but still decidedly impressive in their authority.

Cavaliere Grimani now moved out from among the ordered servants and stood ready to introduce himself and his wife. When the applause dwindled, the Swiss Guard parted, and Grimani, accepting Louis' hand to kiss, addressed the king with grave solemnity. "My wife and I are honored Your Highness has deigned to attend our fête. This entire nation and all of Europe is pleased Your Majesty has come to honor a great son of France, Monsieur de Voltaire."

"Did I make a wise choice, I wonder?" boomed Louis. "The torrents of rainwater that spew from the clouds tonight tell me otherwise." The king's proud smile left his face. "Madame de Pompadour did not accompany me this evening. As you may know, she spits blood."

Gasps came from the waves of onlookers who ringed the monarch while Grimani's face remained expressionless.

"I understand," Louis sniffed, "there's to be a presentation of sorts. Before that moment, this monarch wants to enjoy himself."

"As Your Highness wishes." Cavaliere Grimani gestured toward the balcony, and the dozen musicians struck up a sprightly tune.

Jacques reassured himself that he would again acquaint himself with King Louis on the presentation dais. Until then, he'd mix with the blue bloods. They were the much-needed hors d'oeuvres for his palate.

Jacques threaded his way through the dancers to an impossibly beautiful buffet table swollen with pâte of partridge, shellfish, turkey, filets of exotic fish, ortolans, larks' tongues, and blood sausage. He popped a plump red strawberry into his mouth while deciding whether to nibble on the blueberries, melons, or peaches. Maybe the white truffles. But, oh—to slurp a raspberry fruit ice from Venice!

While he sampled the confections, the creams and puddings, the elaborate vegetable dishes, and assorted meats and delicacies—while he salivated over the endless delights—he chatted amiably with a pack of gluttonous nobles, who congratulated him on his exchange with Voltaire. Jacques was elated.

Tonight my good fortunes begin! At this very moment wagging tongues throughout this party bolster my repute. Certainly my presentation of the religious manuscript to Monsieur will cement my triumph with these aristocrats and the king. Moreover, I'll be richer by a purseful of Grimani's gold. And most importantly, I'll see that he recommends my return to cherished Venice. What do I care if I wear a shredded costume!

Jacques wanted to shout in jubilation, until he spotted the toothless Marquise D'Ampie loitering at the perimeter of the ballroom. He turned quickly on his heel and headed into a throng of celebrants.

While the night wore on, the thundershowers grew fiercer; yet the storm seemed to drive the partiers into a gayer humor. Guests chattered at the buffet; another hundred danced the contra dances. Servants poured champagne while the mass of partiers swilled and swooned.

"It's time to demonstrate my dancing skills," Jacques smiled. "For that I will need Madame Dominique Casanova."

- 16 -

AFTER SEARCHING THE GROUNDS and hunting Francesco throughout the ballroom, Dominique discovered her husband on the stairway to the balcony. She led him to a partially-concealed alcove located beside one of his battle paintings.

While small bands of partiers paraded by, Francesco squatted on his haunches, eyes downcast. Dominique stood over him, one hand on the ceramic mask resting on his head, her other hand stroking a scrap of his outfit.

"Stand up, please, Francesco," she said. "It's important that you show your handsome face and that you and I promote your work."

Francesco's response was a loud exhale.

"I do no good here," Dominique fumed. "You'll quit fretting when you wish to quit fretting."

A shrill creak distracted her. She glanced at a man in knight's armor, dressed as Mars, the god of war. The fat man, gripping the steely visor of his beaver, studied Francesco's canvas. An audience of old women, all of them with cowls spilling over their cloaked shoulders, circled behind Mars.

"Battle," flapped the fat cheeks of Mars. "Artist's colors—all wrong. Base should have been dark, not light. Underlying perspective—execrable." He flung his arm upward making his armor squeak. "And all these billows of cannon smoke certainly hide details that this tyro is too inept or too lazy to paint."

Dominique seethed. *Descending vultures, these people.* She noted Francesco still hunched over, motionless; she stepped from the recess, clenching her fists, wondering how she might squelch fat Mars' grating squawk.

"This artist has never been to war—as I have. Does not comprehend it—as I do. Just look at the soldiers' angelic faces." The old women nodded.

That instant, Francesco heaved to his feet, eyes dull and distant.

Fat Mars continued. "These are not the faces of horror. They are the faces of ... Punchinello." The man held his armored belly as he vomited a guttural laugh.

In a single, swift movement, Francesco drew a small knife from his boot and lurched from the alcove to stand nose to nose with his critic. The old women shrieked and backed away.

Francesco whipped the knifepoint just below his own chin. "This is the face of horror. This is the face of the artist. Casanova!"

"Husband," wailed Dominique, rushing toward him.

Francesco leapt at his painting, plunging his weapon into the canvas. With one powerful rip, the painting gaped wide. Just as quickly he was back before Mars, hissing viciously.

A shudder ran through the fat man's body. His armor clanked.

"Francesco," Dominique pleaded. She positioned herself beside her husband but dared not touch him.

Francesco, barely glancing at Dominique, made his way again to his painting, and sinking the knife into the canvas, let it stay. He spoke flatly. "I destroy all that I love."

Mars, in the meantime, withdrew from the scene and crept warily toward the entourage of old crones who grimaced and one by one covered their heads with their cowls. "Feeble-minded f-f-fellow, my dears," Mars' voice trembled. "I ... I ... I shall insist he not bother us again."

Dominique wiped her eyes and in a whisper tried to console herself and Francesco. Before she was able to touch his shoulder, he spun toward her, speaking rapidly, heatedly.

"I've robbed you of joy. I've clawed away your confidence. I'm a vandal." He quickly fled into a crowd of passersby.

"Francesco!" Shaking mightily, Dominique slunk back into the alcove, pressing herself hard against the wall. Through watery eyes, she watched the gawkers hurriedly return to their drinking and discourse. "What's happening? What am I to do? What?"

She rubbed a tear from her cheek and edged from the alcove. "Among these unforgiving people, I will comfort him." Dominique hovered just above the crowd on a stair step and stared out into the ballroom.

She spotted familiar tattered clothes. Jacques was finishing a dance at the far end of the ballroom, and judging by the servants' activities and the tides of people mulling in that direction, the time for the manuscript presentation neared.

FROM A SERVANT'S TRAY, JACQUES SCOOPED a glass of champagne, congratulating himself for the superb vintage he'd substituted at the last minute for the *oeil de perdrix*. Tipping his glass to his mouth, he glanced at the small dais that had been erected near the entrance of the ballroom.

While the servants made their brief announcements, he finished his drink and headed toward Cavaliere Grimani, who signaled the orchestra to end their music. The king was immediately seated at the head of the chattering crowd.

Cavaliere Grimani stepped to the platform, then stood next to the lectern holding the manuscript. Warily, he eyed Jacques on the floor to his left, bowed to Louis Quinze, then nodded to the Swiss Guards and noble guests.

Without delay, he issued an introduction of Monsieur de Voltaire, who ascended the dais and faced the sea of guests, all clapping hard as they might. After the crowd calmed, Grimani stepped down, leaving the sprightly philosopher—Roman robes adorning his thinness— roosting above the king and ranks of nobles.

Voltaire took a sidelong glimpse at Jacques and hailed his audience.

"I once estimated the average longevity of a Frenchman at twenty-two years," he began. "I've already lived three times longer than the average human of this century, and it's my age, I suppose, that has motivated even my critics to credit me with certain attributes, among which is eloquence." He grinned impishly. "The Abbé Galiani, as you may know, defined eloquence as 'the art of saying something without being sent to the Bastille.'"

Nervous laughter trickled from the crowd

The philosopher rested his eyes on the Louis Quinze. "Tonight, I hope to be eloquent."

The king proceeded to drain his champagne glass, the crease of a drunken grin crossing his mouth. He dipped his head at Voltaire. The onlookers sighed a relief.

"For forty years, I've railed against the Church and its god," Voltaire said. "And I will rail another forty. If *God* grants it."

Laughter pitched the air.

The playfulness on Voltaire's face disappeared. "In my theological studies, I have begun to look into the very beginnings of Christianity. What I've discovered is that in the first three or four hundred years after Jesus of Nazareth's death, there were many variations of Christianity. One variety of early Christianity that greatly interests me was called Gnosticism. This is why we are here tonight." Voltaire gestured toward Jacques and his manuscript. "Some of us think that the true and original form of Christianity was Gnosticism."

Several grumbles rippled through the crowd. Jacques' gut pinched in anguish.

"To digress, the Catholic Church believes that their god—Jesus the Christ—through His gift of sacrifice allows us a free pass to heaven. The Gnostics, conversely, believe a man may create his own pass to heaven—that a man or woman, without mediation from others, has the potential in his lifetime to achieve godhead. Gnosticism maintains that God is to be found exclusively within one's own self."

Loud and disagreeable shouts now pierced the air. Jacques snuck a nervous peek at Louis. Clearly he scowled.

Voltaire was undeterred. "This belief, as you may well surmise, was upsetting to the Church of Paul—and to the later hierarchy of popes, prelates, and the like who made a good living by intervening with God on behalf of sinning souls. Like me. Like you."

Jacques blotted a bead of sweat from his forehead. Even if the king didn't draw and quarter Voltaire—and Jacques, by association— the good Christians in the crowd might flog them to bits.

"This Christian Gnostic philosophy—in conflict with Roman Catholic theology—obligated the early Church patriarchs to eliminate— to destroy—all Gnostics and all traces of Gnosticism. Yet *some* Gnostic documents did manage to escape destruction by the Church of Rome." He pointed to Jacques' manuscript. "Because I've done previous investigations upon this particularly rare manuscript, I deem it to be an authentic Gnostic text that was written in the second century Anno Domini."

Voltaire shot a look into the crowd, then lifting his arms, wordlessly beckoned Jacques to join him on the dais. "And this particularly rare gentleman, Jacques Girolamo Casanova, has graciously consented to turn this text over to my care and safekeeping. It is the munificent act of a discerning man."

Voltaire led the light applause. The king, Cavaliere Grimani and his wife, and scores of guests showed their approval likewise.

Jacques' excitement seemed to expand all the way to his fingers and toes. He wiped the remaining sweat from his forehead, straightened his shoulders, and absorbed the glittering moment. He bowed to the king with as much humility as he could muster, then stepped forward on the dais and hushed the crowd. "I've only to say that I, like so many others with whom I've spoken tonight, feel honored to be in the company of one of the most eminent men of this century." Jacques beamed at Voltaire. "This gentleman of France has an unequaled wit, an all-encompassing intelligence—"

"And nearly fleshless buttocks," trumpeted Voltaire.

At this remark, the crowd convulsed. Jacques, caught completely by surprise, held his sides trying to smother his own laughter, a battle he lost. Through watery eyes, he watched Louis Quinze double over in mirth.

Minutes passed before the uproar settled and the bacchantes returned to their studied politeness.

Jacques cradled the precious text he'd smuggled out of Constantinople, had doggedly transported throughout Europe, a text that he'd always felt deep down would in some manner lend exquisite specialness and unconditional adulation. This night, he'd experienced just that. Tonight, he belonged.

Jacques wondered: was he giving away his magic charm? Suddenly, he felt disinclined to part with the manuscript. But with some formality—and a large smile—he handed it to Voltaire, then left the platform. He could relinquish center stage since another of his triumphal coups would soon take place: his receipt of Grimani's gold.

Francois Voltaire raised his arm. "Times are changing. Men and gods are changing," he said. "This—from the mouth of that soothing English author and statesman, the fourth earl of Chesterfield: 'I foresee,' said he, 'that before the end of this century, the trade of both King and priest will not be half so good a one as it has been.'"

The stunned crowd seemed almost to tip back on their heels as if a blasting wind raged through the ballroom.

To Jacques' surprise, King Louis offered a sardonic smile and began to clap. Here was an enlightened monarch—or a drunken one—who gave the crowd his royal permission to applaud Voltaire's courage, if not his opinion.

Applause rose slowly throughout the room.

Voltaire took his cue. "In earnest shall I study this priceless manuscript and soon report on its significance to all Frenchmen—who are once again my fellow countrymen. I thank Cavaliere Michele Grimani and Signor Jacques Casanova, two generous and true gentlemen." Voltaire paused. "Yet how extraordinary this world is: two Venetians—sharing a radical text they cannot read—coax a Frenchman out of the bowels of Switzerland. What unexpected wonder and strangeness."

While the savant descended the dais amid heavy applause, the orchestra struck up another minuet.

Behind the dais—out of view of the guests—Grimani's manservant placed a velvet purse into Jacques' palm, then strode briskly away.

Jacques fondled the gold coins. All doubts, compromises, and contingency plans dissolved, including the last thread tethering him to Vicomte de Fragonard's proposal. The gold—a thrilling elixir!

As joyous as Jacques felt, he became somewhat miffed that Dominique was not near. He'd not seen her during the presentation, nor had she met him behind the dais. Where was she at this, his moment of triumph? With Francesco?

Jacques tucked the purse between two tatters in his breeches and stepped gingerly from behind the platform to take in the mass of revelers who were beginning to clutter the ballroom floor.

At the near end of the floor, a woman attired as the goddess Diana—and arching like a proud fawn—pranced toward the doors leading to the garden. Even from a distance, Jacques' keen eyes could make out the black silk *mouches* in the guise of hearts and teardrops pasted to her temple, frolicsome marks he adored. He was further invigorated by the gauzelike costume wrapping Diana's body. *Shall I swallow her whole or have her piecemeal?*

From one of the waiters, Jacques filched two glasses of champagne and shuttled across the ballroom, looking through the doors. A thin drizzle of rain teased the flames of the torches outside so that, in the garden, Diana was nowhere to be seen.

Turning slowly around, he spotted Dominique halfway across the room. For the moment, she did not see him.

"This way," purred a female voice.

Jacques spun about, again peered into the garden, and saw the fleeting figure of Diana. He peeked back in Dominique's direction, but then veered straight out the door.

Navigating the labyrinth of wet shrubs he slugged down his champagne just before he heard a whispered "Here, right here."

A fan snapped shut. A hand clamped his groin.

"Ah," Jacques groaned. The hand loosened but immediately slid across his waistcoat, then under his tattered shirt and found flesh. A nipple.

"Oh." He squeezed his eyes closed. "Oh!" Clutching a glass in each fist, he barely managed to remain upright.

"I thought we'd never have one another," pouted the woman. One hand kneaded Jacques' chest while the other tugged his head low, allowing her mouth to slither across his.

Jacques recognized the stinking breath. Overcoming his mortification, he uttered a faint "Marquise D'Ampie?"

"Yours for the taking."

"Where's Diana, the fawn?"

Another salacious kiss from the woman repulsed him. He jerked upright, stood tall, downed his other champagne, then dropped both glasses to the slick grass. He glanced at the Marquise, recalling that this was Carlo Brose's woman, the one whom he was to marry. Wrecking Brose's plan might please Jacques greatly.

"All night I've wanted to suck your flesh," growled La Marquise.

"Your wantoness is, umm, *not* infectious," murmured Jacques, rainwater dripping down his nose. "Or your drunkenness." He felt his member stemming. It grew erect and, discovering an oblique path, peeped through one of the holes in his breeches.

The Marquise dropped to her knees. She broke into sobs—hugging, caressing, kissing Jacques' hardened manhood through the shredded breeches.

"Madame! Do you suppose the involuntary response of my flesh grants you permission to ...?" Jacques tried to regroup his reeling senses. *What to do?*

Before he could say the word "insatiable," Jacques was neatly tossed to his back.

La Marquise pounced.

A quarter hour and three positions later, Jacques was incensed. And to his added consternation, another pair of lovers in an adjacent arbor began a whine of lust.

"More. More," bawled D'Ampie. "Tonight, my lover, I want to die the little death a thousand times."

"No doubt," muttered Jacques, continuing the act of fornication mechanically.

He toiled in a heated sweat, most of it pouring from his head. The drizzle offered little relief while allowing soaked strands of his well-dressed peruke to droop to his eyes.

Amid carnal howls from the adjoining shrub and frenzied dance cadences exploding from the ballroom, Jacques flipped his wig on to the nearest hedge and strained to view Madame Marquise—bluish teeth and all—now on her back.

D'Ampie, you have drifted from flirtation to lechery to—perhaps not satiation but to exhaustion ... "Marquise, I won't continue this rut."

The by now nearly formless creature didn't answer. But during a flash of lightning, Jacques caught her wistful grin.

He disentangled himself, stood up, and shook rainwater from his back like a sodden wolfhound, then groped through the shrubbery maze toward the candlelit ballroom.

His tattered costume and disheveled appearance in the garden doorway surprised neither the drunken dancers nor the servant whose champagne Jacques began to thirstily guzzle.

Before he could finish his drink, a plump woman masked as a shepherdess drew alongside him. In a startling gesture, the fleshy shepherdess struck the bold opening pose of the violent Venetian *furlana*, a dance that had no equal in all of Europe. Jacques—soaked to the bone, drained of his faculties—declined the woman's invitation, but she, as well as several insistent others, would have none of it. The shepherdess yanked Jacques to the center of the floor.

They danced six furious furlane, one following the other. Jacques, at the finish, was out of breath and nearly insensible, but the sizeable shepherdess stood absolutely still without the least sign of fatigue, as if to defy him. The furlana continued. During the most demanding part of the dance, the whirl, Jacques' partner seemed to hover over him like a thick shade tree. Three times she executed the double grand *cercle*. Gasping for air, Jacques felt tart champagne rising up his throat.

A lone violinist, standing beside a bright torch high in the orchestra balcony, plucked a frenzied pizzicato, then stopped midphrase. The orchestra broke off.

On the ballroom floor, the few remaining dancers, glancing to the balcony, froze in place. Jacques, too, came to a standstill. Before starting to stalk away, he glimpsed toward the violinist.

Above and behind the seated musician, a long, slack object swung like a padded pendulum from one side of the narrow balcony to the other. A man. A man in a gay and tattered costume dangling from a rope wound around his neck. A mask attached to the back of the man's head was in view until, shortly, the twisting pirouette of the body offered a snatch of his greenish-blue face. A bit of tongue protruded from the mouth. Everyone in the ballroom stood immobile, engrossed in the unnatural spectacle.

Twirling in front of his painting—my brother! He's finally done it, the shit.

A horrible choking gushed from Francesco.

Jacques blinked in confusion. His brain spun. His heart thundered as if a sword thrust had breached his chest. His eyes, his burning eyes, again followed the rope from a ceiling rod to the body as it labored back and forth.

Jacques tasted the sickening tang of champagne as the contents of his stomach rolled onto the back of the shepherdess who stood beside him. Even before the woman realized what had befallen her, Jacques was running toward the side stairs leading to the balcony, knots of revelers barring his path.

"Help!"

He recognized Dominique's cry, which was quickly drowned by appalling screams.

A dozen strides from Jacques, a man dressed as Mars thrust his fist to the balcony toward Francesco. "That's the madman who slashed the Cavaliere's painting," he shouted. "That ghoul is—"

Jacques pressed forward toward the stairs, driving fat Mars to his knees when he passed. His eyes darted to the balcony, to Francesco, then to a musician who reeled toward the balcony railing, his hands clapped over his nose and mouth. The panicked musician toppled a burning flambeau before plunging into the crowd below. More cries of terror.

"Fire, fire in the balcony!"

Jacques, reaching the bottom of the stairs, saw Dominique stumble in the balcony just before new mayhem commanded his eyes back to the ballroom floor. The king's Swiss Guard had sprung into action. The huge men, arms outstretched, swept through the crowd like scythes through grass, thrusting aside lords and ladies, pulling Louis Quinze toward the reception room and entrance. Shrieks ripped the air; revelers trampled one another.

Battered by the frenzied onslaught on the stairs, Jacques barely remained standing. His throat was scorched. The reek of vomit roiled his senses. "Not dead, must not be," he found himself yelling. "Save him!"

Just then, a bone-thin Voltaire, stripped of his toga, swept past. The bewildered philosopher was steered toward the entrance by a maelstrom of screaming people.

Jacques—tottering, shoving, helpless against the mob—fixed his eyes above the ballroom tumult to the fire. The sinewy flames lashed wildly about. With renewed vigor, he battled through the bunched crowd, charging up the stairway. At the uppermost landing, searing hot smoke greeted him. Clamping his nose, he watched a musician, wits gone, fling himself from the height.

Dominique came into sight, hauling a chair toward Francesco's limp body.

"Dominique!"

When Jacques reached her, she had stretched tiptoe on the chair's edge, struggling to separate Francesco from the rope. Quickly, he pulled her down, then drew his dagger, bounded up, and furiously sawed the cord until Francesco, like a sack of grain, crumpled upon his shoulder, sending his ceramic mask plummeting to the floor, where it smashed to pieces. Dominique dropped to the floor, weeping openly, insanely.

"Fight, Brother, fight," commanded Jacques, as he laid Francesco down. Smoke clogged Jacques' brain. Flicking his eyes momentarily to the crackling flames one tier below, he crouched over Francesco and wrestled the rough cord from around his neck. The noose had crushed the throat. He placed his ear to Francesco's mouth. No breath. He put his ear to Francesco's body. No heartbeat. No life.

"Stay, Francesco. Stay with me." Jacques felt his strength collapse. "Don't give up." He wiped away foam from Francesco's lips and stuffed the contorted tongue back into his mouth. He cradled Francesco's head. "Nothing," he said. "Nothing to be done."

Coughing on the harsh smoke, Dominique heaved herself to sitting.

Jacques' gut jerked fiercely. *She mustn't see him.* He ripped off his jacket, laying it over Francesco's face, but the bulging, blood-red eyes peered eerily through the tatters. When Dominique craned toward him, Jacques turned away to see three musicians smother the balcony fire.

Dominique grasped the lifeless hand of her husband and folded it to her bosom, wailing piteously. Jacques turned and pressed his fingers to her cheek, watching the warm tears brim her eyes.

He lay down beside Francesco, hoping his brother might again bloom to life. Tenderly, he stroked his hair and cheek, then wrapped his arm around Francesco's massive chest, drew him close, and leaned into his ear. "I've never held you in my arms." He paused to calm his speech. He placed a quiet kiss on Francesco's lips. "You're my brother. Until the day I die, you'll always be my little brother."

The candles in the chandeliers burned lower, then lower still.

When the storm passed and the dawn of day began to break, Jacques, Dominique, and Petrine carried Francesco down the balcony stairs, settling him on the empty ballroom floor, while servants offered what little aid they could to the few injured spectators who yet remained. No one offered assistance to Jacques.

In through the garden door trudged Carlo Brose, staggering past the wretched and grief stricken. The husky man, mud caking his costume, champagne bottle swinging from his hand, full mask fixed to his face, sprawled to the ballroom floor amid the debris. He throated a thick drunken laugh. "What a sight. Bread, blood, defecation, death." Raising himself to his elbow, he waved a finger about. "But then, hearing those swaddled bluebloods screeching like hares in a trap. And also my Marquise. Probably somewhere face down in the muck, where she ..." Brose's eye found the vanquished Jacques Casanova. "Herr Adventurer, you must depart this tawdry—you don't belong— you, a much-dejected fellow. I could forgive you if you slobbered on great God. But this?" Brose let loose a brazen howl.

From out of nowhere, Brose produced a small book. "Hah! Stole this from your pocket last night!" He thumbed the pages awkwardly and gloated for some time until, lifting his masked head, he stared at Jacques.

"Horace—born before Jesus—*speaks*, Herr Adventurer. Speaks to us in this very room." Brose sucked up a breath, held it, then bleated. "'We are but dust and shadow,' says the Roman. 'Dust and shadow.'"

Brose pulled the book to his bosom, rolled to his back, and closed his eyes. His mask gave the appearance of an innocent, slumbering child until he spoke again: "You don't belong, Jacques Casanova."

- 18 -

FRANCESCO CASANOVA WAS BURIED TWO DAYS LATER in unconsecrated ground. The interment of suicides in consecrated ground, which included all the cemeteries in France, was forbidden by the Catholic Church. And it was only by sheer luck that Francesco's corpse avoided being drawn naked through the street, pelted with mud and stones, and hanged, as civil law required.

What now of Dominique? Eviscerating grief raised a stone wall around her; this she told Jacques, and for the time-being, he understood.

Despite the great sadness in her heart, there was still an urging, a deep desire to live. But there was aimlessness, too. Clarity was gone. Pressing and immediate obligations and duties seemed trite.

Even so, her common sense, albeit considerably shaken, whispered it was, in fact, her duty that would see her through all this—her common sense would be the means by which she might wrest her soul from the ether of uncertainty, of anguish, of confusion, guilt, and grief.

Walking the streets of Paris at daylight, she found herself repeating words that must have originated in a hymn or a sermon or maybe from her father's mouth. Perhaps they were the priest's words when her father was laid into the ground. "Man that is born of a woman hath but a short time to live and is full of misery. He cometh up and is cut down like a flower. He fleeth as if he were a shadow." Great sorrows washed through her.

Dominique prayed, but more, she wanted to stand on a mountaintop and scream to humanity that all is false, sham; then, in a calmer voice, she might speak with grace. *Take notice,* she wanted to say. *Our lives are ending. Grasp close those whom you love. Clothe their souls with significance. Tell them true stories. Give them stories with meaning and matter.*

Roaming Paris, Dominique heard nothing of substance communicated, only the trivial, inane chatter that people blathered day in, day out. It was as if all mankind were unaware their lives were finite, for if they possessed that knowledge, how could they possibly wallow in the fatuous, in the mindless, in the emptiness?

Less than a week after Francesco's death, Dominique entered her room, kneeled at her chair and, saying a "Hail Mary," closed her eyes until the last vestiges of the day's sun played through the window. "Good Lord and Savior," she prayed, "I come in humility, to ask again for Your forgiveness. Let me be grateful for Francesco. Bless him, I pray. He was gentle. Kind. Untarnished by the world. He was my friend. You allowed us a time together. I pray, let all this not be ... I ask that you forgive Francesco."

Dominique's head fell forward. She wept rueful tears.

* * *

Amid the morass of bewildering events and feelings, certain commonplace actions were still required, one of which was unusually difficult for Jacques. He informed Petrine that, funds being what they were, there would be no more wages or even room or board.

He doesn't know about the gold Grimani paid me at L'affaire de Voltaire. And he could not possibly know I lost it, probably while swaying in the arms of D'Ampie. "I can assuredly be a future reference for you," Jacques tried to cheer the valet. "And when I have your back pay, be sure that you'll receive it."

Petrine, a proud Spaniard, seemed puzzled, but offered his trust in his master's good intentions, then thanked him for being forthright. "Have you a notion for the future, sir?"

Jacques began nodding, then looked Petrine in the eye and shook his head no.

Without a further word, the valet pulled together his few effects, tramped down the stairs, and melted into the teeming crowd, knowing he would never collect wages from his master.

Late that night, Jacques gathered together his brother's possessions, now his inheritance. With grim and ghastly effort, he sat on his bed and examined each item. There were less than a dozen articles of clothing, including Francesco's flannel stockings, a sleeping gown, a pair of shoes, gloves, and trousers. "I once purchased seventy-five shirts of the finest linen, Francesco. And as many Masulipatam handkerchiefs. And you have but two of each."

Francesco's other assets were a pair of sunshades, his smallsword and oilcloth sheath, tools and paints, canvases, and numerous paintings and sketches. Jacques would pack everything.

"Brother," he suddenly cried, "you've hurt me to the quick! I must not think of you again."

Night passed into day. That morning, Dominique found succulent vegetables at the market and accepted a loaf of bread from a neighbor while Jacques worked in the kitchen baking sole. Together they silently prepared for the day's main meal, knowing it was one of the last at the residence.

Jacques took it upon himself to see the tablecloth was clean and well-appointed with Dominique's prettiest utensils and hollowware. Between the two settings—his and Dominique's—Jacques laid a small flower. He knew then, more than ever before, this tenderness toward this woman to be a singular, exceptional privilege.

Soon midday sunbeams streamed through the small window of the room and goldened the bloom.

"I've a white wine that compliments the fish," Jacques said to Dominique while she readied herself for the meal. "And for dessert, I have a sack full of nonpareils."

"Shall we sit?" At table, Dominique blessed the food.

"Your presentation is excellent," Jacques said, indicating the colorful food set before him. "Excellent."

"Thank you. I've done my best." Dominique unwrinkled her lips into a slight smile. "I must say, everything smells wonderful, Jacques. And even though Francesco convinced me that you're not much of a cook, yet he'd surely welcome this."

"He would." Jacques raised his wine glass to Dominique.

By her third bite, Dominique was sobbing.

She'll seek my eyes if she wants sympathies. I must remind myself that this daily outpouring may continue—

"These"—she held up her fork, knife, and spoon—"were a present from Francesco in our first year. I'd forgotten until now."

"I understand."

"He's gone. He'll never sit at the table again."

"He's gone, Dominique. We must accept it."

"Why?"

"Why accept it? Or why is he gone?"

Dominique snorted.

Jacques felt the hot blaze of his cheeks.

"Why?" she said. "Why?" She began a hoarse laugh, which ticked into a sharp upsurge. "Francesco was miserable. His dreams were crushed. Did you know that on the night of L'affaire de Voltaire—potentially his greatest success—Francesco slashed his battle painting? And held a dagger to his throat?"

"I'd no inkling."

Dominique continued, tears rushing down her face. "Francesco lied to you. Small lies. Big lies." She bent forward over her plate. "I lied, too. I once told you your brother had firsthand knowledge of his models, his pretty models. None of it was true. Francesco never had any of the girls. Nor me. Francesco and I never consummated our marriage. We never once made love in seven years. He tried. But—never."

Jacques' hand slid from his chin to the table. In that instant he realized why his brother had so keenly sought the erotic miniatures.

Dominique's tears streamed faster. "For a long while, I believed he found me repellent, that I was the cause of his failure. Until one odd afternoon, he revealed he'd made several attempts with a favorite model. To no avail, he said. He couldn't make love to anyone—as vigorous as he might appear. It humiliated him. Made him bitter and unkind. Slowly changed the quality of his paintings. Why did Francesco kill himself? In the misery of his impotence and in the desecration of his artistic dreams, he felt powerless. And if he knew about you and me, well, he turned that displeasure inward, and the black, helpless hole captured him. He was not the same man I married. I knew, I sensed it, but I did not foresee his death."

"Dominique—"

"Francesco understood, yes, *knew* I wanted children. And I deluded myself that when his paintings sold at the fête, he'd have money, standing, and maybe greater confidence. Maybe then be *able* to have children." The woman cupped her forehead with both hands and let loose a shrill lament. "I've hurt him so terribly, planning the fête. I drove him to ... I killed him." Hard pain suffused her face.

Jacques—his whole frame trembling—rose, crossed to the grieving woman, and kneeled beside her. He waited some time before speaking. "This is, no doubt, the time to be frank," he said. "Even in our boyhood, Francesco never ... partook of the girls. One night in particular, several of us gave over to sharing a willing young lady's favors. Francesco begged off, claiming he was ill. During those times, I might have suspected he wasn't able to perform, but I never, ever considered that his unnatural state would last. Into marriage." He placed his hand upon Dominique's. "I assume he didn't tell you about his condition before you married?"

Dominique nodded.

"He should be faulted for this. And moreover, you must not now feel responsible for his end."

A long, long silence passed.

Giving her the flower on the table, Jacques led Dominique to the bed in the adjoining room where, saying nothing, he sat beside her and kissed her cheeks, then her mouth. He desired her. He said this. But she replied that, for her part, this was not the time.

"Lovemaking might put you at ease, make you feel better," persisted Jacques. "Why discourage our pleasures?"

Dominique's reply was firm. "I feel ample satisfaction in your delicate affection, Jacques."

We begin with affection. But let us not end there. Let us taste ecstasy.

Gazing at Dominique, Jacques lay down beside her, temporarily aligned to her wishes.

To feel, to touch a woman where her waist sloped to her hip would never lose its fascination for Jacques. When his fingers sensed that indefinable fullness, tiny raptures stirred within him, a tingling dizziness held him enthralled—all but arresting his desire. This refined enchantment of nature he'd puzzled on but never unlocked—an elusive message of womanhood he couldn't decode, a fact that only enchanted him further.

With hands—he often looked forward to holding a woman's hands, appendages he explored and kissed in endless admiration.

Beyond these particular treasures, Jacques adored all parts of women and the discoveries that exploration afforded. He cherished a woman's closed eyelids, which might at any time open with the surprise of passion to reveal her most ardent secrets.

Too, the warm, moist breath and unique flavor of a woman's mouth— these offered refined fulfillment. And woe be to the lover who did not find kissing an exquisite delicacy to be enjoyed on its own merits.

He relished the revelation of a woman's nipples: pink or light or dark brown, large or small, and above all, their sensitivity to plucking, pinching, sucking, and caressing.

The ferocious odor of his lover's most private possession was his sweetest harvest. The scent of the feminine treasure reassured him. Reassured him that this life was real, was of substance.

He was at ease with the most unfrequented portions and passions of women, and rarely did he disdain an action or behavior that might bring his partner more pleasures.

To an onlooker, Jacques Casanova might be considered a connoisseur of the carnal; in his own estimation, the act of love merely granted him a neophyte's naïveté—which led him to discover and rediscover all that his female counterpart had to offer. His gift was a fascination with the female.

And yet, to gratify his own senses was his intention.

For him there was no moral dilemma, no vexing inelegance, no taint of religious sin in the act of gratification between a man and a woman. Man and woman were only natural creatures sharing in a mutual earthly paradise. Innocent and inventive as a child, Jacques rejoiced in this paradise.

But here he was. His ardor was pressing. Insistent.

He nevertheless spent the better part of the afternoon only in the tender worship Dominique so warranted.

When the light dwindled and the afternoon air lost its warmth, the pair lay side by side holding hands, enveloped in blissful reverie. The streets of Paris, the cares of life, the future—all seemed distant. When the twilight deepened in the small room but before a candle was needed to see, heartfelt words escaped Dominique's lips. "You don't yet know how to surrender your soul, Jacques *mia*, but you give me your body in the most pleasurable manner."

As was Dominique's wish, Jacques again went to his own bed. He stared at the ceiling, troubled. He was concerned with Dominique's welfare, yet there existed in him subtle reservations he couldn't explain. In past times, he'd been able to extricate himself from a woman by shuffling her to a "worthier gentleman," as he soothingly made clear. That maneuver had worked more than once. But now?

Before Jacques' breathing grew heavy, before sleep came, he thought hard upon the delicate lies and secrets Dominique had shared that evening.

*   *   *

The following morning Jacques was disturbed by a loud clatter in the courtyard. Looking out the window, he spotted the imposing coach and horses—trimmed with argent and crimson—from which stepped Michele Grimani, Cavaliere della stola d'oro. The man, sporting a smartly painted walking cane, approached, his expression sullen. The pommel of his sheathed sword glinted in the sun.

"Jean-foutre," cursed Jacques.

Jacques tore from his bed, threw on clothes, pushed his dagger into the back of his breeches, and moments later stood at the open doorway of Francesco's apartment.

Jacques spoke first. "If you've come to comfort Dominique, she—"

"I do not endeavor to greet Madame this morning, although—" Grimani sounded gruff.

"Were she here, I'd make certain you'd not see her."

"Bitter?" Grimani chided as he reached the door. "Well, let me furnish you additional bitter meat on which to chew. And I strongly suggest I provide it indoors," he pointed with his stick, "unless you wish the passersby and neighbors to know your present lot."

Jacques hesitated, then grudgingly moved aside.

Cane in fist, Grimani barged past Jacques and planted himself, legs wide apart, in the long entrance hall.

Jacques felt his chest swelling. *I shall beat the arrogance from this man.*

"As you know, perfect success for L'affaire de Voltaire was paramount," Grimani said, offering Jacques a sour frown. "But success faltered. My family's victory was denied. Your brother's reprehensible and all too public suicide devastated my grand plan."

"Not *your* plan. Dominique's grand plan." Jacques moved toward the man, but Grimani's menacing cane forced him to reconsider.

"Dominique's plan, then. In any case, important members of the nobility were seriously injured by your brother's stupidity that night. Fortunately the king's coach was one of the first to depart our home. Monsieur de Voltaire's was not. He, like a hundred other lords and ladies, bogged down in the storm-soaked quagmire. This—in addition to the ballroom panic—seems to have horribly humiliated Monsieur. He's left for Switzerland—without even your religious manuscript, it seems. France, you should be ashamed to know, will not clasp to her bosom her greatest son."

Grimani strode down the hallway toward the door, passing close to Jacques. Instantly, Jacques ripped the walking stick from the man's hand and shattered it across his knee.

Grimani backed away. "I'll add this petty feat of yours to my list of grievances," he barked as he clutched the hilt of his sword.

Jacques quickly reached for the dagger in the back of his breeches.

"Your poniard challenges my rapier?" hissed Grimani. "A sorry choice."

Grimani leisurely removed his hand from his sword's hilt, then began spitting words at Jacques. "Everlasting exile from one's home is hardly bearable, and I think you now recognize there'll be no letter to smooth your return to Venice. Further, I intend to reclaim the gold I paid you." Grimani's tone deepened, then swelled into a cry. "You've violated my home. You've sullied my family name. You've debased Venice. Debased me!"

Jacques matched his adversary's high passion. "I'll not bear your blunt load—"

"You've no more leverage, Casanova. No one cares what you do."

"I care what—"

"You're an adventurer," Grimani snarled. "Find an adventure. Quit Paris. Take the widow with you. Or I shall make certain your gambling debts make prison your next rat hole."

With that, Grimani streaked past Jacques, grinding slivers of walking stick under his shoes. Thrusting open the door to the hot morning sun, he twisted his head back around. "Oh, yes, the rumors are rife: King Louis is certain to issue a *lettre of cachet* should you mean to stay in Paris."

Grimani trotted out the door, slammed it closed, and was gone.

A rare sick ache tormented Jacques' gut. *Banishment! By the king.* He felt hot bile rising up his gorge. *Who has conspired against me? Grimani? Francesco? Dominique? Grim Nature herself?*

- 19 -

HIS STRENGTH RETURNED, Jacques lumbered up the stairs to his room, only to find that a half hour later he was again at the front door—this time facing a servant of Vicomte de Fragonard. *Is the Vicomte's favor still obtainable*, Jacques wondered? There was no mention of any such thing. Instead, the servant's request was that Jacques finish Francesco's business arrangements with the Vicomte. At this news, Jacques let go a sigh of disappointment.

It was nearly noon when Dominique reappeared from her early stroll. Jacques explained softly that, though he was legally entitled to his brother's estate, he wished to assign Francesco's belongings to her. These possessions, he suggested, might possibly be stored at the Vicomte's, a request, in fact, he'd made to the servant.

Jacques then asked that Dominique accompany him to the old gentleman's chateau.

She nodded, sadly affirming that, by contract, the following evening must be their last night in the apartment.

By dusk, Jacques and Dominique stood outside the entranceway of the Vicomte's home. There were no servants to be seen, so Jacques knocked on the door, waited, then carefully pushed it open. In the passageway beyond the antechamber stood Vicomte Honoré de Fragonard, scratching his sparse gray beard.

A whiff of bitter castoreum greeted Jacques, quickening his blood and forcing his own urgent and bleak situation to the forefront of his mind.

"Monsieur Casanova," the Vicomte said, "good to see you, good to see you. And this lady as well, although I did not expect her. I

dismissed the staff for this evening. I therefore welcome you myself."
The old man, using his shillelagh for support, offered as deep a bow
as he dared and ambled into the circular antechamber.

Dominique waited until he stopped several paces from her. She
returned his welcome with a curtsy and hurriedly glanced at Jacques
as if to say "You told me he might be old but ..."

Jacques shrugged. "Vicomte de Fragonard does not customarily
stand on ceremony, madame," he said, "although he seems to do so
tonight."

He shut the front door, turned toward the old gentleman, and
bowed. "Good evening, sir. May I introduce my sister-in-law, Madame
Dominique Casanova?"

"You may. Charmed to meet you, madame."

Jacques and Dominique advanced to the center of the antechamber.

"Follow me, please," said Fragonard.

Castoreum fouled the air more. With a shudder, Jacques recalled
the cabinet of curiosities.

"You look well, Vicomte," Jacques said, passing a handkerchief
to his nose.

"You need not equivocate, young man," chided the old gentleman
as he led Dominique and Jacques into a sparsely decorated sitting
room containing three chairs figured in a triangle. "I grow weaker
with each passing day, but as long as I'm in the vertical vein, most
Frenchmen consider me alive. But then Frenchmen are relatively
polite. They, for instance, step around a starving peasant. The Russians?
They slay the peasant, slice open his belly, and shove their feet inside
to warm their toes."

Jacques glanced at Dominique's blanching face.

"May I request," he growled, "you save these tales for another
evening?"

The old man whirled around and spoke firmly. "These are not
tales, I assure you both. I have witnessed such things, things most
human beings might find more than extraordinary."

Dominique gave a heartening nod to Jacques while the old
gentleman lowered himself into a fragile-looking chair facing them.

"Come, madame, if you please."

The Vicomte again spoke to Dominique, who now stood between him and Jacques. "I'm glad I lit this small room well, for I see that you are lovely, dear woman. Exquisite. Unblemished."

Dominique nodded. "I thank you, Vicomte de Fragonard. As I thank the Lord above for bestowing what qualities He deemed necessary to make me worthwhile in His sight."

The Vicomte's lips parted in a smile while Dominique moved to the remaining chair and sat.

Once all were seated, the old man bowed his head graciously, raised it, and setting his shillelagh across his knees, eyed Jacques. "Dismaying as it is to admit, the failure of the Voltaire ball has sealed your fate. To be plainspoken, your role is written out. Henceforth, you are persona non grata in Paris."

Although he was convinced of the Vicomte's steadfast truth, Jacques wanted to protest the declaration; instead, he sat stunned, wordless, his gut churning, wondering how the old man had even found out about the tragedy.

The Vicomte addressed Jacques and Dominique. "Naturally, I will retain all the nautilus and landscape paintings Francesco reproduced for me, and tomorrow my servants will deposit to my cellar all of his personal paintings that you brought. You have my word—all of his possessions will be safe until you're ready to reclaim them."

"Sir," Jacques said, twisting his fingers together, "a small kindness I ask of you? If for a while I'm to be without an address, may I have my mail forwarded to your home? There are many acquaintances far and wide with whom I correspond, and it would—"

"I will think on it and have an answer for you by the end of our meeting." Fragonard smiled. "I've something to say about your well-being, your eternal well-being, but let us converse a bit more."

The three talked of Francesco's death. No, Dominique had not fully sensed the desperate despondency that caused Francesco's suicide. Yes, she believed God would take Francesco to Him, in spite of what the Church said.

The Vicomte offered his opinions on the matter and ended with: "Yes, Time brings death to all individuals. *Ars longa, vita brevis,*" he intoned. "'Art is long, life is short.'"

What sort of consolation is that for Dominique? thought Jacques, who was growing impatient to resolve his brother's business.

The Vicomte, his eyes reflecting brightly the flames of a dozen candles, invited Dominique to stand, which she did. Pulling on his shillelagh and pushing hard against his chair, he rose and hobbled his way next to her. He bid Jacques join them. When the small circle was complete the old man stared deeply into Jacques' eyes, then Dominique's. Without saying a word, he tugged both at the waist and began to warble a melody, then to sing in an unrecognizable language.

The man could not hold a tune, but what bittersweet feelings he brought forth. Jacques saw Dominique's tearful eyes and feared he might be drawn into the sentiment.

When the Vicomte finished, he asked the woman to sit. Then he beckoned Jacques.

The perplexed adventurer glanced at Dominique's puzzled face before following the crippled man into an adjoining room with one narrow table set with several lit candles.

As Fragonard turned, the jittering flames illumined half his countenance.

"Jacques Casanova, as I appealed to your heart, I now appeal to your spirit. You once said that you try to obtain the greatest possible knowledge."

Jacques began to speak, but the Vicomte, standing at the edge of the table, slowly raised his shillelagh. "I belong to a fraternity of men who share that strict goal. I'll say that, in searching for truth and wisdom, we have been mocked, and what's more, threatened. With excommunication. At one time there was an interdiction on our lodge meetings. Now Louis Quinze neither helps nor hinders our order. In any event, the band of brothers who have surrounded me for the last forty years has provided a shelter where intellectual unrest, worldly ambitions, and moral confusion could be addressed. And satisfied." The old man shifted his stance. "I presume you will leave Paris as there is no tangible opportunity for you here now. 'Many thy boon companions at the feast but few the friends who cleave to thee in trouble'." The Vicomte put both hands on his shillelagh and leaned toward Jacques. "It is my greatest sorrow that I shall not now have the pleasure of introducing you to, or possibly inducting you into, my community, the underground stream. But knowing the genuine tragedy that has befallen you, who you are and who you might become, I offer you—as I did some time ago—a different turn in your life."

Putting a hand over his heart, the Vicomte stared into the candlelight, then looked back to Jacques. "Let me say simply that I've decided to gift you with something." The Vicomte searched for words. "Nothing on this earth can prove of better fortune. A treasure of inestimable value."

Jacques felt his pulse quicken. "Treasure? Riches?"

The Vicomte offered a stern face. "If that is what you believe you need." He inhaled deeply, loudly. "You have a path to choose, as I did at your age. That is all I say to you."

The old man set his shillelagh against the table, dug deeply into his waistcoat, and produced what appeared to be a rolled vellum the length of a man's hand. The two men exchanged an earnest look.

"Here is a future, my boy. I no longer have the cover for the scroll. But given your ingenuity, this scroll may suffice." The old man gripped Jacques' shoulder. "Are you familiar with the Knights Templar, the Knights Templaris?"

"Some, yes. What I've heard over the years. I know they were warrior-monks of the Roman Catholic Church. Monsieur de Voltaire spoke of them derisively, I recall."

Jacques' heart pounded furiously. "Weren't the Templars persecuted—?"

"Yes, Jacques. Persecuted in the early 1300s by Philippe the Fair. For their heresies, their orgies—King Philippe falsely claimed. The truth is that they were tortured for a long-kept secret they held." Fragonard's hand quivered. "The Templar order dissolved. But listen to me closely. Rely on their good name. Their *good* name. Remember. I entrust you with a secret of a lifetime. A hundred lifetimes." Vicomte Honoré de Fragonard held tightly the rolled document before placing it in Jacques' hands. His eyes welled with tears.

Jacques felt blood rush to the end of his fingertips and toes. He carefully cradled the scroll—which seemed not vellum but a fine linen or parchment—before placing it in his waistcoat pocket. "I'll remember the Templars' good name, sir. And I greatly, greatly thank you for your trust, for this opportunity."

The Vicomte gestured toward the door as he picked up his shillelagh and blew out the candles. Moments later, the two men were in the room where Dominique sat.

The Vicomte addressed them both. "You may have your letters delivered here as you asked, Jacques. My majordomo will save them all. And for you, madame, here is the sum I owed your husband. He was a superlative copyist, as you must know. And a fine artist in his own right." The Vicomte handed a small bag to Dominique.

As she accepted the money, her lips trembled, but she took the old gentleman's hand and lightly kissed it. His cheeks puffed out; he was embarrassed.

"Please go now. The coach I've provided is ready and waiting for you. If God is willing, we shall see one another again, Jacques Casanova."

Jacques led Dominique to the door, where Vicomte Honoré de Fragonard executed an elegant and beautiful bow. He then turned away from his guests and shuffled toward the candles, blowing out each in turn. "Let us not stand on ceremony. You may find your own way," he mumbled as he blew out the last candle, disappearing completely into the darkness. "*Dieu vous garde.* God keep you."

Jacques took hold of Dominique, and leading her through the house with which he was somewhat familiar, they made their way outside to the waiting team of four.

Jacques helped Dominique into the coach and sat beside her, wondering at her calmness.

It was not long after their departure, however, that he felt his ears grow hot from the words issuing from her mouth.

"As you are aware, I have of late been in a vaporous condition. With time, Jacques, this will pass. What shall not pass is my general situation. I've few means. And I've no protector."

He felt Dominique's arm and leg growing stiff.

"After prayer and reflection these last few days," she said, "I've decided my domicile shall be a convent."

Jacques squirmed. He was pleased and displeased. *A convent?* He studied the shadows that played across the coach window, feeling ill at ease. *Circumvent.*

He explained that in his homeland Venice, a woman did not enter the convent for religious devotion. Many women simply wanted to gain freedom from the ways of the world. They were able to entertain visiting friends, their physical needs could be met, and so forth. In brief, the convent might be the answer Dominique sought.

Jacques rubbed his pocket containing the scroll. "But hold off on your decision, Fragoletta. A bit." Her darkened shape for a quick moment was outlined brightly in the moonlight. "Is that reasonable?"

Home by midnight, Jacques hurried to his room, lit a pair of candles, and plopped on the bed. He reached for his snuffbox, took the last of some crab's-eye, and snuffed it, while from the pocket of his silk jacket he pulled out Fragonard's scroll. The thing was neither vellum nor parchment but a material with which he was not familiar. Unfurling a small portion of the scroll revealed a strange figure -^— ^- in its uppermost corner. Drawn on the opposite corner was the number *1300*, and in the middle a series of very small concentric circles. Jacques unrolled the document with great care. *Very fragile.* On the inside were four Latin sentences:

Ab Uno disce omnes. "From one, learn to know all."

Next, *Scire omnes, tres tantum requirit.* "To know all, you need but three."

Then *Est modus in rebus.* "There is measure in all things."

Finally, *Siste viator.* "Stop, traveler."

In the wide margin to the left were ten letters in a vertical column: "S-O-N-B-O-I-S-I-L-A." Jacques rubbed his chin. He'd seen "bois" before—"woods" in French, not Latin. But he'd never before heard that word included in the middle of a word, French or otherwise. No other characters or letters were visible. Jacques pawed his scalp. *This—this—is the greatest secret of Fragonard's life? This unfathomable nonsense? Was it Fragonard who composed this puzzle?*

Jacques pressed his fingers against his forehead. The Vicomte was an irascible character, yet he appeared sincere when he spoke of the value of his treasure and of his experiences. But is not sincerity a device of all charlatans? What had the old man to gain, however, by misleading Jacques? *I've been deceived before, but … no, I do discount the old man's scroll. And his promises.*

Jacques choked for air. The night was tepid with little breeze coming through the window. His head pounded. Conjecture overpowered him at every turn. He arose, perhaps too quickly, only to become lightheaded.

Curling up the scroll, he placed it in his jacket pocket. He blew out the candles, undressed quickly, and slid under the coverlet. *Time is short. Other decisions must be made.*

- 20 -

A KNOCK ON THE DOOR startled Jacques.

"The sun is up. Are you awake?" asked Dominique.

"Barely, but come in, Fragoletta." The door swung wide, bringing with it welcome fresh air and a pair of familiar faces.

"Petrine," exclaimed Jacques.

"At your service, sir."

"But you aren't—"

"Petrine returns to the fold," Dominique said. "He'll explain while I cross the street and speak with the landlord." She smiled and left the room.

Jacques rubbed his sleep-filled eyes, climbed out from under his covers, and sat upright on the bed opposite Petrine. For a time, both talked of small matters until the valet interrupted.

"Sir, Madame is correct. I've returned—for board only—if you'll have me back. I've decided to cast my lot with a man of your stature, there being few about who are as bold and brilliant as yourself. But, sir—you know me—I'll not be importunate in my request."

Jacques' brow briefly furrowed, dubious of his valet's return. "I thought a wage was your paramount interest. I reiterate: a manservant remains a luxury I cannot afford. For now."

Petrine laughed. "Understood." Then the valet pressed his finger across his lips, shut the door, and crossed back to Jacques. "Sir, it's miraculous. Have you *not* been visited by the debtor's prison authorities, sir?"

"No, Petrine, it's probable that I've been shielded by Cavaliere Grimani's great name. At least until the night of the ball. But I thank you for your concern. As you know, fear does not motivate my actions but—"

"Even prison, sir?"

Jacques squirmed uncomfortably.

Neither man said anything until Petrine spoke. "Sir, I hear footsteps in the hallway."

Dominique's voice sounded. "Jacques, Petrine—are you plotting something? Why is the door closed this hot summer morning?"

Petrine leapt to the door and swung it wide.

"Oh!" Dominique started. To Jacques she marched. "The landlady has softened a bit. We have until noon tomorrow to be gone from here."

"Yes, time is crucial," Jacques muttered. He looked at Petrine. "Did you know Dominique intends to join a convent? 'Forbear, lady, forbear,' I bade her."

Petrine turned slowly toward Dominique, rolling his brown eyes in their sockets.

She frowned.

"I smell a skirmish," Petrine said, wagging his finger. "But I don't take sides. Believe me, I know how to hold my tongue."

"Hmm," replied Jacques, arching an eyebrow. He did not look at Dominique but stammered in her general direction. "I've asked this lady to delay her decision. For … just … until tomorrow."

"Until tomorrow?" asked Dominique.

* * *

By twilight, Petrine had finished his assigned chores. He requested the evening off so that he might see one or two Parisian acquaintances, possibly for the last time. Dominique and Jacques took a coach to the Tuileries, then strolled the promenade until Jacques found a secluded café, where the two shared wine and melancholy conversation before returning to the apartment. Their lovemaking lasted late into the night, when gentle sleep overcame them.

At dawn, Jacques reentered his own room. Everything—upside down! *Robbed!*

He snatched the jacket he'd thrown on the bed the night before and frantically searched its pockets. Fragonard's scroll was safe. He quickly draped the coat over his shoulders.

Dominique appeared at the door, plucking at her sack dress. "Heavens, what's happened?"

Jacques confirmed the break-in, when Petrine suddenly appeared, ogling the disaster. The three stood quiet until the valet broke the stillness, asking if he should put the mess back in order. "To this wary Spaniard, sir, this is a clear sign," he said. "We should rid ourselves of this town."

Dominique grimaced.

Visibly shaken, Jacques stayed Petrine's actions and began to sift through the shambles himself. He immediately discovered that his keepsake, his gold snuffbox, was gone. Yet his pistols and case of smallswords were still in the room, as were the paste jewels. He scoured the floor under the bed.

"My purse! French louis from Michele Grimani! Missing!"

"*What* purse?" Petrine cried. "What—?" He looked queerly at Jacques, then closed tight his eyes for several seconds. "Are you sure?"

The valet's face showed a strange fleeting expression, something that did not escape Jacques' quick notice.

"Gold has been stolen? And your snuffbox?" repeated Petrine.

"Yes," Jacques said solemnly, noting Dominique's great distress.

Again he looked under the bed, then stood up, and stared out the window at churning gray clouds. From the courtyard, below he heard horses snort and whinny. *I must not bring myself to confess to Dominique that no thief stole the purse, that it disappeared the very night of the ball, probably while I swayed in the arms of D'Ampie.* Several times he ran his fingers through his hair. *Shall I tell Dominique of the scroll?*

At last he turned to Dominique and Petrine.

"I'll pore through my belongings shortly. I suggest we leave this jumble of a room and go to the loft. To think. To talk."

Standing under the loft's overhead window moments later, Jacques stared at the large empty room, then with Petrine at his side, spoke softly and intensely to Dominique.

"Because Paris has relieved me of my name as well as most of my worldly assets, I intend to head to Rome. Lateran Rome has more scoundrels per square meter than any place in Europe. The princes of the Church relish the game of faro, and if I bank, we shall win. Despite the fact that great God is on their side."

Dominique did not seem pleased.

Sucking in a deep breath, Jacques turned to his valet. "Let me further say, Petrine, that this woman must not go to a convent. She must accompany me and become a *très* elegant adventuress."

"Odd," Dominique said. "I've decided that you, Jacques Girolamo Casanova, should accompany me to the convent and become a nun."

The two men howled.

When the frivolity cooled, Jacques again spoke. "Now, Madame Tigress, knowing both choices—the convent or Rome—which do you prefer?"

A forbidding luster in her eye, Dominique paced a wide circle while she talked, her arms tucked across her chest. She explained that she had never traveled more than one hour beyond Paris. She knew that a long journey would mean different languages, diverse religions, strange habits.

She affirmed that she knew several languages, but that was little help when dialects were spoken. She didn't know the roads or the customs, or even the measurements. And the different systems of money might make her head fog.

"I'm ignorant in the ways of the world!" she blurted out.

Listening to her fears, Jacques chafed. Tiny specks of dust hovered stock-still in the air until he, after a wait, dug into his jacket pocket. "Come here, please. I've decided to share my prospects, Fragoletta. To do so at this instant," he said, astonishing himself.

Petrine and Dominique both stepped closer.

For several minutes, Jacques made a showing of the Vicomte's scroll—translating the esoteric verses and pointing out the intriguing symbols, all the while adding as much invigorating emotion as he could muster. "Inestimable treasure" was uttered several times during his talk.

"I sincerely believe my room was not ransacked for gold," he said, "nor for my snuffbox. The thief's target was this scroll. For this treasure riddle from Vicomte de Fragonard—which sat right in my coat pocket!"

Noting Petrine's wide eyes, Jacques was confronted with Dominique's knitted brow.

"I know," he said. "The riddle is mystifying. But, Fragoletta, taking a cue from the Vicomte, we must begin our search with the Knights Templar, an extinct military arm of the Roman Catholic Church. And because the center of the Church lies in Rome, it's there that we'll uncover information about the Templars and proceed."

"My master's brilliance will prevail. I'd wager it," Petrine said, turning to Dominique. His full, round face burned with fervor.

The loft seemed to shrink in size as Jacques' eyes blazed with newfound eagerness. He spoke in one long breath. "I'll study this with utmost attentiveness, and we shall triumph. The old gentleman has set us upon a quest for riches. His scroll will guide us. I say to you both, this is our main chance. We, a brave band of adventurers. In pursuit of an inestimable treasure. With thoughts like these, my heart is afire. If you, too, Dominique, have a truly venturesome spirit, then the quest, the riches to be gained, or both shall propel your spirit aloft with my own."

When Jacques' hands dropped to his side, Dominique reached and held them. Her eyes moistened. "It's a true and rare gift to rouse men and women. I do possess a venturesome soul, Jacques mia. And my soul is willing to sail aloft."

"Good news! Great news! A nun no more," Jacques laughed and laughed. Kissing her hand, he then turned to Petrine. "It's decided. We're given over to the enterprising spirit."

"A treasure hunt!" cried the valet.

The three broke into a spontaneous dance until the hot sun shining through the window forced its conclusion. All sat down.

Jacques watched Dominique. He knew that without coaxing she would offer Francesco's commission money for the venture.

Curious that it vexed him so to use the woman. *She gives—and expects little in return. So different. And what do I do? Use my dead brother's wife, this unfortunate woman, for gain.*

- 21 -

ALL POSSESSIONS WERE PACKED THE NEXT MORNING as swiftly as the flick of a mare's tail, and at the behest of his master, Petrine trundled trunks and the mahogany sword case to their destination, a coach station in the Faubourg Saint Germain.

By four o'clock, Jacques marched back and forth beneath the station sign *Loueur de carrosses*. A pair of men walking past tipped their hats to Dominique but moved quickly on when Jacques' surly expression hurried them away. Thrusting his hand at Petrine, he emphatically counted five fingers. "Five days to Lyons. From there to Turino, to Florence, thence to Rome. I say again, a diligence is our one and only choice."

"Permit me to say, sir, that on that coach I'll have to ride topside, and the roof makes me afraid, deathly afraid."

"Tie yourself to the roof."

"I shrivel at the thought."

"Then ride in the great basket in the rear of the diligence with the chickens and rich peasants."

"The rumble is too hot in the dead of summer, master."

"Then ride like the *poor* peasants, rent your own ox and cart, and be damned, you ronyon."

The Spaniard's nostrils flared. "Maybe for the trip I could hire on as a postilion," he fumed.

"Yes, that suits you, Petrine. Postilions frequently ride drunk, are mostly untrained, and are universally thought to be dishonest."

Now Dominique interceded and, with comforting words and a bit of logic, ended the squabble.

Less than an hour later, the diligence set out to Lyons. Petrine rode on top while Jacques and Dominique sat inside opposite three male passengers.

After brief introductions, one of the travelers voiced an opinion.

"I, for one, am grateful we travel in our diligence and not that clanking *carabas* we just passed."

"As am I," said another, straightening his jacket. "The carabas is nothing but a cage atop a wagon."

"Exactly," said the first traveler. "But if you ask me, it's criminal that twenty or more peasants should be allowed to crowd into that cage—"

"When it could carry a hundred," said a third man.

Jacques and another passenger laughed, ignoring Dominique's scowl of contempt.

"Dear acquaintances," persisted the swarthy fellow, "the clanking carabas runs twice a day between Paris and Versailles. And twice a day in my youth, the steep iron ladder up to the carabas provided me rousing entertainment."

Jacques leaned forward.

"That ladder," snorted the fellow while he lightly elbowed the passengers at his side, "forced the ladies, young and old, to show their thighs and much, much more."

All the men in the coach brayed in unison.

Dominique glared.

The trip progressed, and the swarthy passenger nattered on, striving to prove he knew everything worth knowing.

Jacques was growing irritable, knowing he couldn't abide the lout the four hours to Fontainebleau, let alone all the way to Rome. He found an opening and initiated his own conversation.

"I'm excited, Dominique, for the joys ahead. In Rome we'll have our own carriage," he said, glancing sideways at the lout, "and we'll surely parade, dear Fragoletta, on the *corso*."

Dominique's green eyes grew bright.

"Or perhaps on the Marina di Chiaia in Naples," smiled the lout. "Has a gentleman ever taken you there?" he leered at Dominique. "Sundays, Wednesdays, and Fridays are the days to be seen." The man brushed off his red-heeled shoes with a flick of his hand and went on talking.

The coach was perhaps halfway to Fontainebleau when Jacques, after a brief but pithy conversation with Dominique, received a stern upbraiding from the lout.

"Actually, what you say makes very little sense, so if—"

Jacques barked. "If I were to make sense, I would most probably be the sole man in Europe who does."

Dominique laughed.

"Moreover, to make sense in this lifetime is not my purpose. There are some things so divine, so mysterious—such as love, such as life itself—that it doesn't profit a man to try to make sense of them. My advice, monsieur, is to suspect everything that is presented as rational and sensible."

The passengers straightened up in their seats. Feeling that he had won the battle, Jacques set out to win the war.

"Atop this diligence, my man Petrine is finding the motions of the coach akin to a tossing sea, something his stomach cannot abide. With each pitch and toss, his wrists turn white from the ropes that bind him to his roof seat. The rope around his ribs, of course, does no good for his guts either. But most men have need of just such an experience to temper their will and wit and thus discover their feeling for the world and their true place in it."

"Not long ago," the lout interrupted, "I had the exceptional idea of installing a stabilizing hold bar atop a diligence. No one has yet shown interest in my practical invention. Probably ten years ahead of its time. But if in the future a diligence doesn't possess a hold bar for passengers," he addressed Jacques, "you—as well your valet— might be lashed to the coach top—so as to find your true place in the world." The lout dashed off a smile.

Jacques' ears exploded with a screeching din until he felt Dominique's hand squeeze his. He bit his lip hard, trying to quell his desire to challenge the insulting fool to a duel or, at the least, to throw him out the window, when at that very moment, the diligence lurched to a halt. Fontainebleau.

While a dozen or so women vendors surrounded the coach hawking scissors and knives, Jacques determined to favor Dominique and himself.

He kept a casual distance from the lout as he entered the coach house, but when the man stepped into the large privy, Jacques quickly and quietly entered behind him, making sure no one else was inside. When the lout began to relieve his bladder Jacques slipped his dagger from its sheath, grasped the blade tightly, and with the pommel struck the man on the back of the head. The man lurched forward, hit the wall, then quickly plopped to the floor, spewing a stream of urine high in the air.

Jacques sheathed his weapon and congratulated himself. "For this I should be thanked—nay, rewarded." He stepped over the lout, on his back in a puddle of piss, and looked about. Then in a swift motion, he hunkered down and began rifling the man's pockets, until finding what he sought, he wrapped his fingers around the purse and removed it.

Before prancing out the privy door, Jacques emptied the purse's few coins into his pocket, save one which he proffered to the driver, whom he found by the coach.

"Monsieur's efforts," Jacques reported, "have been abundantly rewarded. He'll be staying on in Fontainebleau and instructed me to offer you this." Jacques pressed the coin into the man's hands.

Not one of the coach passengers peeped a word when the gallow-faced lout failed to appear and the driver cried, "Whip up, postilion."

- 22 -

"IN FRANKNESS, DEAR FRIEND, you look older."

"You must remember it's not what a man looks like, dear Casanova. It's how he feels," said Cardinal de Bernis. "And I feel like a centaur." From the edge of his chair, the churchman leaned across the expansive oak desk toward Jacques. "Why, when last we saw each other … in Paris … I—"

"You'd acquired the sheath from St. Peter's knife, one of the nails from the true cross, as well as Prester John's big toe—rock hard, of course, since it was centuries old." Jacques winked. "Those relics, as I recall, were to bring a pretty penny to a lowly bishop's purse."

"Unfortunately they fattened the Pope's coffers," smirked the churchman. "But as recompense, the Most Holy Father—who continually bemoans the dissoluteness of the age—offered me a position here in Rome as a cardinal. Prester John's big toe smoothed my advancement."

Jacques laughed. "And now I sit across from the majestic *Cardinal de Bernis* and tremble in awe."

"As well you should, my young friend."

"Consider, then, that I have nothing in this world but the good grace of the goddess Fortune. And an adventuress with whom I travel—and who shall not hinder our private debauches."

"But the goddess Fortune. She has abandoned you—is that what I sense?"

Jacques nodded reluctantly. "Yes, Your Eminence."

Cardinal de Bernis, his bulk enswathed in scarlet, leaned back in his chair. "In Paris I said I'd write you letters of introduction if ever you came to Rome." He adjusted the scarlet biretta over his white wig, then in a grand gesture tore them both off and threw them on the desk. He scratched his scalp fiercely. "I hadn't known you'd want to visit the Pope himself."

"Benedict, you probably know, was my master and I his student in my seminary days." With his fingers, Jacques brushed his cheek. "And although I do have a special request for His Holiness, I'll not beg the man for money," he joked.

"Anon, anon," answered the fat clergyman. "You know, of course, that *any* Christian is at liberty to appear before the Pope once the Pontiff opens his door?" Staring at Jacques, the cardinal tapped on his desk. "Something in this smells of urgency," he said. "My advice to thee? Do not be in a hurry in this agitated city. Rome is a silly woman, with indolence being one of her primary vices. Even the Vatican cannot escape her slothfulness."

"A dwindling purse hastens my actions."

"Your misfortune has a great deal to do with the merciless French society about which I warned you, doesn't it?"

"Do I dare mention Marquise D'Ampie—on her back—in a garden?"

The cardinal returned a throaty laugh. "When you wrote from Paris, you might have included the scandalous details," the cardinal said. "The sweltering man in scarlet who sits before you wants details. Tawdry details. None of which, I assure you, shall I repeat to the Pope—when I request an audience for you."

Jacques smiled. "I thank you, Your Complacency."

Both men joined in jolly laughter that rang through the hallways of the holy Vatican. Jacques stood, then bowed deeply. "And may I congratulate you, Your Eminence, on your promotion to cardinal?"

"It goes without saying that I deserve the admiration, if not the position." The clergyman threw back his head in a cackle, coughed a raw cough, and slapped his wig and biretta back on his pate.

* * *

At the inn early the following morning, Jacques smiled when he opened the note Cardinal de Bernis had sent: "You will meet Pope Benedict at Palazzo di Monte Cavallo, the summer residence of the

Pontiff. Cardinal Allesandro Albani, Imperial Ambassador in Rome, is assigned to conduct you to Benedict."

Jacques readied himself, gave minor instructions to Petrine, and sat briefly with Dominique. He told her of his friendship with Benedict from long ago and spoke in vague terms of an earnest request he would make to the Pontiff. Dominique was disappointed to stay at the inn but reminded herself that she knew little Italian, something that might hamper the mission. Jacques bid her adieu with a long kiss, which he hoped hid the slim mistrust he'd had of the woman since the debacle at Grimani's *fête*.

As soon as he left the lodgings, he began to chart his stratagem—how to launch his subtle diversion, where to direct his fusillade—in a word, how to trick His Holiness, the Pope.

Jacques knew that the smokescreen he planned—his request to the Pope to reenter Venice—could easily be read as impudence, and at the smallest nod from the Venetian State Inquisitori, the Pontiff might, with a papal ordinance, demand he leave Rome.

This request to the cleric, however, was a risk worth taking—for Jacques' true objective was access to the *Index librorum prohibitorum,* the Church's 'Index of Forbidden Books.' As certain books were condemned by the Church, so, too, were the Knights Templar condemned. In searching the Index, Jacques hoped to gain esoteric, noteworthy knowledge of the Templars.

He had a starting point for his search but, he worried, perhaps the ending point as well.

*   *   *

Jacques, bedecked in his best attire, sat in Imperial Ambassador Albani's meticulously arranged office. The portly cardinal spoke with great solemnity.

"I am instructed to introduce you to the Pontifex Maximus, he who bridges the void between this world and—"

"The kingdom that is not of this world," Jacques repeated in unison with the cardinal, thankful at last for his school days in seminary.

Albani looked up. "Follow me," he said, pushing by Jacques. "You may kiss the Holy Father's foot this morning at nine o'clock."

Now Jacques stood before the Pontiff almost fifteen years after they'd first made their special acquaintance. Cares had worn the man, but certainly he was recognizable, his features agreeable and regular. With a bow, Jacques acknowledged the head of the faithful who sat atop the papal throne; then he kissed the cross embroidered on his holy slipper.

The two exchanged warm and earnest greetings. It boded well that the Pope had invited no one else to view the audience.

"We keep in mind," said Benedict XIV, "that as a student you attended mass every day, often went to sermons, and were exemplary in the recitation of the *Oratio quadraginta horarum*." He extended his right hand to rest lightly on Jacques, whose stomach now tingled with excitement. "We also recall, signor, that you often *forsook* our services in Padua when we intoned the rosary."

"Holy Father, I've worse transgressions," Jacques mustered as sincerely as possible. "Although I've never taken the Lord's name in vain, I've sinned exceedingly. I've not used the talents God gave me to exult His name. It's no secret."

"No secret."

"I prostrate myself at your feet to receive absolution."

The Pontiff removed his hand from Jacques' shoulder and paused for a great while before giving his benediction. At last he asked what he could do for Jacques.

The adventurer stood straight and tall. "I ask for your intercession so that I may freely return to Venice."

His Holiness interlaced his fingers in his lap. His features grew harder.

"It's true, Your Holiness, I escaped from the Inquisitori's dreadful prison in Venice, which makes me well aware of the risk I take in coming to Rome. I'm alert to the prospect of expulsion, and I would hope that you too might find that possibility distasteful." Following this, Jacques did not look at the Pope, but resumed his speech, his eyes remaining downcast. "God has the power to change those creatures that require it. I'm in deep need of His salvation, His love, His joy, His authority."

"We recall, Giacomo Casanova, you possessed at all times the cloak of sincerity, whether it was genuine or no."

Jacques felt his neck tighten.

The Pope continued. "If you were to return to your motherland, you would be required to present yourself before the secretary of the tribunal of Venice."

Jacques was prepared. "I'm willing to hazard that if Your Holiness might supply me with a letter of recommendation in your own hand. With such a letter, I would not risk being imprisoned in I Piombi again."

Pope Benedict leaned back in his throne and steepled his fingers over his lips.

He doesn't figure my strategy. Good. "Most Holy Father," Jacques exclaimed, "profound remorse eats, devours my heart—for not living my life as a servant of the true Church," he lied. "As a penance, I beg your permission to defend the Holy Roman Church with my intellect. Consider—for an infamous libertine to attack and defeat those hostile to religion and the virtues it prescribes—wouldn't this be powerful propaganda to aid the Church? To explain: I've settled in Paris—"

"A wicked city."

"A malevolent city, Your Holiness. One that is infecting the remainder of Catholic France. I've witnessed Monsieur de Voltaire and the philosophes assault the Holy Church in every conceivable manner, while throughout Europe other heretics also poison the minds of Catholics." Jacques went to one knee. "I request access to the Index librorum prohibitorum."

"Access to the forbidden books?"

"Yes, Most Holy Father. That I might study the vile arguments of the heretic to refute their godless logic. To defend and uphold your Holy Church."

"The Vatican has theologians who act in this capacity."

"But none such as I."

His Holiness, the Pope, stared at the cherubim and seraphim on the ceiling, stroking his garments.

Jacques' stomach grew hard as an oak bough. Moments passed. And now—although his bended knee was beginning to pain him— he forged a sparkle in his eye, cleared his throat, and whispered softly but firmly. "Even in these days, Eminence, you've the physique of a poet. And I've not forgotten your sweet—and most holy—touch."

Benedict's cheeks reddened. But at Jacques he gazed, tendering an ever-so-slight and lecherous smile. Jacques returned the kindness.

In good time, His Holiness answered with a benediction, then spoke plainly. "No, you may not return to Venice with our blessing and recommendation. Not until I see and read six pamphlets and two books from your pen. All defending the Church. For this ambitious task, you may have access to the Index."

Jacques could barely hide his elation. "Your Eminence, in his wisdom, pleases me so. Before long I'll return, pamphlets in hand."

Jacques rose and made his exit.

Winding his way back to his lodgings, he turned the corner of a narrow Roman street and, feeling a newfound spring in his step, broke into a loud laugh. His strategy had succeeded! For the time being, he was free to concentrate on the day ahead.

* * *

Jacques knew that Dominique would be as exuberant as a foal in a field to see the sights of the Eternal City. The Coliseum, the Piazza di Spagna, the Trevi Fountain. A leisurely tour began when he fetched her at the inn.

The lovers strolled away the early afternoon, marveling at a few local sights around the inn until, toward the end of the day, Jacques hired a cab, blindfolded Dominique, and read poetry to her as the hackney proceeded to the far north of the city. When the driver stilled his horses on the Via Cassia, Jacques carefully guided Dominique out of the cab. He stood the woman facing in the direction he wished. "You may now take off your blindfold and open your eyes."

It took a moment for Dominique's eyes to stop fluttering, then at the first view of the still far-distant St. Peter's Basilica, she gasped. Her eyes fully roved the landscape. A minute more passed before words came.

"Unforgettable." She turned to Jacques. "This is the heart of my religion. The Roman Catholic Church. Surely if the spirit of Christ lives on this earth in the hearts of men, he does so in this magnificent and dignified temple."

A vivid image of Vicomte de Fragonard rushed through Jacques' mind. "Here on this earth, I have met God," the Vicomte had said. Jacques shuddered and squeezed Dominique's hand.

On the hackney ride back to their lodgings, Dominique expressed her jubilation.

Not so Jacques.

From his carriage window, he'd caught sight of a passing coach. The colors of the coach's trappings were argent and crimson. But what was the coat of arms on the door? Jacques could not be confident of what he'd barely seen. *If it happens that the Venetian dog named Michele Grimani wants his gold louis returned, let him sniff someone else. I'll not abide him in Rome.*

- 23 -

AT DAYBREAK, JACQUES and the frail Cardinal Passonei ambled toward the humorless exterior of the Vatican Library, the sun blunted behind the stone building.

"Yesterday after your audience, His Holiness spoke exceedingly well of you, Signor Casanova," said the old cardinal, peering over the top of his spectacles.

The man's shallow breaths and an unusually high-pitched tone convinced Jacques the clergyman lied; he'd probably not even *seen* the Pope, let alone spoken to him. Assigned a lonely, humble duty, the clergyman simply yearned to feel important.

"Are you previously acquainted with the Pontiff?" Cardinal Passonei asked while ushering Jacques inside the building.

Jacques smiled and nodded, resolving to prevail in silence. He would let his silence inspire gossip. And gossip would enhance his reputation and give him standing with those in the Vatican. He might need allies in this new realm.

The clergyman and the adventurer continued their walk through a long corridor, passing several rooms filled with studious men, quills in hand, laboring at their workbenches.

Cardinal Passonei spoke. "These scribes copy old and important documents, many of which are decaying. So sad." After a dozen steps more, he stopped, held up a thick black key, and inserted it into the lock of the door. "Shall we enter the Index forthwith?" Moments later, Jacques stepped into the most secret of places and was pleasantly surprised that the sun shown through enormous Palladian windows and that the interior granite walls kept the temperature reasonable.

"Welcome to the Index librorum prohibitorum," the Cardinal said. "On that table is the guide to the codices in this archive. But the manuscripts have been shifted from shelf to shelf over the centuries, so at times the guide may be of little help. As you see, most of the leather-bound books are laid horizontally, according to the ancient custom. Return them to their stack that way, please." Cardinal Passonei wagged his finger. "Remember, please, you're not permitted in any other room in this building. And I shall be outside the door to accompany you when you find it necessary to come or go for any reason. Have you any questions?"

"I have a single question," replied Jacques, "and it appears you are most qualified to answer it, Cardinal Passonei."

The old churchman broke into a sudden broad smile that further wrinkled his pale, worn countenance. Jacques took a step closer.

"For reasons I had best divulge to you later, I seek knowledge of the treacherous Knights Templar. I've been assured," Jacques lied, "that you, of all churchmen, know this Index intimately. Before I review the guide, would you show me the particular books in this room that contain the Templar writings?"

Cardinal Passonei looked wide eyed.

"I hope to be able to report your good works to the Pontiff," Jacques added.

The frail man seized his thick key with both hands, then pointed with it. "Why, that entire wall of books over there," said Passonei, "is heretical in one way or another. On that wall you will unquestionably find what you search for."

Jacques glanced across the room. His toes seemed to curl in his shoes. He shook his head. "All those? All those books and ... " He turned back to the Cardinal. "Thank you," he choked. "Of course, there will be some whose language is incomprehensible to me, and there may be others ..." He watched the cardinal's head slowly wilt. "But you've greatly reduced my burden. The Pontiff shall hear of your excellent assistance, mark my words," Jacques lied again.

Passonei's eyes lit with joy.

"And now, I begin immediately."

"I shall be in the hallway," said the cardinal, stepping out the door.

Jacques stood as immobile as the books on the shelves. His ruse with the Pope had worked; he had admission to the Index. But now a formidable challenge: to find a book title that matched a line from Fragonard's scroll. Jacques clapped his hands together in anticipation and began. The path to riches was before him.

After several hours, he had scrutinized hundreds of proscribed books by title. He wished to read many of these, not just to inspect their titles. Paracelsus, Ramón Lull, and the Persian Jābir ibn Hayyān. Philosophers and mystics, misunderstood by Christians. Misunderstood — and therefore the Church of Rome declared their works heretical and forbidden. *And Lull, himself a lay member of the order of St. Francis. What irony.*

Jacques examined a copy of the *Picatrix* for conjuring up the devil, as well as the infamous book on magic, *Clavicula Salomonis*. He perused a treatise by Artephius on the philosopher's stone. Setting it aside, he picked up another text. It was one he had owned: Aretino's *Sonetti Lussuriosi*. He sat down at a long table, opened the book, and began. Soon he was laughing aloud. If only he'd an hour to study this profound work with its thirty-two erotic positions.

At noon, Cardinal Passonei entered the room unannounced. He carried with him a lunch for the important guest of the Vatican.

Jacques knew that the more authority he presented, the more rumors would buzz about in theological circles. He decided to test his power.

"Tomorrow for lunch, I'll require a five-egg omelet."

The cardinal was momentarily dumbfounded. "I, sir, am neither a cook nor a servant," he muttered, wandering back to his hall chair. "But you shall have it."

By late afternoon, Jacques could do no more. He rubbed his eyes and pushed his chair from the table. But how fortunate he felt to browse books human hands had not touched, some for hundreds of years. A number of these most likely were the single existing copy of an original text, maybe something as pagan as Homer—the originals destroyed by ransacking barbarians or the burning of the Alexandrine Library by the Roman legions, or by floods, by book burnings, by book lice even. To actually hold these manuscripts—many containing the most precious knowledge of mankind—in his two hands: astonishing. How precarious was Truth that it could be bundled up and forgotten, shut away in a forbidden library, or utterly destroyed by marauding man?

Jacques did not tarry. His immediate antagonist was time. How much time would be required to scour hundreds, thousands of manuscripts? How long would it take before a title, a trace, a line, leapt out at him?

Jacques dug in his jacket pocket and pulled from it Fragonard's riddle. "From one, learn to know all. / To know all, you need but three. / There is measure in all things. / Stop, Traveler." And there were the vertical letters "S-O-N-B-O-I-S-I-L-A." The letters, the verses—all of it remained opaque.

He replaced the scroll in his coat and considered what the evening had in store. Cardinal de Bernis had asked him to a private dinner party but, contrary to Jacques' request, had not invited Dominique. Of course, to Jacques the gist of de Bernis' action was clear: debauchery.

He would have to invent a lie for Dominique to swallow.

He stood, stretching and yawning, before making his way to the archive door. He soon followed Cardinal Passonei down the hallway.

Wandering past an open door, Jacques noticed the scribes affixing stamps to *volumina* and marking notations with their quills. In the corner of the cluttered room, he also saw a water clock. He'd not seen a clepsydra since his youth. He'd arrange to take a closer look. Tomorrow.

At nine o'clock that evening, Jacques sat at table. Before him spread a culinary splendor that had been catered by Cardinal de Bernis—great epicure or great glutton, Jacques could not decide which. The cardinal's vintner had supplied an excellent champagne with which Jacques refilled four glasses. He set the bottle under the table next to another empty.

"For my second toast of this young evening," Jacques announced while raising his glass, "Cardinal, the loan—or shall I say the gift—you furnished has brought a sheen to my eye. And an itching to my palm." Jacques held up the small bag of gold coins that de Bernis had earlier bestowed and flopped the purse on the table. "Be so good as to gift me any time it pleases you, Your Flatulence."

The two actresses who sat at either end of the table joined in De Bernis' laughter. The response rattled the table china and silverware of the intimate room, setting the two girls to more snickering and allowing Jacques to cast a further critical eye on the two votaries of Thalia that the Cardinal de Bernis had procured.

Charlotte—"La Catai" on the stage—*luminous*, thought Jacques. There was a reserve about her, somewhat incongruous with the abundant bosom she displayed.

The other actress—whose age could not exceed twenty—was likely the ingénue of the theatre company. Ample, attractive, with alabaster skin and blonde hair that made her nearly translucent in the candlelight. *Giselle must be perfection on the stage.* Downing a morsel of food, Jacques sat back in his chair, once again satisfied with the cardinal's choice—on both counts.

Jacques guessed what was forthcoming: with two young women, a competitive rivalry often ensued, and little by little one would attempt to outdo the other. He knew that at these times his principal chore was to hearten the competition, then allow feline nature to ...

Two hours and six champagne bottles later, Jacques and the girls lazed in the center of a bed in a room of discriminating decor. The room belonged to Cardinal de Bernis, and though he was nowhere to be seen, yet he was seeing. That is, he'd taken a position in the adjacent room where, through a special notch in the wall, he could partake of the amatory exploits of Jacques and the actress pair.

Jacques, himself unclothed, reclined between the two nude girls. He cradled one in each arm so that they were face-to-face, lying on his chest. Giselle wreathed her hands, stretched her arms ever so slightly toward Charlotte, and brought the young face to her mouth before licking the full lips of the girl. Charlotte trembled, but Giselle's hands held soundly.

Jacques drank in the soft bodies that seemed to float upon him. His mind drifted, while the lazy strum of a guitar mingled with a resonant flute in a nearby street.

As time slowed and bodies wove into surprising patterns of delight, Jacques found the two girls kneeling over his torso, each holding one another in a gentle hug. The girls kissed sweetly, lovingly, as they fused together.

For some moments, Jacques took in this amorous picture, but he was not one to admire art without conversing with the artist. He slowly, carefully extricated his body, rose to his knees, and repositioned himself next to the embracing girls—the three blending together like swaying willows—in the center of the bed.

Placing a hand around each girl's buttocks, he began stroking, squeezing, caressing. Sliding his hand below Charlotte's buttocks and between her spreading legs, Jacques reached his other hand likewise, between Giselle's thighs, his fingers investigating the glossy hair of each, while he gently maneuvered toward their warmth. In Giselle, Jacques found what he desired. Then, in Charlotte.

He guessed the cardinal was also finding what he craved, that he might be particularly in the mood for the rich sensuality of the ménage à trois. In times past, Jacques had excited the clergyman with athletic feats and wildly imaginative sexual displays. But tonight, Jacques and his lovers excelled in slow and desirous lovemaking.

For this, the Cardinal would be indebted.

Jacques felt tender convulsions from the girls who, still embracing, kissed longingly. Giselle opened her eyes momentarily, turned toward him holding his gaze, until soon her eyelids fluttered closed once again. Charlotte's lips, now gliding to her neck, sucked covetously.

Jacques watched and resumed his massage of the girls' wetness— the gift of their subtle scent amplifying his desire. So firmly were the pair pressed together that Jacques' fingers stroked each at the same time, advancing his delicate work.

This pleasing task continued, a rhythm establishing itself: from time to time Charlotte sobbed, throwing back her head, allowing her deepest passion to fly up. Giselle then covered Charlotte's face with lingering kisses.

Whenever Charlotte leaned briefly away, Jacques offered his mouth to Giselle and was rewarded with a warm, pliant tongue flitting across the arch of his lips. His body further flooded with need. He worked his fingers steadily, faster in the wetness—both girls now loosed in abandon.

Giselle and Charlotte gasped, then hastened their bodies to full excitement. Growling ardently, they released one another—Charlotte giving way to her back, pulling Giselle slowly on top of her, facing her, kissing her.

His manhood hardened with strength, Jacques saw no reason to part the two. He fit his slick hands around his jewel, lubricating his hardness, and from behind inserted himself into the lushness of Giselle's sex. The girl moaned when Jacques began his gentle push.

In a blink it was over—as Jacques, animated well beyond capacity, delivered his heated thrust.

Presently, the girls began to sigh. The moment slowly passed, and lying side by side, both closed their eyes and fell into sleep. Jacques savored well the gratifying sight before chuckling to himself. *Although the cardinal may have expected his amatory enthusiast to provide entertainment of a far-longer duration, he will undoubtedly find his own path to bliss.*

- 24 -

"**THIS WOMAN** is a vital part of my studies," Jacques stressed. "You may be sure of it. Now, shall I bring this matter before the Pope?" The marble hallway echoed Jacques' stern voice. This early morning, he was not sparing in his forceful words to Cardinal Passonei. Even Dominique, who stood at Jacques' side, appeared disgruntled.

One or two scribes shoved into a hallway door to see the disturbance.

Passonei's head swiveled like a sparrow surrounded by feral cats. "There's no need to trouble His Holiness. If she—this woman— facilitates your work, as you insist, she's permitted to join you in the archives. But only in this room," sputtered the cardinal.

After the cardinal removed his spectacles and shuffled into the hallway, Jacques smiled: at his side in the Index was his helper for the stout undertaking ahead.

The morning passed quickly.

Because Dominique could not read, she aided Jacques by removing manuscripts from shelves, returning them, even dusting them, all the while ignorant that the archive contained writings prohibited by her Church.

Jacques had told her only that he'd received admittance to one of the Vatican's theological libraries.

No reason to trouble her conscience, he reasoned.

With her naïve hands, Dominique brought him book after book: Agrippa's works on magic and alchemy, including his *De occulta philosphia*; Nicholas Copernicus' *De revolutionibus orbium coelestium libri VI*, which proved the heliocentric system; a scripture entitled *Sinaiticus*; licentious stories by Crébillon the Younger; Blaise Pascal's elegant *Pensées*.

Jacques did not read Hebrew or Aramaic, so the *Midrasch-Na-Zohar* was passed over. He riffled through works on Freemasonry, magic, witchcraft, and necromancy—works he'd heard of while a young man in Venice. As the morning progressed, he found himself appalled that the Vatican churchmen had not categorized or sorted the books.

At noon, Dominique approached Jacques. After confiding her need for a lavatory, he stood, and the couple traipsed through the Index door where—just outside it—they found Cardinal Passonei snoring loudly, the long hallway redoubling his every wheeze. From the ceiling, a painted flock of tiny *putti*, fat little cherubs, grinned.

Jacques woke the sleeping man and requested his counsel: Dominique had a necessary function to perform. But where? To this, the yawning cardinal pointed to his right far down the hallway, then dropped his head back to sleep.

Strolling to the lavatory, Jacques noticed that the low bustle of the scribes in other rooms was not to be heard. Perhaps it was time for their meal. Or possibly it was their daytime prayers that kept them from their duties.

What Jacques did not see was the old cardinal, his eyes slivered open, watching the couple move down the hall.

When her necessaries were finished, Dominique joined Jacques, and the pair began their walk back to the Index.

Through a crack of an opened door, a light struck Jacques' eye— a reflection emanating from the water clock he had seen the day before. Glancing down the hallway at the sleeping Passonei, Jacques cautiously pushed open the door before coaxing Dominique into the large room. He scanned the room.

"I want you to see this," he said to Dominique. "Are you familiar with a clepsydra?"

She shook her head.

A number of manuscripts lay on the workbenches. From the Latin inscriptions Jacques noted, it was clear these codices belonged to the office of the Holy Inquisition, and in this copy room, all were opened to an identical place.

Jacques eyed the water clock over Dominique's shoulder, then glanced back at a codex. Its date: 1310. Its title: "Interrogation of Bertrand de Saint-Clair, Deputy Master of the Knights Templar. Domenico—." He couldn't make out the text that followed, but no matter.

He placed his finger to his lips to indicate silence before guiding Dominique to a seat. Sighing, she gave a quick shake of her head and sat but said nothing, while Jacques joined her and began to inspect the musty codex, his fingers attuned to the roughness of each page.

He read: "'Where is the document?' asked the Inquisitor again and again.

'I, a Templar, have taken the vow of poverty and of chastity. I will never in battle seek mercy or seek to ransom myself or my fellows.'"

Jacques turned a page.

"'Where are the documents? You know of what I speak. Where will we find them?'

"The Templar begged to be set free.

"'What is the meaning of Baphomet?' urged the Inquisitor over and over. 'What did your brother Templars find in their excavations at the Stables of Solomon?'"

A shiver shook Jacques' neck and shoulders.

"*Quoi?*" whispered Dominique.

"I'll share in a few moments." He lowered his eyes to the codex.

Jacques felt his palms grow sweaty; he rubbed them against his waistcoat. Four hundred years after the Templars' interrogation, the Holy Inquisition was still reviled in many quarters as a fanatical arm of the Church made up of men who'd employed monstrous cruelties to achieve their religious ends.

Suddenly, Dominique jolted. Jacques turned and saw a shadow envelop her face: Cardinal Passonei loomed beside her while directly behind him hulked a stranger larger than any man Jacques had ever seen.

The cardinal leaned on the edge of the table and spoke in a disquieting tone. "You are not permitted in this room. Mark well what's before you for there will be no more reading in these rooms. Regretfully, I've no choice but to inform His Holiness."

"No choice," agreed the onerous stranger.

Dominique squeezed Jacques' knee under the table, then turned to him. "Let's leave," she said. "Please. Please."

Jacques pursed his lips, glanced once more at the codex—then rose with great solemnity.

"This matter will be dealt with," said Cardinal Passonei. The hulking man snapped his head in agreement.

* * *

Late that afternoon, Jacques sat in his lodgings, foot tapping against his chair, fingers scraping across his unshaven chin, wondering what Cardinal Passonei might tell the Pope. How severe an indiscretion was it to enter an off-limits room in the Vatican? To read a codex of the Holy Inquisition? What chastisement would the Pope give? Had Jacques squandered his opportunity?

Another worry: finances. Jacques had secured a stake from de Bernis, but he knew that any future loans would come with further obligations. He supposed there were worse burdens than having carnal relations with attractive actresses for the stimulation of the cardinal. But he didn't relish being a prostitute for another man's gold. He was his own man.

The chatter in Jacques' head seemed unending.

For two days, he waited at the lodgings for some news from the Vatican. Making love to Dominique lessened his frustrations, but as the hours rolled by and no word came, he ached to confess his scheming. But he knew: honorable as Dominique was, she would not tolerate his unprincipled behavior. He must not confide in her.

On the third morning, Jacques decided to pursue more practical matters. Deciding that in any future audiences at the Vatican it would be in his best interest to appear an imposing personage, Jacques borrowed from Cardinal de Bernis a number of jeweled rings, a snuffbox, and a watch chain studded with diamonds, emeralds, and rubies. With the jeweler's finest wire wrap, he attached some of the larger gems around his smallsword and scabbard. The clergy, for all their religion, were men of the temporal world.

It was later that day when Jacques received at his lodgings — much to his astonishment — the much-needed company of a *cameriere* of His Holiness, the Pope. The man, on his Most Holy Master's behalf, conferred a diploma fixed with the papal seal that declared Jacques a doctor of civil and canon law, an apostolic prothonotary *extra urbem*. Further, the cameriere placed around Jacques' neck a broad poppy-red ribbon to which was attached the cross of the Order of the Golden Spur.

Dominique was overjoyed at the award.

Jacques was mystified, yet enraptured. After the Pope's man left, he rushed from his lodgings and took a cabriolet straight to the Vatican office of Cardinal de Bernis.

Jacques stood before the cardinal's broad desk, his shoulders pulled back, his chest blown forward.

"This is an honor I must share with *you*, good friend," he said to Cardinal de Bernis. He proudly fondled his ribbon and cross.

"Ho, ho" de Bernis snickered. "Ho, ho. The Pope has hit upon your weakness." The fat cardinal sat behind his desk drenched in sweat, fanning himself as if his life depended on it. "Yes, two centuries ago the Order of the Golden Spur was presented to the Catholic great, but for as long as I can remember, the popes have presented that handsome cross and imposing ribbon to heal superficial vanities. When you broke the Vatican's rules, it proved to His Eminence you can't be trusted. But he's been gracious to present you a fancy ribbon and prize rather than turn you out."

It was as if a freezing wind invaded Jacques' veins. His mouth dropped open, then twisted into a grimace.

"The Order of the Golden Spur plays to your self-importance, you see?"

Jacques did not see. He slapped his hands together. "I'll not be laughed at, not be outdone by a mere Pope."

"Are you not grateful for *some* of His Holiness's good favor? You spent time in the Index librorum prohibitorum, after all."

"You *know* what dispensations I asked of the Pope?"

"Don't be naive. I've ears in all places."

"And eyes, as I recall."

"Yes," Cardinal de Bernis laughed, "and eyes. But to continue — you were permitted in the archives, but what information you desired, I don't exactly know."

"Knowledge of the Knights Templar."

"And did you find what you hoped for?"

"None. Passonei cornered me."

"That feeble old cardinal cornered you?"

Jacques blanched at the question. "My mistress and I — we were caught in flagrante delicto, in the act," he lied, stamping his heel on the floor.

The cardinal slapped his palms to his cheeks, laughing.

"Wait, wait!," cried Jacques. "What is Baphomet?"

"Baphomet? Never heard of it."

"What are the Stables of Solomon?"

"Stables of Solomon?" De Bernis quit fanning, wiped his sweating brow, and folded a hand across his paunch. "Mm. I've visited those chambers. I believe it was on an excursion years ago. To purchase relics for—"

"I overlooked your expertise."

"Yes, I suppose I am an expert. Relics," reflected the cardinal. "My excursion must have been to—oh, yes, it was Jerusalem. Perhaps to purchase the cloth from Edessa on which Christ imprinted his face. Or the hair of John the Baptist or—"

"But you were at the Stables of Solomon?"

"Yes. A plain, if extraordinarily large, stable—the chambers in the Temple Mount—where it's quietly rumored the Knights Templar buried a fabulous treasure. Or dug one up. Or some such strange thing. What is the Stables of Solomon to you?"

"Probably nothing." Jacques felt a tickle in his stomach when he realized his quest might take him across the seas into another world altogether. "But with the slimmest of chances, it may lead me to— well, let us say I hope to reward your financial generosity soon, and in full measure." Jacques clenched his jaw. "Would you intercede with the Pope to allow me into the archives again?"

"It seems that in the brief wag of a tongue—for the time being— I'm no longer in favor with this Pope," said de Bernis. "The instability of alliances in the Vatican amazes even such a jaded one as I."

The dire look in de Bernis's eye told Jacques that this was the truth.

"What are the chances of reentering the Index?" asked Jacques.

"Surreptitiously, you mean?"

Jacques nodded.

"Impossible. I truly and sternly advise against it. The Church can dole out, shall we say, stringent punishment when it pleases to do so. We here in Rome are our own kingdom, as you know." The cardinal chewed his lower lip. "You've reached a stalemate with the Vatican."

Jacques sat in the chair opposite the clergyman, elbows on thighs, chin in hands. "Then to Jerusalem," he finally said. "I accept this quest as my private challenge. I'll see this to the end. And when you are again permitted in the Pope's company, you may whisper in his ear that I, not being an easily manipulated puppet, plan to—"

"Do not make promises you cannot keep," huffed the fat cardinal as he rose from his seat. "It might interest thee to know," said de Bernis—trying to redirect the tone of the conversation—"I took a meeting yesterday with one of your Venetian countrymen, an imposing gentleman. We talked of your homeland. He said the Republic of Venice was in a precarious condition. One wind or the other might topple it. 'God's blood,' I told the knave, 'that's been obvious for—'"

Jacques raised his hand. Hearing the sad truth about Venice, his home, even dressed up in the cardinal's humorous language, did not please him.

"Also of note," said de Bernis wistfully, "I've heard your mother is again on the stage."

Jacques flushed. "And who might care?"

"It was her introduction that initially brought you to me, was it not?"

"No."

"It would appear I'm digging a deeper hole," confessed de Bernis. He leaned across his desk. "Let me be forthright. One of us is always leaving just when life becomes fascinating. Why not settle for a while? Your apostolic prothonotary from the Pope is useless in securing a law clerk's position for you, but I'm certain I can find you employment, Jacques. Secretary for a notable, perhaps? Something in the diplomatic circle? Rome is handwoven for a curious, intelligent, and quick-witted person like you."

Jacques thought for a moment.

"I can't tolerate the morals here."

At this comment, de Bernis' eyes glowed. He dissolved into a jolly laugh.

Jacques joined him almost at once.

"At the least I can provide another private dinner to send you off."

"To send me off? Or to send you off?"

Again the pair laughed. Cardinal de Bernis held his sides, then leaned back in his seat, nearly exhausted from the merriment.

Jacques said: "I'll make my decision after conferring with my Frenchwoman. Then you shall hear from me." Jacques stood up. "But to think I would consider leaving Rome without playing a single hand of cards. What's happened to me? In the meantime, I return the accoutrement you loaned me."

"Fine, sir."

"As asymptotes to the hyperbola—to speak in mathematical terms—we will meet somewhere. It's certain." He took the fat, sweaty hand of his friend de Bernis, kissed it, and placed it against his cheek.

The cardinal smiled a sweet smile and spoke. "I love you, too, young friend."

Just before Jacques left the room, de Bernis spoke with a profound intensity. "A subtle warning, Jacques. I mentioned a Venetian gentleman a moment ago: Cavaliere Michele Grimani. He knows you."

Jacques covered his surprise. "Yes, he knows me. And I know him." *And I'll kill him if he nears me.*

- 25 -

AT EVENTIDE, THE AIR WAS STIFLING. Dominique stood on an empty Rome street corner wrangling with Petrine about whether a day's visit to Pompeii was feasible. It had been her father's fondest wish to see the ruins of the city. Besides, the trio could set sail to the Holy Land from Naples, just a short distance from Pompeii.

Jacques smiled at the thought that each of his companions had a vote for *his* future.

"We'll be sailing to Jerusalem," he said. "We'll not visit Pompeii or Naples, Fragoletta." Jacques passed a knowing glance to Petrine, then turned to Dominique. "Carlo Brose, the devious man to whom I introduced you at L'affaire de Voltaire, has many powerful friends in Naples and Pompeii and virtually owns the authorities, especially after the success of his pamphlet praising those cities."

Dominique crossed her arms, waiting.

Jacques smiled faintly. "When living a life of adventure, it's often easy to be misled by underhanded rivals. I'll not be hung for trifles."

By late evening, Jacques had booked three passages to Acre and arranged a guide and camels from there to Jerusalem. During that time, he also dispatched Petrine to deliver a note to Cardinal de Bernis—the note firmly declining the clergyman's offer to stay in Rome.

"And it's worth repeating," Jacques said when he, Dominique, and Petrine were finally face-to-face in their lodgings that night. "We must be cautious on this journey. We're on to dangerous and unusual endeavors. Let's purchase unadorned clothes and sell these we wear. Dominique, you will be especially looked to. A plain dress and domino will arouse no pity nor dazzle fellow passengers or seamen. I, myself, will drab down and—"

"I'll select and buy a muslin shirt for Petrine," Dominique said.
Petrine's eyes showed he was much astonished. "A gift? I've never been given a gift. Thank you greatly, madame."

*   *   *

By noon the next day, Dominique stood at the stern of a lateen-rigged caravel, bracing herself for each short roll of the ship. "Rome is fading," she said to Jacques, who stood at her side. "I'd gladly return."

"If the hunt were not before us."

The voyage proved a long—but not difficult—trip. The breezes—there being few true winds on the Mediterranean—were good for sailing, which allowed the caravel, alert to bad weather or pirates, to navigate within the sight of land. Brief stops in Sicily, Crete, and Cyprus charmed Dominique, for she'd never imagined such exotic locales.

During the clear nights, the brilliant stars seemed to light a waterway toward Venice, but Jacques surmised the many vexing obstacles. He promised himself again that when the quest brought great wealth, he would return to Venice and gain the respect he deserved.

The caravel sailed into Acre, where a stout sea wall encompassed a city of ancient marble. Before the overland journey to Jerusalem began, the adventurers were taught by their Ottoman guide Omar Ibn Khalif how to ride and handle a camel.

Almost as soon as they took their new mounts, the scorching winds began to spit sand so fiercely that Jacques feared his exposed face would scour to the bone.

*   *   *

For several days, the caravan followed the ancient byway that wound through the desert panorama. At the beginning of one evening, the sunset melted the bleak landscape of ominous Judean hills into soft shades of purple, pink, and orange. There, on an immense plateau, glittered the revered city of Jerusalem.

The caravan moved slowly toward the walls of the city, but the sun had not disappeared before a sighting of the Temple on the Mount gave Dominique a triumphant excitement.

"To think I walk the same ground that Jesus, my Redeemer, walked," she cried. The adventurers and their guide pitched camp outside Jerusalem.

When the next morning arrived, Jacques sat atop his camel thinking, wondering if his purse would be adequate in Jerusalem. He laughed aloud. *So I now should concern myself with thrift?*

Khalif collected his pay, his animals, then bid farewell. By the time Petrine had arranged food and lodging, twilight had nearly swallowed the ancient city, but armed with Khalif's hand-drawn map, Jacques was able navigate to an old and rugged dwelling on a narrow and sinuous street.

Jacques glanced at his companions—one at each elbow—then knocked on the thick wooden door before him. Far away, a yelping dog seemed to respond.

"I don't want to be standing in this street in total darkness," Jacques said. He knocked again.

"Who! Are! You!"

Petrine and Dominique recoiled in alarm. The timbre of the sound suggested a screeching woman.

Jacques' neck hairs stood on end. He took a moment to regain his composure, then decided upon his best French to communicate. "My name is Jacques Casanova. You come highly recommended to me by Omar Ibn Khalif."

In the center of the door of the clay-brick house, a peephole flipped open. A voice barked back in staccato bursts. "How is it you know Khalif?"

"He led us from Acre to Jerusalem." *Is this a woman? A woman guide?*

Silence.

"Khalif promised we would find a porter, a guide worthy of our task." Not a sound.

"He gave only your address," Jacques whispered.

"No name?"

"No name. You see, I trust Khalif. Just as you must." Jacques stepped farther from the peephole, hoping that whoever was inside might have a better view. "I'm from Venice."

"Fool, your clothes and sword already tell me you're an outsider. Hah! Never are Jerusalem's streets empty of strangers. Let me see the color of your coin," croaked the voice from within.

Jacques opened his purse and sprinkled his palm, making the coins jingle as loudly as he could.

The voice again sounded. "You're a fine figure of a man. Are you a Jew or a Christian?"

"Christian."

"Prove it."

"Yes, my ..." Jacques stopped, then slowly lowered his hands while the startling realization dawned on him. He turned slowly to Dominique and Petrine.

In the last remnants of daylight, Dominique's eyes gleamed from within the hood of her domino. A sprightly smile broke across her lips.

"Pardon me," Jacques turned to the peephole, "I'm a professed libertine who has done a great deal of odd service, but in truth, I've never utilized my penis as a passport!"

The stillness from the other side of the door brought a rising heat to Jacques' cheeks. *How badly do we need this guide?* He snuck a sidelong glance at Petrine, who, snickering, turned his back and faced the empty street.

Dominique crossed her arms, a smile still on her lips.

Jacques let out a loud sigh, stuffed the coins back into his purse, then reluctantly coaxed his member from his pants for the inspection of someone he could not see.

"A Christian indeed. A Christian of prominence," cackled the voice. The door creaked open, and a rough-looking woman, eyes ablaze, took a step toward Jacques while he hurriedly buttoned up.

Jacques looked at the woman. Rather short, about Petrine's height. Lively brown eyes. Fifty years old, give or take. Rotund body stuffed into breeches, blouse, and vest—but one that was no doubt voluptuous in its prime.

"Muslims are circumcised too," said the woman. "Nevertheless ..." She stroked her chin from which several silver hairs protruded. "I'm Esther the Israelite, a descendant of the patriarch Jacob. And I could care less if you're a Jew, Muslim or Christian. I rarely see naked men." Esther again began to cackle.

While Dominique and Petrine moved to Jacques' side, a terrifying shriek came from inside. "Who. Are. You?"

Jacques nearly jumped out of his stockings. Past the open door, he spied a parrot.

"That is my child, Maimonides," Esther said. "A rare intelligence who speaks in three languages."

Petrine burst into laughter. "Your child has wings and a beak?"

Esther glared Petrine into silence.

"We mean no discourtesy, Esther the Israelite," Jacques said.

"Maimonides the parrot is peevish this evening, but you'll treat him with respect."

Esther took several steps past Jacques and looked both ways down the winding street before asking him, "Are you a gentleman? Have you a visiting card?"

"I am a gentleman, madame, but I balk at the trite custom of announcing one's rank in life on a small card," he boldly lied. "My father convinced me that a man's heart should be figured in his tongue."

Esther opened her palms to the adventurers. "I trust that old heathen Khalif, but if you've come to harm me, know that I own nothing of value."

"We've not come to do you harm, madame," said Dominique, removing the hood of her traveling domino, which Jacques at once understood as a sign to introduce his companions. She then made clear to Esther the adventurers' wish to see the Stables of Solomon, to know the story of them, to possess all the information the woman could impart.

Esther stepped from the dark street back into the entranceway, then faced Jacques. "I'm the person for your task. Regardless of each pasha's rules, I've been sneaking into that huge, if dull-looking, chamber for forty years. And so, too, my father and his father before him. The money you showed me will remain yours for tonight. I will consider your mission and decide how much it shall cost you. Return to me at the morrow's sundown."

At dusk the next evening, when they arrived at Esther's door, their knock was met with another unnerving parrot screech.

Jacques promised to throttle the bird.

Esther unlatched the door, greeted her guests, and invited them inside.

Jacques looked about. Rough-hewn table and chair. Fire in the hearth. Mattress with straw poking from its insides. Scattered books. A large mushroom-like ceramic on top of a stand.

Jacques shuffled his feet across the dried flowers covering the dirt floor. These at least disguised the odor of the chamber pot. And Maimonides' droppings.

At that instant, the gray parrot whistled. Jacques glanced at the bird. *A peculiar fellow, with his roving eye and wiggling tail feather. Not unlike myself.*

Esther asked Dominique to remove her cloak and motioned for the three to sit on the round rug that adorned a portion of the floor. The Israelite dipped behind a primitive curtain strung across an archway and returned with drinks, only to disappear again.

Poisoning. A favorite pastime in the Near East, thought Jacques while he discreetly sniffed his cup. *But my nose detects nothing untoward.*

Esther came back with several lit candles that she placed at the center of the rug, then sat between Petrine and Dominique, completing the human circle.

"What do the words on your tablet say?" asked Dominique, her eyes fastened on the burnished letters of a wooden slab on the near wall.

"That is from Isaiah, daughter," Esther said. "It reads: 'You shall see, and your heart shall rejoice.' I find many meanings in that scripture. My grandfather and father were rabbis—teachers—and they introduced me to the wisdom of the scriptures."

Jacques addressed his companions. "May we get to—?"

"How did you travel to Jerusalem?" interrupted Esther.

"Boat and camel."

Esther let out a raspy laugh. "By boat, eh? That pagan contemporary of Jesus the Nazarene, Seneca, wrote he would travel twenty years on his way by land rather than pass by water to any place in a short time, so tedious and dreadful is the sea."

"We didn't find it so," Dominique said.

"So, the Knights of Christ?" cried Esther suddenly, her eyes growing intense. "The preceptory of Jerusalem, *Palatium Solomonis.* According to the stories passed on to me, the Knights Templar in the twelfth century built their quarters on the foundations of the ancient temple of Solomon, as they believed the temple had stood on Mount Moriah."

Jacques nodded. "I was told that one of the Templars' primary tenets was the reconciliation of Jews, Christians, and Muslims, was it not?"

Esther shook an admonishing finger in the air. "An intelligent woman might ask if reconciliation was their aim, why the Christian Templars expended twenty thousand of their knights in the taking and defense of the Holy Land and why they perpetrated the abominable slaughter of thousands and thousands of Muslims and Jews."

"But," prompted Jacques, "we are all men, in our own natures frail—"

"And few are angels. Yes, I know the passage, Signor Casanova. Frail or not, men have a choice." Esther clasped her palms together as if praying and spoke in a lighter voice. "Good, says the Kabala, is that which draws one closer to the sense of the center of creation or the divine. The Kabala allows for good. And evil. The choice between good and evil allows men free will."

"Boethius, too, felt that human will is free," Dominique said. "He believed that, though the end is planned by the Creator, the manner in which the end is attained depends upon the reactions of human beings to situations created by fortune."

Jacques and Petrine turned their heads toward Dominique in surprise.

"As you say, Esther, with free will, men may do good or evil."

Esther clapped onto Dominique's nearest knee. "It is a fine thing to meet a learned woman, daughter. *Shalom aleichem* and *salaam*."

Dominique smiled. "My father, and my husband, too, taught me a great many things." She lowered her eyes to the rug. "Long ago."

"I don't mean to trample on the education you women provide," Jacques said, "but as to men's fortunes, may we talk of the Stables of Solomon? That is the task at hand." Too late, he realized he'd sounded gruffer than he meant to.

"You are but a few of those whom I have led to the stables, Signor Casanova. I'm aware of what you seek."

"And what would that be?"

"Everything in its time, Signor." Esther tugged at the hairs on her chin, then placed her fingers against her lips, as if the words that were about to leave her mouth should not be revealed. "Old grandfather said legend had it that in the stables, the Templars found a treasure beyond compare. But neither my grandfather nor my father in their entire lifetimes could discover if the Templars took treasure with them or secreted it here in the Holy Land."

Jacques' stomach jumped with excitement.

Esther continued: "Be warned: the current pasha forbids anyone in the Stables of Solomon, so you will pay me ten silver coins for my risk, for my services. You will bring haversacks, shovels, water pouches, and candles. And you shall see the stables tomorrow night. But my prescript dictates that we first seek a blessing through a purification."

"A purification?" blurted out Jacques.

"Many years ago," Esther said looking at Jacques and the others, "my brother discovered a cache of oil on one of our journeys."

Jacques scratched the pox scars on his face. "You *sanctify* your sojourns with anointing oil?"

"Yes. You have noteworthy business in Jerusalem, don't you?" said Esther, reaching into the coarse garment she was wearing. "I burn this tonight for a successful guiding."

Jacques raised his eyebrows, then nodded.

Esther pointed to the vial in her hand. "The recipe for the oils were closely guarded by the priestly house of Avtinas but I discovered that the *Mishna* specifies the principal ingredients as kannabus, myrrh, balsam, Chinese cinnamon." Esther pointed over her head. "I am a tool of Him whose name shall not escape my lips. We are all His vessels. As His instrument, I guide men through Jerusalem, a site sacred to Jews, Christians, and Muslims," she said. "A purification, then. Shall we not seek the holiness of men and women?"

Esther did not wait for an answer. Taking one of the lit candles, she rose from the rug while Maimonides the parrot trilled a note and articulated several words.

"Is that Hebrew?" asked Jacques.

"My parrot speaks Hebrew, Latin, and Greek. And he's an extremely quick and able learner."

"What? No Italian?"

"Not a word of that vulgar language," Esther frowned. "And I plainly forbid anyone to use Italian in my household. Need I be clearer?"

Esther gestured to herself and her guests. "The four of us will continue with our French."

"As a Parisian, I agree with your sensible declaration," smiled Dominique, who leaned toward the candles at the center of the rug, then glanced up at Jacques.

Jacques flapped his hand. "Positively no Italian."

Tiptoeing toward the parrot, Esther took a piece of nearby fruit and placed it between her parted lips. She bent toward Maimonides, who flailed his wings several times before taking and swallowing it.

Crossing past Dominique to the small cook fire near her bed, Esther removed a burning ember and dropped it into the chute of the mushroom-like ceramic. Carefully holding the vial, she poured its contents into a side hole of the ceramic. In a short while, smoke drifted from the ceramic stand.

This swirling smoke has an intriguing tang, yet I must be on my guard. Jacques took a peek at Dominique and Petrine situated on the matted rug, while Maimonides the parrot commenced a lilting whistle.

Petrine waved at the bird and began to talk, but Esther placed her finger against her lips.

While thin smoke wisps lengthened and curled around the faces in the room, Jacques watched, amidst the cook fire, small bursts of flame leaping among the embers, sometimes orange, sometimes yellow, then blue and white and red.

Petrine, whose attention was fixed on the parrot, crawled toward the bird. He was met at the foot of the table by Esther, who supported the valet's arm, then helped him to his feet. She sat him in the straw-backed chair before kneeling close to Maimonides—the diminutive bird maintaining a low and leisurely croon to which Esther added a trilling harmony, further sweetening the song.

The red-tail has prepared a lullaby, thought Jacques, *for my Venetian heart. His song echoes my homeland—the warm, sun-filled days, the luscious, sensual nights.*

Sitting cross-legged on the floor, Jacques interlaced his fingers with Dominique's while she lay down atop the strewn dried flowers. *On my life, I've never encountered such a feeling. My muscles repose, yet my mind, enervated, is alert to the moment.*

Through the aromatic smoke, he saw the outline of Petrine, head bending forward to the table, then head in hands—his back heaving mightily. Esther stood and placed her fingers upon the servant's head, stroking his hair slowly, steadily.

I know this pantomime, thought Jacques, patting his own hair. *What each moment is to be before it happens.*

Maimonides leered briefly and continued his song. The bird pitched lower while Esther wrapped her arm about Petrine and led him toward the archway at the far wall, Petrine continuing his doleful sob. He and Esther disappeared behind the entry's red drape while Maimonides weaved his small head in rhythm with his melody.

I'm in tune with the parrot's whistle, like the pleasing of a lute. Jacques caressed the tender palm of Dominique, who stretched before him in sensual innocence. Her hand had never revealed itself so willingly. He felt the form and suppleness of each and every finger. He coursed the paths that lined her hand.

Through the thin haze, Dominique raised herself to sit, then leaned toward Jacques. "My lover, I sigh warm desire into your ear," she murmured. "And this gentle wish makes its presence known. In the service of the queen." Dominique laid back, a curl of smoke swirling round her.

"In the service of the queen," mused Jacques as he studied her green eyes, so much like emeralds. He smiled at Dominique, then artfully lay down between her legs, the back of his head upon her stomach.

"Ahh," she whispered.

"You are the sweetest of pillows, Fragoletta."

Feeling the ebb and flow of her breathing Jacques paused to consider this essential of life—the breath. In and out it came and went, having a resolve of its own and yet always obeying the body wherein it resided.

Jacques measured his breaths to coincide with Dominique's. He reached his hand above his head and placed it against her side, feeling her ribs expand—ever in unison with her inhalations. The unhurried thumps of Dominique's heartbeat seemed to inform Maimonides' melody. All was in time with the inhalations and exhalations.

Hark, a concerto. Wondrous and strange.

Jacques observed his thoughts encompassed in a colorful soap bubble. *In the service of the queen,* he pondered. *This woman is the queen. I serve her. And yet I breathe the same as the queen, I breathe with the queen.*

Maimonides breathes with the queen. Maimonides breathes and warbles and plays the lute. Jacques lay rapt in awe at his fleecy soap bubbles and the myriad of thoughts they contained. *Dominique, Maimonides, and I—we are flesh and blood, yet breath and nothingness. This is profound. This is paradox. This is absurdity!*

Jacques' fingers grazed Dominique's ribcage. Her breath halted. Her stomach stiffened—jostling Jacques' head, bursting all the colored soap bubbles. He laughed. And tickled her ribs.

She let out a hollow laugh. "No!"

"But tonight your quivering belly encourages me." Jacques rolled over and with both hands pressed Dominique, touching and tickling. Struggling to escape, her shrill mirth increased the tempo of Maimonides' tune.

Jacques' eye caught the bird bobbing and weaving, now in time to Dominique's gasps of laughter. He stopped his amusements and lay next to her face-to-face, too contented to move. They positioned their hands together. Their lips touched in a melting kiss. A simple hello from mouth to mouth.

They kissed again. Without passion but with desire. A desire to connect, to be joined together, commingled. A desire to beget sublimity, tranquility, grace. A desire to discover a berth where two souls might greet in endless ethereal elopement. A desire for deliciousness to dissolve expectation. For shared ecstasy to become eternal.

This lovers' kiss—utter feeling. A kiss, an effortless kiss, becomes anew to me. I who claim pleasure as my game am now unfolded, unfettered. This is what we mortals seek. This especial kiss, this kiss of kisses. Oh, heavens. It's this exalted kiss to which the world accords infinite compliment.

Now, beneath the caprices of seduction, I feel a weighty need: oh, let this be she. The she who takes me, connects me, fills me. Let her embrace be the one to raise my hopes, keep me sure, stay my shame, renew our flesh, release our dance, gift us time, ensure our glow. Let her caresses be those which prove the two of us endless.

In an instant, Jacques' lips left hers, and he invaded her eyes, Dominique's eyes. *Behold this helpless lamb. She who feels my secrets.*

He plunged toward the crook of her neck, her vulnerable neck, and grunted his scalding breath on her flesh. He, stung to his marrow with a grim, cruel impulse, seized her suppleness with his sharp teeth and prepared to consume her, to devour her.

As a fragile leaf yields to a potent wind, she offered herself up, freely, bravely.

His hot breath cooled. He loosened his bite. He knew: *in her surrender, she becalms my vilest passion*.

Now frightened, Jacques nestled into Dominique's side and sensed his heart reeling with questions long unasked, with answers never dared.

* * *

A loud whistle broke the still morning air.

Jacques woke midsnore and wondered where he was. He pulled his hands from between his knees and shaded his eyes from the sliver of light spilling under the door. Rolling to his back, he looked up to find Esther the Israelite, tousled and towering, above him.

"Good morning," Esther said.

A cold drip smacked Jacques squarely on the forehead. It fell from the fruit upon which Esther champed. She moved to the far side of the room.

Rousing himself, Jacques turned and saw Dominique behind him, sleeping on the mattress, hardly a wrinkle in her clothes or on her face. His arms felt shod in lead. He wondered at the things he'd experienced in the darkness of the long night.

"Pssst."

Jacques turned toward Esther, who motioned him to table. He rose and, sweeping dried flowers from his shirt, approached. "As I don't see Petrine, I suppose he, too, has been purified to exhaustion."

Esther ignored the remark.

"You and the other two must gad about Jerusalem today," said Esther in half voice. "Purchase the necessaries—small shovels and so forth—the things we discussed last night. Be prudent."

"Yes."

"You will meet me here at noon. We must spend the remainder of the day touring the city. I want us to be seen by the Ottoman authorities." Esther slopped the last bit of fruit into her mouth and wiped her fingers. "Now, wake up your friends, take this veil for the woman, and haste you." She tossed a bundle at Jacques and headed to the archway before squeezing past Petrine, who groped his way into the room.

"A pathetic entrance for a practiced actor," laughed Jacques. "You shame Thespis."

"Water," choked Petrine. "Some water."

"The same, please."

Soon the three were ready. Maimonides, preening and strutting, bid them adieu in Latin, Greek, and Hebrew just before they glided onto the ancient street into the early morning.

*   *   *

The white-hot sun stood at the top of the sky before Jacques again knocked on Esther's door.

Standing next to his master, the valet voiced his complaint. "Esther the Israelite, I bake in this noonday heat."

"Then you'll be well cooked and ready to be eaten by supper," said the woman as she opened the door and invited her guests inside.

"There is hardly a breath in all Jerusalem," added Dominique, waving her hand in front of her face.

"And it will grow hotter," Jacques said.

Esther spoke. "We'll find cool comfort, especially in the Temple Mount."

Esther dragged the trio through Jerusalem the entire afternoon, a full tour, replete with rambling talk on local legends, politics, philosophy, history.

The day proved trying, but at Esther's, after a meager dinner, the real tour began. Jacques felt that his shrewd intelligence, coupled with Fragonard's scroll, would unlock the secret of the stables and that a startling treasure would be his.

By midnight, the group was silently picking their way through the rubble of the city's east wall, using the sparse moonlight to funnel them to the mouth of the underground chamber, the Stables of Solomon.

Jacques patted his pockets to make certain his pistols were at hand. He felt for his dagger, glancing back every so often to make certain they had not been followed.

At the entrance, Esther handed them candles, then lit them. "We can be reasonably confident of solitude from this spot on," she reassured them. "At this late hour, no self-respecting Muslim would chance meeting a demon here."

"Demon?" asked Jacques.

"Yes, Muslims believe that evil jinn—demons—lurk among the dark pillars here."

Jacques felt the hairs on his arm stand tall and straight. He twisted his head in each direction, then joined his companions hurrying onward in the demidark.

A short time later, Esther lifted her candle overhead. The adventurers mimicked their guide's action.

Dominique gasped. "A forest of pillars. I've never seen such a huge place that's so overwhelmingly brown."

Esther chuckled. "Animals might have been tethered to these eighty-eight pillars, which are divided into twelve rows." Esther made her way around a massive column of stone. "Over the years, there have been numerous men who searched here. Dirt, rock, and the fetor of centuries are all anyone's ever found. But perhaps you have unique wisdom or superior revelation."

Jacques' jaw clenched. "Perhaps."

"A thousand years after Solomon," Esther continued, "Herod built this grand vault to support the Temple esplanade that sits above us. What you see here below is mistakenly called Solomon's Stables, but a Jewish monarch would never desecrate his Temple above by stabling horses and camels so near. But then came a contingent of *Christian* Crusaders who proceeded to use the chamber for just that. A stable. Those mangers over there," she pointed, "belonged to the Templars. Twelfth century."

Jacques craned his neck.

She lowered her candle beside her face. "Already I see that all of you have lost your bearings in this labyrinth of columns."

"Which is why we hired you," Jacques said. "The Templars?"

"You need not raise your voice, monsieur. The Christian Templars. Yes. The story often told is that they excavated this entire rock floor. For years."

"Why?"

Esther shook her head and marched in the direction of the mangers. She held her candle out into the darkness, revealing piles of substantial boulders. "When Salah ad-Din retook Jerusalem, he piled these rocks over the supposed excavations in the stables so that the demons might not escape."

I've not traveled all this way to be told that my treasure is rock or hardened horse dung.

"If the Templars excavated here, what were they looking for, Esther?"

Esther stiffened. "Am I the sibyl?" She turned away, offered a terse "Follow me," and headed farther into the darkness. The trio of adventurers quickly followed.

"Watch yourself. Watch your step." The flame of Esther's candle illuminated a series of hollow recesses along the pocked wall. "A handful of tombs," Esther said, "with no corpses." She walked straight to Jacques, held her candle at eye level, and spoke in his face. "What have men hoped to discover in the Stables of Solomon? I give you many answers. Choose what you will." Esther's flame cast an eerie shadow on her face and the high stone vault above. "Why not the Ark of the Covenant? Or holy anointing oils perhaps? Gold? Silver?" Esther thrust her fist toward the empty tombs. "Some say that the Templar Crusaders dug these. Or removed contents from them. What treasure might have been contained in a tomb?" Her voice strained. "Other parties speculate a particular Jewish document that was precious or sacred in some way was excavated here in the stables. Possibly a marriage certificate."

Dominique began to speak, but Esther waved her hand in the air. "A Talmudic tradition holds that in this chamber a violated altar and a golden blade should be found and that these somehow contain the most secret name of the Eternal."

"Are there stories of the philosopher's stone, *Lapis philosophorum?*" interrupted Jacques.

"To convert base metals into gold? Yes, tales," snorted Esther as she trekked into the darkness toward the entrance. "Material reward. Is this what you seek?"

Her voice echoed through the darkness. "—You seek, you seek, you seek?"

Near the Single Gate in the east wall, Esther stopped and held her ground. "I'm willing to bring you to this chamber for three nights. That's how long your money ensures my services. After that, you'll know the subtleties of getting in and out of the stables, you'll have all the history and knowledge I can supply. Then you may decide if you'll return. But from that point on, without me." She told the party to snuff their candles. "Let's move. We'll find our way out in moments."

Jacques threaded his way over the rocky ground, tugging his haversack tighter to his shoulder, wondering what they'd uncover in three nights' time.

The night air parched the throats of the wary band as they slipped through the ancient gate, watching the moon slide from behind the clouds, bunching the landscape with lean and fearsome shadows.

- 26 -

EACH NIGHT AT MIDNIGHT, the group—bundling candles, leather pouches of water, digging implements, various tools, and rations of food—entered the oppressively dark recesses of Solomon's Stables. Esther remained on guard near the Single Gate as the three adventurers tested their mental and physical stamina.

After a night of exploration, the group had uncovered scant evidence of treasure. If tribulations in Rome had not given them a sober outlook, their failure to detect anything of substance in Solomon's Stables certainly had.

Jacques contemplated digging a tunnel at a cant under Salah ad-Din's boulders to see what might be found, but eventually he agreed that tunneling by hand was impossible, and as Dominique pointed out, the boulders would have been an obvious choice for previous treasure excavators. If Templar treasure of any sort existed deep under the boulders, it had most likely been retrieved during the past six centuries. Besides, constructing a tunnel for the current search required apparatus that could not clandestinely be moved to the area or easily employed once in place.

What of the tombs? These subterranean cemeteries should have contained corpses, but none remained. And of what interest would a corpse be to a treasure hunter unless it were gilded? Why take a corpse? What substantial reward could it bring?

These conjectures offered a theme for discussion, yet when all was said, there seemed no explanation as to what treasure might have been deposited or removed by the Templars—or others—from the Stables of Solomon.

Near the end of the second night, Jacques heard a loud summons from Dominique, who, with Petrine, was somewhere behind a distant pillar.

"Jacques, come quickly, I may have something," came a scattering echo.

Jacques rose and, while picking his way, brushed away beads of sweat from his forehead. When he arrived next to Dominique, she held the candle flame chest high.

"This carved decoration, this intaglio, Jacques," she said, pointing repeatedly at a column, "doesn't this match the tiny circles on Fragonard's scroll? Have you seen others in the stables? Is there an intaglio on any other pillar?"

"Well, I don't know. My valet will have to examine the other eighty-seven pillars and tell us."

Petrine whipped his head toward Jacques.

Dominique grinned sideways at Jacques. "Before your valet makes a thorough examination, look at this."

Petrine focused on the pillar. "Circles within circles. The biggest and outermost circle, the size of an apple."

Jacques looked at the circles inscribed into the pillar, then dug out the scroll from his caftan. "Yes, this matches the one on Fragonard's scroll. Wait! Look! These pillar circles are not spaced evenly from the center point. I hadn't noticed that on Fragonard's scroll. Too minute." Jacques traced the stone intaglio with his finger. "Circles—unevenly spaced with one another—is a mathematical abbreviation for Plato's Theorem," he said. "Briefly, the Theorem dictates that specific triangles and squares may be drawn within these circles. And these geometrical derivations may be repeated ad infinitum." Jacques scratched his shoulder. "I don't know the significance of the mathematics of the intaglios but it must not be coincidence that these circles are cut into rock here in the stables and also drawn on Fragonard's scroll."

Petrine eyed his master sheepishly. "I should show you something." He marched into the darkness, his candle guiding him. Jacques and Dominique followed until the valet stopped and thrust his light toward a pillar. "I hadn't thought anything about this when I saw it earlier."

Dominique's tone rose. "Yes! Someone cut only the two smallest circles and part of a third. It's an intaglio only partially finished."

"And unevenly spaced like the other."

"Let's dig," Dominique said.

"What?"

"What might have happened," Dominique said, "is that chiseling, incising, these stone pillars created rock chips, spall—as my father correctly termed it—that may have fallen to the dirt at the base of the column."

"Meaning what?" asked Petrine.

"I'll tell you if we find spall. Let's start digging at the base of this pillar."

Petrine shrugged in disappointment, took a short spade from his haversack, and began.

And it was he who soon announced that, for civilized cultures, it was considered quitting time—nearly sunrise, by the valet's guess.

This was spoken while Jacques uncovered, two feet below the general level of the ground, fragments of white stone matching the limestone of the pillar. There also was animal or human dung, an awl, a fishhook, a damaged bridle rosette, and adjacent to fragments of chipped stone—a coin.

Dominique spit on the coin to scrub the dirt from its surface. She held the coin to the candle and inspected it.

"Well worn from usage, but some points of the bronze can be deciphered."

Jacques leaned closer.

"I can't read the words, but the date is clear: 1181," Dominique exclaimed, her voice fired with exuberance. "Material links! The fact that this coin is in close proximity to our limestone chips—well, this may possibly mean that whoever chiseled this intaglio did so around 1181, give or take a few years."

"From 1100 on, the Crusaders occupied these stables," came Esther's voice.

The three spun around.

"The Crusaders occupied Jerusalem until 1187 Anno Domini, before Salah ad-Din and the Saracens drove them out."

"The Crusaders? Here in the stables, that may mean the Templars, is that not so?"

"Most probably," Esther said.

"So I may suppose the Templars carved these intaglios into the pillars before they were driven out?" Jacques asked. "Where does that lead us, Dominique?"

"I'm thinking."

"Think quicker, girl," Esther chimed. "Outside, dawn is breaking. We must withdraw from this chamber. Now."

The three, tired and dirty, did as they were told.

They traipsed their way through Jerusalem's backstreets back to the inn, to their room. Petrine and Dominique no sooner sat on the floor than they fell deep asleep.

But Jacques sat speculating, occupied by the puzzle at hand. His mind glutted with circles within circles, and shortly, before exhaustion overcame him and before he fell into the chasm of sleep, he thought on Fragonard's advice, to remember the *good* name of the Templars. *What good,* Jacques wondered, *had the Templars done?*

He keeled over in sleep.

*   *   *

Surveying the gloom of the underground stables, Jacques shielded his candle's flame before speaking to the Jewess sitting opposite him. It was Esther's final night; after tonight's search, the adventurers would have no guide.

"While we take our rest, Esther, I've more questions. In the late—"

Esther interrupted. "Why is your Spanish man not here to dig?"

"Petrine? He stayed home. Twisted back, he claimed."

"What surprises me is that you choose to quarry through layers of Christian horse dung. For what?" cried the woman, pointing toward the hollowed trenches at the base of the nearest pillars.

"We have our reasons," Dominique said firmly.

Jacques stroked his chin, thinking. *To sit in this dark and dirty place ringed by these half-dozen candles as if they were a campfire. And Esther, our oracle? No wonder the valet professes injury. To be rid of this!*

"Help me understand, Esther," he said. "In the late 1100s, the Crusaders, the Templars, were slowly losing their stronghold in the Holy Land to the Saracens, the desert Arabs. And the Templars retreated to avoid total defeat?"

"Yes. Many retreated to Acre, which fell to the Saracens four years later."

"Did all these Crusaders die at Acre?"

"On the contrary," Esther said, "my grandfather strongly believed a contingent of Templars departed the Holy Land on Portuguese ships."

"Portuguese?" asked Dominique incredulously.

"Yes. Years earlier, an army of Christian Crusaders had defeated the Muslims—the Moors—and had liberated Lisboa. In 1147, I think. Most naturally, Portuguese Christians would rescue brother Crusaders from the Holy Land—from the heathen Muslims—a scant thirty years afterwards."

Esther shifted her weight and passed her hand through a candle flame. Dominique grimaced at the sight.

"My grandfather believed the Portuguese extremely seaworthy. Three centuries later, their progeny were the most celebrated seamen in the whole world. Prince Henry the Navigator, da Gama, Dias, Magellan."

Jacques rested his chin in his hand and glanced in the direction of the catacombs. "If the Templars had managed to excavate some sort of wealth here in the stables, would transporting it have been safe, even among other Crusaders? Or conversely, would the Templars leave their treasure here in the Holy Land if it were plain the Saracens were on the verge of taking control?"

Esther turned to the candles and, with the tips of her fingers, extinguished one's flame. "My grandfather wasted his life and what family fortune we had to hunt treasure. My father followed his footsteps. Ha! Thank the Creator, I realized the riches to be excavated were not from these grounds but from fools' pockets." She removed a coin from her purse, tossed it in the air, and caught it.

Esther redoubled her passion. "I've taken some of your money but not all of it. Before greed perverts your remaining decency, before you squander your fortune on treasure hunting or have your throat slit by other rapacious men, leave this land and give up your search. You will find nothing but calamity." She looked up momentarily into Dominique's face and smiled gracefully. "Find a worthier aim. Bring a child into the world. It's true, I've none of my own. But as a woman, I say again, have a child. Have two."

A fragile mist sparked Dominique's eyes. The glistening looked to be the beginning of a dozen tears, but not a single one came.

Esther waited no longer but threw her coin to Jacques and brushed her palms together. "I return a small portion of what you have paid me. I trust our contract is fulfilled." She quickly snatched a candle from the few remaining, stood, then took her leave. Before she disappeared near the east gate, she spoke, her voice without rancor. "Say goodbye to your Spanish man for me. And may God grant you peace."

"And God be with you, Esther the Israelite," Dominique said, while staring at Jacques.

The pair used the remainder of the night to search for more spall around the intaglios and to discuss the scroll that obsessed their waking thoughts.

*   *   *

"There was another important question I wanted to ask the Jewess," whispered Jacques when he peeped out from the chamber into morning's first light. "I knew there was." He pivoted around, making sure there were no witnesses to their departure from the underground.

"And what would that be?" asked Dominique as she pressed herself upright, dusted off her garments, and tried to straighten her legs.

"When we first met Esther, she mentioned that Godfroi de Bouillon, a Jew, led the Templars." Jacques threw his bundle over his shoulder. "Why, I ask you, would a Jew lead a *Christian* army of Templars, of Crusaders?"

"An intriguing question, but one that we might refrain from asking Esther after her scolding last night."

"Possibly. But why not ask? All she can do is refuse more of our money, order her bird to attack us, and shut the door on our toes."

Dominique laughed, then threw her bundle on her shoulder and blinked at the morning sun. "Hmm," she said, staring at Jacques, "a woman could use more adventure on this adventure."

"Madame, your stimulation shall be tended to, sped by the wings of Mercury. Administered by the tongue of Casanova." He winked.

*   *   *

"Is that you, Petrine?" asked Jacques, poking his head around the corner of the bed.

"It is. I return. And my back seems mended," Petrine said as he shoved open the door. "This lodging lacks charm, if you ask me," he declared. He set down the objects he held in his arms and closed the door. "I've spent time at the market, mixed with the local inhabitants, and attended to the thousand duties required of my position, sir."

"You've been gone all day? Did you manage a—?"

"And I managed two fine bottles of wine."

"Good. Dominique and I are just rising."

Not long after, Jacques sat at table with Dominique, Petrine, three cups, and a bottle.

"You, my good man, are a favorite of Esther's," Jacques said, "so be your best behaved. Where our gold might be of no use, your appeal may be."

"She'll not want me there, Master Jacques," Petrine slurred. "I shouldn't—"

"You are the main chance when we return to the Jewess."

"Then I must have more wine before we set off." A forced grin crossed the valet's face. "To enhance my appeal, you see." He emptied his cup and immediately refilled everyone's. The three raised their cups several times, drinking a good deal, voicing their displeasures with the little progress they'd made with the search.

Early twilight was descending upon Jerusalem when the trio of adventurers made their way shoulder to shoulder down the narrow meandering corridor that led to Esther's. There were no human beings in sight, the late afternoon heat still working its will.

Petrine cocked his ear and cackled. "That perverse melody I hear? Maimonides, the parrot, I'd wager my life on it."

"Yes," Jacques said. "The bird that speaks Hebrew, Greek, and Latin. I marvel that this rare intelligence does not defecate in one of those languages."

"How do we know the bird is a 'he'?" laughed Dominique.

"That's another question I'll put to our former guide." Jacques playfully swung Dominique's hand in his as the three advanced toward Esther's dwelling. "Maimonides the Maniacal, I'll find you a maiden to mollify your madness."

"Who will mold your madness into memorable misery," garbled Petrine.

"Rascals!" Dominique laughed. After batting Petrine's shoulder, she removed her veil, shrieked like a parrot, and pantomimed a madcap—hands on ears, silent scream on face—then raced toward Esther's.

"Delightful—her silliness," Jacques said.

He and Petrine watched in amusement while Dominique took a ridiculous stance in front of Esther's door, knocked, then quickly covered her nose.

Striding toward Dominique, Jacques wheezed with laughter until a disturbing odor stole the smile from his face.

Dominique frantically jabbed a finger toward the hulking wooden door.

Suddenly Jacques felt too weak to shut out the putrid odor. Or the parrot's strident squawk. Finally, he shouldered the door open. The last vestiges of twilight overran the dingy room. The parrot went silent.

"Esther? Esther the Israelite? We've come to ask one more question."

Dominique pointed to the overturned incense burner and to the straw mattress, upon which two books lay open.

Jacques stepped further into the room. He pulled a pistol from his caftan just as Petrine rustled through the doorway behind him.

"Light a candle."

"No matches."

"Here, take these," Dominique said.

Jacques' free hand trembled. He fumbled it into a pocket underneath his caftan and, producing a handkerchief, thrust it in Dominique's direction. She covered her mouth and nose while Petrine crept to the table and lit two tapers.

Jacques closed the door quietly behind him and aimed his pistol at the curtained archway opposite. "Petrine, where does that lead?"

"It's a smallish room with a wardrobe and an assortment of books. That's all."

Jacques—grim concern straining his face—shouted a bit too loudly. "Esther, we're entering your back room." His fist tightened around the pistol's handle. With the gun's barrel, he prodded the heavy makeshift curtain.

A throng of flies, like hissing arrows, swooped past.

Jacques' scalp seemed to lift from his head.

He glanced at Petrine and Dominique, signaling them to stay behind him, then plied the curtain wider.

Before him lay a corpse splattered in blood.

"Horror. Oh, horror," exploded from Jacques' gut to the tip of his tongue. Ripping the curtain closed, he staggered back from the gruesome sight. He pressed his hand to his mouth to quell the possibility of retching, then pointed Dominique across the room to the table and chair.

"Petrine, you and I must see what can be done. Stay at the table, Dominique."

The woman buried her face in the handkerchief wrapped around her hand.

"Old Maimonides—dreadfully mute," Jacques said. "As if his world is forever changed."

Laying his pistol next to Dominique, Jacques stepped toward the curtain and opened it. He stepped into the room that was perhaps five meters long and well lit by a single small window in the opposite wall. Seeing now the offal and the crusted blood that pooled the floor, he felt as if a sharp spur rode full-length down his back.

"The woman is rotting. From the heat," Petrine said, trembling. He closed the curtain behind them, genuflecting while he knelt.

With his dagger in hand, Jacques examined the wardrobe in the wall niche of the room. Two garments, nothing more. Stooping beside Petrine, he stared at the unblinking wretch whose pale face was speckled with splotches of gore. Jaw agape, sunken eyes, body sprawled and twisted in an ungainly manner—all evinced the terror she'd assuredly experienced in her last moments.

Jacques rose to his feet. "She has quite a decent collection of books in these shelves," he said in an attempt to divert himself.

"Yes, master."

"Who would do such an unspeakable—?"

"A monster," Petrine said, blistering pain in his voice. "Stabbed several times."

"Excruciating death. What did this old woman do that brought her this end? She has no means."

Jacques peered again at the books: philosophy, history, religion, and the Templars. Then other titles quickly seemed to leap at him. Unexpected titles: alchemy, magic, excavating, mining.

"Why did Esther say she owned nothing of value?" Jacques muttered. "She has a worthy library here. Perhaps she lied about her possessions."

"Pardon?"

Jacques handpicked several small books from the shelf. When he did so, he discovered—out of sight behind the others—a small book flattened against the wall. He freed the book from its resting place, and when it fell open in his hand, he saw a word that his brain—though feverish from the grisly scene—immediately imprinted: *Olissibona*. He shut the thin volume and put it and several others in his caftan.

"We leave Jerusalem at once, Petrine. We're not involved in this affair. If we tell anyone, we risk our lives."

"I agree."

"Quickly," snapped Jacques as he exited the foul-smelling room and looked to Dominique. Head bowed, she stood opposite Maimonides, clutching the ivory crucifix on her necklace. Her lips moved silently.

"We leave immediately, Fragoletta. We'll send a messenger boy to Khalif. He is a man of character. He'll know best."

"I've prayed for Esther, for all of us," Dominique said, her voice quivering. "Her God will fetch her soul. Of that I'm certain."

Jacques pressed Dominique's hand gently to his chest. "Is everyone at the ready?" He proposed an answer to his own question but was cut short by a rude and disconsolate source.

"*Illustrissimo, si. Illustrissimo, si,*" screeched the gray parrot perched in the corner.

Instantly, Jacques turned toward the bird as if an invisible puppeteer maneuvered him. A single thought shot like a lightning bolt through his mind: *Maimonides knows three languages only. The bird speaks no Italian. Who, then, does the parrot mimic? Who's been saying "Yes, Illustrious One" in his presence? Esther's murderer?*

Jacques looked to his companions. Their dismay suggested the same alarming questions.

*   *   *

Jacques contacted Khalif not only for Esther's sake but also for the safest and surest transport back to Acre. With Khalif at their head, the adventurers hastily departed Jerusalem, camping on the far outskirts of the city.

Stirring the fire, Petrine glanced at other campfires on the far perimeter before fastening his eyes on Jacques and Dominique. "No treasure yet."

A noise at his right attracted Jacques' attention.

"Van Doormolen's as fine a sailor as there is in the Mediterranean," reported Khalif, walking into view, "but like many men from his land, he's as hardheaded as a block of stone. Antonius van Doormolen is his name, but he'll answer to absolutely nothing but Captain."

Dominique shot a puzzled look to Jacques.

Khalif stood beside the fire, shifting his feet in the sand. "As for Esther, I've made arrangements. She was a spirited woman, a woman with great learning, and an ally to me in difficult times."

Jacques thought he detected in Khalif's voice more than a passing friendship.

"Do her honor, sir."

Khalif bowed a goodnight before pacing towards his far shelter.

"And take care of that prattling parrot," Petrine shouted.

"I shall," answered Khalif in the darkness.

Dominique watched sparks fly upward from the campfire. "I've prayed," she said quietly. "Aren't God's mighty heavens beautiful?" She waved her hand across the night sky. "I'll be glad to return home. Shall we be bound for France tomorrow?"

"No." Jacques blew on a piece of meat he held in his hand. "We've not yet found treasure."

"A good woman has been murdered," Dominique said. "We may be in some way responsible. Or we ourselves may be killed. Your scroll, Jacques—we go round and round."

"Part and parcel of our adventure."

"Adventuring—I now see—is no more than wandering whichever way the wind blows."

"I prefer to call it freedom, madame." An ember popped from the fire. Jacques cleared his throat. "I've given my all to our endeavors, you may agree. There have—"

"The violence sickens me," barked Dominique.

Jacques sniffed the meat he held on a spit and lowered it over some coals. He motioned for Dominique and Petrine to come nearer. Only Petrine moved.

Glaring into the ruby-red cinders, Jacques continued.

"What I discovered in Esther's library, and what appears on this," he said as he produced Fragonard's scroll, "confirmed to me that we must sail ..." From beneath his caftan, he produced several small books and set them in the sand next to him. He chose a thin one, held it near the fire, and showed its title.

"Have you forgotten?" snapped Dominique. "I don't read." She tossed the remainder of her meal into the fire, blasting a shower of orange sparks into the air.

"*Lisbon: Favored City of Christians* is the book's title," Petrine read as he leaned toward Jacques.

Jacques held out the book in his palm. "Ah," he said, "it again falls open on the twelfth page—just as it did at Esther's. Here is the sentence that struck me. 'Under the Moors, the city had various names: Lisbon, Lixbuna, Luzbona, Ulixbone, and Olissibona.'"

"I'm far from ignorant, master, but I see nothing here that tells us—"

"Look closely and cleverly. The word on our scroll, "SONBOISILA," is an anagram. An anagram made up of the letters from Olissibona. Lisbon."

Petrine's jaw dropped. "It is, master."

"Knowing I could probably make no headway with the esoteric verses on the scroll, Fragonard—with his personal advice—tied our mystery to the Templars. Researching the Templars in Rome lead us to the Stables of Solomon. I figure that past treasure hunters, hearing old Templar legends, excavated the stables. But they didn't have our advantage: the scroll. Those treasure hunters certainly found the intaglios—as we did—but the intaglios led them no further.

"The carved intaglios for us, on the other hand, connect to the intaglio on our scroll. Further, we've uncovered, in anagram form, a new scroll clue: Lisbon. My theory is that in Lisbon we'll discover other clues—and that the esoteric verses on our scroll will eventually specify the exact location of the treasure."

Petrine spoke. "So what Dominique shared with me—Esther's little tale—that the Templar Crusaders, upon leaving Jersualem, sailed to Lisbon—may be true?" His eyes reflected the frenzy of the campfire flames. "Treasure," he repeated in a crisp voice.

Dominique spoke. "Even if that were true—that they sailed to Lisbon—we can't be sure if they took treasure with them or buried it in Jerusalem."

"If the escaping Templars had the means to flee with their treasure aboard friendly Portuguese ships, why would they possibly chance leaving the treasure to a Muslim enemy? Well," Jacques said, stealing a look at Dominique, "the Dutch ship captain, Van Doormolen"—he sturdied his voice—"we're contracted to meet him in four days' time at Acre to sail west to Lisbon."

"What? Contracted? You've no right. What of Paris?" Dominique smashed her heel into the sand. "I'll not go to Lisbon."

"I'll not go to Paris."

Jacques' mouth felt dry. He glanced over his shoulder to make certain that no one was near and, calming his stormy gut, shifted around the fire closer to Dominique and took her hand in his. His face softened at the sight of the implacable woman who sat before him. "Fragoletta, I wish you to sail to Lisbon. The treasure we'll find there will allow you whatever you desire. If we find nothing in Lisbon ..." Jacques paused. "If we find no real treasure there, I promise it shall be our last destination, Dominique. I give you my word."

The wind began to whistle and whirl.

"You had no right," Dominique said. "No right." She jerked her hand, stood up, then marched toward their small shelter.

After Petrine bundled a blanket about himself to sleep, Jacques lay next to the fire and inspected Esther's six books, again pinching through each page of each thin volume as he had done a day earlier, but nothing of note met his gaze until he reached the last page of *Lisbon: Favored City of Christians*. The tiny identifying colophon matched the odd painting Francesco had made for Fragonard: the cross section of a chambered nautilus. Jacques' mind quickened. He stared at the inked device until, soon, the flickering fire invited his eyes to close, his mouth to open, and his nose to snore.

The book fell shut.

* * *

The next night of the journey, Khalif, warming his hands over the campfire, thundered aloud about the conquerors who had held sway in the region over the centuries.

Uninterested, Dominique gradually drifted a distance from the fire, where she found Petrine sitting, using his stiffened finger to draw on the surface of the cold sand.

"I didn't realize you can write," Dominique said. "What word do you mark?"

"I wrote my name," Petrine said without looking up. "Long ago I learned. The man who managed our acting troupe taught me to write and read. And to speak with big, important words." He picked up his cup, took a sip, then let out a braying laugh.

"Why the amusement?"

"He also taught me to avoid women whenever possible. I remember, and I laugh. But those are stories for another night." Petrine looked back at the ground. "Watch. With a sweep of my hand, I demolish the sand that briefly immortalizes my name."

Dominique stared out into the starry night. "An actor?" she mused. "An interesting existence?"

"I suppose. But after a time, I realized that trooping from town to town was a proposition whose charms had faded. I'm a very good actor, they say, and I enjoyed maneuvering people to laugh and cry. But there was little money. My stomach was weary of hunger, of starvation even." Petrine knifed his fingers into the sand. "So my teacher showed me how to better my station. To better my plight." His mouth warped into a grimace. "All I need now is—is *not* to be desperately poor. When I have much money, my name will not be obliterated by the sweep of a hand, my belly will not cramp hard from hunger."

Dominique sat listening intently.

"So I must—may I speak to another subject that troubles me, senora?"

"Why, surely."

Rubbing his wrist feverishly, Petrine glanced toward Khalif's campfire. "Esther's parrot," he uttered. "From whom do you think Esther's parrot learned those words Illustrissimo, si? Yes, Illustrious One?"

"Well, that subject—"

"Those words stay with me. Give me shivers. In the night. As does Esther, who comes to my dreams. Do you think the bird repeated what he heard from Esther's killer?"

"It seems possible.

"I wish I'd—we'd—never gone to Jerusalem. Never met that woman." Petrine quickly glanced at Dominique, then lowered his eyes.

"Disturbing, I agree."

Dominique watched Petrine stare into his coffee cup and waggle it round and round, its steamy contents sloshing over the lip of the chipped vessel. He poured his drink in the sand, sniffed at the cool night air, then bounding to his feet, hurried back toward the campfire.

Sensing the valet had spoken more plainly than he wished, Dominique called out. "I enjoyed our talk, Petrine. Again, soon."

She stood captivated, gazing at the glory of the starry threshold until before long her awe transformed into the sense that she might be only an immaterial speck in a vastness of sky and sand. "Sweet Jesus, protect us. Guide us," she prayed. "All of us."

- 27 -

ARRIVING IN ACRE, THE ADVENTURERS located Captain Van Doormolen's serviceable-looking *senau* that would provide sail across the waters of the Mediterranean—this time to Lisbon. After the passengers were boarded and their belongings had been stowed, the ship pushed out to sea.

The first day and night were uneventful. Things were about to change.

"*Videlicet*—that is to say, 'from one, learn to know all ...'" Jacques mouthed, his closed eyes not yet detecting the weak light of dawn seeping into the ship's hold.

As his hammock pitched to and fro, his mind hazily awoke, his nose assaulted by rotting timbers and brine. "Another day," he mumbled. "Seneca is correct. Sea travel is tedious."

Jacques vaguely recollected Captain van Doormolen in Crete. That was yesterday. Or was it the day before? His mind seemed unclear, numb. The last thing he was able to recall was the spry old captain cursing his crew when he'd uncovered the barrels of brackish water aboard. What a stink that had been.

"Help me survive this voyage," Jacques muttered while he drew in a chest full of air and opened his eyes.

He began to lift his arms but found both lashed tight to his hammock. A coil of thick hemp rope firmly encircled his body!

"What in the devil?" With all his strength Jacques struggled, but the rough rope only raked at his arms and torso. His smallsword was missing. And the dagger with which he'd slept? *Gone.*

"Pssst," came a popping of lips from behind him. "Jacques."

He stretched hard over his right shoulder and found Dominique's green eyes staring wide at him. She, too, was bound to her hammock berth, rocking back and forth at the mercy of the sea's watery pulse.

"Are you all—" Jacques fell silent. Just beyond Dominique, he saw a stark and perpendicular object. A knife. Buried in a passenger's belly. Jacques' innards grew cold.

His eyes remained on the sight a moment longer before glancing quickly around the small ship's hold. He saw two dozen passengers asleep—or scared silent—men, women, and children. All held fast by rope, rags, even articles of clothing. Jacques felt as if an anvil crushed his body.

"Dominique," he gasped again, "are you all right?"

"Yes," came the whisper.

"Is Petrine—?"

"He sleeps directly behind you."

"Sleeps?"

"I believe. Or drugged. We all must have been."

"Bound tight?"

"Yes."

Jacques listened to the stamp of boots on the deck above, his heart galloping. For a moment he thought he understood the strange language, but surging water against the ship's hull drowned out the voices. While daylight wavered its way into the senau's hold, he decided a course of action.

"Petrine," he announced.

No answer.

"Petrine," Jacques said. "Do you serve me?"

"*Certainment*, master," came the groggy reply. "Certainly."

"Dominique—"

Jacques stopped himself cold when indistinct shadows stole across the walls of the hold.

A half-dozen ruffians with long knives at the waist appeared among the rows of hammocks. One gruff man wearing a red felt cap and embroidered red waistcoat ordered the release of the children, one by one, until a half dozen were directed at musket point to the deck above.

The red felt cap and the scimitar, Jacques knew, signified Turks, known for—his next thought made him tremble—a fearsome cruelty toward Christian women and children.

Several of the men eyed Dominique while they strode by. Moments later, Jacques spied Petrine—his body like a sack of potatoes—being lugged between two ruffians.

"Till we meet again, master. At our port of destination."

"In Lisbon, Petrine, Lisbon."

The Turks disappeared topside. For most of the trip from Acre, Petrine had been as sick as a cat at sea. Now the sorry Spaniard would no doubt be sold into slavery. Jacques' stomach knotted in pain.

He clenched his fists and strained his head sideways to give Dominique a heartening look, but her eyes were closed. He wanted to howl. *It was I who persuaded her to sail!*

The ship creaked and groaned. Beleaguered by the immediate future, Jacques shut his stinging eyes.

"The last time I saw you, you cradled a corpse like your lover." The voice was coarse, malicious.

"That corpse was my brother," whispered Jacques forcefully. The reek of alcohol annoyed him. He glared into the dark liquid eyes of Carlo Brose, longtime nemesis, sometimes accomplice, and always, it seemed, persistent shadow.

"Last time we met, you owned a nose," Jacques said. "Now, whoremaster, you've a flat black patch where it should be."

"You may recall that at your Voltaire fête I had on a mask that covered my face. Yes, I did possess *some* nose that night, but it was decaying even then. Ulcerated."

Turning his head away, Jacques spat. He felt sickened. Brose faced an impending and painful death. He glanced back at his rival. "So, the pox then?"

"Sadly, yes. And such a magnificent nose it was."

"Sadly, no."

Brose shoved a small crate under his rump and sat next to Jacques' hammock, pushing it to and fro. "No need for me to be brief. Seeing as you're not going anywhere and the Turks won't be back soon, we might even find time to—"

"How do you manage to be onboard this ship, Carlo Brose? And who holds us captive?"

"You shun my playfulness?" Brose swigged from a small bottle. "Let me see, let me see. It was not long after you were hounded out of Paris I peddled my exceptional chair to a certain Comte. My chair, you may recall, guaranteed success with the opposite sex. I would—"

"Your diabolical chair, you mean. To mechanically subdue a woman in a chair—to render her helpless—so that some depraved aristo might notch a rape? I cringe at your revolting perversion."

"Calumny, Herr Adventurer, calumny."

The wail of a passenger momentarily interrupted Brose, but he turned back to Jacques.

"My exceptional chair seemed inadequate for the Comte's needs," he continued. "The Comte complained—whereupon I was bid, at the king's pleasure, to depart Paris. Given the state of my health, I decided a cruise might do me good. And it was, in fact, restful. Until these Algerine corsairs, many of them Muslims, some of them *renegadoes*, captured and sank my vessel in early September. Such is the life of adventuring, is it not? So since you ask, *that* is how I came to be on this ship."

"And yet, you're not bound as am I and these others?"

Carlo Brose ignored the remark, placed his lips to the bottle, and drank. "As for discovering your whereabouts today, Piccinio, the renegado captain, was informed the prisoners stank of foul garlic. At once I knew Jacques Casanova to be aboard," Brose laughed.

"Our situation is hardly a matter for jest."

"Do you not wonder how you and the rest of these passengers came to be captured so easily? One of the Algerine corsairs masqueraded as a paying passenger aboard this ship. He drugged the water in the barrels—the brackish water, remember? These corsairs, you see, rely on their cannon and flintlocks only as a last resort. They much prefer deceit. Oh, I saw their methods: once the Algerines had been signaled that most everyone aboard your ship was drugged, they put a small boat afloat. They tied strips of sacking round the oars to deaden the sound of their rowing, and upon scaling your ship and taking it, the first thing they did was roll your Dutch captain and his men in rugs and heave them overboard. There's a burial for you. The rest of you are fortunate."

With his head, Jacques motioned to the corpse with the knife in it. "How is it you are free and these passengers are not?"

Brose scratched the black patch that covered what used to be flesh. "Providence seems to provide for those in need, Jacques."

"Hah."

"These Muslim Turks are reasonable enough, I suppose. It's the renegadoes—the Christians converted to Muslims—that seem to possess a special vindictiveness." Brose flapped his lips. "You ask how I saved myself? I have, to my eternal credit, shown my fellow poxers different ways to administer the great cure."

"Mercury?"

"Yes. Having the choice of booty or curative, it was the medicinal mercury these Turks went for first when they captured our sail. I was quick to realize, naturally, that I should be the one to demonstrate they could inhale mercury, take it by pill, or even swallow a decoction. Till then these corsairs—who understand my French, by the way—only knew to mix the element with fat and rub it on different body parts. I'm therefore a revered healer to these barbarous dogs."

"Healer?" Jacques said. "If mercury does not poison a man outright, it will rot his teeth and guts."

"You should know."

"I do know."

"And did the great cure make you piss blood?"

"Too many times," admitted Jacques. Both men laughed.

Brose offered a sip from his bottle and Jacques accepted—Brose dispensing the liquor to Jacques' lips.

"Well, in a world where two sword thrusts, a broken leg, and bad water have not killed me, I've been favored by fortune to be missing only a nose."

"Yes, and I avoided the smallpox, yellow fever, influenza, bubonic plague, and other assorted pestilences so that I might end my days as a captive of piratical Turks and the confidant to a poxy adventurer. Carlo Brose, we've both been favored by fortune."

Laughing aloud, Brose again pushed on Jacques' hammock.

After his gaiety subsided, he spoke softly. "I'm a favorite with the crew. They look at me, realize what may happen when the disease goes too far, and they take their mercury cure like good schoolboys." He coughed into his fist. "So it's true, I've actually witnessed these renegadoes take sensible action on occasion. Nevertheless, it appeared to me that, even though I administer the cure, it was possible they might enslave me at some future date. So I supplied them with two further reasons that keep me securely aboard."

"Which were?"

"A miraculous demonstration convinced them I could convert glass into diamonds." Brose's eyes danced with devilish merriment. "You know the trick, fellow, do you not?"

Jacques grinned and nodded his head. "You'd previously secreted gems in your anus that they could not—or chose not to—recover?"

"Yes. And reason number two that keeps me aboard?" Brose lingered, his faltering speech indicating a confession of sorts. "I turned Turk. I converted, Jacques, to Muslim."

"Apostasy? Catholics and Protestants alike will roast you alive when they get their hands on you."

Brose took a long draw from his bottle and waited an even longer time before he spoke. He then bent to whisper, his deep bass rustling Jacques' ear. "Let's not equivocate. I've not long to live. My nose is gone. I feel the sickness in my bones. My mind, I must tell you, is baneful. I rant on occasion. Nevertheless," he said, giving Jacques' hammock another slight push, "why should I not accept Allah? I believe Jesus the Christ is the Son of God—while I acknowledge Allah as the true God. In essence, I've adopted a variation of Monsieur Pascal's wager. I've accepted two gods and therefore double my odds that this riddled body will be healed and this diseased soul may be saved." Emotion fogged the voice of Carlo Brose. He looked away.

"So your soul may be saved?" Jacques smirked. "What soul?"

A sudden roll of the ship produced a gasp from the nearby prisoners.

"You did what you had to do," Jacques said with kindness.

Brose gave a neat, sad smile.

Jacques knew it was time to voice his concern for Dominique. "Carlo Brose, I'm troubled for the safety of the woman in the hammock behind me as well as my Spanish manservant, who has been taken topside."

Brose glanced at Dominique, who lay with her eyes shut.

"Yes, I recall your blonde beauty. But as for your servant, I make it a point not to have a valet in my hire. That way I'm certain I'll not be robbed nor have a spy at my heels."

"I tell you, I'm anxious for the both of them."

"Why, I've never known Jacques Casanova to be unselfish." Carlo Brose finished off the bottle and plunked it to the floor. "You're much changed."

"Doubtful," Jacques said. "Find out how I can be released. And discover what you can about the tall Turk who to me appears to be primo lieutenant. More especially, uncover the corsair captain— what's his name—Piccinio?—uncover his aim."

"Herr Adventurer, you may be assured I shall put spurs to my flank." Brose took a last look at the passengers bound in their hammocks and, leading with his disfigured face, stumbled toward the deck ladder and the streaming light from topside.

Jacques lay still, hoping the base fellow would remember his drunken promise.

*   *   *

Later that morning, two of the crew came round with a sponge of water and a few bites of porridge for each prisoner. Many begged for release from their berth, but no deliverance came. What did come for many was vomiting and defecation—and the vile stench from those acts.

If there remained anything tolerable, it was that the ship sailed smoothly. The sea was quiet.

During the course of the day, Dominique spoke with Jacques, who was beginning to pale in face and spirit. The conversations she held, she figured, becalmed others around her and allayed her own fears as well. To be sure, she was grateful to God that she still had her wits—which was much more than many of the others. *But Jacques and I must make a plan. We must.*

In guarded talk, Dominique let Jacques know he'd been spouting Fragonard's verses aloud in his sleep the night before.

"Most likely, it eases the chatter in my brain, Dominique. But I'll think on Fragonard's verses here and now during my waking hours." He closed his eyes. "My salvation in previous times, especially in I Piombi hellhole, was my imagination. I'll yet use that resource, weak as I feel."

"We're being propelled toward the ineffable rewards of the Lord," Dominique answered.

During the afternoon, the gentle rock of the hammock, the creaking of the ship's timbers, and the warmth of the hold encouraged Dominique to nap. But before the light began to wane, her eyes flickered open. What she smelled put a quiver on her lip: the musty sweet scent of moldering blood.

A tall man stood with his back to her. Tied across his shoulder with a thick cord was a cloth sack caked with dark red blood. Peeking from the open end of the sack was the instrument causing Dominique's abhorrent feelings: a cat-o'-nine-tails. She'd never felt the sting from the lead tips of a scourge, but she'd seen it in action. To witness the flaying of a human being was one of the sharpest regrets of her life. The experience had bred nightmares for years.

Sensing that Jacques was fast asleep, Dominique dared another look at the profile of the corsair who carried the foul, bloody sack. Judging from the embroidered red waistcoat and red felt hat, he was the Turk who earlier that day Jacques had styled the "primo lieutenant." The man had undistinguished eyes, black hair and mustache, and a complexion burnt rough and dark by the sun. He strutted back and forth between the hammocks before motioning to a squat mate.

A moment later, Dominique felt rough burlap ride between her teeth. She choked on the gag. It seemed her head was exploding but her mind worked frantically.

Maintaining his swagger, the tall primo lieutenant surveyed the prisoners, all of whom were now gagged as well as bound. Wheeling about, he wiped his mustache with his hand, then stuffed his hand into his bulky pants. Daylight in the hold was quickly fading, but enough light remained for Dominique to catch the glint in his eyes when he stared at Jacques.

The primo lieutenant signaled his friend. Moments later, Jacques was double gagged. With bound legs and arms, Jacques—now fully awake—struggled to no avail.

The squat mate climbed above deck, leaving the primo lieutenant alone with the prisoners. The man moved to Jacques and bent over, grabbing Jacques' throat with both his hands.

Jacques! Dominique tried to scream but her gag made it impossible. Streams of sweat burned her eyes while she watched the corsair loosen his grip. *The scroll*, she feared. *The scroll!*

The corsair lowered himself to his knee to tighten the rope that restrained Jacques. He gently drew his hand across the adventurer's face.

With his remaining strength, Jacques arched. The lieutenant clamped Jacques' nose and mouth. Jacques stopped his struggle. The corsair released his hold.

Jacques panted through his gag, his frenzied wheeze slicing like razors through Dominique's heart.

The primo lieutenant—bulbous eyes pitching back in his head—paid no heed to the muffled cries of the passengers when he tore open Jacques' shirt and began to caress his flesh.

The primo lieutenant's hand continued its slithery journey.

Dominique thrashed against the hammock, infuriated to a degree she'd never felt before. She squeezed her eyes shut.

When at last she persuaded herself to look, she saw, in the last daylight of the ship's hold, the corsair stroking himself.

Jacques' face was hidden from view, but Dominique saw from his taut neck and stiff shoulders—his seething. A vast rage boiled in her.

For what seemed to Dominique an eternity of debasement and horror, the mustached corsair continued his depraved work. When his pleasure slaked in a deafening groan, scalding tears shot down Dominique's cheeks.

While the primo lieutenant plodded toward the deck ladder, Dominique choked back her revulsion.

Her long night overflowed with desolate and desperate loathing.

* * *

"Who put these nauseating gags in your mouth?" croaked Carlo Brose.

Dawn's rays snuck into the hold while he leaned close to Jacques, inspecting the filthy cloths. "I likely risk my life if I remove these. Well, remove them I shall." He scratched the patch on his face and undid the cloths.

Jacques sucked hard breaths into his lungs.

"Quick! Untie Dominique's," Jacques said. "See to it." Jacques paused. "I ask your help."

"What has come over you?" Brose grinned. "You again *ask* my help?" He moved to Dominique's hammock, loosed her gag, then scuttled back to Jacques. "She sleeps peacefully," he gestured. "As for the Turk you wondered about, Jacques—your primo lieutenant— I found out he's out of favor with most of the Algerine crew," he said, standing over Jacques' hammock. He narrowed his eyes, then sputtered. "What goes on? Ah, nose or no nose I smell the situation. That swarthy heathen! Thought he had the look about him. Well, for the Muslims to have a young boy—their religion does not discourage that. To have a man of your years—well, I see you inspired the Turk's fancy," he sniveled gleefully. "May I tell him you've amused yourself with others before him?"

Jacques glanced over his shoulder. Dominique still slept.

"It's true, isn't it? With the handsome Duc de Longueville and also with ..." Sweat bubbled Jacques' forehead, but he said nothing.

The two men glared, each daring the other to speak.

Then Brose's eyes softened. "I recall you liked it rough, Jacques."

Color rose in Jacques' cheeks. His tone was gentle. "You're mistaken, Carlo. A fond nature was more to my liking."

"I remember. We could afford to be tender to one another. We were young and did not know the devilish world as we do now."

Jacques nodded.

"You broke my heart," said Brose. He looked away. When he returned to Jacques' gaze, he had a playful gleam in his eye.

"So shall I relay to the primo lieutenant that you have experience?"

"No, do not tell him, Carlo. It would lessen my worth with him. Let him think that he means to possess me, the maid."

Brose placed his palm on Jacques' cheek before he spoke.

"One thing else. It would be helpful to your cause if you yourself turned Turk."

"I will not. I prefer to—"

"You're not a Christian! Well, you might die like a Christian." Brose coughed. "Let me be honest, Jacques Casanova. I came to you this morning already knowing you'd caught the big Turk's fancy— for I overheard certain things late last night. You now may as well know that a ransom for you was agreed upon by the crew and paid by the lieutenant."

Mindful of any signs or sounds of captors on the deck above, Jacques spoke quietly. "Ransom me? What does the captain say?"

"As nearly as I can gather, there are no rules to govern this particular circumstance, but these corsairs—who fancy themselves a floating republic—cast votes on most all issues. The corsair captain? His response was 'Keep the prisoners alive. No one will ransom dead men.' He also forbids the rape of women and children because he knows rich Muslims relish unsullied Christian prisoners for their bagnios and harems. Practical man," Brose repeated softly. "So if you, Jacques Casanova, are as impoverished as I suppose, and with no one on the mainland to pay for you, the Turk lieutenant has ransomed you from certain slavery.

"To be a private, special slave."

- 28 -

SHORTLY AFTER BROSE SLIPPED AWAY, two corsairs entered the hold, released Jacques from his hammock, manacled him, did the same to a dozen other prisoners, then led all topside. Before long, other male and female prisoners were brought on deck, some glaring at the red half-moon flag that fluttered on the mast, some staring blankly out to sea.

Squinting sullenly into the bright sun, Jacques found he could hardly stand. His legs wanted to fold in two. But glimpsing the pale blue sky, he saw a magnificent morning on the Mediterranean—blustery, but beautiful. He wondered if this would be his last day as a free man.

Here came Dominique, lumped into a group coming topside. From his position in the front row of prisoners, Jacques managed a reassuring nod to her before she was shoved into line not far to his left. Her eyes, he could tell, were swollen.

Trying to calm himself, Jacques surveyed the cargo strewn haphazardly around the mizzenmast: indigo, silk, damask, and velvet. Spices and exotic wine bottles piled near the bow. Many vessels had been plundered by the corsairs and probably many prisoners sold into slavery.

Jacques' breaths clustered sort and shallow. He reined back his maudlin thoughts and forced his mind into quick service. He saw no loose weapons in sight. He wondered how he might bargain for one. And from whom? He considered that his card playing might somehow rescue Dominique, Petrine, and himself. Or later, could he possibly persuade Carlo Brose to cut his bindings, to release him from his hammock prison below deck?

The masts and rigging quaked as a gust of wind billowed the canvases. While spume shot over the bowsprit and onto the deck, Jacques stared angrily at the manacles on his wrists. *I'll first rid myself of these.* His body shivered uncontrollably while the sprays of seawater continued their drenching. Maybe it would cleanse him; he'd soiled his breeches several times in the ship's hold.

From the corner of his eye, Jacques spied a red embroidered waistcoat; his mind fumed when he realized the primo lieutenant stood across the deck.

A pair of corsairs positioned themselves in front of Jacques; the two twisted his manacles until his palms turned upward.

Jacques winced. He knew the Turks would learn much from the prisoners' hands: If a man had no calluses, he was a blue blood. If there were telltale ink stains to see, the corsairs would know the prisoner was literate and bring a higher ransom. *Who would think these soft hands would determine my fate?*

It seemed to Jacques his body had never ached with such pain. *My future, though, is not the same as these other prisoners. I'm already ransomed.* He flinched. *But a month or a lifetime with the Turk will be worse than a coffin.*

The corsairs continued down the line of prisoners. Examining hands took time— time for Jacques to peek at Dominique. She was haggard, fragile. What would he not give to turn back the clock?

A voice whispered from somewhere just behind Jacques. Carlo Brose.

"The man conferring with your lieutenant—the thickset fellow cloaked in the frayed burnoose—he's the *rais*, you see. He made a name for himself by capturing and plundering a papal galley. Since then he's vanquished everything on the horizon while fighting his jihad, his holy war, for Allah. The sexton, on the rais's orders, calls these Muslims to holy prayer to Allah six times a day. Anyhow, from what the crew says, this captain, this rais, makes up for his short stature with enormous ferocity. To me it also seems the rais has a talent for leadership. To me—"

Suddenly, the man about whom Brose spoke threw off his burnoose and strode forward, facing the three rows of prisoners.

"Happiness belongs to those who honor Allah and also fear him," he shouted. The crew standing behind the captain clapped raucously.

"Years ago I turned my back on a false religion. I encourage you to do likewise. You shall be blessed by Allah; this I promise."

Speaks a little like a Venetian, thought Jacques. *And with brimming confidence.*

The sails overhead snapped loudly in the breeze as another buffeting spray rained down.

The rais motioned to the captives. "There's one of you who is ready to join my Algerines, my crew. I am Piccinio Rais, and I welcome this man."

A pack of Algerines scurried toward the line of prisoners, unshackled Jacques, and led him forward.

At once, Jacques saw his chance. He instantly plunged himself to one knee before the rais—which placed him nearly face-to-face with the short captain.

Jacques felt the points of two Algerine knives at his back.

"Piccinio Rais," Jacques cried without moving a muscle. "Your reputation on the seas is a great one. I'm pleased to be aboard your ship and in the grace of Allah. Is it true I've been ransomed by a fine and loyal Algerine?"

The rais made a quick sign, and the Algerine corsairs lowered their daggers.

The man understands my words. And his cunning tells him to be content until I have my say.

Piccinio Rais stepped forward, placed his fingertips on Jacques' head, made an emphatic gesture with his opposite hand, then with a flick of his fingers motioned the primo lieutenant forward. The lieutenant, dark mustache bristling, complied—leering at Jacques.

Jacques sprang to his feet. He felt two daggers press deeper at his shoulder blades, and—although immediately forced back to his knees—he shouted in a booming voice.

"I'm a free man. I'm not to be purchased like a cheap sow. If this corsair chooses to ransom me—if he wants me—let him fight me for my freedom."

There was silence from all on deck.

The rais held his dagger at the ready.

Sails again ruffled in the wind until another commotion—the rattling of manacles—brought attention to a slight figure who thrust her body apart from the line of captives.

No one on deck was more shocked than Jacques. His mind raced. What? Had she lost her senses?

"This corsair wants the prisoner?" Dominique nodded toward the primo lieutenant. Her brows knit in a furor. "I say I want the prisoner. Whose prayers shall Allah answer?"

The Algerines taunted, some clapped.

Dominique continued, shrill anger in her clear-born voice. A handful of prisoners—encouraged by her passion—rattled their manacles in support.

This was not overlooked by Piccinio Rais, who, Jacques saw, seemed enthused by Dominique's display of bravada.

"If this mustached swine wants the prisoner, let him win the prisoner," she shouted full throat. "I mean for this ugly pig to fight me. Whoever draws first blood wins the prisoner."

Jacques' heart crashed through his chest. "She must not fight," he screamed toward the mob of corsairs. "She can be ransomed. Ransomed. You'll get riches for her!"

A multitude of voices roared across deck.

The rais thrust his dagger into the sunlight for all to see, then whipped the blade to Jacques' throat.

The bold move had its effect. All hushed.

The rais, reducing his eyes to slits, surveyed the prisoners, Dominique, the lieutenant, and his corsairs. "Let it be known I command this ship," he cried. "And I propose to slice the prisoner in two. A half for each party." When he met the moist eyes of his kneeling prisoner, he paused before removing the dagger from Jacques' throat.

He marched to Dominique, striding a proud circle around her. "Let it be understood that this fair-haired woman—she has the heart of a lion. But for this suffering prisoner," the rais pointed to Jacques, "this woman has the heart of a girl. Allah esteems such a spirit."

Piccinio Rais now motioned toward his lieutenant. "This Algerine, too, has a fortitude Allah admires. I have witnessed him in battle. He's daring, he's strong." The rais spoke to the sky above. "Which of these two shall Allah deem worthy to carry the day?"

A fiery voice delivered itself from the crowd. "Let them draw first blood."

The crew erupted in a clamor.

The rais raised his dagger for silence. "It's true, we corsairs pride ourselves on our independence. In this world we take our bearings, make our rules and sail our own course. This is why we allow the woman prisoner to speak her heart. This is why my brethren shall vote theirs."

The corsairs hastily retired to the stern of the ship, leaving several Algerines to guard the shackled prisoners. Jacques was manacled, then jostled back into line. He glanced toward Dominique, who was being shoved back into her place with the others.

Afternoon came while the corsairs deliberated. Soon the warm sun and breeze had its way: two men abreast of Jacques passed out on their feet, crumpling to the deck. A violent jerk of the ears from their captor was enough to bring each prisoner stirringly awake.

After a long interval, the rais returned with his crew.

"It is decided. This corsair," shouted Piccinio Rais as he pointed to his lieutenant, "and that woman," he said, pointing to Dominique, "shall fight."

The crew lauded the decision with whistles and clapping.

The rais took an ominous tone. "My brethren have altered one condition of the combat. The fight will not end with first blood. The fight will end with death. The living combatant shall own that prisoner." He indicated Jacques with a nod of his head.

Jacques' knees buckled. He summoned his strength to speak, but it was the rais who spoke first.

"Either fighter may withdraw from this combat, and Allah will place no shame on either. I await your choice."

Dominique was the first to step forward. "I fight."

"No!" Jacques screamed. "No!"

The cries that arose from corsairs and prisoners alike drowned his further screams.

Jacques' back grew taut as a tree.

The lieutenant—opposite Dominique—advanced. In his native tongue—most likely Berber—he turned and shouted to the crew. He was met with jeers.

He addressed his captain, who then wheeled and faced Dominique and the prisoners.

"The corsair offers you the choice of weapons: knife, pistol, sword"—the captain turned to the crew—"or belaying pin." He was favored with hoots from his men.

Dominique did not flinch. "Smallsword," she said. "You will kindly retrieve my belongings and the belongings of your prisoner, where you will find a case of smallswords. Two smallswords." She thrust her manacled hands toward the lieutenant. "That ship swine shall have one of them."

"Stop," cried Jacques. "Wait. I have treasure. I have a map to treasure."

"No, Jacques, no," Dominique cried.

"Here. Here in the back of my shirt. Piccinio Rais, look for yourself."

The rais advanced toward Jacques. "Treasure?" he said. He promptly ripped Jacques' ragged shirt from his body, and out fell Fragonard's scroll. A corsair fetched the furled parchment and handed it to Piccinio Rais, who unrolled it and studied it momentarily. He sidled next to Jacques and spoke coolly. "These Algerines must search you better next time, fellow." He threw a glance to the primo lieutenant and gave a yelping laugh.

A thousand fears tumbled in Jacques' heart, but he could find no words for them; the best he could do was keep from squirming before the captain.

Piccinio Rais tucked the scroll in his breeches and marched to the center of the deck, where he motioned to Dominique, then the lieutenant.

"Smallsword," he commanded. "To the death."

"No," Jacques cried as several corsairs grabbed him by the shoulders. His struggle was of no use, and he knew the outcome inevitable. *She'll die. And I'll be a minion of the Turk.*

- 29 -

WHEN PICCINIO RAIS LOWERED HIS HAND to his side, Jacques was quickly carted to the ship's mast, hoisted up, and lashed to the spar several meters above the deck. The spar rope tightly squeezed his arms and upper body, leaving his feet to dangle loosely. He felt as if a vulture prodded his insides. His whole lifetime he'd practiced a chivalry that demanded he defend the damsel. Dominique now defended him. He stared down at the adventuress. *After she's gone, I'll find a way to kill the primo lieutenant.*

A contingent of Barbary corsairs ran below decks and minutes later crowded topside, attired in fine garments.

Salt to the wound! Jacques struggled against his rope bindings. *Do these cutthroats think they attend a wedding? Dressed in their dandified, plundered clothes. A killing should not be a cause for such celebration.*

Blazing sun now washed the ship's deck. When the breeze stilled, the rais ordered sentinels posted on the mast high above Jacques. He knew no rescue would come. The Muslim captain was too shrewd to be taken at sea like a floating turtle.

To further the bizarre atmosphere, Piccinio Rais gave orders to a host of Turks, who soon came back with kettledrums, oboes, bugles, and cymbals. *These heathens play for sieges, battles, boardings, but why would ...* Sweat rolled from Jacques' forehead as he realized the answer. *None of us has ever seen a woman—Muslim, Christian, or pagan—fight a duel. To bloody death.*

As soon as the Turkish band raised a strange and heinous overture, Jacques wanted to stop his ears. The rais was doing everything in his power to make the odious contest a memorable affair and thus promote his fame.

While the tumult continued, Dominique and the primo lieutenant were conducted to positions opposite one another on deck. The frenzied mob, bundling into a human ring around the duelists, matched the tempestuous martial music.

Jacques studied Dominique's face below. Her assurance was still present. She stood bravely, keenly sighting her enemy. As for the lieutenant—he held a very small sword in his huge hand. *It feels too light to him*, Jacques thought. *He's used to a far bigger weapon.*

While Jacques' eyes ranged, his heart ached at the spectacle below him.

Among the onlookers, he spied Carlo Brose propped weakly against a barrel, knotting his stringy hair. *A painful, poxy death will be too good for him.*

All hushed. The circle of corsairs spread wide as Piccinio Rais stepped to center deck. His eyes gleaming, he cried out a short speech before situating himself prominently on deck stairs above the scene, then with a grandiloquent gesture, initiated the duel to the death.

The rope hugged Jacques' ribs hard when the ship slowly listed back and forth; he sucked in shallow breaths—all that his constraints allowed.

The Turk slashed the air with his blade, the menacing hiss severing the silence. He slashed again. To gauge his new weapon. To unnerve Dominique.

"Stay brave, Dominique!"

She had time for one doleful glance at Jacques before the hulking Turk advanced, slicing. At his back, stuffed into a wide belt, bobbed a sack with his cat-o'-nine-tails. It swung wildly until the Turk stopped at the middle of the deck and opened wide his arms, a taunting invitation for Dominique to attack him.

Her sword point shook uncontrollably, but as quick as a hare, she charged the Turk. Instantly, he cut at her head. She ducked as she passed and deftly sunk the point of her sword into the Turk's bare foot. The man shrieked in agony as his blood showered onto the deck.

The captives and corsairs who encircled the fighters howled. The martial band doubled the tempo of its freakish tune, the kettledrums generating wailing bloodlust from the mob.

"Finish it, Dominique," Jacques cried. "Finish him."

The Turk clapped a hand on his spurting wound, then calmly wiped blood across his face. His eyes protruded through the crimson smear, revealing a heart of butchery. A new spray of blood gushed from his foot as he lurched at Dominique.

She evaded the vicious hack, but the Turk's cuts came faster and fiercer until she was in full retreat. Barely sidestepping another killing blow, Dominique edged away from the blood-smeared Turk to the railing of the ship.

Writhing against his bonds, Jacques watched the incensed lieutenant forge his way across deck. There was no place for Dominique to go but the sea.

Dominique held her *en garde* while the Turk advanced. Suddenly his feet flew skyward in a stream of slippery blood. He thudded to the deck, flailing on his back. Dominique rushed forward.

The mob's roar erupted when the Turk managed to beat away Dominique's attacking sword point. She turned and redoubled her effort, but her second assault, another thrust, missed the Turk completely when she lost her footing in the gore. The Turk leapt to his feet, his cat-o'-nine-tails banging to-and-fro behind him.

He picked his way to the drier perimeter of the deck, the crowd creeping back as he drew near Dominique. With features black, the Turk began a grim stalk. Around and around.

He'll wear down her nerve, expects her to falter. Jacques' throat felt raw. His nose drew in the sweet smell of blood. How long could Dominique prevail against the behemoth?

Jacques saw it. Swinging loosely at the Turk's back, the cat-o'-nine-tails roped itself around an object—a belaying pin on the railing—braking his advance. The Turk glanced over his shoulder.

At once, Dominique executed a jump-lunge—her sword in full extension—and hurtled toward her opponent.

Spinning, the Turk parried too early, missing her blade entirely. Dominique's sword point shot through bone and brain and out the back of the Turk's head, splashing flesh, blood, and bits of skull skyward. The man toppled to the deck. The martial music waned and died.

Dominique twisted away from the sight, then collapsed.

From the crowd, Carlo Brose reeled forward, coughing. A moment later, Piccinio Rais stepped to the main deck.

Blistering sweat raced down Jacques' face as he joined the explosion of shouts.

Within moments, he was unlashed from the spar, and his manacles were removed. He was positioned near Dominique, who now was propped upright, flanked by a pair of corsairs. Jacques watched while the remaining prisoners were shuffled down into the hold. *Dominique is well enough. She breathes.*

Piccinio Rais marched forward through the blood, parading round about the dead lieutenant. "I salute our valiant mate, who forfeits his earthly life. May he consort in heaven with seventy-two virgins."

Raucous shouts split the morning air, and many of the corsairs raised a fist toward the clear blue sky.

Jacques recalled what Brose had first confided, that the primo lieutenant was out of favor with the Algerine crew.

"It seems, prisoner," Piccinio Rais said, strutting toward Jacques, "that at present, you belong to this woman. Praise be to Allah, who inspired her with the courage to win you." The rais stretched his arms tall and wide. "As all Muslims know, however, a woman must not own a man. Therefore, as rais of this ship, I declare you to be free. You'll be placed on the next passing ship—bound for your home."

Jacques bit his cheek hard and, as best as he could, made a sweeping bow. *This cannot be. I must act.*

Piccinio Rais motioned at Dominique, who stood in shock. "It seems also," he said, "that Allah has determined a favorable fate for you. A private ransom will be paid for your person by this gentleman." The Muslim ship captain brandished his fist to his left and watched Carlo Brose stagger to his side.

What? Brose ransoms her? Jacques thought. *Why? To gain revenge against me. With his ransom, the man snatches Dominique from me! Retaliates for all the indignities I've ever heaped on him.*

Jacques stared at Dominique, who, panting like a dog, seemed unable to comprehend what had transpired.

Carlo Brose veered toward the rais and managed a shake of his head. He turned back to Jacques.

"O abominable rival, compound of the base and the noble," proclaimed Brose, "you and I have pointed the dagger at each other's hearts for years." He stabbed roughly with his fingers toward Jacques.

When the corsairs hooted out their approval, Carlo Brose spun, faced the bulk of them, and flicked his other hand toward Jacques. "Now it seems chance has favored me to be the instrument of this man's fate."

Jacques felt the breath burn out of him.

Brose tapped the patch on his face. "Great Piccinio Rais, my nose is not so far decayed that I do not sniff a good thing. Jacques Casanova is a free man, and I will presently have ownership of this woman."

Jacques seemed to sag with every word Brose spoke.

Carlo Brose pointed toward Dominique, then took from his pockets two small objects that glinted in the sunshine. He held them, one in each hand, high overhead before presenting them to the Rais. "I now purpose, with these two diamonds," Brose said, "to ransom this woman. I then purpose to furnish Jacques Casanova this woman as a means to make amends for the wrongs I've done him."

Jacques gawked at the man who marked the speech.

"Allah has granted this wisdom," cried Brose, "and I pray He shall look favorably upon my deed."

Loud acclamations rang from the corsairs.

Dare I believe my ears, thought Jacques? *If captain and crew allow Brose's proposition, Dominique and I will be freed—to be reunited.*

He turned toward Dominique. Her gleaming green eyes told him his hearing was true. He swallowed hard on the lump in his throat.

Piccinio Rais slapped his hand against the back of Carlo Brose, who nearly collapsed from the blow. Brose then moved unsteadily toward Jacques and, for a long moment, managed a salutation, his fingers against his forehead. "Tired, so tired," were his drawn-out words as he shambled past toward the ship's hold.

* * *

By early afternoon, Piccinio Rais had fed Jacques and Dominique with the best food aboard and allowed them to choose garments from the pile in his cabin. Surrounded by nautical instruments and a number of sea charts, the three relaxed around the captain's table over their fourth glass of Scopolo wine.

"So you now know from my own mouth," Piccinio Rais said, "I was once a citizen of Venice."

"And a Christian, *n'est-ce pas*? Is that so?" Dominique said, her face red with the flush of alcohol.

"Yes, a Christian," nodded the rais. "Before Allah lightened my spirit." Piccionio Rais fixed his bloodshot eyes on Jacques. "But to put a finer point on our previous conversation, I, a son of Venice, heard of a dazzling feat carried out by a certain citizen of that republic. Are you the one, the only man, ever to escape from that infamy called I Piombi, the Leads?"

Dominique swung her face toward Jacques.

Elbow on table, chin in hand, Jacques lifted his head and lazily bowed it. "I am he, the one who had the grand misfortune to be out of favor with the Inquisitori de Stato."

"You are? You are he?" Piccinio Rais smacked his lips. "Had you confirmed your famous name this morning when I first addressed you, you'd have been paladin of this vessel."

"What's the time?" Jacques asked. "Am I too late for renown?"

Dominique and the rais laughed.

The rais pushed a dish of *kavurma* past Dominique toward Jacques. "I wish you to tell me of your exploit," he slurred.

"It's a long tale," Dominique warned, "but a worthy adventure. I've heard this man's story, and I wager he has the memory and the wit to do it justice."

"This woman is emboldened by the excellent wine, Piccinio Rais. But she's correct. It's a lengthy and improbable tale."

"But genuine?"

"Yes."

The rais spoke. "I spent, it seems, several hundred years in that prison, Signor Casanova. I ask you—I insist—you share your escape." He opened both hands in a friendly gesture. "If you recount your deeds, you may expect bounty in return. What is it you desire?"

"The freedom of all captives aboard this ship."

The rais spoke, situating both palms flat on the table. "These hands do not possess that power. Nor would I ask the crew to relinquish the prisoners and the ransom those prisoners will undoubtedly bring. It cannot and will not be done."

Jacques waited some time before he again responded.

"Then find and release my Spanish valet, Petrine. If he still lives. And return my scroll."

"The return of your valet," the rais laughed, "and your scroll piece, both of these are within my power."

Dominique pointed at Jacques. "It goes without saying that this man will need his two pistols, his smallswords, and his dagger."

"It goes without saying."

Dominique smiled.

"One added thing ..." she said as she tipped her chair toward the short man, scooped her hand around her mouth, and leaned to whisper in his ear.

"Lisbon?" bawled the Captain. "Lisbon!"

Dominique shook her blonde locks. "Lisbon," she said. "To further expand the deeds of this adventurer seated next to me. Jacques Casanova, more than other men, requires a life filled with exploits, with secrets, with swordplay, with—"

"With a French lioness who shares in the same?"

Jacques caught Dominique's fine glance.

"Well, I suppose"—the rais languished on the word suppose—"I suppose I could sail past the coast of Algarve where I first initiated my holy war for Allah." After the ship swelled up and down, the rais put his hands in his lap. "So if I'm to hear the full tale of I Piombi, we'd better begin, Signor Casanova. We have only till nightfall before we must alter course toward the lovely port of Lisbon. Oh. And yes, here." He reached into a small drawer behind him, then handed something to Jacques. "This scroll may lead someone to treasure, but I find the thing taxing. My treasure, I find it on the seas. You understand?"

Dominique applauded, then looked to Jacques. Her eyes sparkled brightly as she planted her lips on his.

It was not long before the rais, although clearly enjoying Jacques' daring story, stopped the teller. "Cavaliere Grimani? You're sure it was he who sent you to the Leads?"

"Yes, a Venetian patron of mine confirmed it on his deathbed. Grimani has been a member of the Inquisitori de Stato for many years. His power is immense."

The rais fell thoughtful. "So he's the man who I'll someday thank in person for a most unforgiving prison experience." He looked up. "I'm grateful, Signor Casanova. Now please resume your story."

* * *

Late that night below decks, Petrine was released to his master. The folds under his eyes hung in dark creases, and stringy hair matted his head.

"Yes, filthy where they worked me, sir. But I'm little worse the wear for my labors." Petrine beat lightly upon his chest. "And I have you to thank for my liberty."

"You may thank Dominique I'm alive to free you," Jacques said. "She is, for the moment, safe with the captain. If you're permitted to move aboveboard, Petrine, find her and offer her your compliments." Jacques reached for his lantern.

"You're staying here below, sir?"

"Yes, for a time. One of the Turks told me that Carlo Brose holed himself up down here." Jacques pointed into the darkness of the below deck. "I intend to discover what Brose, weak or not, has in store." Jacques tapped his dagger, took up his lantern, bent low, and stared into the bowels of the ship. "I'll find you and Dominique later."

"I must go with you."

"No, I can manage."

"It would be wise if—"

"I can manage him."

"All right, master. But have a care. I still desire to hunt treasure with you."

When Jacques found Carlo Brose, he lay stretched out on his side, his head crooked in his bent arm, eyes glazed and distant. His skin looked gray. Certainly he was in no shape to do material harm. He cocked his head and feebly offered a wooden cup that Jacques declined.

"Two lanterns are too bright," Brose mumbled to the floor. "Extinguish yours."

Jacques did so.

"Lay opposite me so I may see you, Herr Adventurer. Neither of us can sit tall. You're too large. I'm too ill." With difficulty, Brose raised his head. "Did Piccinio Rais direct you here? It's well. Strangely, I've come to believe our captain is an honorable man. In his own manner, of course."

The ship's hull groaned disturbingly.

Brose jingled coins in a small pouch and nudged it towards Jacques.

Jacques ignored the pouch but, before stretching to his side, double-checked for his dagger, then adjusted his weight on his forearm.

"For what wickedness did you ransom Dominique?" he scowled.

A shiver shook Brose before he spoke. "Wickedness?" He presented a fragile smile. "Well, I was tired of fingering through my own shit each morning looking for the diamonds I swallowed the night before. I figured I had two left. Those gems might as well do good for someone."

"Why not yourself? Why'd you ransom Dominique? What trap do you plan for me?"

When Brose feebly bolstered himself up onto an elbow, the lantern light caused his face to look more somber. He stared into his wooden cup. "I'll be brief as my temperament and the times dictate. I've known many women who weren't worth a sou," he said. "Your companion seems worth a vast fortune. Furthermore, shouldn't a man perform at least *one* noble deed during his short, miserable life? Ransom a worthwhile woman?"

"I know you too well. Why did you not save the diamonds for yourself?"

"Myself? For what?" Brose wheezed. "Herr Adventurer, I have position here. I'll stay with these men, with this ship. Yes, they're revolted by my marked face, they know I'm dying. And yet they revere my powers of healing. Or at least they patronize me enough to make me believe so. I'm a kernel of hope for some of these wretches. Why would I relinquish my unique status?"

Brose choked down a short swig from his cup. "Praise the wine and the opium," he gurgled. "Besides, Jacques Casanova, you once accused me of detesting life. Perhaps a just indictment. It seems, however, in these past months I've discovered a sweet, sweet taste for life. It's dear. Life is dearer than ..." Brose's voice faded. Settling back down on his shoulder, he spoke hoarsely. "I pay a reasonable ransom for a woman, and you dare ask why?"

At this pronouncement, Jacques condemned himself to silence.

"Here, take this back, fool." Brose fumbled with his grimy pocket and produced a small book, one that Jacques recognized. The book that Brose had stolen from him at L'affaire de Voltaire.

The sick man feebly pushed the volume toward Jacques. "Open it where the black ribbon lays."

Jacques opened the book.

"Read the quote I underlined. Your man Horace is correct. Read it. It's no secret." Brose managed another sip from his cup.

"Seize the day," Jacques read. "Put no trust in the morrow."

"Sums up the wisdom I've gained these last several months. When Allah finds me—" The wooden cup tumbled away. It was empty.

At the clatter, Jacques looked up and found the hollow eyes of Carlo Brose.

He crawled close and touched Brose's hand. It was cold. He touched his face, confirming that life had fled from the man who once detested it.

Unhurriedly, Jacques reached for the pouch of coins Brose had offered and withdrew two gold pieces. Rolling Carlo Brose to his back, he closed the man's eyelids, then placed a coin upon each.

He skirted the lantern and reopened the small book.

"Cease to ask what the morrow will bring forth," he read aloud, "and set down as gain each day that Fortune grants."

Jacques lingered while the flame burned low, reading on, imparting the wisdom of gentle Horace to his longtime rival and long-last friend.

AUTUMN – 1755

- 30 -

"NO MORE PROTESTS, PETRINE," repeated Jacques. "You grow tiresome."

Petrine rammed his finger into the soft puddled candle wax before flopping his forearm on the table. "We sit, doing nothing."

"We've not yet lodged a full day here," Dominique pointed out.

"But why don't we start? We came to Lisbon to uncover Templar clues."

"We'll begin when I—" Jacques voice began rising. "Enough of your prattle, ronyon. Perhaps a box on the ears would satisfy you."

"Jacques, please," Dominique said, crossing the small room. "It's late. You'll wake the whole inn."

Jacques slapped the table.

The muffled voice of someone in the next room could be heard.

Dominique tramped to the corner, returned, and stood next to Petrine. Her toe began tapping while she unlaced the strings of the purse she held.

"As Jacques has told you," she explained, "we need a respite from our eventful voyage. Come back in three days, then we shall explore, if need be, every single church—to advance our search." Opening the bag wide, she set it in front of Petrine. "Trust this agreement."

The valet stole a look at Jacques before stuffing his hand into the purse. "I adore gold, gold, gold," he said mischievously.

Jacques tightened his jaw and cleared his throat. Several coins— released by the valet—clinked back into the bag.

"But you see, I take only what I have need of, master," Petrine said, offering a meek smile. He blew a strand of hair from his face, pulled his hand from the purse, and stood up. His brown eyes beamed when he turned to Dominique. "I'll return in three days' time." He charged to the door. "Enjoy yourselves in Lisbon."

"You also," groused Jacques.

Shortly after midnight, Jacques and Dominique finished their supper. They dressed warmly with some of the clothes Picinnio Rais had given them and ventured from their lodgings. Guided by a brilliant moon, the couple strolled arm in arm across the sand of the town's squares, down wide avenues, past pink marble façades. Fresh paint on the signboards, doors, and lintels told the lovers of the upcoming religious celebrations in Lisbon, the most Christian city in Europe.

Feeling carefree, Jacques hugged Dominique. From the moment they'd stepped onto the Cais de Pedra, he'd marveled anew at her artless charm, her curiosity, her vivacity. He went to one knee, cradled Dominique's hand, and kissed it.

"In the Portuguese fashion," he said, staring intently into her eyes. In the moonlight, he savored her blush. "It's true, life is meant for these moments."

The woman's smile reflected Jacques' earnest charm. As the breeze rustled past, it brought to Jacques a feeling of hope, a firm gladness in the fact that he shared the evening's air with the darting birds and the thousand other amiable creatures that belonged to the night.

* * *

Late morning found Jacques in his lodging sitting at table with pen and paper. In the corner, Dominique busied herself mending a plain dress. "To whom do you write, Jacques?"

"Vicomte de Fragonard."

"And what do you write?"

"That for a time we explore Lisbon, the town to which the mystery has led us.

And that in spite of setbacks and imbroglios, we feel confident we'll solve the riddle and return to his home for Francesco's worldly goods and my friends' correspondence."

As the words left Jacques' mouth, he knew he'd made a mistake. He allowed himself a glimpse at Dominique. Her barren looks wrung his heart. Why had he mentioned Francesco?

"Do you hope the Vicomte will resolve the mystery we've set ourselves to? Out of pity, perhaps?" Dominique asked.

"Perhaps," Jacques said. "But truly, I find I have a fondness for the old man. And, too, for the quest he's sent us on."

By evening, Dominique had relaxed and was chattering gaily. After sharing a glass of wine, the pair made love until night was almost upon them. In Dominique's soft eyes, Jacques found surprise, innocence, and contentment. With himself, he felt fire, then stirring admiration.

A loud pounding on the door startled the two at sunrise.

"Manstur, mashure," stammered Petrine.

Jacques, in a dressing gown, opened the door. The smell of liquor met him.

"Pare, prepee, prepare—"

"Prepared?" Jacques barked. "Prepared for adventure, valet? So my nose informs me." Jacques fanned the air.

Petrine stumbled through the doorway, fell down, then rolled over, face up, unmoving.

"One of your duties this morning, ronyon, is to unpack my pistols. And lay out my smallsword and dagger," Jacques said, running the bottom hem of his gown lightly over Petrine's face. "Do you hear?"

"With so—some dilliculty," answered Petrine. His open eyes wandered the ceiling.

"Are you too drunk to begin your chores?"

"Not a'all, mashure. I'll be on ther—those—hores—chores in the flap of a wing's dove."

Dominique laughed.

With great effort, Petrine lifted himself and slouched his way toward the travel trunks. "Set t' go in no time, mashure."

Some hours later, on a hillock above a church, the trio of adventurers stood. The intense late afternoon sun showered the basilica, throwing attention on the dome's regal but long-faded colors. By Jacques' count, it was the eleventh church they had scoured today.

"Look down there," Dominique said in a hushed voice. "That man—the one in the frock."

"Where?"

Dominique tugged Jacques' sleeve. "There," she said, subtly nodding. "Rubbing that sheet of paper against the church wall."

Jacques shaded his eyes with his hand and saw the profile of a fellow with a light complexion and gray hair. His narrow eyebrows signified—according to Lavater's doctrine—that this was not a man given to anger. "I note him, yes."

"See what he rubs? An intaglio! The intaglio we hope to find."

"Intaglio," Petrine said. "Same as the Templar intaglios we found in the stables?"

"Seems so. I see it clearly, now that he's lifted his arm." Jacques peeked quickly at Dominique and Petrine. "Step behind that rise of earth over there—we'll have a bird's-eye view of the church below and be mostly concealed."

Petrine moved at Jacques' signal and, arriving at the appointed spot, whispered to his companions. "Our hunt's not in vain—"

"See the pale-skinned ruffian crouching beside that far colonnade?"

"Where?" Dominique and Petrine both asked.

"Dozen paces to the right of Signor Intaglio."

"Lurker on the far left, too, Master Jacques. And he—"

"I see both. What troubles you, Jacques?"

"They hang back—either side of Signor Intaglio—loitering. Performing no industry. Both keep a keen eye on him."

"Yes. And an eye on the few passersby on the street also," Petrine said. "Irregular."

"Shall we intrude? A risk."

"Let's not give ourselves the go just yet," Jacques said. "If the frocked man is in danger, it's not our business. He makes a simple gravestone rubbing. May be an innocent, even a fool. May—"

"But if —"

"He might know much more," Petrine quickly added.

"You read my thoughts, Petrine," Dominique said. She turned to Jacques. "If Signor Intaglio is a piece of our treasure puzzle—if he's privy to information—we mustn't allow him to come to harm."

"Voices low, please. I'm thinking," Jacques said, surveying the scene below. Snaking his hand around his back, he felt his dagger. "We'll undertake to scare the ruffians away. But we're new to this town. No unnecessary trouble."

"Agreed."

Jacques handed each of them a pistol.

"I'm not as good with this as I am with a sword," Dominique whispered, pointing to her pistol, "but I'm good enough."

Petrine and Jacques smiled.

Before the sun could dip behind the basilica, Jacques trod down the stairs to the cobblestone street, then motioned Petrine and Dominique to veer left. Placing his back momentarily to the church, Jacques unsheathed his smallsword, obscuring it behind his leg, then turned around and began a leisurely flanking movement to the right of the ruffian, who, he now saw, clenched a low-slung knife. From the corner of his eye, Jacques monitored Dominique and Petrine while the pair stalked their prey at the opposite side of Signor Intaglio.

A pistol fired. Smoke. Near Petrine.

Immediately, the nearest ruffian sprang into action toward Signor Intaglio.

Sword raised, Jacques stormed forward. The ruffian redirected his blade at Jacques, who, like a torero, arched free of the man's fury, then with his sword met his enemy's forearm, sending the knife clattering.

The ruffian screamed in pain and hurtled down the nearby lane.

All passersby had scattered from the scene. The street was empty.

Beside the church wall, Dominique's head lay in Petrine's hands, her face contorted.

"Master!"

Jacques ran fast, knelt beside her and, seeing the open cut in her pant leg, sucked in a lungful of air. His gut stung as if the barbs of a spiked hook dug into him.

"Here," Signor Intaglio said, arriving at Jacques' side. "Will you use this?" Without waiting for a response, the man tore a portion of his clothing and shoved it toward Jacques, who, already pressing on Dominique's thigh, strapped and tied it just above the crimson gash. He twisted the cloth.

"The ruffian attacked, I shot at him," Petrine said, huffing. "I think I hit home."

Jacques glanced quickly about. "Let's hope neither man has friends close by who want cold revenge."

The tie slowed Dominique's bleeding.

"You've lost some blood, young woman," Signor Intaglio said, stepping closer. "And I've lost some smock. Ho, ho, ho." The man began a belly laugh that brought a meager grin to Dominique's lips. "Yes, you'll be fine. And well taken care of. I shall see to that. My name is Quentin Gray, and unless I've miscalculated, you three have prevented my early exodus to heaven. But I believe I'll get there soon enough, so I forgive your mistake. Ho, ho, ho, ho."

Quentin Gray was unscathed, but his laughter seemed to reveal his distress.

While the man daubed blood from Dominique's leg, Jacques studied him.

"Signor Gray is right, Dominique," Jacques said while he used another piece of cloth to swab her leg. "The cut, I'm glad to say, does not look too serious."

Dominique squeezed her eyes shut, then looked up at the men kneeling around her. "Get me back to the inn?"

"Yes. Right away."

"Your perfect pronunciations tell me you're from France," Quentin Gray continued in French. He wiped his bloody hands on his ripped smock. "I live humbly, since I no longer have a vocation. Yet I do have a calling. You must stay with me and share my modest means as long as you care to."

"I'm not sure that—" Dominique stammered.

"Perturbation," the man declared. "I'm sure. I insist. After all, madame, you require my medical aid and I have a cask of hydromel at home. Let us make the proper introductions, let me gather today's work together, then we shall fetch your belongings at the inn and be started before you can say 'Alameda de São Pedro de Alcantara'." The man burped another "ho, ho."

Quite soon, Quentin Gray led them away toward the hill country.

"You'll see when we round that last knoll ahead, I live on a hillside where there is less humanity. Then, too, rent is cheaper the higher up Lisbon's seven hills one travels. Not that I pay rent." Quentin let out a laugh. "I have no colleagues left in Portugal. I find myself quite alone," he sighed. "Quite alone. Certainly none of my English countrymen to share my good fortune with—my good fortune being the Conde de Tarouca's palace, the roof over my head."

In truth, Quentin Gray did reside in a palace. But arriving at the destination, the adventurers saw that the roof looked as if it might collapse any day, as did the crumbling walls.

Quentin snickered. "As you can see, the actual construction was never completed. But the grounds, while not hugely expansive, are more than sufficient for my needs. Credit the good Lord." Quentin slung his bundle from his shoulder.

"The Lord works in wondrous ways," Dominique replied as she slipped from Jacques' shoulder. "We accept your invitation to stay, Signor Gray." She clutched Jacques' arm and gave him a sideways glance.

He returned it, dubious.

"An adventure," Dominique said, smiling.

Inside, Quentin examined Dominique while she rested on a makeshift bed.

"Lie still and gather your strength," Jacques said. "And allow this gentleman to apply his medicines."

"We'll either fashion a litter or some crutches. But that will be tomorrow."

Within a short while, Quentin Gray stood by an earthen fireplace just outside his palace walls stirring a pot of olla podrida. "Your valet's pistol shot may have been on its mark. But the assassin might have been saved by the silver plate he wears over his abdomen."

"Silver plate?" asked Jacques.

"Yes. To prevent a hernia. I fit it to Fernando myself. It was in consequence of a saber cut he'd received at some previous time."

With Jacques' help, Dominique scooted closer to the fireplace. "You know the man who attacked you?"

"Both men, I believe. The man *you* wounded, Monsieur Casanova, did he have a brand on his hand?"

"I believe he did."

"Well, that is most probably Jonathan Tillson. You see, in England, my home, they brand a manslayer's hand. Mr. Tillson has that brand."

"So Tillson is a known criminal?"

"Yes. Certainly a known Catholic." Quentin threw his head back and howled a long laugh. He straightened up. "Seldom is the twilight breeze this bothersome," he observed. "Come, let's take these dinners inside. The walls won't provide much of a windbreak, but they'll help."

Quentin led the group into the abode, set down his lantern amid a circle of primitive chairs, and invited Jacques and Petrine to partake in some rappee. Petrine accepted.

Jacques knew the tobacco was far too pungent for his taste, but he also knew it was judicious for him to accept the man's offer. He wrapped a blanket around Dominique's shoulders, helped her into a chair, and sat down between her and Petrine. Quentin offered an ember he brought from the cook fire and lit the men's pipes.

Jacques needed information about the intaglio rubbing. He'd take Quentin into town for the main meal tomorrow. Food and drink. Men spoke freely with the joy of Bacchus in their belly.

"Well," Quentin began, "one great advantage with having a scant roof—I'm able to see the emerging stars in the firmament on an evening such as this."

"Signor Gray," Dominique said, shuffling her feet, "why were you doing a gravestone rubbing on the wall of the basilica?"

Jacques choked on his pipe.

"Rubbing? On the Basilica de Santa Maria's wall?" said Quentin, his voice rattling higher. "Hmm. Well, the patera—the pattern of the circles—intrigued me. I wished to copy it, bring it home, and admire its beautiful simplicity. Let it saturate my thinking."

"Ah," Jacques feigned, overstating his earnestness by blowing a smoke ring— which a gust of wind promptly dispersed.

Quentin Gray carefully reached into the rock cranny beside him. "Shall we enjoy the rubbing this evening?" He smiled at the adventurers before he carefully unrolled the sheet and held it to the light. "Familiar?" he asked nonchalantly.

Simultaneously, Jacques and Dominique gave opposite answers. Their eyes met at once.

Petrine began to chuckle. Which drew Dominique into outright laughter.

"To be forthright, sir," Dominique said after eyeing Jacques squarely, "the three of us saw that exact intaglio carved in stone in Jerusalem at the Stables of Solomon."

Jacques kneaded his pipe vigorously while observing Quentin Gray's face.

Quentin Gray took his time relighting Jacques' pipe. "Stables of Solomon? Hmm," he said. "What can that mean?"

Jacques spoke up. "Most frankly, we hoped you could tell us what an intaglio is doing here."

"Most frankly, Monsieur Casanova, I don't know. And I've sought an answer for some time."

Dominique let out an audible gasp. Jacques, too, stirred with excitement.

Quentin Gray continued. "Yes, I, too, desire to know the significance of a carved intaglio on the wall of a church." From his position in the chair, he pulled his legs to his body and wrapped his arms about them. He glanced over both shoulders, then spoke quietly. "Well, I suspect the Lord wishes me to show gratitude: you all did save my mortal life. So ... mesdame et messieurs, what you witnessed today—it was not the first time I've been attacked by Catholic assassins."

"What?" Dominique cried.

Quentin explained that for a score of years, he had been a member of the Society of Jesus, the Jesuits.

"And there were attacks on your life?" barked Petrine. "For what reason?"

"Are you as impatient as I, sir?" laughed Quentin. "Believe me, we work toward the point," he said as he reached behind him, lifted the lantern, and placed it near his feet. "Holding high office in the Jesuit order—an immensely powerful organization—meant I was privy to many sensitive matters. Yet it was almost pure chance two of my Jesuit brothers and I uncovered what may prove to be the most nefarious subterfuge in the Church of Rome's seventeen-hundred-year history." Quentin's face grew intense. "Several years ago, my brethren and I divested ourselves from the Jesuit Society to discover the truth of the matter for ourselves. And because we left the order, some allege we work against the Church. Perhaps that's why my Jesuit brothers were murdered and I myself put on the assassination list."

Jacques sensed Dominique's coming grimace. *She believes the Church to be unsoiled in the ways of the world.* He squeezed her hand gently.

Petrine spoke up. "If you don't work for the Church," he said, genuflecting, "then you work for Lucifer?"

"No, Petrine. I serve God. And the truth. I was placed on earth to that purpose. There is—"

Petrine looked directly at his master. "Perhaps I work for Lucifer."
He grinned slyly.

Jacques glared.

Quentin began again. "Aside from the basilica's wall, I too have
seen the patera—what you call the intaglio—somewhere else." He
reached deep into his garment and pulled out a fine parchment
scroll. He hesitated, then extended the scroll toward the lantern.
"Here. A group of warrior-monks, religious men, called the Knights
Templar produced this."

Jacques leaned forward; he could hardly believe his eyes. The
visible outside corner of the scroll was inscribed with the miniature
circles, the -^—^- figure, and *1300*. He squelched the surprise in his
voice. "Ahh," he said as he pulled Quentin's hand and the scroll
closer to the lantern. "That strange design on the scroll looks like a
sign for the Egyptian adept Ormus."

"Or perhaps the astrological symbol for Virgo." Quentin Gray
drew the scroll back. "I tend to believe this figure—the two-humped
camel as I christened it—is possibly some stylized letter of a long-
dead alphabet." Quentin ran his hand across his stubbly beard. "The
Pope did not officially dissolve the Templars until 1312 Anno
Domini. This map must have been created by them anytime before
then, or more to the point, before 1307—"

"Could the *1300* on the scroll indicate the date, the year it was
created?"

"Possibly."

"Could this all be a hoax?" interjected Dominique.

Jacques held his tongue in anticipation of Quentin's answer.

"No. As I was about to say, my brother Jesuits had proof positive
that several scrolls were made by the Templars before their persecution
in 1307 by Philippe le Bel. Men do not craft hoaxes when they are
about to die."

"Truly, sir, truly."

"Philippe the *Fair*?" Petrine asked, scratching his front teeth with
his thumbnail and smiling impiously.

"1307," Jacques said, raking his hand across his stubbly beard.

Jacques locked eyes with Dominique, then gave a look to Petrine
before digging deeply into his clothing, where he found his own scroll.
He handed it to Quentin Gray.

Glancing at the symbols on the outside of the scroll, Quentin rushed his palm to his gaping mouth. "Alike. Indistinguishable," he muttered when he held it closer to the light. "This is the third I've seen. The second I knew of disappeared with the murder of my colleagues. It was for their scroll, I'm sure, that they were murdered. If your scroll contains text—does it have text inside it?"

"Yes."

"Then it may be authentic. What do you make of the miniature concentric circles?"

Jacques offered a smug smile to Dominique. "If we examine the scroll more shrewdly, we see the miniature circles are not actually concentric. They are drawn so small that they *appear* to be concentric. In reality, they match what the Templars—most probably the Templars—carved into the columns of the Stables of Solomon and on your Basilica de Santa Maria. Such circles indicate Plato's Theorem. I believe these Templar intaglios imply mathematics as part and parcel of this riddle, although I don't know how Plato's Theorem may come into play. Specifically, I mean."

"The theorem, that was the conclusion I came too also," Quentin said. "Well done!"

Petrine turned to Dominique. "I told you my master was a virtuoso."

"Yes, you did," Dominique smiled.

Jacques unrolled his scroll and pointed to the letters in the vertical column. "S-O-N-B-O-I-S-I-L-A. An anagram for 'Lisbon'. That is partially what directed us here to this city."

Quentin nodded.

Shortly, he and Jacques compared the verses of their scrolls. Identical. Quentin read the first two lines aloud, then shook his head. *"Obscurum per obscurius."*

"Explaining the obscure by the means of the more obscure," translated Jacques.

Quentin continued, his legs still wrapped comfortably to his chest. "In truth, there are additional carved intaglios I can show you. And where—I'm thinking—maybe there's some physical association I've missed."

"But do we know for certain that the Templars from Jerusalem brought a treasure?"

"I fully believe the Templars had the capability."

"The most important question," Jacques exclaimed. "Do we know what the Templars brought? What is the treasure?"

"A secret which, if kept, will preserve the Church's *status in quo*."

Dominique shook her head in confusion.

Jacques asked, "Could the treasure, the secret, have to do with the philosopher's stone?"

"Ha, ho, ho, ho." Quentin's gray hair shook with his laughter. "If you believe my Jesuit brothers and I risked our lives to search ninety convents, numerous libraries, countless cemeteries, two universities, a dozen provincial churches, nearly forty parish churches—most of which were Jewish synagogues until their Christian 'reconversion' in 1497—to unearth a temporal treasure, even for the fabled *lapis philosophorum*—ho, ho, ho—it seems that, above all else, you treasure the material. While the treasure I seek is monumental. Would I pit myself against the whole of the Church of Rome for anything less?"

- 31 -

DOMINIQUE WEPT. "When I stabbed his foot, drew first blood, I thought he would quit the fight," Dominique confided. "I'd neither desire nor will to kill the Turk. The Lord sustained me."

Jacques, lying on his propped elbow next to Dominique, felt his stomach tense while he wiped her tears. "I understand, Fragoletta. Tell me more, if you will. He stroked Dominique's hand in hopes of quelling the pangs of her heart and the pain of her leg wound.

"Francesco taught me how to disable an opponent. During a duel, I saw him stick his sword point through a soldier's foot. The soldier quit the fight straight away."

"I'd no idea Francesco—"

"There's much you didn't know about him. I've told you that, Jacques. As for me—I often defeated Francesco when we bouted. Which, in turn, means I fence better than you, at least from what I've seen."

"You have not seen me at my finest. In fact—"

Dominique lifted a bit of Jacques' hair from his face. "I was a skillful dancer, don't forget. Early on, Francesco convinced me I could easily learn the footwork and arm work of swordplay."

"Footwork and arm work are one thing. But from where did your courage—"

"Frightened out of my skin, Jacques. But making the hard choice, I figured I'd have a better chance against the Turk than you. He would discount me, a woman, as a fighter. Which would be a benefit. Also, I knew the weapon the Turk was most likely familiar with was the scimitar. And the scimitar is mostly a *cutting* weapon. He would be used to cutting." Faint moonlight illuminated Dominique's arm as she slashed the night sky. "Francesco impressed upon me that a slash with a sword is slower to arrive to a target than a thrust with a sword point. I would have an advantage with the thrust, the *stoccata*, of my smallsword."

"Your unique intelligence, your exceptional daring, impresses me more than you know, Fragoletta."

Dominique's voice lowered. "I'd no choice but to risk everything. I did what I did—for us."

Jacques found himself blinking rapidly. His breathing halted.

"The stars seem distant tonight," whispered Dominique finally. "I didn't want you to duel the Turk, Jacques. You're not a fighter. You're a lover."

"You know what you name me, don't you? In the classics, the seducer is always pictured as a jester."

"Does that thought bother you?"

"Demeaning laughter brings me to my knees." Jacques adjusted his forearm on the straw mattress. "Perhaps I've trifled away my precious time on earth chasing the rustle of soft silk. Perhaps I'm a jester," he said. "Tonight, I'm regretful. Since I was a young man, I've chosen to live, really live. But I've not stopped to discover if vice or virtue has lead me onward. And sometimes, late at night, a distress gnaws at me."

"Don't you know you're known throughout Europe as one of its great gamesters, as the only man to escape I Piombi, as a lover of repute, as—"

"Yes, I've been famously sweet with women." Jacques could hear anguish in his voice, and he knew it would compel Dominique to answer.

"I sometimes feel your need to accomplish great things. I feel your urges." She pressed her hand against his cheek. "What drives you is the agitation, the turmoil lurking in your heart, Jacques. You may not realize it's there, but I know it to be so. That's a woman's way."

Jacques turned on his back. "I congratulate you on your womanly talent."

Dominique was momentarily dumbfounded. She spoke softly. "Your detachment doesn't trouble me, Jacques. I was married to your brother. A phlegmatic temperament was my daily diet."

She boosted herself up on her side as the bracing wind raked branches against the stone wall behind her. "I want to ask—in Lisbon you said you wanted us to dream together. Do you carry a *special* dream in your heart?"

Keenly aware of his pounding temples, Jacques closed his eyes. "I do."

A long pause followed.

Dominique smiled and slapped playfully at Jacques' shoulder. "Would you care to reveal that dream?"

"Oh," Jacques smirked, "would I care to *reveal* it?"

Dominique nodded.

"My dream is to return to Venice," he said, opening his eyes.

"An admirable goal," said Dominique too readily. "I also long to visit Venice. After all, isn't it the home of the Casanova brothers?"

Jacques did not answer but saw the strain in Dominique's smile.

"Have you thought that the city may not be the same one you remember from your boyhood?"

"Venice is ageless. She will always enthuse."

"Perhaps. And perhaps she's only a Venice of memory."

"Memory? My closest friends, our pranks, my boyhood, the beginning of manhood, the home where I dreamed my *first* dreams. And Venice herself. A city, a republic. Truly like no other. Long live La Serenissima, Venice."

Dominique's short sigh transformed into a cloudy mist, then dissolved. "I may be able to walk with a cane or crutch tomorrow, though my leg throbs mightily just now. Hold me, if you will."

"A moment, please. Give me a moment."

The moment stretched into minutes until Jacques, still not having honored Dominique's appeal, could just make out in her soft whispers— a prayer for their safety and salvation.

Soon afterward, he fell asleep.

* * *

Quentin Gray rose early and prepared coffee, which he gave to each of his guests before training his eyes on the dawning sun. "Phoebus in his triumphal chariot brings us another day."

Jacques paced to the small fire to warm his hands. "Phoebus is a pagan god, not suited for a Christian tongue like yours."

"Filtered through the alembic of so many brilliant Hellenic minds, somehow I cannot find the Greek gods pagan."

Quentin maintained his matter-of-factness: Lisbon's cathedrals would be packed with churchgoers, today being All Saints' Day, when the church remembered the descent of the Holy Ghost to the apostles. This, then, would be the ideal morning to explore the deserted citadel on a promontory above Lisbon—to view the intaglios.

Although Dominique was in pain and felt that her wound would slow the expedition, Jacques insisted that, with the aid of the crutch that Quentin had fashioned, she would be fine to make the journey. Petrine would be there, if there was a need.

Dominique's resistance to traveling fell on deaf ears. Contrary to the previous night's sentiment, Jacques' gruff manner began to sting.

When the sun edged above the horizon, Quentin—packed and eager to go—gathered the adventurers and led them from the Conde de Tarouca's palace. After a long walk and a demanding climb, during which the mournful religious chants of the *saetas* sounded from below, the four arrived nearly atop the plateau.

"We're not so high up as one would think, but this jutting terrain affords a remarkable vista, almost the whole of Lisbon," Quentin said, glancing at Jacques.

He pointed out the River Tagus that led into the dazzling Oeiras Bay, then the opera house, the magnificent library, and the dozens of church spires and towers. "You all may recognize the pink marble of the Royal Palace this fair November morning."

Jacques felt like a gull that, encircling the panorama, spied upon the great houses of the wealthy, the offices of the government, the merchants' shops. He watched human figures sally across the Cais de Pedra, where Piccinio Rais had landed them, and soon his mind conjured up the sailors who transported Templar Crusaders—and their treasure—to a new home, hopefully Lisbon.

Jacques turned and looked at the substantial edifice just above, one that abutted into the steep hill behind it.

"The old citadel's in decay," Quentin said, "but, believe me, the tower itself has withstood time and will outlast me. The intaglios we seek are at the top." When he began to climb the rough stairs upward, the trio followed.

Greeted at the base of the tower by the peal of church bells rising from the city, Quentin came to a stop in the stone yard and nestled himself against the rough parapet wall.

"And arising from fine Lisbon," he said, "do you hear the music of *Gaudeamus omnes in Deo*?"

"The introit," Dominique said. "Yes, I do."

No sooner had the words left Dominique's lips than a yawning rumble filled the air.

"Haaah!" exclaimed Dominique and Petrine.

Jacques looked below. Lisbon's tall buildings began to sway like saplings in a wind.

He felt bewitched, his mind confounded. Insensate fear engulfed him as he watched the city's stone structures ripple to-and-fro.

A rumbling, deafening roar tore his ears before a cry of terrible surprise sliced a path to his throat. "Oh, my life!" As if cruelly wounded, the stone yard shivered and the earth dropped from under Jacques, slamming him to his back. The others, like straw dolls, were likewise flung to the yard.

Regaining his feet, Jacques spun about. Not far away, Dominique strained to sit, struggling for her crutch. In the same direction sprawled Quentin and Petrine. All were moving, alive.

Jacques braced himself tightly against the parapet wall. The clamor was of a hundred bombards blasting the town, but he dared a look at the grisly sight below. Stone missiles from massive belfries and cathedral spires hurtled downward, killing innocents by the drove.

Deadly crevices opened wide, swallowing slews of victims.

Dust began to choke the ruins. Human figures stumbled through the mess.

As the welter battered his ears, Jacques folded into the wall— every dram of spirit drained from his body.

Suddenly, his heart pumped a terrifying message to his brain: be strong. He turned to his friends and rushed toward them. The feral groans of the earth ceased. He collapsed to his stomach beside Dominique, who, lying face down, turned to meet his eyes.

"Stopped," he said. "Stopped."

GREG MICHAELS

With both hands, she clutched his arm.

"Are you hurt?"

Dominique shook her head frantically.

Jacques, glancing over his shoulder, watched Petrine and Quentin stagger toward the parapet wall. Tears rolled freely down Quentin Gray's cheeks. His lips mouthed unheard syllables.

"Let's go to him, Dominique," Jacques said, trying to steady his voice. He raised her by her arms, and together they labored across the wrecked yard to the wall, staring at the sight below.

A ravaged carcass of a town lay below them. The earthquake had wrenched Lisbon from its foundations, shattering it.

In the mangled wreckage, fire began its vicious work. Ten thousand church candles, hearths from a thousand homes—flame in all its malevolent patterns—were unleashed. Hell danced among the rubble. Mothers threw themselves over the flaming bodies of their infants. Men afire skeltered in hopeless circles till demon flames burnt the life from them. Fiery animals bolted through the ruins, forming unearthly images. The howling agonies of beasts, the hot whistles of the gross inferno, the groans and dark cries of the maimed—all tortured the air.

Jacques and Dominique panted in confusion. And watched.

Fire infused panic into the victims, impelling many to flee to the bay. Others stumbled back into the holocaust.

A fiercely hot wind advanced up the hillside, forcing Petrine and Quentin together, seeking safety in each other's arms. They crouched—hugging, weeping. Drawing abreast of them while clutching Dominique, Jacques cried "Make haste, we—"

Another jolt tore the citadel's courtyard wide, plunging Dominique into a gaping hole, followed by Petrine and Quentin Gray.

"Dominique!" Jacques screamed.

The earth stilled. The tremor stopped.

Jacques edged to the pit. "Where are you?" he screamed.

Quentin, in the chaos, moaned fitfully.

Swirling dust stifled Jacques' lungs, but not far below he spotted Quentin's arm. Bloodied and nearly dumb with fright, Quentin clawed furiously while Jacques tugged him up to what remained of the stone surface.

"Dominique? Petrine?" Jacques screamed.

More coughing was the reply. Amid the veil of dust, Jacques caught sight of Petrine beginning an ascent from the rock-strewn abyss. "Climb, Petrine!"

Jacques, wresting the valet up to the ruptured courtyard, gently rolled him away from the edge before scrambling again on his side, scouring the chasm below. A raw, bitter taste rose in Jacques' mouth; warm trickles of blood laced his cheek. Tears burned his eyes.

"Dominique!" he shouted. "Dominique! Where are you, Dominique? Answer me." Jacques twisted toward Petrine and the Jesuit.

"Rescue—impossible," Quentin whimpered, "even if she's alive."

Jacques swung his head back toward the hole, squeezing his fist to his temples as if to force his desperate mind to a decision. "Go! Both of you," he cried to Quentin and Petrine. "Find safety."

Quentin nodded and lent his hand to a bewildered Petrine.

Batting at the whirling dust, Jacques descended into the crumbling abyss, his bare hands and feet searching for any handhold. "I come to you, Dominique," he whispered.

His step sent a rock tumbling downward. "No," he cried.

Jacques probed into the darkness, his stomach knotted. An eddy of dust swirled past, allowing his eyes a view. "Dominique!"

On her back she lay, blonde hair sprawling around her head like a crown of gold.

"Dominique."

"Jacques," came the weak reply.

Jacques' back burned in pain, but he hurried his descent until he was at her side. Blood coursed her mouth; her body trembled.

"Can you move?"

"I die."

In mute horror—every part of him—Jacques felt his courage wilt. "I'm putting you over my shoulder. Hold me wherever you can. Don't let go. Do you hear me?"

"Yes."

He began to lift her. Dominique shrieked.

"We're climbing out of here," Jacques cried. He scratched through the thick gloom toward the light—every feeble step a torment for them both.

He stopped to rest on a crag of stone. *My lungs will surely burst.* He lay Dominique down and, as best he could, rested beside her on the narrow ledge.

"Afraid, afraid to die." The words from Dominique, in a barely audible whisper, were accompanied by a look that vouched for its truth. "I've sinned. And asked so many times for forgiveness. For deliverance from my weak flesh. Help me, dear Jesus. Let me die confessed."

"The good always are forgiven, Dominique." Jacques wiped blood from her lips and mist from his own eyes.

"I've tried to be worthy in so many ways. But God does not grant children to a woman who …" Dominique coughed more blood. "I want *you* more than I want a child, Jacques mia. You should know—I have grown to love you. I love you."

Jacques' lips twisted shut until he managed to kiss Dominique's pale cheek. He rose to his knees, his whole body quivering from the pounding of his heart.

Gently, he helped her. "Hold on to my neck." Her face contorted in pain.

The pair inched their way toward the light above until they reached the brink.

With what remained of his strength, Jacques deposited himself and Dominique on the flat of the tower courtyard. He embraced her, then kneeling, rested her head on his knee so that he might see her tender face.

A low rumbling compelled his attention. He raised his head. Through a breach in the parapet wall loomed a spellbinding sight: the Bay of Oeiras—suddenly and with alarming speed—emptied itself as far as Jacques could see. Without the watery support from the sea, tall-masted ships bottomed and heeled over. Stranded fish writhed in the muddy reaches. Small craft smashed against rocks—rocks that had never seen the light of day.

"It can't be," reasoned Jacques. Yet he watched the sight, as did the still-living wretches in the rubble below, in fascination. All saw the sea before them recede and utterly disappear.

Soon a phantasm appeared on the horizon.

The phantasm, minute at first, moved inexorably closer—its appearance that of a barber's steely, glinting straight razor.

Now larger, the phantasm surged.

A wave.

A wave of such magnitude that, for a moment, Jacques could only marvel and try to comprehend.

Dashing lingering vessels to bits, the water advanced.

Below in Lisbon, thousands of hapless souls, coming to the realization of their hideous fate and seized by unbearable terror, cried out to their god. To these masses the thunderous raging brine brought swift, savage death. Mothers, fathers, children—all were swept into its irresistible grip.

Mad with fear, Jacques dragged Dominique from the breach in the parapet away from the tower.

On came the rapacious wave.

He covered her body with his.

The murderous wall of water crashed up the hill, hurtling itself against the citadel tower—and driven by an invisible fury, speared past the adjoining gorges, its crest persisting onward.

Jacques and Dominique careened against each other, against the rock, slammed this way, then that.

To the far wall he was tossed, suffocated by the sweeping water while it rushed over him, around him, through him, before receding.

His ribs, his insides, felt liquid. His lungs existed only as grueling pain. *Where is she?*

He spotted Dominique, crumpled against a parapet wall. Spitting, choking, Jacques struggled to her side. After making certain she was alive, he cleared with his fingers her mouthful of sludge and vomit. Her body jerked when he stroked her shivering arms.

For the longest while, only her eyes could speak.

Cradling her head, he wiped the tangled hair from her forehead, then held her hand.

"Fragoletta?" he asked. As he gazed at her, the lump in his throat made it almost too difficult to form words. "You are special to me. The greatest joy life has ever brought is to hold you."

"You, Jacques mia, always give me your body in the most pleasurable manner," she whispered. "And you long ago allowed me to surrender my soul. Tell me you've never called anyone else your Fragoletta." Dominique closed her eyes and smiled, but her shivering would not stop.

"Fragoletta—my little strawberry?" he said, embracing her closer. "Never, Dominique, never."

"I'm satisfied," she said. "Is my crutch at hand?"

"Yes," Jacques smiled. "I'm here."

A calm joy connected the pair until a thundering noise lanced Jacques' nerve.

The horror reappeared, this time gushing back down from the higher ground.

Jacques' screams disappeared in the roar of the roiling brine. Like a wounded animal, he curled himself around her.

The world turned black.

- 32 -

JACQUES RAISED HIS HAND to block the noonday sun from his face. "How ill-beseeming your breath," he said, looking up at Quentin Gray.

Quentin frowned and continued to administer eye drops from his quill. "Again I remind myself you're no longer master of your moods, Jacques. Even so, you need not be boorish."

"You need not reek."

"My breath may stink, but I have a fine set of teeth."

"So does a mooncalf."

"Perturbation, man. Hold still or my quill will stick you."

"Where's my lackey? And where's Dominique?"

"Petrine sits behind us, leaning against the wall. There." Quentin straightened a thumb over his shoulder.

Jacques lifted his head from the ground and stared somberly at Petrine several paces away. "It seems I view the man's shadow. And that shadow has a rather saturnine façade for a saucy Spaniard. Petrine," Jacques yelled. "Petrine."

Quentin tilted his chin, gazed at the crumbled walls of Conde de Tarouca's palace, and released a long sigh. "Your valet does not answer to his name. He cannot tell you who he is nor where he is. Even what year—"

"He does not know the—?"

"The quake of the earth knocked him about. He is concussive. Rest, food, and prayer are what we can provide him, and I'm thankful God has spared, for the most part, my dwelling for that. A fair amount of wall caved in, as you see. But, yes, we're blessed to have this refuge. As for you, Jacques, you should be grateful that you've no broken bones—though your many bruises and this ragged wound still hurt, I'm sure." Quentin indicated Jacques' forearm. "For days now I've cleaned you, comforted you, and repaired you the best I know how. Only this morning have you become mindful enough—"

"Where's Dominique?"

"Dominique?" Quentin stammered. "Petrine, uh, Petrine is senseless, but he may, in a few days or a few weeks, recover his faculties. We shall pray for him." Quentin supported Jacques as he sat up. "Take this cup from me, O Lord," he said quietly. He caressed the quill of his feather and steadied his voice. "Dominique's left us. Gone."

"Gone?"

Still kneeling, Quentin lowered his head and mumbled words that seemed an incantation. "Because of your quick actions, Petrine and I made our way to higher ground. From there, I saw the backwash sweep Madame Casanova from your hold. How you survived—well, that's God's mystery."

"She's not—"

"The Psalms say that God's loved ones are very precious to Him, and He does let them go lightly. Two days ago, God chose to take up thousands and thousands. Others were left to live. We must be grateful we remain to do God's bidding."

"I held her in my arms. Yet she is lost." Jacques fiddled his brow, uncomprehending.

"You and Madame Casanova endured so much together—"

"She's gone," Jacques said, bereft of emotion. "Promised her—if we found no real treasure in Lisbon, this would be our last destination." With his fingernails, he raked the length of his cheek. "Her last destination."

"Bosom," muttered Petrine.

Jacques turned. "What?" he hissed.

Petrine's black hair framed his vapid face. "Bosom," he repeated. "Bosom of Abraham."

Turning around, Jacques found Quentin Gray choking back tears.

"I recall a lesson, Jacques, I learned long ago. In times of great suffering, tears are an infallible remedy."

Quentin stood, walked several steps away, and wept for a long while in the midday sun.

When the bulk of his grief had passed, he prayed aloud for Dominique, Petrine, and the people of Lisbon. He prayed for Jacques. Most of all, he prayed for the strength he would need in the coming days. Jacques lay back down, pulling at his lower lip.

* * *

While the clouds sped ominously overhead, Jacques crept from beneath his blanket, crawled past the rubble of the dwelling walls, and huddled over the solitary flame of the cook fire. His body ached, his mind chattered.

"A rather sullen sky," cracked a voice from behind.

Jacques did not answer. He felt a hand on his shoulder.

"Bread and porridge?" Quentin asked. "I prepared it earlier at daybreak and have already fed Petrine over there."

Jacques shrugged off the Jesuit.

"Bread is hard to come by. We mustn't squander what God provides." Quentin sidestepped a thin column of smoke to the opposite side of the small fire and stood, hands on hips. "I dislike leaving you and Petrine each day, but there are others in Lisbon who also need succor. I welcome you, Jacques, to accompany me. Perhaps it will do you good. Perhaps you will do others good."

Jacques spat at a burning ember.

"Let us talk sensibly before I depart, Jacques. My Templar scroll has disappeared in the earthquake, although, needless to say, I long ago memorized its Latin verses. You possess the remaining copy, if indeed you still have it." Quentin moved in Jacques' direction. "In my recent forays to Lisbon, I've seen many, many animals that were freed by the earthquake, so I've no doubt that other beasts—criminals and galley slaves—escaped their confinements, too. Stay doubly alert and keep your sword and dagger close. We must think of your well-being. And Petrine's. And the remaining scroll."

"Well-being?" Jacques pointed to himself. "Hook your eyes on the valet there who is senseless and—well-being? A fruitless endeavor."

"Perhaps," Quentin said, kneeling next to Jacques over the smoldering fire. He blew into the coals, and a flame arced momentarily.

Jacques again spat at the fire, dousing the flame. Dropping to all fours, he crawled across the ground, removed two stones in the wall, returned with his scroll, and tossed it into the fire.

Quentin scrambled madly before retrieving the scroll. He raked the horizon with his eyes, then spun around and quickly tucked it back behind the stones. He spoke gruffly. "I tell you to keep the scroll here where either of us may have access to it." Slinging a small leather sack across his shoulders, he retrieved a piece of bread from his pocket and turned into the morning sun. "I'll be back here to the hill after sundown. If your mind is changed and you wish to go with me now, you could be of great value to those whose bodies—"

"And souls need restoring," Jacques bleated, finishing Quentin's thought. "Your efforts are wasted on me."

By afternoon, Jacques was hunkered on the ground like a squirrel, nibbling from his cupped hands the nuts and bread Quentin had left him.

His mind now wandered fitfully far.

"Am I in Spain? Or am I dreaming?" he whispered to himself. "Spain—in former times I imbibed the Peralta wines from Pamplona, supped choice white truffles, excellent oysters, and shellfish. In Seville— heard the enchanting hornpipe played by blind musicians, danced by naked girls. Great times, those. Yes, marveled at castratos' duets, danced the seguidilla with ravishing partners, mimed copulation during fandangos. Ahh!

"And isn't it true I was handsomely paid to advise the government on mining? That I was received, in times not long past, by some of the most prominent grandees in Spain? Now I've no need to mix with those titled few, be their honorifics genuine or factitious. Of late, I have other callings."

A light flared into his eyes. Jacques slapped his hands to his face. "Be gone," he muttered. "Be gone."

The maddening glimmer persisted. Jacques, charging to his knees, howled. "I do not stutter. Be gone!" The irritating glint disappeared.

"I do command the universe," he smirked, his lips twisting into a scowl. Before he bent to finish his bread, a small patch of light shimmered again upon his body. "What reflects the scalding sun?

Bores holes into the sockets of my skull?" He smacked his chest, then jerking his head up, glared in the direction of Petrine, who sat propped upright, a rumpled blanket supporting him. Scattered around Petrine were some of his belongings.

"This irritation stems from the lackey," Jacques threw his victuals at the dilapidated wall and stumbled across the rocky soil. Standing at full height above the valet, he crooked over, then yanked an object poking out from Petrine's shirt.

Suddenly, Jacques' stomach churned. "My gold snuffbox," he whispered, "reflects the sun. My prized snuffbox! The lackey," he said, "how did this come to be here in his possession?"

Petrine's face remained hard and blank.

Jacques stood before the valet and calmed himself. "If I somehow confirm he stole it, I'll watch—uncover his game." Jacques slid the snuffbox under Petrine's blanket. He rapped the stuporous valet on his head, shuffled back toward the wall, and squatted. *Keep your friends close and your enemies closer ...*

* * *

The days passed onward, and in the chill of an evening's twilight Jacques, toying with a weed sprouting from the dirt, recalled Corneille's great play *Medea*. The distraught heroine, after losing her husband and murdering her sons, is asked what she has left. "*Moi, dis-je,*" replies Medea "*et c'est assez*. 'Myself, I say, and that is enough.'"

"I've relied on myself all these years," Jacques said aloud. "Myself. My clip of courage. My adaptability. Notoriety. The force of my person." He spit at the weed. "I no longer have myself," he said. "Who am I? Who do I deceive? It seems I'm perpetually within the grasp of some magnificent solution to a problem, to squaring the cube, to finding a treasure. Have I accomplished one single thing on this earth? No! The children I've sired are indolent and inept. My mother is foreign to me. I've hardly known a father for I am unsure to which father I belong. I've been cut adrift in this seething madhouse called society. I want, I need the howling voices in my head to stop."

He ripped the weed from its home soil and offered it as a sacrifice to the gloom of the swollen sky. "I've told and retold my story of escaping prison to whoever would listen. That is the ringing achievement of my life, the sole thing I've accomplished. Escape." Overhead but not far away, soot-colored birds winged in random patterns while plucking a banquet of bugs from the air. They squawked their triumphs before fading into the bone-thin clouds and oncoming darkness. Jacques stared in cold amazement.

*   *   *

Over a small cook fire, Quentin Gray—returned home—removed food from his pack, then closed it up. "Earlier this afternoon, I was nearly shot." He shook his head, smiling. "Nearly shot. For looting."

From his seat on the ground, Jacques looked up after Quentin coughed hoarsely. "Me, a looter? I wasn't robbing the woman and her sister but giving them last rites."

Quentin planted his fists on his hips and took up a mock stance of arrogance. "I, Sebastião José de Carvalho e Mello, the king's man in Lisbon, brook no disorder. I conduct executions immediately, publicly. These mobs of refugees will behave. Lisbon sits atop property owned by the Crown. It will remain the property of the Crown."

Quentin grinned with embarrassment at his imposture, then offered a parcel of bread to Petrine, who, taking it in his mouth, chewed monotonously as a cow its cud. "Thank the good Lord," added Quentin "that Sebastião José de Carvelho e Mello recognized his error: I am unshot." He smiled.

"Error," repeated Petrine lifelessly.

Quentin again smiled, rolling his eyes at the remark.

Slurping from his spoon, Jacques threw it aside and pitched forward on his knees. He tossed his half-eaten plate of food over his shoulder before leaning back against a pile of stones and snorting loudly into the night air. "You, Quentin, stink of corpses, of rotting flesh."

"Yes, most likely. My mission is among the maimed who are slowly dying."

"A nosegay, Jesuit, must be of little use with the stench of Lisbon's carnage," Jacques laughed. "Lisbon's rotting flesh. What we all are, Quentin Gray. Hark! Look next to you—my valet. Here by the light of your cook fire he appears more cadaver than man."

Quentin sat down, staring hard across the fire.

"You gawker."

"I'm at loose ends," Quentin said. "I barely keep my eyes open tonight. Such is my fatigue from the duties in Lisbon. We need not quarrel about the dead."

A mule brayed in the distance. While Quentin rubbed his forehead with the heels of his hands, his eyes glowed yellow, reflecting the bounding flames. "In this frivolous era," he said to himself, "I ponder the tragedy of Christian Lisbon and wonder how Europe may view it."

The earth rumbled, clattering several cook pans against one another.

Quentin tensed. In a brittle voice, he intoned, "God is our refuge and strength. Therefore will not we fear, though the earth be removed, and though the mountains be carried into the midst of the sea." The swaying stopped as Quentin repeated his litany. "God is—"

"A rancid and skulking scum, if He exists," Jacques screeched. "He's a drinker of blood. A cretinous filth who filches life from the innocent, yet requires the guilty to live. I defy heaven. I piss in God's face. God sucks dark-brown shit from my ass." Jacques angled his head and thrust out his tongue at the drab heavens.

Quentin staggered backwards from the fire into the dark.

When he again appeared in the light of the weak flame, his face was rigid. To Jacques he spoke. "I've dealt with foul sinners, with blasphemous heathens. My fortitude has not once wavered amidst the shocking scenes of Lisbon. Yet a guest, who must be—who is—out of his senses, has caused me extreme suffering." Quentin managed a mea culpa and stumbled away.

Minutes passed before Quentin's voice bellowed from the blackness of the night.

"Tomorrow morning, signor, I will share something that may save you from your inexcusable temperament."

* * *

Harsh morning sunlight skeltered across Jacques' eyelids but it was his profusion of nightmares that awoke him.

From across the palace wall, Quentin addressed his guest. "Will you hear me out, Jacques Casanova?" he said, striving to avoid the unkind sun. "I've withheld particular information from you. Information regarding the treasure."

Jacques, fingers in his mouth, crooked his head. He leapt up abruptly and strode imperiously toward Quentin and Petrine. "My disconsolate shadow leads the way," he cried.

"This is important, vital." Quentin unrolled a leather article the length of his forearm, sat on the ground, and in his lap smoothed out the delicate antique object. "This is the cover—the cover—that accommodated my scroll. An oiled animal membrane cloth. I always kept the scroll and the cover separated for various reasons, but primarily as surety for my safety." Quentin's lips drew tight. "My safety." He motioned Jacques closer, then displayed the article. "On this thin cover, I count forty-seven pinpricks—"

"Meaning?" muttered Petrine, hunkered near a corner of the roofless dwelling.

"Meaning?" repeated Quentin without taking his eyes from Jacques. "I don't know its meaning."

"Meaning. Life has meaning," sang Petrine, who promptly fell listless.

Standing above Quentin, Jacques cackled. "Forty-seven random pin-sized dots prick your scroll cover. Ha! Vital information. Momentous clue."

"This is pertinent, I'm certain. You and I will find where it fits in our puzzle."

"*We* will?" Jacques howled.

Quentin carefully set the scroll cover on the ground, roused himself to standing, and spoke with firmness. "You, Jacques Casanova, were put on this earth for a reason. I do not guess at your ultimate purpose, but it's not by accident that the Lord placed you here to twice spare my life, allowing us to solve this mystery together. Look at me, Jacques! I've practiced patience a long while, seen my share of treachery and death surrounding this secret. I have, God forgive me, participated in deceit myself." Quentin pointed a finger at the cover, drew a long breath, and went on. "As for your lack of character and courage—about which you hourly rant—you revealed your character in the crisis on the citadel parapet. For that reason, I choose to believe I can trust you. Also because Dominique Casanova told me of your character, I trust you."

Jacques slapped his hands to his ears and stamped his foot violently at the ground.

"She confided in me," Quentin said emphatically. "Does that stun you? Yes, she confided while I oversaw her wound. Yes, she was a Christian who knew she had sinned. She sought my spiritual comfort and advice. She told me you two were not husband and wife, as I suspected. She told me of your brother's death, of his lack of faith. She admitted her adultery. She spoke of your weaknesses, Jacques."

Jacques tore his hands from his ears. "Did she recount that she saved my life? But I ... I could not return the kindness."

"I saw you with my own eyes make a decision that imperiled your safety. You descended into that chasm. You chose to save her. You were willing to sacrifice yourself."

"I insisted—I demanded she come to the parapet that morning, leg wound and all. Jacques' voice shifted. "She needn't have been there."

"Dominique was willing to sacrifice herself for you against the Turk and for your search to find the treasure. In order that you might return to Venice. She had her doubts in the beginning, she told me, but as time went on, she was unambiguous. She supported your wishes, regardless of the cost. She performed 'the difficult task of loving you.' Those were her precise words." Quentin closed his eyes and rubbed his brows. "My advice is to examine yourself deeper. In God's world, we are all deserving of love."

Jacques threw his arms over his belly as if cinching in his guts, then slunk out the doorway shambles of the palace. His head drooped lower with every step.

"God delivered you for a reason," Quentin said quietly.

For the whole of the day, Jacques lay on his back, receiving little solace from the elements. All of nature seemed hushed. The sky, a barricade of gray, provided little antidote for his ill feelings. No activity of mind stirred him, and if asked what he was experiencing, there would have been no obtainable answer. When insolent clouds chased the weary sun to nightfall, Jacques pulled himself up, trudged back inside the palace, and dumped himself opposite Petrine.

A crackle in the brush. Jacques' ears tingled. *Beyond the wall,* he thought. *An intruder. So be it.* Jacques sat still, all too ready to meet his fate.

"It's early, but I've returned nevertheless," Quentin said, stepping across the threshold and brusquely slinging his pack to the ground. His cheek twitched as he clamped his jaws tight. "A stern and final rebuke from the king's minister, a staunch adversary, it seems, of the Society of Jesus. A man who considers even *former* Jesuits enemies. Today he ordered me to quit my mission, to allow the king's authorities to dictate policy. My helping hand in Lisbon is no longer welcomed." Quentin collapsed to a rock near Jacques and Petrine, smashing his fist into his palm. "As for good news, King Joseph escaped the catastrophe, as I have said. Several portions of the city are left undamaged. Neither quake nor flame has harmed them. God has spared them. But my spirits wane when I tell you of the fire-consumed Patriarchal Church, the many government offices, the Royal Palace, and scores of other notable buildings, private homes, and museums. All destroyed in the fire. Alas, too, the greatest of Lisbon's cathedrals have perished. Only the glorious city library remains whole. A very large portion of it, anyway."

"What cost in flesh?" Jacques yelped.

Quentin, ignoring the remark, stopped his quivering hand. "All seven of the Jesuit houses in Lisbon are destroyed."

"Seven, heaven, forty-seven," muttered Petrine.

"What?"

"Seven, heaven, twenty-seven. Seven, heaven, thirty-seven. Seven, heaven, forty—"

"Enough, Petrine. Do you understand? Enough!" Quentin buried his face in his sleeve and said nothing until, suddenly raising his head, he pinched his chin. "Seven Jesuit houses. Forty-seven pinpricks on the parchment. Forty-seven. Heaven … heaven. Saint. Forty-seven." His eyes turned toward the orange-streaked evening sky as he stroked his mouth rapidly. "At that time, at the time the treasure scroll might have been devised—1181, I believe—there would have been forty-seven monasteries in Europe. Not Jesuit monasteries, but

Cistercian. Forty-seven Cistercian monasteries." Quentin sprung from his rock, hurried to a bit of broken wall, and slowly extracted the scroll and its cover. "Can this association ..."

Jacques watched him with indifference.

Quentin returned and quickly squatted between Jacques and Petrine. "If these pinpricks indicate monasteries, one of them may hold the treasure."

"Search forty-seven monasteries?" Jacques sneered. "Over all of Europe?"

"Yes, if these ..." Quentin repeated the Latin verse, "*Ab uno disce omnes*. From one, learn to know all. This verse could affirm that from one monastery we could know all," Quentin said. "In the twelfth century, Bernard, founder of the Cistercians, designed all his monasteries with identical floor plans for the buildings. Identical. A blind man, it is said, having learned one, might enter any Cistercian monastery and find his way about. Saint Bernard was a man who prized discipline and uniformity, so he demanded—in the initial charter for the order—that in all future times there would be forty-seven monasteries, no more, no less. From my searches about our mystery, it's clear Bernard was well known to—and very influential with—the early Templars." Quentin scanned the parchment. "The second verse says, 'But to know all, you need but three.' Could this mean that to know where the treasure is hidden, you need but three?' Search three of the monasteries? That's not too many to solve a mystery of this magnitude."

"Magni—tude," replied Petrine in idiotic singsong.

Quentin turned toward the lethargic servant, whose long, rumpled hair obscured his face. He drew in a breath, shifted his body, and thinned his eyes. "It is held, Petrine," Quentin said, choosing his words syllable by syllable, "that the mystery will direct us to something of enormous value." He tucked gray hair behind his ear and made with his hand the sign of the cross before circling it around his mouth and whispering loud enough for Jacques to hear. "We seek the Son of God."

"Yes, the Son of God," Jacques said, defiance rising in his voice. "He's someone whose acquaintance I must surely make. It goes without saying. Be that as it may, my future is determined. I shall write a firsthand account of the horrific scenes in Lisbon, return to Paris, and sell my account to the public. I'll again be the talk of Europe. Indeed, the toast of Venice."

Quentin's jaw dropped. His voice flared. "Making money on the miseries of others? This is the time for righteous actions—a noble enterprise—that may go a long way toward healing you."

Ignoring Quentin, Jacques mused further to a vacant Petrine. "I may be nothing now, valet. But I'll again be respected, recognized, recognizable." Jacques paused. "Maybe even to myself."

- 33 -

"UNFORTUNATELY I'M MORE DELICATE than I appear. I'm not used to riding." Quentin laughed nervously, his eyes reflecting the scarlet sunset. "One trip up from Lisbon city on this mare, and my skin is raw." The horse boxed, its flailing head barely missing Petrine, who stood next to Jacques.

Quentin's face turned ashen. With extreme delicacy, he climbed from the saddle. "I also found—without intending to—the old girl gallops like the wind." He laughed again and fiddled the horse's mane. "Perhaps I shouldn't have rescued her, but she was loose, with no owner or rider anywhere in sight."

Quentin pushed the reins into Jacques' hands. While scanning up and down the path adjacent to his dwelling, the Jesuit lowered his breeches and examined his inner thighs.

"The skin has been excoriated from the flesh," Jacques said, looking around Quentin's shoulder. "Well done, well done. Or should I say rare? Bloody and rare?"

Quentin's attention was all for his legs. "I've some aloe as well as other medicines I shall apply. In the meantime, you're welcome to the horse."

Without a second thought, Jacques shook his locks and, tightening the surcingle, hopped into the saddle and kicked his heels hard into the mare's belly.

That night, Quentin pulled a blanket around his shoulders, while the mare, tied up inside the palace wall close by, whinnied and continued eating the scrubby grass. Through the smoke of the cook fire, Quentin glanced at Petrine, then up at Jacques, who stood over the limp flames.

"Now that the mare is in our possession," Jacques said, "I'll be going down to Lisbon."

"To minister to the needful people?"

"No, my mind is not changed. In Lisbon, nothing—or no one— will touch me. Nor I them. My plan is to take notes on what I hear, see, and smell, then based on close observations, each night I'll write my pamphlet within the confines of these walls."

"My opinion is you will also recommence our scroll search, with me or without me," Quentin said. "What I know for certain is that I'm a weary man who no longer has the vigor to carry on. By myself. Yet still, still my deep desire, my need, is to find the Christ, to know the truth of this matter. That necessitates utilizing your youth, Jacques Casanova, and your worldly wisdom." Quentin's voice grew staunch. "In the search, you've been a catalyst for me. My heart, Jacques, knows you'll continue to seek. And because of who you are, the treasure you may discover is greater—"

"I don't require you, your speeches, or your nag."

"Let us be forthright, signor. You may be at times beyond reason. But you're keen enough to stay near me. For my purse. For my foodstuffs."

Jacques found he did not have a response. He turned away. *The Jesuit speaks true. I use him. All my life I've used people for their purse or for what I could secure from them. My brother. Cardinal DeBernis. Dominique. Perhaps I am a leech. A mere parasite, as Cavaliere Grimani insisted. A parasite that needs a host on which to feed.*

Quentin raised a finger. "Yes, you need my assets. But I require your back and brains. In order to help each another, God has seen to it that our destinies intertwine."

An ember burst from the fire, offering brief light to the black night.

"Very well, borrow the mare!" Quentin barked. "Join me in my treks into the capital each day. Go your own way while in town. Write your pamphlet each and every night. But know that I, in spite the warnings of the king's men, intend to minister to those in need as well as continue our scroll search as best I can." The Jesuit leapt to his feet and marched away.

* * *

At early morning, walking side by side with Petrine, Quentin chattered. Jacques, on horseback and lost in his distemper, paid no attention.

"I've noticed the number of refugees has decreased," Quentin said. "Many of these displaced souls have probably been detained for lack of proper papers; some, sad to say, have succumbed to wild animals or starvation; some turned back because of the weather." Quentin looked up at Jacques. "This route down into Lisbon has not been hospitable for some."

"Whoa." Jacques jerked the reins. The mare halted, frosty air gusting from her nostrils.

Ahead on the precipice, a naked corpse caged in the hoops of a metal gibbet, a man's body broken on the wheel, and a pack of wretched onlookers blocked the path.

Quentin whispered to Jacques. "A warning that uncivil activity will be punished by the king's authorities."

Jacques gave the horse a heel, leading Quentin and Petrine with a solemn plod until they reached a standstill alongside this omen of doom.

From within the abject crowd, a child's voice rang out. "Mother, do you think a man, even if he be sinful, can go to heaven?"

There was not a murmur until a woman sternly answered. "The Church says when Christ returns at the Last Judgment, the chosen ones will ascend to heaven with Him."

"Yet another belief tells us that Christ does not lead us to heaven. We may make our own way," Quentin said, words spilling from his mouth. "Man can learn. Man can change. We make our own way."

"Without a priest?" piped a voice.

"Without even a Pope," Quentin said.

"You speak heresy," rumbled a voice.

"Heresy. Evil," barked someone else. "That which the heretic Voltaire spouts."

Before Jacques' eyes grew round and glassy, he cried out to the onlookers from atop the mare. "Many, many eons ago I met the illustrious Voltaire. I can state to you he is long, lean, and without buttocks. He needs flesh. Or he needs heat."

Several rumblings buzzed through the crowd while Jacques tugged his coat collar about his neck, regally dismounted, and tied his reins to the gibbet. "*This* poor fellow," Jacques pointed to the naked corpse in the gibbet, "needs more than heat. He needs heat and light. Light. Illumination."

Jacques, spying a young woman at the front of the mob, flapped his hand. "Mademoiselle Stench, do you stare at me? Or at the gibbeted fellow whose head has been shaved and tarred?" he asked, all the while jiggling the red ribbon on his coat. "Allow me to introduce myself. Pope Benedict himself presented to me this Order of the Golden Spur." Several in the crowd strained for a view. "'Tis my reward. For trying to outwit His Holiness. 'Tis."

Jacques left the gibbet, meandered toward the girl, words sliding from the side of his mouth. "The world's not sane, I know." He pushed out his chest and plucked at the red ribbon. "Touch, if you like, mademoiselle." Towering over her, he purred. "Touch me. Any of you. All of you. While I yet exist."

The woman extended her hand timidly, placing it on Jacques' medal. Moments passed before Jacques removed her hand, batted his eyes like a budding ingénue, then sauntered seductively toward Quentin Gray. "This man has a map. A map to find the Son of God. He does. And he's hinted," Jacques smiled wickedly, "he's told me if I abide with him, I, too, shall find the Son of God." Rolling his eyes, Jacques threw his head backward toward the corpses confined in the gibbet and wheel. "I say I've as much chance of finding the divine as the pair behind me."

"Man's a lunatic," snarled a woman's gruff voice.

"Heresiarch," another cried.

The grumbling grew louder while Jacques casually retrieved the reins of the mare, mounted, and squared himself in the saddle. He scarcely noticed Quentin hustle Petrine around the crowd and down the road.

"Do not ask yourself too many questions," Jacques cried to the wretches. "You may find answers that make you unhappy." Jacques' voice faltered. "Answers that may do you damage. Destroy you." He dug his heels into the mare's flanks. "Farewell. Peace be with you. Peace be with me," he shouted into the frigid air as he galloped onward toward Lisbon.

Riding into the capital later, Jacques found desolation. Buildings, churches, shops, homes—crushed and burnt civilization, mangled ruin. From beneath an enormous, jagged stone a half-dozen human arms could be seen, resembling, for all the world, an ungainly gargantuan spider. Further along, a friendless colt, stained fetlock deep in burgundy-black blood, neighed. Scene after curious scene presented itself until Jacques, sick at heart, galloped away from Lisbon—the stench of ubiquitous death in his nostrils.

* * *

The wind wheezed through the uneven stones of Conde de Tarouca's palace wall, producing an odd, aggravating clamor while Jacques, at the far corner of the dwelling, took a seat astride one of his traveling trunks—for the present, his table. Off to his side, Petrine sat, still and quiet.

In the nearing darkness, Jacques couldn't see what he furiously scribbled on the paper, but he loudly voiced the words he wrote. "Half-expecting the Scylla to ensnare me while I tailed through the catastrophic mess past the library of Lisbon—incredibly, still intact, and able, without apology, to accommodate Human Truth—a dreadful odor assailed me, giving notice that pathetics must lie close at—"

A crunch of boots on rocky soil announced Quentin's approach. Jacques glanced at him, then bent further over his work.

"A good evening to you both," Quentin said, squatting across from Petrine to hand him his cup.

Petrine drank greedily, soon emptying the vessel. Retrieving the cup, Quentin sat on the ground while Jacques, giving no salutation, grunted threateningly.

After a while, Quentin began lightly mouthing words. Soon he could be heard just above the bursts of racing wind. "*Ab uno disce omnes.* From one, learn to know all."

Jacques rolled up his sheaf of papers and gripped them as if choking the life from an enemy. Out of spite, he cited the third verse. "*Est modus in rebus.* There is a proper measure in things."

"That's your translation of the Latin? Is that how you interpret it?" Quentin asked, setting his cup aside. "No. *Est modus in rebus*, I say, is 'The golden mean should always be observed.'"

Jacques shot a fierce look.

Quentin pressed his palms together. "Could it be that in some manner both translations are valid? Equally valid?"

Jacques turned his backside to Quentin and Petrine.

Brief flashes of lightning silvered the sky. The mare, tethered not far away, pawed the ground.

Petrine snorted. "One of these days soon," he crowed, "I shall be a titan and travel in a well-appointed coach and six. With robust horses, a coachman, two footmen in liveries, a postilion, a jolly gentleman on horseback, and a young page with a feather in his cap."

"Well, there's a lofty ambition if ever I heard one," said Quentin. Astonishment slowly claimed his face. He turned toward the valet. "A full thought, Petrine! The first and complete thought you've uttered since ... and what a protracted thought it is, man! Well, I'm glad your firmer nature has—is—returned. Well, well, well."

"Tomorrow, Petrine, you'll forage for us," Jacques snarled without pause. "Understand me?"

Petrine nodded his head. "Yes. Yes, sir. And when we find the treasure trove, then the coach and six?" he asked.

Quentin laughed. "Once you have your coach, be so kind as to ride me down into Lisbon each day. That would be the lap of luxury." His eyes toughened when he turned to Jacques. "*Est modus in rebus*. The golden mean should always be observed. Think on it. Please."

*   *   *

Jacques awoke fitfully the next morning—a cruel, hard wind etching all that remained of the palace walls. At a distance he saw Quentin holding the reins of the mare.

"Shall we make our start down to Lisbon?" asked Quentin.

Petrine, demeanor grave, stood nearer, unbundled to the cold, enveloped in a bank of fog, switching at his leg with a slender twig. He appeared more apparition than man.

"Ronyon, bring me my snuff," Jacques yelled. "And my gold snuffbox."

Petrine stiffened. "Master, I have no snuff. And certainly not your snuffbox."

"Certainly not," Jacques cried back, a tinge of skepticism in his voice. He flicked his hand in an imperial wave as if to say *never mind* and pulled his blanket tighter to his shoulders.

Quentin joined Petrine, handed him the reins, then approached Jacques, telling him that the valet would use the horse to forage, and that he himself would walk today—to keep from reaggravating his thighs.

"Are you in a right way—in a right mind, Jacques, to accompany me?" asked Quentin. He was ignored.

Petrine climbed into the primitive, worn-out saddle. The mare clopped forward. Horse and rider crossed through the bank of fog and were soon out of sight.

"Well, we're a bit late," Quentin said.

Jacques pivoted from his makeshift bedding. "Is there a soul?" he blurted.

Quentin tucked his chin to his chest, then gazed at Jacques. "In a group of budding theologians, I would expect this question, but in the light of your peculiar humors ..."

Jacques clicked his teeth together rapidly.

"Is there a soul?" Quentin repeated calmly.

"*Sola scriptura,*" Jacques said. "*Sola scriptura.* The scriptures are the sole authority, true enough? The scriptures should have the answer." Jacques squawked like a bird.

"Yes, the scriptures are *most* important," countered Quentin, "but even as a Christian, I believe the proverb that warns us to beware the man who has read only one book to discover his truth."

The wind erupted, forcing Quentin to pull his ragged coat closer to his body. "Shall we begin our journey? We shall talk of this on our way to Lisbon."

For several moments, Jacques stood back, staring only at Quentin's face.

* * *

Jacques slammed the top of his trunk shut, making Petrine jump. "What are you doing here at the close of day with my papers in your hand? What business have you with them? What else of mine do you have? What else?"

Petrine stood straight as a sword blade. He handed the sheaf of papers back.

"You seem less than repentant."

"Please don't shout, master. I can explain." Throwing a look across the dusky sky, Petrine pulled his fists to his sides and resumed. "I wanted to find out if your pamphlet is nearly at the ready so that we might leave for Paris soon."

"I scarcely believe that—"

"As is the custom, you'd want your arrival announced in the gazettes, wouldn't you? And I would be in charge of—"

"Perhaps, ronyon, I don't want my name known to all of Paris. Especially with Cavaliere Grimani and his ilk. Perhaps I've changed my mind about the pamphlet. Perhaps you've overstepped your—"

"Hello there," came Quentin's voice, carried on the blustery breeze. "So many clouds. Barely a sun to tell us it's sunset." He crossed toward Jacques and Petrine. "What passes?"

Jacques flung open the trunk, threw his papers inside, slammed the lid, and stalked a few paces away.

Quentin ignored the behavior and stepped to Petrine, placing his arm over the valet's shoulder. "A miracle—that your faculties returned. A true miracle," Quentin said loudly—and in Jacques' direction. "One for which we might express thanks to God."

"Tomorrow," Petrine said bluntly. He flinched at a sudden flash of lightning, slipped out from Quentin's arm, and wandered toward the mare, glancing from the corners of his eyes at his master.

*   *   *

It was the next morning when Jacques awoke with a start. He was tense. Day after day, hungry thoughts had clawed his mind. He thirsted for something—but he knew not what. At night he toiled with desperate dreams that engendered a yearning unlike any he'd ever known.

He stared out across the rocky soil while the invisible wind lofted debris high into a dull, gray sky. Bleary, he gazed through a peephole in the palace walls and saw, at a fair distance, refugees tramping by, their heads bent toward the pathway before them, as if hitched with a yoke. *Dreary monotony of endless manhood.*

He rose and relieved himself, a dozen thoughts in his head competing for attention. At this hour of the morning, the sweet fragrance of perfume used to please his nostrils. Now, piss and stale dung.

While he scrubbed fiercely at his rough beard, his mouth filled with words. "I must go back," he said. "I must return."

In short order, he gathered food, water, and what items he deemed necessary for the journey, then woke Petrine. "I want you with me. Rouse yourself now."

A short distance away, Quentin was waking. "What cryptic needs have you this morning?" he called out. No answer came back.

Jacques faced the cold wind, mumbling to his valet. "I've made up my mind to travel to the seat of my present miseries: the citadel."

By noon, Jacques and Petrine stood at the foot of the citadel ruins. The tower was gone. The spiraling stairs upward—those few that remained—were caked in mud and refuse. The rest of the steep incline looked as if a phalanx of infantry had trampled it to grit.

Jacques said nothing, his mouth grim, fixed.

Petrine spoke. "The parapet wall, some of it, is still there, but ..." he shivered "this place does not please me."

"Stay here at the base."

"Should you need me, shout from above."

Jacques did not acknowledge his servant but, with eyes pitched upward, began his ascent in a crawl.

After reaching his destination at the top of the hill, he peered about, his breathing ragged and heavy. For a time he lay on his belly, lingering, looking. Fouling the rock yard were numerous fish skeletons, battered bits of human refuse, and pulverized dead trees. Hoary clay and coffee-colored mud melded together in rivulets. Jacques seemed a spectator to the upheaval of the underworld.

He clambered, finally, across the uneven stones until, arriving at the edge of the pit, his initiative gave way.

When at last he brought himself to peek into the hole, Jacques saw nothing more than mud and rubble.

On his elbows, he wrenched in each direction. No Dominique. His body curled up. Then, as if he were being crushed by a heavy atmosphere, he flattened to his back, unable to move, to breathe, to cry out. He felt fragile, frail.

A beaded raindrop struck his cheek. Then another. His hands fumbled against the surface of coarse stones, his fingers earning no relief until a thing of a different texture piqued his senses. He clasped the object tightly, fingers gliding over its slippery, rain-soaked surface before bringing it to his eyes.

"A nautilus, a chambered nautilus." Faintly he spoke. "My good brother painted and painted and painted the lustrous cross section of your inner shell, so elegant, symmetrical," he confided to the object. "Should I again find symmetry in this world, I'll think upon you, nautilus. And upon Francesco."

More, even dearer words, flowed from his lips. "A creature of the sea, a thing of beauty—Mademoiselle Nautilus. Abandoned here on an earthen hill? So far from home. Belonging to nothing, to no one. From what distant ocean did the furious wave carry you? The wave that stole our Dominique." Jacques, blinking away the rainwater from his eyes, gulped for air. "You have your shell to protect you. What have I?"

He swabbed his skin and hair with the once-living nautilus, feeling its rain-cold chill. It was as if Fragoletta's fingers stroked his face. Cool comfort.

He settled into his solace until a greater cascade of rain cut it short.

His search persisted through the devastated ruins until, driven by the storm, he descended the tangled stairs, nautilus in hand.

The rain pelted with formidable power by the time Jacques reached his valet at the foot of the stronghold.

"Were your pamphlet studies worthwhile?" Petrine asked.

"I'd no business with the pamphlet. I sought to reclaim ..." Jacques ran the nautilus shell across his chin. "It feels as if the Fates commanded me here. As if Dominique wished me here, purely for this simple gift." In his palms he framed the nautilus before placing it into his shirt. With nothing more to say, he turned and scuttled down the steep road. Petrine hauled his pack to his shoulder, wondering.

* * *

The breeze blowing through Lisbon's hills was cold the following afternoon, but once the sun begged the clouds for a breach and those clouds allowed the fiery sphere to give out its glories, Quentin and Jacques slowed their pace. The Jesuit had questions about the adventurer's outing the previous day; about his continued, solitary trips to Lisbon; about the scroll. Jacques remained silent.

As the pair rounded a wood, an inky crow drawing down the wind careened past, practically unseating Quentin from his saddle and extracting a harried glance from Jacques.

Jacques lagged next to the mare, pointing past a crooked tree just ahead. "Bring me my snuff. My snuff, Petrine. And snuffbox," he shouted.

"You left your valet at my place early this morning to forage again. To whom, my friend, do you now talk?" Quentin asked, shaking his head. He tightened the reins.

"We have snuff to trade," rang a voice from behind.

Jacques spun on his heels while Quentin wheeled the horse about as best he could.

Both observed, at a dozen paces, two figures in hooded cloaks and a third man, his exposed face worn and pale.

"Refugees on the move," Jacques muttered.

"We have snuff to trade. For food," insisted the first hooded man.

Astride the mare, Quentin took a quick glance down to Jacques as if to say, "Do you really want tobacco?"

"Food for snuff?" Jacques asked. "We have food."

One stranger tramped past Jacques, who stood beside the constricted path. "Our companion—the one behind us—has crab's-eye, sir. Help yourself."

"*Aide-toi, le ciel t'aidera*," mumbled the other hooded man as he passed.

"Help yourself, and heaven will help you," translated his snickering companion.

English. He sounds English. "The man on the horse has the food," Jacques said to the strangers' backs.

The pair of men trudged toward Quentin, who reined in the skittish mare, barely urging it away from a tree onto the path. Once the horse was adequately under control, Quentin jabbed into the bundle behind his saddle.

The third man offered his trade to Jacques. "Besides tobacco, good sir, you may want to occupy yourself with this, if it pleases you." From inside his cloak, the man brought out a snuffbox and pressed a button on its side. When a small compartment opened, he held it up to Jacques' eye.

Jacques grinned. He pressed his palms together. "Why, yes, I truck with these. Yes," he said, noting the man's hand.

I've seen that scar somewhere.

A dull thud of hooves struck Jacques ears. He looked back at Quentin, extended over the fragile neck of the mare, offering bread to the two men who crowded his horse. In an instant, the larger man took hold of Quentin's arm, flinging him to the ground. The mare reared.

"Murder!" Jacques cried.

A hand tightened around Jacques' wrist. He reacted by driving his free elbow into his assailant's face. Just as quickly, he faced a pistol barrel. He slipped sideways, then redoubled the attack on the man. The hood recoiled from the attacker's head while Jacques, dry with rage, pummeled again. A pulp of bloody flesh. He'd crushed an eye.

The man crumpled to the ground, but not before Jacques seized the pistol, pushed the barrel into the base of the man's limp neck, and fired. The head exploded like a red firework, spraying nuggets of bone, blood, and brain.

Racing toward Quentin, Jacques swiftly ensnared the assailant's dagger, stabbed the man to death, then spotted the third stranger, who had clumsily drawn back into a gnarl of trees.

It was as if a tiger had cornered a hare. But the hare immediately found courage in the guise of a pistol. The gun belched smoke. A deadly ball jumped from the barrel, sizzling with swift death as it passed Jacques' face.

From beneath his cloak, the man jerked out another pistol and aimed.

Jacques sprang, brandishing his bloody dagger. There were only gasps—no screams—when the man sagged to the mushy ground. Jacques stood flat-footed while the body shook violently from head to toe, then ceased to move.

Panting without stop, he marched back to Quentin. He gaped at the thick pool of blood that outlined the Jesuit, then knelt.

"Beg their forgiveness," the Jesuit choked. His eyes remained closed. "Peace I leave with you, my peace I give unto you," was the final utterance of Quentin Gray.

Jacques wiped red ooze from his arms, fingers, and face before sitting cross-legged. He was cold, chilled. Wrapping his arms around himself, he surveyed the carnage before him and behind him.

After a time, Jacques unsheathed his poniard and plunged it into the damp soil, overturning a large chunk of brown earth. He dug again and again until he growled, "Deep enough."

He examined Quentin's body before laying it in the grave. "*Mors ultima linea rerum est,*" he shouted. "Death is the final boundary line of all things."

After finishing the burial, Jacques moved toward the mare. Approaching the alarmed animal, he took several determined steps; then gently reaching for the reins, he coaxed the horse close. The animal stood firm while Jacques whispered in its ear.

"Much chatter jangles in my head, friend. How much between your ears?" He moved to the other side of the mare. "I want you to know," Jacques said in a plaintive tone, "I'm not responsible for his death. Truly, I'm not."

Jacques wrapped the reins around a thick shrub. To the dead man in the gnarled trees, he marched.

"Weeds will soon grow through your ribs, fellow." He ripped the man's shirt from his abdomen, then trod to the second assassin, again tearing the shirt away from its owner.

"As I supposed." Jacques stared at the gut of his victim, took his dagger, and thumped the pommel against the man's abdomen. "Didn't Quentin say he'd fit this silver plate? For a saber cut?" Jacques threw down the bloody shirt, spit into his palms to scrub away the blood from his hands, and eased the dagger's blade beneath a lanyard around the dead man's neck. He cut the leather thong. From it, he unthreaded a crucifix.

Jacques plodded back to the grave, hunkered down, then sat and propped his back against the mound of earth that bore down on the Jesuit's corpse. For a long while, a cloud bred a shadow, encasing the dismal scene.

"Old Quentin Gray, you claimed that assassins from the Church murdered your Jesuit brethren," Jacques said while dangling the crucifix. "I believe you now. Now that you, too, are murdered. By Catholic assassins. So my curiosity pleads: what treasure is so vast, so prized, that the Church of Rome is willing to kill its own holy men? What treasure? What secret?"

After he unpinned the Order of the Golden Spur that rested on his bosom, Jacques smudged his fingers across the ribbons. He placed the medal and the crucifix in his hand and slung both into the woods.

- 34 -

INTO CONDE DE TAROUCA'S UNFINISHED PALACE tramped Jacques, his shoulders hunched against the merciless rain, the mare he led looking as exhausted as he himself felt.

Petrine gingerly lifted himself from a rock, took the animal's reins, and signaled Jacques to take his place. "You look soaked. And you're wan," he said. "But I'm happy you're back."

Jacques said nothing.

"Where is Senor Gray?"

When there was no reply, Petrine, for a time, went about his business with the mare until he again broached the subject. "When shall we expect Senor Gray?"

"He's gone. For good."

"For good?" Petrine sputtered. "To where? Where would he go? He's not coming back at all?"

"Didn't say."

The mare snorted. Petrine jerked the bit. He balled his fist, punched the mare's neck, and again yanked the mouthpiece. "Did Senor return your scroll?" Petrine demanded, looming over Jacques.

"A scroll, a scroll cover, an intaglio rubbing, and a replenished purse," Jacques said, tapping the tips of each finger for emphasis. "All mine."

"How is it the Jesuit's so openhanded?"

"He's murdered."

"Murdered?" Petrine's features turned black. He fixed on his master's eyes, swollen, rheumy.

"The man with the silver-plated gut. And his fellow assassins. The Jesuit's dead."

Petrine crooked over toward Jacques, leaning into his face. "But you say we have the scroll, cover, and purse?"

"As I say."

The valet tied the horse to a rock on the palace wall, and unable to build a fire in the rain, he prepared a cold meal while Jacques sat. Afterwards, the valet busied himself nearby.

In a much measured manner, Jacques, rainwater streaming his face, nodded his head, and taking his hand from his pocket, he held close the nautilus shell from the citadel and began to imagine it neatly cross-sectioned.

A sudden epiphany emblazoned his brain. He sat straight and whispered hoarsely. "The mathematics for our mystery."

"What?" asked Petrine. He turned and quickly crouched opposite his master. "The mystery, the treasure?"

What little light that was left of the day was so submissive to the rain that Jacques could barely see his valet before him. He planted his elbow in his lap, rested his chin on his hand, and began talking with himself. "Must now fuse all drawn-out thoughts in my head. You may stay. Or you may go."

Petrine stooped even more forward, his scowl beginning to reappear. "Obliged to stay."

"A riddle is a delicate item. And multifaceted. An item unlocked by the means of clues."

"I'm well aware, sir, that clues—"

"Our assumption," Jacques said lazily, not looking at Petrine, "our assumption is that the symbols and verses on Fragonard's scroll are clues. The cover of Fragonard's scroll is also significant, is also a clue.

"However, any of these clues may have been created by their originators, the Templars, to be false lures, decoys. Or perhaps the Templars constructed a clue symbol that's useful only if utilized in concert with another symbol or verse. And what of the possibility that our scroll and cover don't possess every one of the clues we need to solve the riddle?"

Jacques persisted. "Further, because our world, our cultures, have changed greatly since the time of the Templars, we also are obligated to keep ourselves open for clues in contemporary forms.

Clues not on the scroll and cover itself but possibly adopted—adapted—from them."

Jacques pulled at his cheeks as if he were trying to wring the rainwater from them. "I've been dwelling—"

"You have a grip on the mystery?" Petrine asked, impatience grating his voice.

Jacques' lips hastened into a fragile smile before he resumed talking to the drizzle as if Petrine were not there. "Inside the Fragonard scroll are four Latin verses and an anagram, S-O-N-B-O-I-S-I-L-A. The scroll also contains—I don't know which—a hieroglyph or stylized alphabet letter forming the humpbacked camel symbol. The number *1300* is written on the scroll. And finally, the scroll possesses an inherent mathematical symbol, the tiny intaglio drawing."

Jacques suddenly rose and, sloshing through the mud, crossed the yard of Conde de Tarouca's palace, spewing words as he went. Petrine attempted to follow but slipped to his knees in the mire. Cursing, he quickly pulled himself up and stumbled toward his master, who stood beside one of his rain-soaked travel trunks.

"Omnipresent," Jacques said. "Everywhere—relatively speaking." With a muddy finger, he drew circles within circles on the top of the wet trunk. "The intaglios. These circles are ubiquitous. Commonplace. On the columns in the Stables of Solomon, at Quentin's Basilica de Santa Maria, on the outside of the scroll, at the citadel, Quentin told us." Jacques slapped the trunk's top, making the water leap. "The Templars could incise or draw this intaglio everywhere, anywhere, and because of its undemanding design, it would be seen only as a simple decorative emblem—concentric circles—by a majority of men. Undoubtedly, others might see that the intaglios are not concentric and comprehend the inherent mathematics of Plato's Theorem, but only a meager few would ever be able to connect it to anything further—unless one had, for instance, our scroll. The cunning Templars created the ever-present intaglios as a test. And if one passes their scroll-intaglio association, the Templars offer a strong hint so we may extend our knowledge about the mystery—with the assistance of mathematics."

"What?" Petrine croaked.

"Harken to this, ye gods," Jacques declared. "Since reading Horace as an adolescent, I supposed his words *Est modus in rebus* to translate as 'there is a proper measure in things.' But of late, of very late, in contemplating this Latin quote in our scroll—and believing mathematics to be part and parcel of our mystery—I have entertained Quentin Gray's translation: 'The golden mean should always be observed.' What more beautiful mathematics than the golden mean?" Jacques hurled his arms at the menacing clouds. "To solve the mystery, one must recognize the mathematical intent of the intaglios: they point to, must be used in concert with, a specific clue, Horace's Latin line—the golden mean line."

Jacques' shoulders shook. He pushed on his forehead, muttered something, then smeared his hand across the trunk.

Petrine spoke. "I enjoy sharing your thoughts, sir, but I must confess my ignorance when you say this golden mean has ..."

"However, this clue has been modified, has been contemporized—and this contemporary clue has been, at times, right before my very eyes—the *cross section* of the chambered nautilus. The nautilus—its underlying spiral skeleton—is what Vicomte de Fragonard commissioned my brother Francesco to paint."

Jacques held the small dead sea creature at arm's length. "Would that I could cross-section this shell to view the individual chambers the nautilus forms while the sea creature inside it grows." He brought the object close to his face, speaking softly, sweetly to it. "As mathematicians know, the spiral shell of the chambered nautilus—to the amazement of the ancient Greeks—grows, spreads in a fixed and definite proportion. Mathematically 1.618 to 1. A never-ending, never-repeating number. The so-called golden mean."

Petrine stared hard at the nautilus while pacing back and forth. "I think we need to be clear what I'm confused about."

"The golden mean," continued Jacques, "was found by these same Greeks to govern *many* phenomena of nature. The whorls on a pinecone, for example, a simple pinecone. Or the spacing of buds on a stem, the shape of an egg, seed-head groupings, and sometimes—the spirals of seashells. The Greeks glorified the golden mean, all but worshipped it."

"As I certainly esteem you, sir."

Jacques' body shook again, his eyes growing wide as if a ghost had crossed his path. He pinched at his lip. "Ye gods, ye gods," he whispered, a catch in his voice. "Thwarted. Thwarted, I confess." After his jaw fell open, he slowly lowered his head. With crossed arms, Jacques Casanova sought to protect the chambered nautilus from the drenching rain. He pried open the lid of his trunk, stuffing the shell deep inside.

"Where's the treasure we look for?" Petrine asked.

Raking and raking his fingers through his hair, the adventurer watched the raindrops, like tears, drown in the watery mud. "Wit's end, sirrah. Stygian darkness is my sole companion. What I've relayed is the absolute sum of what I know."

"That's all?"

Jacques Casanova laughed with such strange glee that Petrine could only blink in amazement.

* * *

Jacques left Petrine early in the week, making clear he would again return to Conde de Tarouca's abode but that his stay in Lisbon would be as long as his investigations required.

"You, valet, will stay here and care for the mare," Jacques said. "My piles, aggravated to distraction, have made riding a less than pleasant prospect for me, but we'll need a horse in future days."

The main library of the city of Lisbon remained in one piece. Although the mighty earthquake had reduced many of the surrounding buildings to odd-angled rubble, yet that stout repository of wisdom stood barely molested. There were, to be sure, breaches in the structure and one major wall slanted uncertainly, but from a quick reckoning Jacques knew he might—and must—gain access to the library, even if it were ready to fall down around him. He also knew that, for reasons of public safety as well as to prevent looting, the library would be off-limits to all patrons.

The immediate hindrances were the three guards, soldiers of Carvalho e Mello who gave vigilant watch at the library's entrance. *Banter and barter must win the day.*

Jacques, charming the soldiers with personal flattery and tales of exotic women as well as monetary tokens from Quentin's purse, soon was slipped through the doors of the institution, only to be met by two gentlemen in the library's sanctum. Coins of the realm did not seem a motivating gift for these two learned men, but Jacques, now the mad fox, had planned well. He expounded on his "obsessive hunger for knowledge," then displayed one of his most prized possessions, his treatise on squaring the cube—the vexing mathematical problem he'd mentioned to Dominique, a solution toward which he'd worked for years.

The two gentlemen well understood the paper's importance, even incomplete as it was; to examine that "honeyed treatise," as they put it, they were willing to grant Jacques what he wished.

Jacques intended, he explained, to inspect as many monastery maps as achievable. Maps from the time of Bernard of Clairvaux, if possible. Ideally, originals. Or, hopefully, exact copies. What Jacques didn't say was that his task was to scrutinize the thinnest of these maps to discover if the unfurled scroll cover could be suitably seen when situated underneath a map.

Jacques was stunned when he was told the library owned no monastery maps. But hundreds of maps of Europe existed. Jacques agreed to see those.

At last within the confines of the library, he stood gazing at the shelves before him. A thorny challenge. Five hundred maps, perhaps, or more. Most all in scroll form—well taken care of, neatly arranged, no sign of bug or rodent invasion, and little dust upon the shelves in which they nestled.

He began his investigation.

Four days and nights Jacques conducted his research, the only disruptions being the naps he took or the sparse meals he had brought with him.

When he at length found his way out of the library vaults, it was difficult to say if the outlandish smile on his face was one of happiness, relief—or one of madness.

*   *   *

On the morning Jacques left for Lisbon, Petrine had planned to secretly follow his master into town to mind his actions. The valet allowed Jacques a head start toward Lisbon, but at the last moment, he'd decided a quick forage for food supplies was needed. Petrine soon delayed his trip entirely, for in an abandoned dwelling he discovered, then confiscated, three bottles of wine.

The spirits fulfilled their role. Drinking from late afternoon to sunup, Petrine deemed it reasonable to hard-gallop the mare.

Just as the newly washed rays of morning spilled over the horizon, the valet slunk from the saddle to the ground. Waking much later, he discovered the result of his rashness: the horse had drunk from a nearby creek till it foundered and died.

"I shouldn't have trusted the beast," Petrine announced angrily.

He soon traded the mare's saddle for an abundance of food and wine and returned to Conde de Tarouca's palace to wait.

On a cold afternoon, Jacques finally returned

Serving the evening meal, Petrine sadly recounted how the mare had thrown him from the saddle and run away. He then took a stone seat opposite Jacques, who did not lift his head but with blank eyes sat bemused in thought.

When Petrine asked about his master's inquiries in Lisbon, there was no response. Instead, Jacques began to slowly rap his knuckles on the stone on which he slumped.

"A mix of intuition, analysis, and raw trial and error—that's who I am, that's why I'll succeed," mumbled Jacques, his mouth barely eking out the words. "My task requires the thinnest of maps, essentially cloths of oiled animal membrane. Maps I can see through. After examining three dozen of these maps, I begin to wonder at my obsession. After a hundred of them, I doubt my mind."

Tottering at the edge of his rock seat, Petrine reached for Jacques' plate and set it on the ground. "What are you talking—?"

Jacques exhaled loudly, then began in a shrill voice. "I unroll Quentin's scroll cover and affix it to the library desk as flat as is possible.

"Now I ask 'Which one of these forty-seven pinpricks, these forty-seven monasteries, contains the treasure?' A line from the scroll helps mandate my answer. 'To know all, you need but three.' In other words, to know everything, to solve the mystery, I need employ just three—pinpricks.

"Three points, as any schoolboy knows, may construct a triangle. Located at one of those points of the triangle may be the monastery I seek. But no. The Templars were more cunning.

"In this matter," Jacques droned, "another line from the scroll neatly directs me. 'The golden mean should always be observed.' This clue furnishes a mathematical proportion that will help me connect three pinpricks—not into a plain, unsophisticated triangle, but into an extraordinary spiral.

"For the time being, I make the assumption that Lisbon is the central locus of the spiral I want to construct. From the general pattern of the forty-seven pinpricks, I ascertain that only one prick—the one farthest from all the others—stands for Lisbon. Using the city as my locus, I very carefully draw a spiral on my scroll cover based on the golden mean proportion, a spiral that, I hope, will intersect only *two other points* of the forty-seven. It seems my rigors are rewarded with accomplishment when I find two—and only two—points that intersect the outward-bounding spiral. 'To know all, you need but three': these two points and my locus are the three.

"Now I must determine where these points lie on an actual geographic map.

"The forty-seven pinpricks of my cover, each representing an existing monastery—all must lie *within* the land boundaries of a European map. Cistercian monasteries, after all, are built on land, not on the ocean. Again and again over the unfurled scroll cover, I position the thin European maps—remembering that I'm looking for a template of Europe that will match exactly the size of my unfurled scroll cover. Days and nights pass with only a dim candle and a small bug to companion me."

"A bug?" Petrine's voice rose adamantly. "I've been quite patient—"

"None of the first hundred European maps I try encompass the requisite pinpricks, but finally a map turns up that does, indeed, hold all forty-seven." Jacques straightened up his body and stopped his knuckle rapping. His head still hung low.

"Carefully steadying this map of Europe on top of the scroll, two—and only two—points intersect the spiral I've drawn. One or both of these points on the spiral must be the geographic location of the monastery we want.

"And then further, glimpsing the right corner of my special map, I spy the number *1300* in the same stylized calligraphy as my scroll's. This unexpected and joyful surprise gives me hope that I hold the appropriate Templar map. Eventually I examine all the remaining maps, but only this one fits all my criteria."

"You know the actual site of our treasure?" cried Petrine.

Jacques jerked his head up, tilting it strangely. "The closest monastery," he said, "if I've properly understood the cipher, the code, and the other abstractions—if I'm precise—the search will lead to a monastery located, by my estimation, somewhere within ten to twenty square kilometers of terrain in southern France."

"Southern France?" Petrine's eyes closed. "Twenty square kilometers? Twenty!" He opened his eyes, jammed his fingers to his open mouth, and began to gnaw. After a glaring silence, he spoke. "I never distrust your taste in women. Nor your brilliance in scholarly areas. Nor your talent to inspire me onward. But in all humility, sir, in all frankness, at this moment I ask, are you in your right mind?"

"Did you speak?"

Petrine rubbed his balled fists against his thighs. "I asked, are you in your right mind?"

Jacques' head fell forward as if ready for the executioner's axe. "I believe … I do believe I'm right—in my mind." Long moments passed before he again spoke in an uneven whisper. "But perhaps my heart is still lacking."

- 35 -

"SLOGGING THROUGH DECEMBER'S RAIN is not taxing enough," Petrine grumbled to himself while he readjusted the packet on his shoulder. "Now a week out of Lisbon, the clouds of France buckle with freezing snow. My master should reward me for thinking to steal heavy coats for us before we left. And he ought to be grateful I thought to hide away his travel trunks in Lisbon." Petrine laughed quietly. "I never supposed in all my days I'd see him part with those and his vanities." He scurried to catch up with Jacques, who was not far ahead.

"The air—tantalizing," Jacques muttered.

Petrine took a sidelong glance at Jacques. "Yes, master. Practically springlike."

He listened to the aggravating crunch of his boots on the hard-frozen earth. "Darkness is close upon us, master. When do we stop?"

"By my judgment, we're a short walk farther to Arques."

"Perhaps it's a *ville* large enough to provide shelter for the night? I can't move one foot in front of the other much longer."

Jacques studied the sky, all the time keeping his steady pace. His face was drawn, eyes red.

Within a half hour, the daylight had all but disappeared—but so, too, had Petrine and Jacques covered a fair distance.

"Can that be the light of an inn?"

"I say it is."

"Even if the place is a chimera, it must suffice."

The next morning, after a well-deserved sleep and breakfast, Jacques and Petrine convened outside their austere and ancient lodging.

"Glad to have found this place last night." Petrine was about to blow hot breath on his fingers when the inn's signboard squeaked in the stout northeast wind. "Master, master," Petrine stammered. "Do you see?"

"I do. I'm looking where you are. And I'm incredulous. But let us take our eyes off the sign immediately."

After a quick "Follow me," Jacques took a dozen lively steps across the wide path that passed for a road and collapsed his back against a gargantuan boulder. Petrine followed, animated with excitement.

"Stand here opposite me," Jacques said, "so I can talk with you while I take this in."

"The sign on the inn reads what I think it does?"

"Yes. *Siste viator.* Stop, traveler." Jacques spoke as a gust swirled snow about his head. "The last Latin line on our treasure parchment is the *name* of our inn." His eyes gleamed fiercely. He clamped Petrine's shoulder.

"Master, master. What? What?"

"In the far distance beyond the inn, I see the formation. A mountain formation. *The* mountain formation. *Ecce signum.* Behold the proof."

Petrine began to turn, but Jacques pulled him back.

"If I could paint this remarkable mountain from where we stand," Jacques said, "it would match Francesco's landscape canvas. And further, a drawn outline of the formation surely corresponds to the double-humped camel on our scroll, what I thought indicated only letters of some alphabet."

Petrine wrung both hands around Jacques' outstretched arm.

Jacques spoke quietly, insistently. "I see now. Vicomte de Fragonard commissioned Francesco to copy that rugged likeness on canvas—an ingenious way to leave behind an important clue. Remember? *Ars longa, vita brevis,* the Vicomte often repeated. Art lasts longer, much longer, than a human. Art can pass on a vital secret with a greater accuracy and for longer—from generation to generation, from culture to culture, if necessary. Francesco innocently copied an image of the unique landscape we view."

"Master, look at me," exclaimed Petrine.

Jacques' warm breath exhaled a ghostly mist in the freezing air. "What I say, Petrine, is that my eyes must perceive the very location the clues provide. We've reached our destination. This is where we want to be."

Petrine wrapped his arms around his master, nearly crushing him with a hug. "Joy! I dance with joy!"

It was quickly agreed Petrine would, in the shortest time possible, glean what information he could and make subtle arrangements for the journey to the mountain. To that end, he spoke with those few locals who wandered about the inn. He began with the innkeeper.

"So, heading south, are there places to stay the night?" Petrine asked.

The innkeeper quit sweeping bone scraps, opened the back door, then launched the scraps out into the yard. With his broom, he pushed the door shut and ran his fingers through his long white beard. "The only place for fifty kilometers to lay your head, young sir, is here. We're surely off the pilgrims' path, I'll give you that, but we're not forgotten. In fact, sir, if you want to stay more nights, our inn's well stocked and well kept. The pious tribe that owns this sturdy place—in the old times it was built as a monastery—gives me full run, and I manage it well for them."

"Monastery?" Petrine asked excitedly. He quieted his tone. "Why, I thought you were the owner, sir. You have that air about you."

"No, just the keep," the old man smiled, tugging meekly on his beard. He set his broom aside and blew out all the candles on the long table. "Every morning my wife and I work to make this place as comfortable as possible in this harsh country. If I—"

"One last question, sir, if I may so put upon you. If we travel south, will we find food anywhere?"

"Not one bit. But my wife had a decent growing summer and might sell you some. As the Spanish say, *Dio provvederà*."

"Yes, God will provide. As long as the devoted valet is here," Petrine grunted under his breath.

All of the day and most of the next morning were required for the arduous trek across the valley, but the glittering white façade of the camelback formation enticed Jacques and Petrine onward. By noon they reached the base of the mountain.

"A marvel," Petrine cried out, new elation in his voice.

"Yes, I feel the same," Jacques panted as he trained his eyes upward. "I feel dwarfed by this towering mass." He slowly turned his head. "Soaring monoliths on either end. The spiring mid-section— exceptional formation, to say the least. Never in my travels have I seen anything like this. How much time will we need to traverse the base for a recognizable sign, an identifying mark, I wonder?"

"I, for one, am up for the contest," Petrine said, his voice crackling with enthusiasm. He offered his waterskin, then took some for himself.

* * *

It was with some luck that, two days later, Jacques detected what he interpreted as a footpath, a faintly discernible route so narrow and overgrown a mountain goat might be hard-pressed to survive its treachery.

"We will follow this as far as we can," Jacques said solemnly. He shaded his eyes, trying to chart what little of the path he could make out.

Petrine tossed his packet to the ground, then raised his bruised forearms. "Might not be able to handle another tumble like yesterday's."

"You've been closer to hell than this, lackey."

"With you, as I recall," the valet replied, batting his master's shoulder.

"Lisbon," Jacques shuddered. He placed his hand firmly on the crown of Petrine's head. "Yes, with me. The both of us."

From the deep recesses of the adventurer's mind, a thought whispered: *The crucial moments are coming wherein I'll need the man most. If something is afoot ... if the valet means to forsake me ... I must sharpen my attention.*

"And we're now about to better our situation, our standing in the world, aren't we?" asked Petrine.

"We'll discover what secret the Church of Rome so greatly prizes that Dominique, Quentin Gray, and especially the old Vicomte would want it so."

For hours, Jacques and Petrine progressed cautiously up the mountainside avoiding, when they could, scrub, loose rock and thick roots blocking the path. Jacques' nostrils smarted with each breath. With care he stood up, folded up his hands, blew on them, and gazed at the sky. Bright day instantly altered to gray when a voluminous gray cloud blotted the sun. He motioned to Petrine, and both proceeded onward.

- 36 -

JACQUES STRUCK THE WHITE ROCK with his fist. "The perilous trail has played out. Played out." He stooped over, hands on knees. "I ache to think this is a false path."

Petrine forced his back against the cold face of stone behind him and slid to his haunches. "Maybe the trail was meant to end here?" he wheezed.

"Perhaps."

It was some time before he recognized the slightest of gaps in the sheer rock—at eye level—but back below him on the path. "We'd passed right by," he muttered. He picked his way down the trail and stared at the irregularity above.

"Petrine, stand on my shoulders."

"Are you certain? Your shoulders, I mean?"

Jacques nodded.

The valet waggled his finger. "No untoward moves. Not from this high up," he said, his voice shaking badly. "Be steady." He removed his goatskin and packet and set them against a brittle scrub that immediately snapped in half.

Carefully he climbed and planted himself atop Jacques' shoulders, then spoke straightaway. "Here, I'm right in front of it."

"Quiet, Spaniard. There could be others about."

Petrine readjusted his weight, then continued his efforts. "Well disguised, these cuts in the rock. Taking all my might to slide this stone over. May need more time. Strength. More than I ... moving— yes—the stone," he huffed. "Now it rests next to the mouth of the cut. I did it!"

"Good, good."

"A long—looks like—horizontal shaft. Very dark. But a bead of light in the distance." Petrine coughed, burrowing his boots deeper into Jacques' shoulders.

"Come down," Jacques ordered, his voice fading. "My muscles are worn." He patted his lips with the back of his hand. "Hard to breathe this high up. I'm parched, too."

The valet cautiously slipped from Jacques' shoulders and squatted.

Jacques slumped on the path next to Petrine and took the water pouch, upending it in his mouth. He stared at the mountainside and rubbed his neck. "A man-made tunnel this high up? What other purpose? A mine?" He took another drink. "The shaft leads to riches. It must."

"No blockages as far as I could see into the murkiness. Room for a man to crawl on his belly, not much more."

"Ready?" Jacques stood. "I'm going up."

"I'll go. Your bruised shoulders."

"This is the main chance. It will be me."

Petrine lurched to standing and snatched the goatskin from Jacques' hands. "Taking the pouch is out of the question," he growled. "Shaft is too narrow for a big man like you—and it."

Jacques glared. "You pay too little heed of your station, valet. I'm the one to go," he said, drawing his dagger.

Petrine took a quick step back.

"Be careful with me." Jacques placed the dagger's blade between his teeth before raising himself on top of the valet's shoulders.

"Hurry. Your weight crushes—"

A moment later, Jacques stared at the entrance to the shaft. "Partly in," he said, painstakingly inserting his body headfirst into the slender shaft.

Anticipation roused his blood, even as the dry, acrid smell taunted his nose. Prostrate on his stomach, he clenched the blade hard between his teeth until, watching his knuckles pale, he stopped breathing. The whistle of a far-off wind played its mournful tune. *If I'm trapped, Petrine will never be able to rescue me by himself. A lonely, ugly end.*

He relaxed his fists, then advanced, clawing the rockshaft bit by bit. His mind tumbled. The cold pressed around him. Each time he rested his chin on the coarse rock surface, beard stubble jabbed his cheeks, the dagger crowded his tongue. He pushed forward, the corridor narrowing as he went.

In a short while his fingertips met ... nothing, emptiness. A drop-off! Jacques' heart hammered. The pinpoint of light Petrine had spotted eked from some source below, but whatever was there—colder, menacing—couldn't be seen.

As best he could, Jacques dislodged a pebble with his dagger and flicked it out into the void. No sound. *A bigger stone then?*

But he hadn't the room to maneuver a bigger stone. He shivered uncontrollably. Fear was upon him. *Dare I send my dagger over the brink? If the dagger's fall is drawn out—my dagger is lost and I'll proceed no further. Not without better—*

He let go of his weapon. A muffled thump. *A short, soft fall then?*

Lengthening his body like a blind worm until it extended over the void, Jacques tucked his chin, covered his head with his arms, and made one last push.

"Aaagggh."

Thudding on the ground, he winced, ribs throbbing.

His fingers pawed the dagger underneath him, rough granules of sand biting into his cold, numb hand.

When his eyes adjusted to the indistinct light, Jacques sat up, straining for breath. He was in a cavern as big as a ship's hull. Squeezing his dagger and pointing it with both hands, he spun round and round, his eyes searching the rock ceiling, then the sandy ground.

The faint illumination in the cavern came through a hole in the wall, smaller in circumference than the one he'd just traveled. Jacques would explore that presently. But first he walked the perimeter of the cavern to discover some clue, something that would give him satisfaction. No detail escaped his grim stare, ceiling to ground.

Bare. Nothing but gritty, bare soil. Where's my treasure? What's the secret? He ached. He repeated his survey. *Nothing.*

Collapsing to his knees, he shouted, stabbing his dagger into the ground.

"Eeeeeeeeeeehhh."

Sand, gravel, rock exploded as he gored and gashed the earth.

"Yeeeeeeeeeehhh."

Exhausted, Jacques let go his weapon and fell to the sandy floor. He lay flat on his belly, puffing heavily, muscles weak, played out. When at length his inflamed eyes flickered open, he observed at arm's distance a small round object protruding on the ruptured surface. He rubbed dusty tears from his eyes. A coin. A bronze coin.

Jacques stretched toward it, his shirtsleeve inadvertently scooping a portion of sand. Another coin peeked through. Silver! His eyes darted about. Trembling, he raked at the sand and gravel.

More coins!

Jacques forced himself upright and began to eagerly shave the cold granulated surface with his dagger's blade. At finger's depth, he discovered a solid, even base—a concretion—dotted with round depressions, each depression filled with a coin. Several more scrapes of his dagger revealed dozens of coins—side by side—all housed in the concretion.

"Yahhhhhhh!"

Repeating his actions in a narrow swath, Jacques worked his way to the center of the cavern. Innumerable coins, resting in the dimples of the concretion underpinning, curved outward from the cavern's center in an ever-widening spiral. A pattern! A pattern imitating the spiraling shell of a bisected chambered nautilus!

Jacques choked tight his fist.

This floor is laden with riches!

The tears in Jacques' eyes turned into a gleam. The gleam of his eyes quickened into a tickle in his gut. The tickle transformed into a heaving laugh, and the laugh exited his mouth in a giddy shout.

"Haaaaaaaaww."

The cavern resounded with grossly outrageous laughter.

"Am I not deserving?"

Jacques held up a gold *maravedí*, then reached out and seized a fistful of the largest coins, allowing sand to drain through his warming fingers. "I'm a man of wealth. From this day forward, I shall never want. Nor shall I ever again tip my hat to an unworthy. I am somebody. And to Venice I will go."

Jacques soon began to scrutinize the treasure more closely.

"This is peculiar. The assortment of money—here in the spiral. Silver thalers laying beside gold ducats. But then lowly bronze—and more bronze. *Doblas* of gold—and Florentine florins—next to humble copper pennies that then are followed by pieces of eight—all silver." Jacques scratched his chin with the butt of his dagger.

When once more he worked his way from the outer spiral toward the center of the nautilus pattern, unfamiliar monies appeared—coins from antique times, denominations he'd never seen. Gaulish coins, silver shekels, gold and bronze. Coins with Greek inscriptions, even Arabic dinars. Jacques' lips twitched fitfully. Why, for God's sake, was the cavern's fortune such a profusion of priceless silver and gold coins, but yet peppered with far less valued copper and bronze?

The answer came slowly. The nautilus pattern spiraled outward, creating a history recorded in coins. The gold, the silver ones—these were placed in the spiral by kings and queens. But the smaller denominations? Men and women of lowly birth had left those.

Still, I'm bewildered. What unites lowborn men with those on high? And men of many nations, of different cultures? Of different times?

Jacques rose to his feet. "I care not a whit to answer that question. What matters is that I've found the cache of wealth Vicomte de Fragonard foretold—and to which Esther the Israelite alluded." He paused. "But can this be the *vital secret* the mighty Church of Rome wishes to keep?"

At eye level above the cavern floor, Jacques found himself staring at the dim light coming from a modest hole in the wall. He stepped to the opening and cautiously leaned in. There were several handholds in the breach that tunneled upward at an acute angle.

A thought stirred fleetingly in Jacques' head. *I have what I want but not what I need.*

A sweet smell pervaded the shaft.

Driven by an acute impulse, Jacques sucked in all the fragrance he could, checked behind himself, stuffed his dagger between his teeth, then hoisted himself into the rocky notch. His skin stretched taut as fear again hardened his muscles.

Twice the tunnel constricted and changed direction, but handholds aided his labor, and the faint light at the far end of the shaft led him forward.

He struggled ahead until, reaching the end of the passageway, he was able to sit on his heels. He blew on his bitterly cold hands.

Immediately, his fright and fatigue vanished as something akin to bright daylight—a radiance that bore semblance to earthly light yet illuminated the span with a supernal glow—drove away the murkiness. Jacques sheathed his dagger and eased himself down into the space below.

At the center of a large chamber, resting on pillars chest high, stood an ogee-sided sarcophagus wrapped in a cerement of diaphanous linen. The coffin's luminance drew Jacques forward while all intention, all restlessness in him dissolved. A sweet and familiar smell welcomed him. Ambergris, for embalming. He breathed in the fragrance, stepped forward, and peered through the nimbus of light surrounding the sarcophagus.

Beneath the linen shroud lay the delicate figure of a man, apparently dead. A close-cropped beard enveloped the face while small beads of blood ringed the temples and forehead. Burnished hair, a narrow nose, and slender lips completed the compassionate face. The hands, Jacques saw—each showed a deep, purplish-black hole in the palm.

Jacques closed his eyes.

He felt a subtle lightness in his limbs and body, yet he was unafraid. Nor did he cry out as the cool air streamed past head to toe. His strange heart opened in surrender.

And when he looked again, he had risen—to the high canopy of the rock cavern.

Jacques existed effortlessly outside himself.

From his lofty harbor above, he saw two men on the cavern floor—one living, one dead.

Below was a material person—the physical person—of Jacques Girolamo Casanova, a flesh-and-blood man who, though standing, was more dead than alive, a man whose lifelong vanities and frivolous pleasures had produced a damp spirit, a stagnated self.

Jacques thought: *I clothed myself in coats of gold. It did not bring peace. I knew dishonorable women. They did not bring comfort. I sought the adulation of others. It gave little happiness. Love was offered me, but I turned away.*

He proffered a wordless cry.

In this same simple tableau bathed in pure and ethereal light, Jacques also beheld the reclining corpus of a man who, though now conquered, emanated yet a placid contentment and serenity, the quintessence of which seemed alive, merciful, loving. The reclining man manifested the beauty of enlightenment in his face, the joy of love in his essence, the grace of God in his celestial glow.

At this moment Jacques felt a freedom he'd never before experienced, the freedom of truth. For a moment there was meaning. Then the veil closed. Effortlessness ended.

In an instant Jacques seemed to melt back to the cavern floor, once again standing beside the open coffin. A soft tear now rolled down his cheek while he quietly regarded the figure immersed in light.

A treasure of inestimable value, the Vicomte had said.

Jacques placed his hand to his throbbing chest, trying to quell the bounding blood within. He leaned over the sarcophagus, peering once again through the nimbus of light encircling the deceased man.

"To the marrow of my bones, I now know the face of god Jesus."

For some time Jacques stood still, fully entranced by the tender serenity that exuded from Jesus the Nazarene. While light continued to bathe the translucent winding sheet and coffin, an ecstasy superior to all other earthly pleasures infused Jacques' veins.

"And now I fathom that which is beyond all earthly value, of inestimable value—the peace that passeth understanding."

*   *   *

When finally Jacques descended to the lower cavern, he reburied each coin he'd excavated from the ground. Then taking his own purse from his boot, he set—with care and precision—half of his money in the outward spiraling tail of the nautilus.

I understand. The Templars—and those after them—guided monarchs and merchants, commoners and queens to this secret, isolated mountain. It was an ordeal, a pilgrimage, all gladly taken. People of different eras, of varied cultures, of stations in life poles apart—all undertook the pilgrimage. To share a most remarkable banquet. An ecstatic feast of the soul. A place where all men can belong together.

Jacques crossed his hands over his stomach. *And now I, too, have been to table.*

He took a final look and began crawling. With prodigious effort, he succeeded in extricating himself from the series of caverns, then with some apprehension, called out to Petrine, who after a time presented himself. Great relief and thankfulness filled Jacques when he was assisted—by his valet—to the ground.

It was a full two days' journey north before Jacques Casanova could, for his inquisitive manservant, put voice to the sublimity of what he had encountered.

When Petrine had heard the last of his master's story, he stiffened into the cold wind, repeating again and again. "You've performed nobly, sir. Nobly."

For his part, Jacques was eager and glad to be heading for Paris—to be carrying a full belly of warm feelings as well as the tale of a singular, extraordinary experience—to Vicomte Honoré de Fragonard.

- 37 -

"WILL THIS ONE DO, MASTER?" Petrine asked. "Of course, by the light of lampposts, every lodging in Paris looks agreeable."

"Any bed softer than the ground will be satisfactory," Jacques replied. "Tomorrow we should be able to complete our journey to the Vicomte's."

An ebony crow, wrestling a morsel of garbage in the street, shrieked in frustration.

"Once in our room, I'll be retiring for the evening, Petrine, and will have no need of your services. Here's a bit of money."

Petrine ran his fingers through his stringy hair. "I was hoping to have time for myself, this being our first night back in fancy Paris. Just one coin though, sir. I won't be talked into more. Keep the purse. You may need it. My wages will come soon enough," Petrine smiled wryly.

"The door will be left open for you tonight."

Dry mouth was the cause of Jacques' waking the next morning. He labored to open his eyelids, but before long—surprised that Petrine's snoring was not irritating him—he reached around his back. When no lump of flesh met his searching hand, he rolled over and saw the blanket next to him remained tucked.

"Petrine?" He sat up. The sun's rays revealed no valet. He worked up some spittle in his throat. "Petrine!"

All was quiet, except for the clopping of horse hooves on the street outside. "We need an early start! Where are you?"

Soon after, with breakfast under his belt, Jacques stood at the front door of the inn. Perhaps the valet had procured a bottle. "There's a twice-told tale, if there ever was one," he said quietly.

Surely trouble had not come upon the valet. But this morning Jacque's gut told him that an excess of alcohol was not the reason the valet was missing. *I refuse to believe Petrine would betray me.*

To the innkeeper, Jacques entrusted coach fare, a hand-drawn map for Petrine, and a note instructing him to meet at the Vicomte's no later than dusk.

Then he was off.

The trip passed swiftly, the destination was attained.

Stepping to the door of the Vicomte's chateau, Jacques was bid a high-spirited "Good afternoon and welcome" by the majordomo who stood outside. The two men entered the home.

"When my valet arrives later ..." Jacques gently smiled but did not finish his statement.

The majordomo crooked his head, then continued. "The Vicomte will be most pleased to see you, Monsieur Casanova. But he is at present asleep. May I wait awhile longer before I wake him?"

"Certainly."

The majordomo crossed the waiting room, then turned to face Jacques. "The canvases and effects you left here, sir—I'll be happy to show you to them. And there are a number of letters forwarded to you from your previous address. I'll have them in your hands posthaste." A large smile widened the servant's face. "The Vicomte refers to you as his prodigal son and has often said—and was certain—that one day you'd return."

Jacques nodded appreciatively. "I've much to impart to your master," he replied, turning away from the majordomo. "*Credete a chi ne ha fatto esperimento.* Believe him who has had the experience."

"Sir?"

Jacques looked back at the manservant. "In the meanwhile, may I see my brother's belongings?"

"Sir, I was saddened," said the majordomo, taking a step forward, "I was greatly saddened to hear of your brother's death. A tragedy." The man leaned nearer Jacques. "You know what Monsieur Voltaire says of the theatre? 'Tragedy instructs the mind and moves the heart.' If I may say so, I have found this true with art—and with life itself."

Jacques raised his head and looked deeply into sincere eyes.

Quite soon he supped—then recognized he was not in the humor to examine Francesco's effects but had a greater want to satisfy that need not wait for the Vicomte's waking.

He sought out the steward and spoke softly.

"The what, sir?" the majordomo asked.

"The écorchés," Jacques repeated. "I'd like to see them once more."

A perplexed expression sat on the majordomo's face.

Jacques asked: "May I be so presumptuous as to have you follow me?"

"Gladly, sir."

In short order, they stood in front of the door that Jacques and his brother had visited months before. The impressive lock was still intact.

"I beg your pardon, Monsieur Casanova. I've ignored this room so long, it's all but erased from my mind."

Jacques gave a sly smile.

"No sir, you see, sir—" stammered the servant, "well, over the years in other quarters, rumors have been spread about a certain cabinet of curiosities and what a strange wonder it is." The majordomo cleared his throat, stopped still, and directed his gaze to Jacques. "I tell you truly. In thirty years' service to the Vicomte, the contents of this room were shared with me only twice. Not that I wish to see the écorchés a third time," the manservant whispered under his breath. "Certainly I know the Vicomte's passion—embalming—but his cabinet of curiosities was far stranger than anything I'd imagined. As for the key to the lock, its whereabouts are known only to the Vicomte. He'll take great pleasure, I warrant you, in showing you his fantastical creations himself. Actually, sir, while we're upstairs here, why don't I go ahead and wake the Vicomte? His room, you may be well aware, is the one at the end of the hall."

Through a side window, Jacques watched while the last vestiges of winter's cold light closed out the day. "I suppose we might rouse him," he smiled. "It's not every day his prodigal son—"

"He'll be much pleased. Allow me a few moments to light these candles, then we'll proceed."

The majordomo moved to the wall sconces while Jacques seated himself in a chair by the locked door from which a hint of pungent castoreum wafted. A different odor—sharp and repellent—led Jacques to recall the contrary feelings the écorchés had engendered at his first viewing.

When the majordomo finished his work, he summoned Jacques to the Vicomte's door.

"Sir, may I awaken you? You've an important guest who wishes your audience."

When no response came, Jacques, on a whim, removed a lit candle from a nearby sconce and edged just ahead of the servant. Knocking briefly, then pushing lightly against the door, he eased into the room.

"Vicomte de Fragonard, please excuse my—"

A blistering stench threw him back, but in an instant he was beside the bed, the uneven flame of his candle revealing the Vicomte's twisted body. The old man's mouth bowled wide, as if blaring a silent, unbearable pain. His eyeballs spilled from their sockets like a gaffed fish.

Jacques turned, thrusting his candle into the darkness of the room. Across the carpet ran a torrent of vomit and syrupy brown excrement.

"Oh, horror," the majordomo cried as he angled across the floor, his hand covering his nose.

Jacques shoved the candle to the nightstand, wilted to the bed, and did his best to straighten the Vicomte's fingers, close his eyes, and wipe his lips.

"Your master," he said quietly to the majordomo, "your master has met his end."

A heartfelt moan escaped the servant.

Jacques turned and scanned the revolting carpet. "Something the Vicomte ate or drank. Swift in its action. Most likely poison."

He stood, eyeing the manservant anew, but it was obvious the man was grief stricken.

"On my life, sir, it was not I. Nor could it be any others of my small staff. This room has three doors."

Jacques' mystification must have shown on his face.

"Anyone might have come and gone," said the majordomo. "The Vicomte on occasion entertains company informally here in his bedroom, as they do in the fashionable Parisian salons. Given my master's egalitarian nature, associates often feel comfortable to enter this house unannounced. Unnoticed, even, I've come to learn. Unnoticed by my staff or by me."

There was a palpable stillness.

The majordomo bent over and, carefully maneuvering the thick candle in his hand, looked at the old man's face. He clubbed the bed with his fist. "A bitter curse on the party who caused this."

At once he stood straight, composing himself. "I must inform the others. Then I must return to prepare my master," he said in a hollow, icy breath.

Jacques laid his hand on the man's shoulder until he once again calmed.

The servant carefully picked his way toward the door, but reaching it, he stopped, glaring at a side table next to the couch. From it he lifted two short-stemmed goblets.

"This is the Vicomte's glassware. His other matching goblets, next to the brandies, are over there," he pointed to a corner cabinet. "But why two? And snuff also?" He set down the glasses and picked up a small silver snuffbox. "My master, I know, hasn't taken snuff since he was a young man." He presented the box to Jacques.

Jacques took a pinch of its contents and held it to his nose. "Fine tobacco. Spaniol, possibly. If a person were here in this room, I believe they made a central error in leaving this snuffbox behind. But the dreadful act of raw murder can defeat even a well-planned scheme."

"Shall we allow the authorities their say and expertise?"

Jacques paused before offering a reluctant "yes."

"Then I will send one of my staff for them. They must surely be shown these objects we have here in our hands." The majordomo looked askance. "It's plain you're not in any way connected to this grim deed, but I understand your hesitance, sir. Given your standing with the king—I was told by the Vicomte some time ago—you may not wish to chance the authorities. Should you decide to leave before they arrive, there need be no mention of your presence here."

"I appreciate your concern," Jacques said. "In any case, you must perform your duties."

The majordomo excused himself.

Left alone, Jacques went to the bed and sat next to the body of Vicomte de Fragonard. "Who has stolen your life? Who has reason to perform such a brutality?"

He held the old man's hand for some time until his anger cooled. "I've come back. And now I understand Francesco's paintings—all to keep the secret alive. You, sir, set me on my journey. A pilgrimage, I recognize, you yourself long ago must have undertaken. One that cannot be described with mere words. Treasure of inestimable value, you said. In my ignorance, I misunderstood." Jacques placed his hand on the Vicomte's cheek. "This evening, I honor your wisdom. I forever cherish your trust. In my heart, gentle sir, I now feel your warm presence. You bow splendidly, you stand tall and dignified, you unwrinkle before my very eyes. So profoundly pleasing it is—that you display such vigor upon the return of your prodigal son."

It was not long before the majordomo returned to place a sheet over the Vicomte. He then handed several letters to Jacques, who, lost in sorrow, offered a nod of his head.

"The post on the very top was delivered only late this afternoon." The majordomo extended his arm. "I've work here. Please allow me to escort you downstairs, sir."

"Yes."

Alone in the antechamber moments later, Jacques trembled, his whole being shaken by the sight of the topmost letter, a letter directed to him from their Excellencies the Inquisitori de Stato, fixed with the official lion seal of the Republic of Venice. *Having this seal, the letter cannot be counterfeit.*

Slowly, he unfastened the seal and read.

We, Inquisitori de Stato, for reasons known to us, grant Giacomo Girolamo Casanova the right and privilege to return, provisionally, to the republic of Venice. He will present himself at the stated address of Signor Zorzi Contarini dal Zaffo at noon on the first day of January M.V., 1756; then as directed, submit the following day to further interview. Until the prescribed time, Giacomo Girolamo Casanova is sanctioned to come and go within the republic, traveling wheresoever he pleases without let or hindrance.

Should he fail to appear for the arranged appointment, his safe-conduct is rescinded, and efforts at repatriation, as stipulated, will be null and void. Such is our will.

Wavering to-and-fro, Jacques kissed again and again the letter he held.

"Is it possible? After all this time I'm permitted to return to La Serenissima? My beloved homeland! But why? Why now?" He wiped his misting eyes and refolded the letter. "What has passed? In what ironic drama do I perform?" he asked himself. "The Vicomte's riddle, which promoted me to an experience beyond the ken of reason, is solved. But Esther died roughly. As did Quentin. And Vicomte de Fragonard, the man who initiated this progress, is murdered. Petrine now is missing. And hard upon the heels of all of this, I'm empowered to Venice by the Inquisitori. To return provisionally, temporarily. Might Michelle Grimani's hand be in this? The Church?" Jacques' neck knotted with anxiety.

That evening he lay awake, feeling the softness of the pillow under his head, pondering the letter. He wanted badly to go home even if there were dangers.

By midnight he was resolved: he would accept this invitation, embrace whatever challenges lay in store. He began to laugh, thinking it was so like the Inquisitori to set up an appointment in a house composed of hideaways—a *casino*.

Quite soon, he realized that if he was to meet the Inquisitori by the first of the year, there were few days left in which to travel. And to wait any longer for Petrine would mean that he would lose this opportunity. Other feelings, too, did not permit him rest.

What should he do for the Vicomte? The majordomo?

It was with the first light of a sunny dawn that Jacques prepared his leave-taking, after which he informed the majordomo, who immediately expressed his understanding by replenishing Jacques' purse.

"I sense the pangs of your heart, sir, and I tell you truly, the Vicomte would have it this way."

"Here, on the off chance," said Jacques, "please set aside a sum of this money for my Spanish valet. Here, too, are my instructions, when he—Petrine—turns up." Jacques replaced some coins in the majordomo's purse.

"He'll come to this destination?"

"Mouth on bottle, most likely," Jacques said, wrinkling out a half smile, now feeling that the valet had washed his hands of the master. Or worse.

The majordomo smiled back, dipped his head, and ushered Jacques forward.

"I shall write to you soon, to inquire of the outcome—"

The manservant interrupted. "You may be assured that—as far the Vicomte—I'll follow through with every means available until there is satisfaction."

Jacques stopped in the anteroom and faced the majordomo.

"For your concern and confidence," Jacques said, returning the bow, "I thank you, personally. When I speak of your master henceforth, I'll affirm he was my compass, my shepherd."

With fond eyes, Jacques looked around the room, then drew a deep breath. "Now Venice calls. And it's certain that, like a wise and loving mother, she'll have answers." With those words Jacques left the chateau straightaway.

By midday he was in Paris. Because the Inquisitori's appointment was now his strictest priority, he purchased a new and modest outfit, then booked a diligence which departed promptly at three fifteen.

Jacques stepped aboard. Bound, at last, for home.

- 38 -

JACQUES LOOKED OUT THE WINDOW of the diligence while it
slowed. He was to travel from Geneva over Great St. Bernard Pass to
Milano, Verona, and Padua. There he would board one of the well-
appointed *burchiellos* that sailed the Brenta Canal. Jacques' brow knit
with impatience. His coach had traveled only as far as Versailles.

It promised to be far too long a journey, but drawing closer to
home, Jacques' heart soared with delight until a thought, exhumed
from some girdled vault of his brain, made its way into his head. *What
drives me home? And why, strangely, am I afraid? Is it a fear that my
dream of Venice—of perfection—is unfounded?* The thought was over
and done with in a moment, yet for a time the anxious residue stuck
with Jacques like dark pitch to a tree.

After he considered what lay ahead, he also judged what had
taken place: "For reasons known to us," the Inquisitori de Stato had
written. In Venice, that always meant practical politics. What would
that mean for him? Whatever the case, it seemed his name no longer
displeased the Serene Prince.

On the deck of his burchiello in the final hour of his journey,
Jacques forced his eyes through the haze of the December dusk.

There it was at last, appearing to float on the lagoon. Venice: a
village that had grown rich by monopolizing the gold, silks, and coffee
from the East; a city never invaded by foreigners; a republic that had
remained intact ten centuries and more; an empire all of Europe
admired and respected.

Most importantly, there was Jacques' home, where all his youth
had been spent.

Through the distant forest of ship masts, he feasted on the umbers, ochres, and siennas of stately palaces, of *pensioni*, of old and crooked houses, and on the immaculate whites of magnificent patrician homes. All blended together to create an exquisite palette—one which, being finely mirrored in the surrounding waters, was doubled in beauty. To Jacques, the balance of the civilized world seemed drab when compared to Venice.

Across a horizon softened by twilight, Jacques searched for the symbol of Venice: the waterside entry to Piazza San Marco. Into view at last came the dignified column throned by a lion, its claws holding an open book with the inscription "Peace be unto thee, my Evangelist Mark."

There was an unmistakable ache in Jacques' breast, but the sights tempered his concerns. He greatly wished that Dominique—even Petrine the Spaniard—could share his homecoming.

Sitting back in his burchiello seat, he could not begin to articulate what home truly meant, but at this moment its sights and sounds whirled everywhere onshore.

His heart now practically jumped from his chest.

Carnivale, the longest lasting and grandest of Venice's celebrations, was under way and would continue until Shrove Tuesday!

How long have I been absent from home to forget that this is Carnivale! Jacques laughed. *Carnivale—farewell to the flesh.*

Drawing closer to shore, he could make out the chirp of mountebanks mixing with the sweet, sonorous songs of the gondoliers; the *improviasatori* strumming their guitars and mandolins; the *calle* comedians entertaining the revelers; the storytellers weaving their spells.

He beamed while a flood of pigeons circled the piazza and poured down in a silvery stream to the rooftops. He laughed, "Can the high-flying pigeons make out the prostitutes from the priests, beggars from patricians—clapping, cheering, carousing—all decked in their pearly masks and black dominos? Ah, to be a bird and take it all in at once."

Soon he was engulfed in the aromas: orange peel, pumpkin seeds, perfumes, pomades, as well as the tempting smells of fried oysters, dried cod, and calamari. *If La Serenissima's best days were behind her, as Cardinal de Bernis and others claim, she would not still dazzle like this!*

Then came a new scent, the mustiness of decay. Jacques tweaked his nose. *Perhaps it will take a little patience to cope with this aspect of old Venice's charm!*

The burchiello swept ashore, but when Jacques tried to step to dry land, he was nearly shunted back aboard by the jostle of partiers. He slapped his hands together in exhilaration, suddenly intent on a raspberry fruit ice, an incessant craving since he'd left his mother's breast. *And it will drip down my chin, just like it always did.*

He leapt like a fawn from the boat.

No sooner had he made his purchase and taken a lick than a strong slap on the shoulder jolted him. Jacques spun about and stared up and into a bautta—a black mask—through which gleamed two brown eyes. The bautta completely enshrouded the reveler's head, face, and shoulders with a hood, short cape, and tricorne hat. Covering the reveler's body was a long domino-style cloak.

"My friend," shouted the shrill voice above the din, "if you are who I think you are, shouldn't you borrow my mask and *tabarro* and stroll this town incognito?"

Jacques stared incredulously. *Does this carnivaler truly know my past? What's this person's intent? I must buy some time.*

"Who calls me friend?" Jacques said loudly.

"The three of us," said the reveler, who gestured to the two disguised accomplices at his side.

Something splattered against Jacques' shoulder. He shrunk back.

Squealing laughter erupted from the accomplices, whose arms intertwined those of their tall companion. One of the pair reached up and picked white specks from Jacques' jacket.

"Scented water in eggshells," laughed the decidedly female voice. She pointed at a man in the crowd. "The half-cracked one over there—the one dressed as a rooster—flings these." The costumed female in front of Jacques began to strut like a cock, to the amusement of those around her.

"Sir, I again inquire," said the tall figure, "tonight would you like to borrow my bautta? You may remember Carnivale costumes are worn to eradicate all social distinctions, all identification—"

"So in secret anyone may satisfy their most frivolous or their deepest desire," giggled the female, strutting past.

The tall reveler leaned toward Jacques' ear. "Are you not afraid the Inquisitori will clap its most infamous escapee in irons, hmmm, Signor Giacomo Casanova?"

I must keep my wits, although the standing hair on my neck tells me it avails me nothing. Jacques took a long, slow lick of his raspberry ice.

The figure spoke. "I will save you embarrassment, sir. I remove my mask, you see."

"Tomaso," Jacques exclaimed. "Tomaso! I should have recognized those brown eyes. Wonderful to see you!"

"Great to see you, old friend," said the handsome man, who immediately wrapped his arms about Jacques, then kissed his cheek. "I knew this fellow in my youth, knew him as the Prince of Macaroni," he bellowed to the two masked creatures who leaned against him. "Together he and I laughed and laughed and laughed. How long, old friend, is it that you've been gone?"

"Long enough," Jacques winced, "to learn to cry."

Tomaso's mouth drooped.

"On the other hand, it *appears* I may be pardoned by the Inquisitori. That's the better news."

Tomaso slapped Jacques' shoulders and placed him at arm's length. "Excellent, excellent. And how's Francesco? Your family?"

"It's been too long since I've spoken of them, Tomaso. But you shall hear."

"As shall these two," Tomaso said, taking each of his accomplices under an arm while quickly exposing a female face beneath each mask. "We are prepared for great wonders tonight, and you, my newly arrived friend, are the very beginning of a miraculous evening."

The girls tittered.

"And now," Tomaso said, "take my mask and mantle. Wear it. For we shall light up this old town."

Jacques feared his face would crack from the broad smile that governed it. He took a last lick of his raspberry ice. *This, and all that surrounds it, tastes exactly as I wanted it to.*

At Tomaso's bidding, Jacques picked up the single bag that contained his possessions, shoved his smallsword out of harm's way, and with friend and acquaintances, stumped madly onward into the crush of Carnivale.

Soon Jacques discovered, to his amazement, that his heart and mind lived in a different place altogether. Not that he wasn't tempted by what Tomaso and his companions offered, but he'd lost his need for carousing.

Too quickly, he also found that his trip from Paris had produced a fatigue he could not overcome, and because Carnivale would continue for weeks, he asked his old friend for a respite from the night's activities. At Tomaso's residence, Jacques slept long and well.

Thirty-six hours later, the first of January, he removed the intricately folded packet from his pocket and reexamined it, confirming one more time that the Inquisitori letter had requested his presence.

Making his way to the interview address, he was again drawn to the Piazza San Marco, drawn to the white-and-rose-colored marble and the lace-like finishing of the Doge's palace—under whose lead roof sat the prison he knew so well. I Piombi.

Jacques' entire body grew stiff. *My captivity provided an opportunity to ask questions of myself. I shunned every one.* Forcing himself to a short bench, he slumped upon it, studying his quivering hands. *All those years ago, I joked at friends' predictions that my behavior would send me to prison. I wasn't innocent, as I've claimed. My public controversies, the seductions, and blasphemous behavior. The rape accusation. My prank that paralyzed that man—forever. Shall I finally admit that I deserved imprisonment by the Inquisitori?*

Jacques looked back at the Doge's lead roof and watched the dissolving clouds beyond it. *I might have saved myself some measure of—had I then possessed a courageous heart. But that time … is over.*

Air rushed back into his chest. He stood up, briefly looked in all directions, then continued his trek.

There were few people on the narrow *calli* he walked, but all the rubbish and refuse confirmed many Carnivalers had passed through. The canals, too, were littered with feathers and confetti, shreds of bauttas, masks, and costumes. Jacques managed a tight smile.

Finally, he arrived before an old structure that matched the address on his appointment letter. The plainness of the exterior, he knew, disguised a refined interior. The peculiar way in which the houses were constructed also meant that the stairs blocked light from the sky, even now at midday. It was therefore customary to provide a lighted lantern, which Jacques now spied at the bottom of the steps.

After climbing a number of staircases, he knew the only door would be at the top. His breathing grew heavier with each turn. Was it the exertions or the chilly air, Jacques wondered? To speak the truth, he was uneasy.

Making his way up the final staircase, he took in several heavy breaths and, steadying himself, knocked. The door creaked open.

"Chevalier Casanova? Welcome."

Jacques frowned at the title before stepping through the darkened doorway. A hand relieved him of the lantern.

Jacques immediately took in the large room. There was one exit only—an impressively carved door at the far end. Ornate sconces illuminated the bright orange walls; on each wall hung a massive vase brimming with flowers. The high ceiling was festooned with gaily-colored silks, each billowing freely above the marbled floor. He noted a low table at one side of the room, while at the opposite side, draped across an ottoman, were crimson velvet robes with furbelows and a hat sparkling with a rosette of diamonds. Overstuffed pillows strewn around the room completed the impression of a sultan's seraglio. Jacques perceived ostentation and wondered whom this patrician endeavored to impress.

"I shall also take your cloak, Chevalier," said the leathery-looking manservant. "And sword."

"I prefer to wear my cloak, and I will retain—" Jacques reached behind his back for his dagger. *It's not on its hanger! I forgot it at Tomaso's.*

"I shall keep my sword," Jacques said anxiously.

"A sensible man must," answered a smooth voice.

For a moment, Jacques thought he recognized the masculine voice.

He directed his interest to the speaker, who entered from the far door. The black silk hood and mantle of Carnivale covered the man's head and shoulders, while his face was hidden under a mustachioed mask. A long tabarro in scarlet—a color denoting nobility—stretched to the floor and was half thrown open, revealing a well-turned calf, then velvet breeches, doublet, and ruff. Jacques knew and recognized the comic character of Capitano, insolent braggart and vainglorious bully who, when acting upon the stage, is rattled by the mere rustle of leaves or cowers when a fellow character simply strikes a menacing pose.

Jacques' insides churned. *What passes?*

"Again, welcome, Chevalier," Capitano said. With two clicks of his fingers, he caught his servant's attention. "Your services will not be required this afternoon, Dandolo."

"Illustrissimo, si. Yes, illustrious one," the servant replied. He bowed and left.

Suddenly, every pore in Jacques' skin burned hot. Red hot. *"Illustrissimo, si!" Are these Esther's murderers?!*

"I welcome you on behalf of the Most Serene Republic," Capitano said.

Jacques slowly slid his hand to the hilt of his smallsword before executing his most stylish bow.

"Captain, with humbleness I ask—do I present myself to Zorzi Contarini dal Zaffo?"

"Your letter specified *your* attendance. It did not, however, say dal Zaffo would attend you."

Jacques' mind raced to figure the game.

"I've taken great pains to have a delectable feast prepared," said the captain. "I do hope you've not eaten your main meal."

"No."

"Do you like this room?" roared the host as he took on the personality of Capitano, showing off his fit and trim physique and twirling the mustache on his mask. Not waiting for Jacques' answer, he paraded to a sidewall and pulled on a short cord. A turntable rotated out of the wall, full with a dozen dishes. "This convenience," he pointed to the device, "means we may dispense with servants so that we may discuss the business at hand." He stepped toward Jacques. "Please take this covered tureen and put it at my place setting on the table. I shall bring us a casserole." He gestured for Jacques to sit on a pillow at the low table.

Jacques glanced at the front and rear doorways, then with one eye on his host, he sat.

The captain removed a bottle of wine from the turntable and walked to the table. "It was my prestige and influence that resulted in your summons today, Jacques Casanova. If you thrive at this preliminary interview, the Inquisitori de Stato is amenable to my recommendation."

I now know the man behind the mask. Jacques placed a hand on the table and abruptly changed the direction of the conversation. "I remind you that I'm a true Venetian who never forgets or forgives a slight."

He succeeded in remaining stoic while the captain removed his tricorne, twisted his Capitano mask to the back of his head, removed his bautta and tabarro. "May I pour you a glass of wine?" asked the moon-faced man with the aquiline nose. "It is, I assure you, an excellent Scopolo." A sparkle flooded his piercing blue eyes as he leaned toward Jacques. "I regret I have no Spaniol to offer today as I did in our first meeting."

Jacques remained calm when he recalled the humiliating slap he had months ago received. He stared at the man who had given him that slap and made certain that Cavaliere Michele Grimani took the first sip of wine.

- 39 -

BIDING HIS TIME, JACQUES obliged his host by recounting inconsequential anecdotes, a favor that was shortly returned.

Two glasses of wine and several dishes later, Cavaliere Grimani, eyes gleaming in the candlelight, came to his point. "I'm prepared to tender a position, a worthy position, to you. It comes with generous remuneration. And a significant title: chevalier. I tried that appellation on you minutes ago. How do you find its fit?"

"Until one knows the true *size* of the position, its fit is both too small—and too large."

"Let me remove all suspense. My proposition is one of agent. For Venice."

"Agent? You mean spy." Jacques coddled his glass.

"Did I say 'spy'? That is your unsophisticated description. Allow me to elucidate," Michele Grimani said, pouring Jacques another glass. "My memory even now recollects the phrases of Jacques Casanova's prison escape letter. 'I beg the Inquisitori de Stato to return my good name and my honor. For Venice is my heart and my home.'"

Grimani sniffed his glass. "Moving words," he said. "The position I offer should suit to perfection a man with those sentiments."

"What are the terms of the position?"

"One limitation only. But of little concern to a man of your bent. You are allowed to travel anywhere in our Serene Republic but not outside its borders."

"My spying would be done only within Venice?"

Grimani nodded and took a drink.

Jacques impulsively blew a breath toward the ceiling and watched the swags of silk flutter. "And I would report to the Council of Ten?"

"Not precisely."

"To you, then?"

"To me alone."

Jacques pushed his wine glass to the side. *Things are amiss, but I'm sorely put to unravel the whole of it. In the meantime, I must try to keep him off balance.*

Michele Grimani's fingers drummed the lid of the tureen. "Venice is on an uncertain course. She teeters on the precipice—"

"As must your prized family."

Grimani reddened. "As I was saying, one nation or another might topple Venice. You've already accomplished an invaluable service for the republic by ..."

Jacques leaned across the table toward his host, whose eyes now were blank. "To what invaluable service do you refer, Cavaliere Grimani?"

Grimani drew a breath to speak. His lips parted. Not a syllable sounded.

"Michele Grimani, it's true I love Venice exceedingly. But it is truer still that I shall never be bound to one man's will. I will never answer solely to you for the fate of the republic."

Grimani's lips stretched thin and stiff, distending his moonish face. Without a blink, he slowly edged the tureen toward Jacques.

The high, lean sound of the scraping dish grated Jacques' ears. He arched away from the table as the tureen reached its position in front of him.

The Cavaliere's blue eyes turned spiteful. "Many of us labor for the republic. I have toiled an entire lifetime for Venice. Even your Spanish valet has performed a service for Venice. Petrine was loyal to Jacques Casanova when Casanova could pay him. When Casanova could not pay him, Petrine became loyal to my wage." Grimani extended a finger, pointing to the tureen. "Lift the lid."

Jacques cautiously removed the tureen lid. A gleam of gold struck his eyes.

He lapsed back into his chair, ears ringing.

"My snuffbox."

"Petrine, you see, was in my employ early. On my orders, he removed the box from your possession at your brother's in Paris."

Jacques' brain reeled. *Deceived by Petrine. It's true!*

"You are to be lauded. You've been summoned to Venice because you—and your lackey—have been for me a tool, have provided an invaluable service, one that will insure the survival of the Republic of Venice."

"I ask anew," Jacques stammered. "*What* service to the republic?"

"This I foresaw," Grimani crowed. "I told myself neither you nor any of my other pawns would recognize the richest potential." He let out a rude laugh. "Oh, I may as well explain. Your treasure, scapegrace! Your treasure! As I suspected long ago, and as you have now *proven*, the man—the god we call Jesus—did not rise from the dead as the Church of Rome insists. No! When He died—as all men do—his corpse was preserved and hidden. Who can guess for what purpose? Well, it's enough for me to declare that, in and of itself, the corpse of Jesus the Nazarene exists. Exists. Earthbound! Hah."

"But you did not know where?"

Grimani nodded. "For years my family had possessed bits of information about the secret: I surmised there might be a vast amount of money as well as the actual corpse. But like others before me—yes, scores of others over the centuries—I could not piece together the clues. I knew, for example, that Nicolas Fouquet, Louis XIV's finance minister a hundred years ago, was bound in an iron mask for withholding an immense secret from the king. But what knowledge, what exact clues Fouquet possessed, eluded me as it had eluded the king himself." Grimani took a breath. "I knew, too, that the Church had for centuries suspected the existence of Christ's dead body—here on earth. And the Church was willing to commit heinous crimes to obtain that boring corpse and dispose of it."

Jacques showed confusion.

"You don't understand?" Grimani cackled, his face growing purple with annoyance. "The corpse that I'll now possess—"

"*You'll* possess—?"

"Why, I need only threaten the Pope—threaten—to expose the fact that the divine Christ did not ascend to heaven as the Church maintains. What choice will the Pope of the Roman Catholic Church

have but to bend to my every wish? Hah, what choice?" howled Grimani
with a pernicious fury. "I see you wonder at my intent? Well ...
because the Pope has influence with every Catholic monarch in
Europe, each royal throne will subtly bow to my will—and help sustain
a triumphant Venice for another thousand years." A grotesque
expression hung on the man's face. "You must admire my plan. You,
too, yearn for Venice to thrive."

"Not by these means."

"By any and all means. Especially by employing the discovery of
a lifetime. Of a dozen lifetimes. Hah. The Grimani family has sought
to unravel this riddle, this secret, for three hundred years or more.
And I alone am the one to succeed."

"You have not yet succeeded."

"I will direct Venice on her path to glory, the Grimani family
name will reside in the Golden Book for another five centuries. Soon
it shall be whispered that I am the power broker of Europe, and
Cavaliere Michele Grimani—*my name*—will be eternally acclaimed
for restoring Venice." Grimani smiled with cloying sincerity. "I'm so
proud I must twirl the mustache of my Capitano mask."

"The Church will not sit idly by."

"The Church of Rome has a formidable, ferocious arm. Yes, they
will try to kill me. But I'm well-prepared to deal with its might."

"I digest your game. I've unknowingly served you. Now to buy
my silence about the discovery, you arrange a position for me so that
I may protect you, to keep you alive, to support your despicable
activities." Jacques glanced at the snuffbox on the table before him,
then eyed Grimani. "But why spare me? I've solved the riddle and
discovered its treasure. You now might easily rid yourself of me."

"My sentiments precisely." Michele Grimani slapped the table.
His smile dissipated. "But, I thought: parasites may be useful in
particular situations. As bodyguards or as spies, for instance."

"And you ordered Petrine—"

"He removes the treasure and corpse from where you discovered it
even as we speak. He will hide it where I command."

Blistering indignation coursed Jacques' veins.

Grimani leaned back in his chair, smiled scornfully, and raised
his glass in a toast. "Petrine is to be applauded. A former actor,

applauded. How apropos." He sipped his wine in satisfaction. "For relatively straightforward tasks, I relied on him. But as you must certainly recognize, Petrine is not to be trusted unconditionally. He was to silence Esther for me, but when at the crucial moment he lost his head, my personal valet was forced to initiate the—admittedly— unpleasant chore of eliminating her. Which, to my displeasure, I witnessed." Grimani sighed. "After Petrine completes his work for me, he must be forfeited. Truly, I don't trust a man motivated solely by the clink of coins, especially a man of his sort, of his station.

Jacques' blood scalded his temples.

Quick as a snake, Grimani thrust his hand across the table, seizing the gold snuffbox.

Jacques reached for Grimani's hand but was too late. The Cavaliere quickly tipped the gold object into his coat pocket.

"Give it here."

"I think not."

Choking the hilt of his smallsword, Jacques growled his formal challenge. "Are you disposed to take a walk?"

"You brave me? Over a snuffbox? How quaint. We need not go anywhere to fight. The privacy of this casino will do." Grimani slowly and casually rose from the table. "I told Petrine," he said, making a flippant gesture with his hand, "I told him you would not accept my career proposition."

When Grimani turned and brazenly offered his back, the Capitano mask on the rear of his head came into view, startling Jacques. "My sweet sword is behind that divan," Grimani said as he pranced to the far end of the room and retrieved the weapon. He promptly unsheathed, kicked away several pillows, and cleared a small path across the marble floor. "Your valet attempted to persuade me that you would bow to my control—if only you could return to your homeland. I countered that your brittle arrogance would not permit you to accept my generous offer."

With his sword, Grimani made an elaborate salute. "I hoped— frankly, I knew—we'd come to this. You may recall that I'm a fencer of no small repute. Why, did you know that just one month ago, I fought and killed the renowned Signor DeLongo with this, my ancestral sword?" Grimani caressed the blade. "As for you, when I stick this sharp through your purblind heart, you will be gotten rid of. Venice will be rid of you. Your body will be taken to sea, shredded, and dumped. You and everything about you will be forgotten in short order. It will be as if you had never lived."

Jacques' cheeks fired red, his heart rippling with anger. He leapt from his seat, unsheathing his own steel. He did not salute but went en garde, the tip of his keen sword eye level at Grimani, who, across the room, posed nonchalantly.

From one side of the casino to the other, Michele Grimani paraded, leisurely booting pillows in his way, smelling flowers in each and every wall vase, chattering incessantly. He plucked a bloom from a wall vase, threw it toward a ceiling silk, and with a crisp thrust of his smallsword, impaled the thick stem of the flower. He slapped the bloom to the floor. "Years ago it occurred to me that twenty heads are better than one. I decided to maneuver others to accomplish my goal. Yes, I'm the master puppeteer of some of those men who had clues as well as some who were fed information I already had."

"Was Vicomte Honoré de Fragonard one of these others?"

"And why should I tell you?" rebuked Grimani. "Oh, well, perhaps for the sake of what we shared."

Jacques' head twitched in confusion.

"A certain blonde woman."

A gust of rage shook Jacques. Squeezing his sword hilt, he advanced toward Grimani, who retreated, smiling wickedly.

"Long ago I figured Vicomte de Fragonard to be vital to my mission, but the turgid fellow wouldn't cooperate. You see, I'd discovered that years before he'd been taken by his Freemason brothers, blindfolded, to a secret cavern to help preserve the corpse. He is, after all, one of the expert embalmers of his time, one of dozens, no doubt, who safeguarded the corpse over the centuries. But without the Vicomte's help ... well, his recalcitrance was maddening." Grimani waved his blade tauntingly, then slashed the air with a breathtaking hiss. "I must confess, it gave me great satisfaction to personally eliminate him. You see, I don't choose minions to carry out all my purges," he sighed. "Imagine: many of my personal pawns are still traipsing the planet, trying to unravel the mystery. Hah. And you? You were the fortunate one able to solve the nearly impossible riddle," he cried taking a step closer. "I say again, before you die, you are to be lauded for your service to my republic."

"It is not service to *your* republic. The republic you desire is one of cold self-interest, of secret police, of false imprisonment, of tyranny, of all that free men detest. You may be willing to bring dishonor and ruin to Venice. I'm not."

Grimani drew *doublés* in the air with the point of his sword. "Shall I remind you it was I who imprisoned you in I Piombi? It was by my order. You would have remained years. Until you'd rotted."

Jacques thought of his flesh putrefying.

Then instantaneously, he recalled the flesh of another, the flesh of a bearded man he had seen with his own eyes and experienced with his heart. A man who, though deceased, bestowed a glimpse of compassion and peace.

Jacques' rage immediately cooled. Calmness overtook him. When his grip on the smallsword loosened, he looked hard at Grimani. "I choose not to steal life from you. I'll not fight."

Jacques sheathed his sword, turned on his heel, and hastened out the front door.

For several seconds while he wound down the staircase, he heard nothing until, from above, his host screeched like a madman.

"Coward!"

Jacques, hustling down the dark flights of steps and into the street, glanced up to see a lantern flying at him. He dodged, but it slammed his shoulder, then hand—and burst into pieces beside him. His fingers seemed useless.

"Scum!" Grimani shouted from the balcony, his ire unquenchable. "Common scum!"

Sharp pain stung Jacques' shoulder. Then, on his back, he felt heat. His wrap was on fire! He tried to unclasp the burning cloak, but his right hand still had no feeling.

Instantly, Grimani was upon him, brandishing his sword.

A vicious thrust forced Jacques backward into a wall. Feeling the scorching flame, he grappled frantically with his cloak, yet his eyes could not afford to leave Grimani.

With his left hand, Jacques squeezed his sword from its sheath—barely—then managed an unwieldy cut, sending his foe spinning away.

Using the blade's razor edge, Jacques sawed the drawstring of his cloak until it fell, a burning heap, to the ground.

Grimani's sword arced above Jacques' face. Deflected by an overhanging sign, it struck just wide of its mark.

Jacques darted to the next street, taking a small group of Carnivale revelers by surprise. Sidestepping them, he glanced back, then stopped.

Grimiani appeared without the revelers noticing; he came to a halt and twisted his Capitano mask over his face. Then sliding ahead of the boisterous crowd, he spun back, capturing their attention by calling out in a high comic voice and frantically shaking his knees. "That dullard, that buffoon, that parasite will not duel," cried Grimani as Capitano. With his smallsword, he pointed down the street toward Jacques. The revelers jeered.

Jacques retreated while Grimani continued his bombast. "Why, I shall slice him, I shall slash him, I shall slay the slabbering slave—the slinking slothful slut."

The crowd roared.

Jacques fled around the next corner.

"Nowhere to go," Grimani shouted. "Our grand finale will be in a box alley."

Jacques saw his mistake. Trapped! Hot sweat bubbled his forehead while he faced his approaching adversary. Jacques beat the fingers of his right hand against his thigh, and although he sensed feeling returning, there was not enough sensation or strength to direct his sword. He began a run toward Grimani, swinging his weapon with his left hand in a wide swath.

Grimani easily ducked the assault.

As Jacques rushed past, he felt the stab in his side.

Cupping his wound, he lurched toward a small open piazza. He reeled about and watched a determined Grimani move his way.

Blood wet Jacques' shirt. Stinging pain marked his face, but feeling was coming again to the fingers of his right hand. He shifted his weapon to it, all the while gauging his fast-approaching opponent. *I've little choice*, he thought. Weak as he felt, Jacques stepped forward, forcing the tip of Grimani's sword to slide along his, producing a sharp, pinching noise.

The two men, circling the piazza, vied for advantage, their steel blades pressing, tapping against each other in preparation for attack. A sudden beat of Jacques' smallsword sent Grimani's askew. Jacques thrust hard. Grimani evaded and backed away.

"I'm told I move exceptionally well. Do you agree?" Grimani said through his Capitano mask.

The response from Jacques was another thrust.

Grimani defended the attack, then riposted.

Jacques parried, allowed his blade to press Grimani's, and in a quick envelopment, ripped the sword away from the man.

Jacques raised his steely point to the center of his enemy's mask. "You're disarmed. And at my mercy."

"Trim Capitano's mustache," someone shouted.

"Give the braggart a shave," another voice yelled. A volley of laughter followed, and Jacques knew a pack of carnivalers ganged behind him. He pressed his ribs. Warm blood oozed through his fingers. He lowered his sharp point and, without hesitation, stepped away from his adversary.

"Look to the bright sky, Capitano," shouted one of the onlookers.

Sensing a shadow, Jacques turned and glimpsed an object flying toward Grimani, who reached out—and caught—a sheathed smallsword.

"Give us more of your boasting, Capitano," a reveler cried. "And more fight!" The crowd applauded.

Jacques felt new fear until a voice rang out.

"Casanova. Giacomo Casanova," Tomaso shouted.

Swiftly, like a flame fanned by wind, the name Casanova raced through the crowd.

Jacques squinted at the carnivalers, astonished by their eager identification.

"We're here, just arrived," Tomaso said. "Watching this gay amusement you present for Carnivale and your friends. And, too, for these important Venetians, men of name and rank." Tomaso raised his arms to the group of onlookers beside him. "Entertain us, Signor Casanova!"

Jacques was too weak to reply.

But Michele Grimani fairly shivered in rage. He tore the Capitano mask from his face and hurled it to the ground.

"Cavaliere della stola d'oro," shouted a reveler, recognizing Grimani.
"Inquisitori de Stato!" someone else said. "The Cavaliere Grimani."

But from the rest of the crowd, there was only silence, no acknowledgement for the patrician.

Jacques watched beads of sweat curl down his foe's cheeks, the jaw clenched in rage.

Instantly, Grimani ripped his newfound sword from its sheath and thrust hard.

Jacques pitched back to stave off the attack.

The crowd cheered its approval.

Grimani edged closer to Jacques, his deadly steel cocked in preparation. "I marvel. You've not asked about your little dancer, Dominique."

"Moments ago, I spared your life," Jacques growled. "But if you spur me, I must kill you."

Grimani advanced rapidly while executing a series of doublés. Giving ground, Jacques attempted to match the weapon's deceptions until, at the ebb of his strength, he let fly a flurry of thrusts—to fearful exclamations from the onlookers.

The attack failed. Jacques withdrew, cupping his side. He wondered if he could go on.

Where were we?" Grimani snorted. His moonish face strained. "Oh, yes, Dominique? I realized early she would be of little direct aid to me. She could not, after all, even *write* to keep me informed, as did Petrine. But I decided it wasn't necessary that I have her cooperation at all." Grimani hardly noticed the surrounding crowd while he continued his harangue. "To maintain the woman as my puppet, I simply impressed her with heroic stories about you. Completely contrived, of course. But because of my delicious stories, I knew she would follow you, would also focus you—keep you on task in the attempt to unravel the secret." He sighed theatrically. "To my chagrin, the woman had somewhat a mind of her own. Eventually she, poor thing, went to her death. With you the cause."

There was uproar from the crowd when Jacques threw himself into a reckless barrage of attacks. The clash of steel echoed across the piazza as Grimani parried several thrusts and escaped the rest.

"My reputation with a sword is well deserved," he shouted.

"Look," a reveler suddenly shouted. "Casanova—he bleeds. This is no sham combat, no entertainment."

"Jacques, wounded!" Tomaso shouted. "You must stop this duel before it ends your life."

The swordsmen continued their fierce fight. When the two veered toward the front of a store, the attending shopkeeper fled.

Grimani sneered. "I know your history, Casanova. To me, you're nothing. Nothing. No aristocratic blood. Your mother, an actress. Your father? Who *is* he? Hah! One does not have to be overly clever to grasp your unending desire for high opinion from society."

Jacques' heart exploded through his ribs.

"My family?" Grimani crowed. "Five hundred years in the Golden Book. It's my breed that has preserved precious Venice—"

"Not the Venice I love. Not by sacrificing people like Esther, Petrine, the Vicomte—"

"What of it? They died for Venice!"

"When has the republic asked you to butcher an old woman or a fragile old man? When has Venice asked you to murder? To lie, cheat, manipulate, and destroy? You bestow upon yourself the mantle of importance in order to gain your own selfish ends." Jacques parried a lethal thrust from his opponent, then spewed more venom. "I know others of your family. They're not corrupt. But you? I shake in fear for the future of the republic. In the control of tainted hands such as yours."

"Just after I cut your lowborn heart from your body, my hands will control *all of Venice.*"

There was a gasp from the crowd. One of the revelers cried out. "This Cavaliere—he does not act like a worthy son of Venice. He acts like a disease." Heads nodded sternly in agreement while others jeered the man.

Jacques, seeing his main chance, thrust. Grimani parried a low *prime.* Then with blades bound, the two duelists arched body to body, only their sharp steel between them.

With snakelike quickness, Grimani delivered a blow with the pommel of his sword to Jacques' chin.

Jacques reeled backward.

"My grand plans will succeed," Grimani cried. "But first, you must die."

Jacques tottered uncontrollably until, from somewhere deep in his memory, he heard his brother's advice. "You may want to use *Maistre* Liancour's lunge, which may save your life someday." Next came the motherly advice of Zanetta. "A young man needs a proper snuffbox. I've given you boys few gifts, but to you I present this snuffbox, my son, so you'll find respect when you enter good society. Carry this gift wherever you go."

A river of memories sped through Jacques—faded faces churning at him, odd singsong rushing in and out. Black-and-white Carnivale masks swirled past. He tried to grip his smallsword. Tinkling laughter began. It was Dominique's, and its music seemed effervescent and beautiful. "Perhaps we should sharpen your fencing skills," she teased. "Beginning now."

Jacques roused with a newborn passion. He retightened his fingers around the sword hilt and spun deftly about, narrowly avoiding Grimani's killing thrust. Presently, he stood granite still and issued a feral growl. "I loathe you, Michele Grimani. Your fiendish ways bring a hideous blight upon the Republic of Venice. Personally, too—you offend me."

Michele Grimani offered a callous smile.

Now, as if animated by a wolflike spirit, Jacques, in one sleek and effortless move, extended his sword's point, lifted his front leg, kicked hard his back one. His voice raised to a pitch so clear and savage the very air seemed to vibrate. In a swift jump-lunge, he bounded, his unpitying steel aimed at the heart of Michele Grimani.

Then—amidst the heat of combat, in the daunting precision of his lethal lunge—Jacques relented. He collapsed his outstretched arm, the needle-sharp point halting a finger's width from the flesh of his enemy who, frozen in place, had failed to parry quickly enough.

Michele Grimani cried out as if a white-hot iron had passed through his chest. His weapon tumbled from his hand. He remained fixed to his spot, staring at the sword point, gurgles of fear rising from his throat.

When Jacques bared his teeth and glared into the frightened eyes of the vanquished man, the shouts from the crowd seemed far away.

"My sword cries out for blood," Jacques hissed, his point pressing mercilessly at Grimani's breast.

Now expectation packed the noiseless air.

In good time, Jacques again spoke. "Neither the unyielding punishment of prison nor a life of ill-advised adventuring could cure my defects. I was not an upright man." He paused. "But I'm changed." Jacques finished the thought in his heart: *For this I'm grateful.*

He slipped his hand into the coat pocket of Cavaliere Michele Grimani and quickly removed his gold snuffbox. He snapped it open. "You lied, Cavaliere. There is indeed Spaniol to be had." Hurling the contents at Grimani, Jacques closed the lid, and tenderly kissed the keepsake he so cherished before placing it in his pocket.

Grimani's face reddened like a fat plum.

Jacques whispered at him. "You have, as the French say, *folie de grandeur*. A delusion of greatness, Cavaliere. But then you yourself must carry that burden."

Jacques raised himself to his full height and cradled his smallsword against his cheek while the crowd of revelers moved toward him. The mass of Venetians—commoners, aristocrats, sirens, shopkeepers, free men and women—heartily cheered Tomaso's childhood friend, Casanova.

A tall, regal-looking man quieted the crowd before stepping toward Grimani. "Cavaliere," he barked, "hearing from your own mouth how you conduct the business of our great republic—by circumventing its laws and customs—I and my colleagues," he gestured behind him, "these distinguished personages, will make certain you shall bring no more dishonor to Venice. There will be investigations, and we will do our utmost to ensure that you be removed from offices of power and your name be stricken from the Golden Book. You are a disgrace. To your family. To the Republic of Venice."

Stooping over, the man snatched Grimani's smallsword from the ground and strode quickly away. Silence covered the crowd.

Every line etched in Grimani's grim countenance seemed to burst with pain.

Jacques—now cognizant only of the streaming sunlight, his face inspired with intense earnestness—raised his sword to the heavens and saluted the broad, blue sky that canopied Venice. It was a good thing—to be alive. He stood a short while before a slight smile creased his lips. *To you, Francesco, and to the woman—the fine woman—who loved us.*

The revelers hoisted Jacques to their shoulders and, bearing him that way, scrambled past the shamed Cavaliere until, near a lapping waterway, he was set down.

"Good Casanova," declared Tomaso, "surely you have regained your name. With you among us—as a friend—Venice will be a far better place."

"Tomaso, please lend me your handkerchief," were Jacques' simple words. "I have a wound very near my ... heart." A single tear warmed his cheek.

He pressed the cloth to his chest, then accepted Tomaso's helping hand.

The throng of revelers, joining with other carnivalers, swelled into larger streets, surged forward in a torrent of carefree voices, and spilled out into the grand piazza called San Marco.

Jacques Casanova, escorted by the jubilant crowd, imagined that glorious Carnivale breathed in ten thousand Venetian hearts—that men, women and children everywhere celebrated and rejoiced.

I, too, rejoice. I'm at peace. I'm home, where I belong.

Then his thoughts turned to Petrine.

AFTERWORD

THESE HISTORICAL PLACES, people, and events were a beginning point, a point of departure, for *The Secrets of Casanova:*

Honore Fragonard (1732-1799) was the director of the world's first veterinary school in Lyons, France. The Fragonard Museum, with a number of unexplained anatomical exhibits, exists to the present day in the outskirts of Paris.

Michele Grimani was a member of the *Inquisitori de Stato.* The Grimani family was initially listed in Venice's roll of patrician families— the Golden Book—in 1297.

The Stables of Solomon may still be seen in Jerusalem.

The Lisbon earthquake killed approximately thirty to seventy thousand people in November 1755. Following the earthquake, the three ensuing tidal waves wreaked further havoc.

The Vatican's *Index librorum prohibitorum* lists some four thousand books forbidden throughout the world. No layman may read or possess any of them without special permission granted only for single books and in urgent cases.

Casanova was imprisoned in Venice's I Piombi prison in July 1755—for unspecified charges—and was incarcerated there when the Lisbon earthquake struck in November. He and a renegade priest (incarcerated with him) made a daring escape—the only men ever to do so. In 1787, Casanova wrote *Story of My Flight,* which he later repeated in his autobiography.

Portugal held a great fascination for Casanova all his life, and although he traveled widely, he never set foot in Portugal.

In December 1759, the Marquis de Pombal (Carvalho e Mello) expelled all Jesuits from Portugal.

Giacomo Girolomo Casanova died June 4, 1798, in Bohemia. His final deathbed words were: "Almighty God and you witnesses of my death, I have lived as a philosopher and die as a Christian."

In the waning years of the eighteenth century, the oldest republic in the world—Venice—in the hands of Napoleon, ceased to exist.

AUTHOR'S NOTE

Dear Reader,

The fiction I write is made up of exaggeration and fabrication, of the evasion or erasure of known facts, of the reordering of events and dates, and of a good deal of prose created by my vivid imagination. Some call this literary license. I've taken immense literary license with my fiction.

Please do not take any of this book as factual; it is fiction.

ACKNOWLEDGMENTS

They say writing is a solitary experience. I agree. Rewriting, however, is a collaborative experience. Following is a thank you to the many people who have supported the writing of *The Secrets of Casanova*.

I lovingly acknowledge Lisa Michaels, "patron of the artist," for giving, in so many ways, love, support and understanding. In my life, there has been no other like her. I have loved her—not always well—but always.

My sons, too, have been a mainstay while I've confined myself to the computer or a pile of musty books. They witnessed their dad's actions first hand—and tolerated his obsession. I love them mightily and thank them from the depths of my heart.

Deepest and greatest thanks to Robin Maxwell, the "carrot and stick" woman who inspired, prodded, and generally used her every trick to support the creation of this manuscript. To her I owe considerable cash, although as I consider it, a friendly and warm "Love ya, dear friend" might suffice. I'm extremely beholden to Robin for her encouragement, her unwavering assistance, and her enduring friendship. And let me not forget her sublime sense of humor!

The manuscript grew immensely under the tutelage of Teresa Hoyer. I laud her for her patience, expert suggestions, compassion, perseverance, and for her overestimation of my abilities. If Robin Maxwell is midwife to *Casanova*, Teresa Hoyer guided the manuscript from infancy into adolescence. Her skills have been indispensable to the creation of this book.

From the book's adolescence to adulthood, there was Charis Conn, the editor who played a substantial role in the shaping of the manuscript. Professional, smart, and frank—great qualities for an editor.

Editor extraordinaire Cynthia White capped the *Casanova* creation with her unswerving dedication, her diligence, and her insight. She performed heroically time and again.

To Jeff and Paula—they will never know ...

To Harold—for truly making *The Secrets of Casanova* possible. Here's to you, Dad, for your faith and sincerity.

Others who were instrumental: Gabriella Herkert and Polly Blankenship, two writers whom I greatly admire, who set the bar just high enough and without whom *Casanova* could never have matured. Much other assistance was given by Todd Herman, Barbara Soichet, Bob Haas, Sam Johnson, Susan Jeter, Alan Adler, Matt Briggs, Natasha Kern, Susan Brandner, Michael Schaitel, Elizabeth Lyon, Max Thomas, Christopher Gortner (whose personal generosity under professional duress was astounding), Billie Morton, and Linda Lazar (who designed a marvelous Web site). I also thank Stephen Les and Sarah Milici who, for inspiration, gifted me with a Casanova action figure(!). Thanks to all, y'all!

It goes without saying that the wonderful folks at Booktrope earned my respect and unflagging admiration: Katherine Sears, Jesse James Freeman, Greg Simanson, and Julie Klein, among a slew of others. These are talented, dedicated, and generous people.

All of these folks are champions, and I thank them from the bottom of my heart.

As for the *many* sources used to write *Casanova*, special credit must go to John Masters for his superb biography of Giacomo Casanova, to Willard Trask, (the "first true English translation direct from Casanova's own autobiography" says John Masters), and to J. Rives Childs, "that dean of Casanova students."

Last, I give great, great credit to Giacomo Casanova's *History of My Life*—a must-read for anyone intrigued by the man. *The Secrets of Casanova* would certainly not have come into being without the adventurer Giacomo Casanova—a man who lived an unparalleled, if not exemplary, life. A life that continues to fire the imagination of all who know his story. I am one who fell under his spell.

Adios ...

Till we meet again.

GREG MICHAELS
SEPTEMBER 1, 2013

MORE GREAT READS
FROM BOOKTROPE

The Printer's Devil by **Chico Kidd** (Historical Fantasy) A demon summoned long ago by a heartbroken lover in Cromwellian England, now reawakened by a curious scholarly researcher. Who will pay the price?

Sweet Song by **Terry Persun** (Historical Fiction) This tale of a mixed-race man passing as white in post-Civil-War America speaks from the heart about where we've come from and who we are.

The Summer of Long Knives by **Jim Snowden** (Historical Thriller) Kommisar Rolf Wundt must solve a brutal murder, but in Nazi Germany in the summer of 1936, justice is non-existent. Can he crack the case while protecting his wife and himself from the Gestapo's cruel corruption?

Discover more books and learn about our
new approach to publishing at **booktrope.com**.

CPSIA information can be obtained at www.ICGtesting.com
Printed in the USA
BVOW03s0304061113

335209BV00001B/8/P